Band of Sisters

Band of Sisters

A Novel

Lauren Willig

HARPER LARGE PRINT

An Imprint of HarperCollinsPublishers

BAND OF SISTERS. Copyright © 2021 by Lauren Willig. All rights reserved. Printed in the United States of America. No part of this book may be used or reproduced in any manner whatsoever without written permission except in the case of brief quotations embodied in critical articles and reviews. For information, address HarperCollins Publishers, 195 Broadway, New York, NY 10007.

HarperCollins books may be purchased for educational, business, or sales promotional use. For information, please e-mail the Special Markets Department at SPsales@harpercollins.com.

FIRST HARPER LARGE PRINT EDITION

ISBN: 978-0-06-306231-3

Library of Congress Cataloging-in-Publication Data is available upon request.

21 22 23 24 25   LSC   10 9 8 7 6 5 4 3 2 1

To the real founding members
of the Smith College Relief Unit,
heroes all:

Margaret Ashley, '14
Marion Bennett, '06
Elizabeth H. Bliss, '08
Marjorie Leigh Carr, '09
Anne M. Chapin, '04
Elizabeth M. Dana, '04
Ruth Gaines, '01
Harriet Boyd Hawes, '92
Catherine B. Hooper, '11
Ruth Joslin, '12
Maud Kelly
Alice E. Leavens, '03
Millicent V. Lewis, '07
Lucy O. Mather, '88
Alice Weld Tallant, '97
Frances W. Valentine, '02
Marie L. Wolfs, '08
Margaret G. Wood, '12

Band of Sisters

Chapter One

Dear Ma and Dad,

~~I know this may come as some surprise, but I've decided to leave my position at Miss Cleary's to join the Smith College expedition to France~~

Dear Ma and Dad,

~~I hope the boys are well. I have some exciting news to share. I've signed up with the Smith College Relief Unit. We're a group of alumnae who mean to sail for France to bring aid to French villagers. I've resigned my position at~~

Dear Ma and Dad,

~~You may have read in the news about the Smith College Relief Unit.~~

Dear Ma,

Would it be all right if I joined you all for dinner next Sunday? I'll be in town and would very much like to see everyone.

> *Your loving daughter, Katie*
> *—Miss Katherine Moran, '11,*
> *to her mother, Mrs. Francis*
> *Shaughnessy*

July 1917
New York

It was a very long way down to the wharf from the deck of the SS *Rochambeau*.

Kate hadn't expected the boat to be quite so large. When Mrs. Rutherford had informed them that a packet boat would be carrying the Smith Unit across the Atlantic to France, she had pictured a cross between the Staten Island Ferry and one of the barges that chugged along the East River, something squat and rectangular and human-sized. Not this behemoth of a ship, taller than a town house, giant smokestacks punctuating the sky, crowded with war workers of all description. American ambulance men exchanged war stories with French aviators; journalists jostled aid workers.

Kate felt smaller than small in the midst of it, among all these laughing, shouting groups, families hugging, mothers kissing their sons one last time, champagne corks—of all things!—popping, baskets of fruits and bouquets of flowers piled into the arms of overworked porters, already staggering under piles of trunks and bandboxes and goodness only knows what else. It felt more like Smith graduation than an embarkation.

Well, she hadn't really expected them to come, had she? Her mother had made her disapproval clear.

"Have you run mad?" was a phrase that didn't leave itself open to much misinterpretation.

There were lifeboats all around, swung out in the ready position in case of need. On the walls, strongly worded notices forbade such dangerous activities as smoking after blackout once they reached the war zone.

Blackout. War zone. Maybe her mother was right; maybe she had run mad.

Blame the day. That July day that had been hotter than hot, her room in the boardinghouse sweltering, the stupider-than-usual student who had come to her for tutoring in French, the sweat dripping down the back of her neck making her itchy and irritable. At that moment, any place in the world had seemed preferable to where she was, to that horrible, stultifying room that stank of cabbage, the brainless debutantes she had elected to teach in what had been meant to be a temporary position but had become six years of mindless drudgery.

Kate hadn't cared terribly much about the cause itself. But the idea that someone would pay her way—there were funds, Emmie assured her; it wouldn't be charity, nothing like charity—to go abroad had seemed too good a chance to miss.

We need you, Kate, Emmie had pleaded, and she'd allowed herself to be persuaded, less from charity than from desperation, desperation to be anywhere other than where she was.

She knew it was madness in her mother's eyes. Here she was, with a good position, a respectable position—a teacher at a private girls' school! She would never have to scrub floors and empty chamber pots, as her mother had; never have to wear a white cap and lower her eyes and curtsy to her betters as they swept past her, making dark prints on a floor she had just cleaned.

She had gone off to Smith, and look what had happened.

Her mother hadn't said that, not precisely, but it was there between them. There in all the things they never said; there in Kate's clothes, her accent, the way her dad (not her father, always her dad, the man her mother had married when she was nine, kind, always kind, but not her father, never her father) called her "our college girl." They were proud, yes, but also wary. She'd become a thing apart.

Or maybe she always had been. Kate was the one relic of her mother's first marriage. You could stick a ring in a drawer, but flesh and blood was harder to hide, especially flesh and blood that was old enough to remember and to mind that her past was being scrubbed away like chalk from a board. The early years, when her father had driven the cart for the brewery and come home smelling of beer and horse to tell long stories in his heavily accented English. And, after that, the lean years, when she and her mother had been all in all to each other, sharing a bed in the one-room apartment where the radiators never worked and the water came out brown, where her mother scrubbed the stairs in exchange for the roof over their heads, where they ate bread and dripping for supper and pretended it was all they wanted. It had been hard, but they had been together. They had been themselves.

But then had come Frank Shaughnessy, member of the Ancient Order of Hibernians, one of Brooklyn's finest, a good man, a steady man, a policeman. Her mother had put cotton gloves over her reddened hands. There had been meat in the stew and sweet-smelling things in the kitchen and four little brothers, one after the other, each louder than the last. Kate had spent more and more time in the local library, reading her way around the shelves as the light shifted with her, the first one there after school, the last one out at dusk.

Her parents might blame Smith for making her a stranger, but it had all happened long before Smith; she'd been a shadow on the edge of their life well before she'd won the scholarship that took her to Northampton.

The one time Kate tried to go back, after Smith, after that summer with Emmie in Newport—well, suffice it to say it hadn't been a success. It wasn't that there hadn't been room for her. They'd made room, even though it was tight in that two-family house with her four brothers all crammed into one room. But they hadn't known what to do with her or she with them. The men her stepfather had brought home to meet her, boys from the force or the sons of friends, had called her "miss" and treated her like someone's maiden aunt—or they'd been defensive, belligerent, as though daring her to look down on them.

No. It hadn't been a success.

That was when Kate had found the job at Miss

Cleary's School for Young Ladies. Which hadn't been a success either but had at least paid a wage. Because if there was one thing that month at home had taught her, it was that she couldn't go home again, not really.

But she hadn't anywhere else to go either.

"Oh, hello! Are you one of us?" A woman bumped into Kate and gave her a long look up and down. Given that she was wearing the same distinctive uniform, Kate rather thought the question answered itself. "You weren't at the luncheon, were you? I would have known you then. I'm Maud Randolph, class of '09."

Kate held out her hand. "Kate Moran, class of '11."

"Moran—do you mean Warren?"

"No, Moran." It was really Moranck, but the gate-keepers at Ellis Island, confounded by her father's excess of consonants, had, in a stroke, turned him from Jiri Moranck to Jerry Moran. He had made a most unconvincing Jerry Moran. Kate had been only five when he had died, but she could still remember his thick Bohemian accent, the way he pronounced his *B*s as *P*s.

"I know some Warrens in Montclair," offered Maud. "Why weren't you at the luncheon? Everyone was meant to be at the luncheon."

Kate felt as though she'd been caught sneaking in after curfew. "I was a late addition. Emmie Van Alden told me you were short a chauffeur and—well, here we are."

"Van Alden?" Maud, who had been looking over her shoulder, searching for more interesting prey, turned her full attention back on Kate at the sound of that magic name. "Oh, you drive? So does my friend Liza. I don't, but I'm rather a dab hand at French, so I imagine we'll get by. Liza! Come meet Miss Warren."

"Moran," said Kate, without much hope.

Straightening her hat, Maud asked, with false casualness, "Do you know them well, the Van Aldens?"

"A bit." Kate had stayed with them for that one summer, in Newport, in the house she had learned to call a cottage, even though it was anything but. It was the summer she had learned to drive; the summer she had learned, painfully, just how little she would ever belong to their world. "Emmie and I roomed together at Smith."

"Of course, my family knows her family—well, slightly. Not to speak to, really. But we move in the same circles. My father's law firm handles some of their legal work." Maud flapped an arm at another girl, who was attempting to press a large bouquet on an already overladen porter. "Have you met Liza Shaw? Liza! Come meet—"

"Katherine Moran," said Kate, resigned to repeating her name for the foreseeable future. It felt like freshman year all over again, milling about, trying to keep track of people's names, liking some people on sight and disliking others. "Class of '11."

"Liza Shaw, class of '09." Hurrying up to them, Liza said breathlessly, "Maud, there's another bouquet for you. From Harry. I've had them put it in the cabin."

"That's two bouquets from Harry," said Maud with satisfaction, "and a basket of fruit. Although those pears are so terribly hard, I don't know what he thinks we mean to do with them. Fling them at submarines?"

Liza swiped at a lock of blond hair that clung damply to her cheek. She had a Dutch doll sort of prettiness, all red cheeks and slightly bulging blue eyes. "Well, yes, but if we leave them out to ripen . . ."

"Where? Have you seen the cabin yet? I swear, the Black Hole of Calcutta has nothing on it." To Kate, she said, "Are you rooming with Miss Van Alden?"

"Yes, and with a Miss Cooper. I haven't met her yet."

"Class of '14. She seems nice enough. You really ought to have gone to the luncheon, you know. It was terribly inspiring."

"We're going to have a killing time!" put in Liza. "I mean, it seems like a very good group."

"Except that doctor woman." Maud gave an exaggerated shudder. "So mannish. Have you met them yet? There are two of them, a senior doctor and a junior one. The junior one's all right, at least, her hat was very pretty, but the older one—I half expected her to try to worm me on the spot! I swear, I saw castor oil and carbolic in her eyes."

"We met them all at the luncheon," put in Liza helpfully.

"Yes, I got that." Kate was beginning to feel as though she'd turned up at an examination having missed the first month of classes; she hated coming in at a disadvantage. She hadn't even known there had been a luncheon; Emmie had come to beg her to join after the Unit had already been assembled, to fill a gap made by someone's leaving. She was, as usual, an add-on. An afterthought. "What made you decide to join up?"

Maud waved her hand in a way calculated to show the engagement ring placed carefully over her glove. "Oh, Harry's unit is sure to be sent to France—Harry and I were just engaged this spring—and I heard they're not giving wives passes anymore. So this way, I get over there on my own. And it's only for six months.

So how bad can it be? With any luck, we'll have some time in Paris before we go wherever it is we're going. I promised my mother I'd shop for my trousseau."

"Won't they be rather short of everything?"

"It's Paris," said Maud, as though that explained everything. "Oh, is that your old nanny come to see you off? That woman over there. She seems to be trying to get your attention."

"Where?" Following Maud's careless gesture, Kate saw a familiar hat at the base of the gangplank, her mother's very best hat, the one she wore to baptisms and wakes. Her mother was trying to push her way through the mass of humanity streaming down and away from the boat; a porter stopped her, pointing her away.

"Poor thing; that was the last whistle. Didn't you hear it? They'll never let her on now. Still, it was sweet of her, wasn't it?"

Maud's voice buzzed in Kate's ear; Kate rose on her tiptoes and tried to wave, but her mother was remonstrating with the porter and didn't see Kate, didn't see that Kate had seen her. She'd come. She'd come despite it all. And they were turning her away.

"They never do realize we've grown up, do they, these old nannies? Mine still comes from time to time and tries to wipe the cookie crumbs off my face."

The porter was quite firm. Kate's mother shrugged and turned, looking back over her shoulder at the boat. Could she see her? Or was Kate too small a speck, way up high on deck? If she could just get down to the gangplank—

Kate looked distractedly at Maud. "Would you excuse me? I must—"

"They're putting the gangplank up now. Oh dear, look at that frantic man. Like a picture of the guilty swain, don't you think? But that collar! And did you ever see such a gaudy bouquet? I wonder who it could be for. Not that it matters now. He's too late, poor man."

Too late. Kate strained to see through the crowd, to try to catch one last glimpse. It was a scrum down there, all the visitors who had been shooed off the boat milling about, getting in each other's way. Her mother, never tall, was impossible to spot, was probably already halfway back to the El.

Had she come to give Kate her blessing? Kate would never know now. She craned her neck, but it was hopeless. She could have wept with frustration. Why did it always have to be this way? Always just missing each other?

"Oh, there's Harry!" announced Maud, waving wildly. To Kate, she said graciously, "I'm sorry you missed your nanny."

That wasn't my nanny. Kate opened her mouth to say it. She meant to, truly.

But Maud poked Kate in the arm, hard. "Oh, there's your friend! Miss Van Alden! Yoo-hoo! Miss Van Alden! So good to see you!"

Kate bit her lip, knowing she should say something, should correct Maud, but Emmie was already upon them, dispensing goodwill and dropped hairpins with equal abandon. "Oh, how nice to see you again, Miss . . . Er! Isn't it lovely to be here?" Kate could tell Emmie hadn't the slightest idea who Maud was, but Kate knew Emmie would never hurt Maud's feelings by saying so. "Kate!" Emmie folded Kate in a hug that smelled like their room at Smith, lavender sachets and cocoa powder and Pears soap. "You're here! You'll have to come see our cabin—I've given you the bed by the window, but the steward tells me it will be awfully hot with all the portholes closed so we might want to sleep on deck tonight."

Emmie's hair, that indeterminate color between blond and brown that looks gray in the wrong light, was already frizzing out of its pins, frothing around her face. She shook the strands out of her eyes, like a horse shaking its mane.

"You're losing your pins," said Kate, sticking one back in for her.

"I know," said Emmie ruefully. "I expect I'll be entirely shed of them by the time we get to France and have to wear my hair in a long tail and all the Frenchmen will make mock of me."

"'Mock mothers from their sons, mock castles down,'" said Kate without thinking, slipping back years in a moment. They'd put on *Henry V* together their junior year, bit parts both, but the dialogue had become part of their personal lexicon. Any use of the word *mock* meant an immediate recitation of the tennis ball speech.

"What are you on about?" demanded Maud.

"It was our junior play," offered Emmie in her conciliatory way. "*Henry V.* The tennis ball speech."

"A very long time ago," said Kate, before Maud could ask her if she played tennis. It felt like a different lifetime. Back when she and Emmie had been inseparable. Back when Kate still thought she was one of them, could be one of them. Back before Newport.

How do you like the latest charity case?

So long ago, but those casual words still stung.

Maud asked Emmie, just a little too avidly, "Did your people come to see you off?"

"My father and three of my brothers came—that's why I was so long, Kate, or I would have found you sooner." Emmie was unconsciously twisting her hand-kerchief between her fingers as she used to, at Smith, when she had to do a recitation. "My mother wasn't able—there were so many meetings—you know how it is. So many committees! But she sent a basket, all full of woolens and wooden toys for the children. And my father brought sherry and crackers!"

"What kind of crackers?" asked Liza with interest.

"DeWitt's, I think," said Emmie. "There's also a twenty-pound box of Bailey's candy and some other things. My father said he'd rather thought we would need them, off in no-man's-land. He was only joking, of course."

"We're hardly going into the trenches," protested Maud.

"Oh, no, he means it as a joke, really. He says he feels quite small in the face of our nerve." Emmie paused, looking a bit uncertain. "And it is marvelous, isn't it? To be going abroad and doing something about this horrible war?"

Or about one's trousseau, thought Kate, but didn't say it. Emmie had assured her that there had been an extensive vetting process for applicants, including a written questionnaire, reference letters, and a doctor's note. Perhaps Maud had been a mistake. Or perhaps the mistake was Kate's, letting herself get swept up in one of Emmie's schemes after all these years, when she was old enough to know better.

Debutante nonsense, her mother called it. Good enough for those that don't have to worry about getting their living.

But this was work too. She might not be paid for it, not exactly, but the Unit was covering her room and board, and how else was she ever to see France, even a France at war?

"But I nearly forgot!" Emmie gave her head a little shake, losing another pin in the process. "Mrs. Rutherford asked me to help gather everyone together. We're to meet in the saloon. I'm meant to be chivvying everyone. Shall we?"

"We haven't much choice, have we?" said Kate. "Unless we mean to swim to shore."

She'd meant it as a joke, but it came out a little flat. Maud looked at her just a little too hard, with those bright eyes that saw too much.

"I didn't bring my bathing costume," said Emmie, bravely making a joke of it. "And I don't think this uniform would hold up awfully well in the water, do you?"

Kate grimaced at her uniform. "I don't know. It seems pretty indestructible."

"Just like us!" Emmie grabbed Kate's hand, just a little too hard. "Let's go before we miss anything."

"Did you know nearly everyone on the boat is concerned with the war in some way?" Maud angled in between Emmie and Kate as they hurried to the saloon. "I hear there's a whole unit of ambulance men on the boat, and also one of engineers."

"Don't forget the aviators!" added Liza, puffing along behind them.

"Did you know Nick Penniston's gone for an aviator?" said Emmie to Kate.

"Really?" said Kate, as though she hadn't seen the articles in the papers, millionaire's son takes to the sky, as if she hadn't stared at the grainy features half-indistinguishable in the newsprint, cursing herself for a fool.

He'd been kind to her, that was all. Sometimes, the girl who got to go to the ball wasn't Cinderella at all; sometimes, when midnight chimed, the prince didn't bother to give chase. She wasn't a princess in disguise. As far as the people in Emmie's world were concerned, she was just another Bridget: Irish, Catholic, and poor.

"The president of Andover is here too," said Maud importantly. "We met him in Montclair last year, didn't we, Liza? He's frightfully nice. Do you know him? And there's Dr. Denison of Boston College, and the president of a university somewhere in Oregon—goodness only knows, but they say he's up for the presidency of Smith, so I suppose we oughtn't to dismiss him. Oh, there are the ambulance men. Halloo! Those two tall ones seem rather nice."

As Maud waggled her fingers at them, one of the ambulance men elbowed his friend, pointing to them. "What are those?"

"Women, Hank," drawled the second man, taking a slug from a flask with Harvard's "*Veritas*" emblazoned on it and handing it to his friend. "They're women."

"No, but what are they doing here?"

The second man shrugged. "They tell me it's a unit from Smith College."

"College girls?" Hank choked on whatever was in the flask and had to be pounded on the back. "D'you think they'll send a platoon from Radcliffe?"

"I'd like one from Gimbels," quipped the second man, snagging the flask.

Kate felt two patches of color high in her cheeks. She resisted the urge to stamp on their feet in passing.

"Harvard men," said Emmie, whose family had all gone to Yale.

"They think we're a joke." It would help if she didn't

feel so much like a joke. The uniforms, which had been designed especially for the Smith Unit, were a cross between the military and the archaeological, crammed with pockets wherever a pocket could be put, an embarrassing display of utility. Kate's was too big on her, which made it even worse. It had been tailored for the girl who had left, who had been built on heartier lines. Kate was, like her mother, short and small-boned. Easy to overlook.

"We just have to show them otherwise, then," said Emmie bravely. "That's what my mother would say."

And when Mrs. Livingston Van Alden spoke, people listened. If they didn't, she chained herself to railings. Or invited senators to tea and harangued them. Or both. Neither of these skills seemed quite applicable to their current situation.

Mrs. Rutherford's voice boomed out over the crowd. "Smith Unit, to me!"

The founder of their Unit was five feet tall in her buttoned boots, but there wasn't anything else small about her. Her voice made the smokestacks shake. She was an archaeologist by profession, which was probably why, thought Kate, their uniforms looked suspiciously like the chosen attire of that much photographed archaeologist Amelia Peabody Emerson.

Mrs. Rutherford waved an umbrella in their general

direction, using it as a prod to herd the slower women into the saloon. "Everyone here? Good."

Kate knew there were only eighteen in the Unit, but the room felt very full of gray uniforms, with their symbolic touch of "French" blue. Some of the faces looked vaguely familiar, but hairstyles and clothing changed and features blurred over a decade's distance.

Except one. One woman she would have known anywhere.

Kate stopped where she was, her hand on Emmie's arm. "You didn't tell me your cousin would be here."

"Didn't I?" said Emmie vaguely. "She's a doctor now, you know."

"No, I didn't know." The one in the pretty hat, Maud had said. It wasn't pretty, that wasn't the word for it. It was elegant. Julia couldn't be anything but elegant if she tried. It was in her bones, her bearing. The fair hair that looked so drab on Emmie was golden on Julia; Julia had the same long bones but not the buck teeth. Put her in a toga and she'd fit right in on any cameo or group of classical statuary, perfectly carved of marble and just about as warm.

Kate had never been quite sure whether Julia deliberately set out to make her feel like a worm, or whether that was merely a by-product.

Julia, sitting next to Nick on the stairs in Newport,

her golden head next to his. *How do you like the latest charity case?*

Kate tried to smile at her but succeeded only in producing a grimace.

On the plus side, Julia looked just about as delighted to see her as she was to see Julia. Those bluer-than-blue eyes narrowed. She looked like a cat who had discovered she'd been given tainted cream.

Kate could feel the boat moving beneath her and stilled a tiny flare of panic. Six months. She'd signed up for six months of this.

Mrs. Rutherford stepped into the center of the room, blotting out Julia's perfect countenance. Instinctively, the women all fanned out around her, creating a circle, private conversations ceasing.

"Welcome, girls, welcome! Welcome to our floating home for the next fortnight as we set out on our grand endeavor."

One of the girls started to clap, and then flushed when she realized no one else was doing the same.

Mrs. Rutherford smiled kindly at her. "Well may you applaud! You have all, by virtue of your very presence, signaled your courage and your kindness, your willingness to sacrifice your own convenience to the good of others." Her voice dropped and she looked around the room, her eyes meeting those of each woman in turn.

"There have been many who have asked me how I can leave my own children to the care of others while we travel abroad on our great work. But all is well with my children. There are other children with whom all is *not* well and they too are precious in the sight of God."

It felt like sacrilege to breathe. Outside the room, the noises of the ship went on, but inside the saloon all was hushed expectancy.

"There are women and children in France who have been forgotten, women and children who need *us*. You ask me what we can do, and I tell you: everything. If they need food, we will help them plant it. If they need shelter, we will find the means to put it over their heads. We will build schools for their children and find beds for the weary. But most of all, the most valuable gift we bring is letting them know they have not been forgotten. As the men wage war, as the guns fire, we remember. We remember them. We remember they are not just statistics, so many left homeless, so many lost. They are people, like us, like our families. And we remember them."

Kate could feel the words like an electric current running through her; she could feel herself standing straighter.

Mrs. Rutherford seemed to speak directly to each one of them. "You have it in you to make children smile again. You have it in you to mete out goodness to those who for the past three years have known only cruelty. Look inside yourself and know that you have it in you to make all the difference to those who have been abandoned by the world, who have lost their families, their homes, their hope. *You* are their hope."

Nobody spoke. Nobody moved.

Mrs. Rutherford smiled at them, a crooked, sisterly smile. "I won't mislead you. Our path is not without pitfalls. We are on probation, all of us. They doubt us—just as they once doubted that women were worthy of an education."

An excited murmur ran around the room.

"The Red Cross didn't believe we would be worth the bother. The American Fund for French Wounded has sponsored us—but only for a time. We must earn our welcome. It falls to us, to each and every one of us, to prove them wrong and show them that there is nothing that an American college girl cannot do."

"Hear, hear!" cried the girl who had clapped, and this time no one reproved her.

Kate found herself alarmingly inclined to cheer. She knew it was all rhetoric—it was all rhetoric, wasn't it? There hadn't been a word of specifics in it—but she still felt like standing up and charging the barricades.

Inspiring, Maud had called their director. Well,

she was right in that. Kate felt like the snake once the charmer had got through with it; it made her wary.

Emmie didn't seem to have any such reserve. "Isn't she wonderful?" she whispered.

On the other side of the room, Julia's beautiful face was still and watchful.

"Now. Back to the practicalities," said Mrs. Rutherford. "We are almost all present. Our agriculturalist, Miss Lewes, has responsibilities at the Department of Agriculture which will keep her through the fall; she will be joining us as soon as she can get away."

"Agriculturalist?" echoed Liza.

"To help us with the chickens," said Mrs. Rutherford briskly. "We have an addition to our group since we last met. Miss Moran, if you would make yourself known?"

Reluctantly, Kate stepped forward.

"Miss Moran is a member of the class of 1911. She is to be one of our chauffeurs. She is also an accomplished teacher of French." Mrs. Rutherford looked blandly around the group. "I know there are those among you who could use some reacquaintance with the language. Miss Moran, if you would be so kind as to offer a daily French lesson during our time in transit, your efforts would be much appreciated."

"Of course," murmured Kate, since that was what

one said, even though she would rather stab herself in the eye with a pocketknife than teach French to anyone ever again.

Emmie beamed as though she'd just done something rather clever.

"You know our doctors, of course. Dr. Ava Stringfellow"—a middle-aged woman with a strong-featured face and a pair of expressive eyebrows stood up and gave a half bow—"and Dr. Julia Pruyn. Please do try not to fall ill. Their services are not meant for us but for the people we go to serve."

A couple of the women chuckled; Kate didn't think Mrs. Rutherford had been joking.

"I have a little gift for you." Reaching into one of her multitudinous pockets, Mrs. Rutherford drew out something that jangled and clanked. It resolved itself into a series of chains, each with a metal tag at the end of it.

"Miss Baldwin . . . Miss Cooper . . . Miss Dawlish . . . Miss Englund . . . Miss Ledbetter . . . Miss Mills . . . Miss Moran . . ."

The tag was warm from Mrs. Rutherford's pocket. Kate ran the ball of her thumb against the lightly incised words, the cuts still rough in the metal.

K. Moran. SCRU. On the other side: *Rue Scribe, Paris.*

"Miss Patton . . . Miss Pruyn—pardon me, Dr. Pruyn—Miss Randolph . . . Miss Shaw . . . Miss Van Alden. Ah, and here is mine." Mrs. Rutherford fitted her own tag over her head, tucking it neatly beneath her collar. "You must wear your badge at all times. They are not the most beautiful of ornaments, but they are necessary."

"But why?" asked Miss Cooper, the girl who had clapped, looking up from her tag.

From the other side of the room, Julia spoke for the first time.

"They're to identify our bodies," said Julia in her hard, beautiful voice. "When the ship goes down."

Chapter Two

Dear Mother,

Don't you like the life preservers all over the
stationery? It's quite different from the last time we
crossed to France together—all the talk is of
submarines and lifeboats. But there's really nothing
to worry about, they say, so long as we follow the
regulations and don't do anything foolish.

They've given us tags to hang around our necks
with our names on them. Mine says "E. Van
Alden, SCRU." It's merely a precaution, of course.
It makes us feel quite military.

—Miss Emmaline Van Alden, '11,
to her mother, Mrs. Livingston
Van Alden

August 1917
Paquetboat SS Rochambeau
Somewhere in the Atlantic

M iss Cooper dropped her tag.

Everyone stared at Julia, who just shrugged. "Don't kill the messenger. It is what it is."

Emmie jumped up, her own tag clutched in her hand. "Well, I think it's rather fun to have a keepsake of our time together. A memento!"

Some of the women smiled back. Some didn't.

"No one is drowning," said Kate flatly, not out of conviction, but because if Julia said the sky was blue, Kate would claim it was purple. Emmie had forgotten what it was like, mediating between the two of them. Or maybe she simply hadn't wanted to remember. "There are lifeboats in plenty and these lovely, bulky life jackets with which they've provided us."

"Ah yes. That's another thing. You need your papers for the lifeboats." Mrs. Rutherford rustled about among her pile of papers, producing thin slips, which she proceeded to distribute. "You are each assigned to a place in a lifeboat. Please do try to remember to keep your papers on you. You will need to show it to take your seat."

"What happens if we haven't our passes or run to the wrong boat?" asked Miss Cooper, looking worried.

"I don't know about you," said Maud, "but if the ship is going down, I'm climbing aboard the nearest lifeboat and asking questions later."

"There's really no need for that sort of thing," said Mrs. Rutherford. "As long as everyone follows the protocols, there shouldn't be any confusion."

"But wouldn't the ship be tilting?" asked Miss Cooper, twisting the chain of her tag around and around her fingers. "What if you couldn't get to your lifeboat?"

"I'm sure it's all moot," said Emmie soothingly, looking to Kate to back her up. "They have to think of these things, but, really, we're not at all the sort of ship the Germans want, are we? And they do seem to have thought of everything, haven't they? I'm sure we'll be safe as—as—"

"One can be in enemy-infested waters," said Julia.

Miss Cooper gave a tremulous smile. "You make it sound like mice."

"Mice have their good points," put in Miss Dawlish, '07, the kindergarten teacher. Emmie had been seated next to her at the luncheon and liked her immediately. She had a pleasantly freckled face, her ginger hair braided around and around like a crown. "We made pets of them in our classroom. The children built a little cage for them."

Maud wafted that aside. "Mice, perhaps, but not Germans. Do you know, they say they give you five hundred francs and a *Croix de Guerre* if you shoot one. I, for one, mean to get a revolver and pot as many as I can."

"Mice?" asked Miss Cooper.

"No, *Germans*," said Maud, rolling her eyes at Liza.

They seemed to have rather departed from the high tone of a moment before. Emmie looked to Mrs. Rutherford, wondering when she would take charge, but Mrs. Rutherford was busy with her notes, shuffling through a pile of lists and papers, unconcerned by the sniping among her recruits.

In desperation, Emmie clapped her hands together. "Has anyone thought of getting a concert together? A charity concert?" Charity concerts were one thing she knew how to do. As she knew better than anyone, the best way not to think was to keep as busy as possible. "We could hold one for the other passengers. There are an awful lot of people on the ship, aren't there? We could have a concert to raise money for the French wounded. It wouldn't need to be anything elaborate. Just a few airs and recitations. Kate, remember *Henry V*? You could do the St. Crispin's Day speech! 'We few, we happy few, we band of brothers . . .'"

"Wouldn't it be band of sisters?" said Kate wryly, but at least she'd stopped glowering at Julia.

"Ugh," said Maud. "You aren't going to ask us each to do a turn, are you? It would be too embarrassing."

"Oh, no, we wouldn't want to take over the program. Just organize it," said Emmie, improvising madly, feeling the mood of the room lightening. There was nothing like a concert for pulling people together. The others were perking up nicely, everyone starting to think what they knew, what they could do. "We could ask those nice Harvard men to sing glees. Maybe you might ask them? I'm sure they would listen to you."

"If you think it would be useful . . ." said Maud, but Emmie could tell she was itching to get out there and put her persuasive powers to use.

Emmie looked around the circle of women; she didn't know them yet as individuals, but they felt familiar anyway, familiar as Smith women, familiar as all the committee women and settlement house volunteers with whom she had worked over the years, women who had helped her drape bunting and serve hot meals and put on comic operettas. She felt a surge of warmth for them all. "There must be other people on the boat with all sorts of talents. We could put out an open call for performers!"

"It will have to be before we enter the war zone," Mrs. Rutherford cautioned, looking up from her notes. "Once we cross that line, there'll be no more music after dark. That will be . . . a week from now."

"We could call it One Last Night of Music," suggested Miss Cooper, and then looked alarmed at her own words. "I mean, not the last night of music forever. Just the last night of music on the *ship*."

"Yes, yes. Ava, if you would come with me?" Mrs. Rutherford gathered up her files, gesturing to Dr. Stringfellow, who served as assistant director of the Unit as well as their primary medical authority. "And Dr. Pruyn?"

Emmie felt her tension lighten as Julia turned to go. She loved Julia, she did. They were first cousins, practically the same age—except that Julia had been born six months earlier, first in that as she was in everything. Emmie had always suspected that she bored and frustrated Julia, but it was hard to tell. Julia kept herself to herself, twisting back her emotions as tightly and adroitly as she did the golden coil of hair at the back of her head, not a strand out of place. Julia's mother, Aunt May, was just the same way. Emmie had always been a little terrified of Aunt May, who lived an exotic, continental existence, returning to New York every so often to drop Julia at the rambling brownstone on East Thirty-Fourth Street "to be a sister for Emmaline."

And they were sisters—of sorts. Sisters who loved each other even when they didn't understand each other very well, which was most of the time.

Feeling guilty, Emmie called softly, "You will sing at the concert, won't you, Julia? No one has a voice like yours."

Her cousin gave her a curt nod of acknowledgment before following Dr. Stringfellow out of the room.

Emmie could feel Kate looking at her. "She means well."

"Hmm," said Kate, which was Kate's way of disagreeing entirely.

"Come," said Emmie, hooking her arm through Kate's, feeling obscurely cheered. She knew that "hmm" of old. It had been six years, but Kate was still the same Kate, and there was something reassuring in that. They said blood was thicker than water, but she had always felt more at home with Kate than with Julia, even if Julia came of the same Knickerbocker stock and Kate from what her father called "those people." "I'll show you our cabin. Don't expect terribly much. It really is pretty dire."

"It can't be worse than my room in Boston," said Kate as Emmie pushed open the door.

"I thought it was a very nice room," lied Emmie, groping her way through the darkness until she bumped into a berth, sitting down with a thump that made the springs squeak. The portholes had been boarded over, casting the cabin into permanent gloom.

"It was a dreadful room," said Kate, and suddenly they were both laughing, as if they were eighteen again, and not twenty-eight and on their way to a war zone. "Be grateful it was, or I'd never have agreed to come."

"I'm so glad you did," said Emmie honestly. "It makes it all feel less . . ."

"Mad?" suggested Kate, lowering herself carefully onto her own berth.

"Daunting," said Emmie.

They were quiet for a moment, the dark room close around them. *Why didn't you ever visit?* Emmie wanted to ask. *Why didn't you write?*

They had never stopped being friends; they had simply stopped being friends who saw one another. She had known Kate was busy, that Kate had to get her own living, but she couldn't help feeling a bit hurt all the same. Her mother would have been so happy to help, to give Kate a job as her own secretary. They might have gone on as they had been.

But, of course, all things changed. Emmie knew

that. It had been an impulse that had taken her to Kate's boardinghouse in Boston. They needed a woman who could drive and who spoke French, and Kate could do both.

But that wasn't the real reason. The truth was that she'd wanted Kate there because she'd felt in some obscure way that if Kate were with her, nothing would seem quite so large or terrifying. Kate would make everything all right, just as she had back in their days at Smith when nothing was so bad it couldn't be cured with hot cocoa brewed on a gas ring.

"Do you remember the cocoa parties we used to have?"

"I doubt there'll be much cocoa in France," said Kate quietly.

"You're probably right." Of course Kate was right. She was simply making a statement. It wasn't a rejection; it was Emmie's own sensitivity that made it feel like one. "I heard someone asking the steward for white sugar. He shrugged and said, *c'est la guerre*."

"I imagine *la guerre* covers a multitude of things," said Kate. Emmie heard the springs squeak as Kate reached up to lift the heavy knot of her hair off the back of her neck. "I take it back. It is even hotter in here than in my room in Boston."

"One of the ambulance men was telling me that

everyone sleeps on deck," offered Emmie. "He said pushing two deck chairs together makes an adequate sort of bed."

Kate grabbed two blankets and handed one to Emmie. "Let's hope it doesn't rain."

It did, of course. Not that night, but the next. The ten members of the Smith Unit who had elected to sleep on deck woke to a deluge and wound up taking themselves, dripping and shivering, into the marble-floored entry hall of the ship, huddling together for warmth.

"Have you noticed," said Miss Cooper in a small voice, hugging her knees to her chest, "that our uniforms *smell* when they're wet? They do say the war zone is awfully rainy."

"I imagine we'll get used to it," said Emmie hopefully.

"And it saves us having to wash our hair," said Kate drily, loosing the tie of her braid to fan out the long, wet strands. Emmie had always envied Kate's hair, a thick, rich chestnut, not all indistinct and flyaway like hers. Kate's hair stayed where she put it. "Have you thought of the lunacy of us all, sitting here shivering when we all have perfectly good beds waiting for us below?"

"Yes, but it's easier to escape from on deck." Liza struggled to a sitting position, kicking her legs free of her sodden blanket. "You know they say that the most dangerous time is just at dawn when the sea is quiet and the submarines can see us but we can't see them."

"Lovely," said Kate.

"But the ship shouldn't list quite so quickly because all the portholes are closed," said Liza importantly, thumping the never-sink vest she was using as a pillow. "So that should give us more time to get to the boats."

"Oh, for heaven's sake!" The blanket-wrapped lump that was Maud flopped over. "If you can't all be quiet we might as well go and smother in our cabins. At least that will be a *quick* death."

"Must we talk about death, please?" asked Miss Cooper in a small voice.

"Nobody is dying," said Emmie soothingly, but it was a lie, of course, and they all knew it. In France, ten days away, six days away, four days away, men were dying by the thousands, dying every day, dying in mud and blood and unimaginable agony. And they were going there. They had chosen to go there. What had made sense on a spring afternoon in Boston made much less sense at four in the morning, huddled under a blanket on the hard floorboards of the deck, listening to the restless pacing of those who couldn't sleep, waiting for the torpedoes to strike.

Emmie did her best to keep busy. In the mornings,

she joined Kate's French classes, where Liza continued to struggle with subjunctive verbs and Miss Cooper spoke very carefully in her correct but cautious French. Miss Cooper had brought a little paint set with her, and while Emmie couldn't paint anything more demanding than flowers, and not very interesting flowers at that, she could look and admire, so she admired to the very best of her abilities.

In the afternoons, Emmie stood on the deck, waving her arms about over her head and jumping up and down along with Liza, Maud, Miss Englund, Miss Cooper, and roughly eighty assorted ambulance men, engineers, and YMCA volunteers as the YMCA physical director led them in a series of setting-up exercises designed to get them into fighting shape or at least scare off any inquisitive seagulls.

Miss Dawlish, the kindergarten teacher, could usually be found in the saloon about that time, drinking weak coffee with brown sugar. Emmie made a practice of joining her, still red in the face from calisthenics, to discuss the innovations of the Sloyd method of teaching, of which Emmie knew only a little, but Miss Dawlish was only too happy to enlighten her, her tired face lighting with enthusiasm as she spoke of the education of children through woodwork and handicrafts.

In the evenings, Emmie and Kate shared a table with Miss Cooper, Liza, Maud, and the presidents, respectively, of Andover, Boston College, and Reed College, during which they had lively discussions about the advisability of education for women, and Kate got far too much amusement out of the president of Andover's insisting on addressing Maud indulgently as "Rosie," no matter how many times Maud corrected him.

"I can't stand his ideas," Kate admitted, "but I do love watching Maud fume."

"I wish we had a table together as a unit," said Emmie worriedly, pulling two deck chairs together to make a bed. The chairs themselves weren't that uncomfortable, but it was always awkward at four in the morning when the chairs were kicked apart so that the decks could be swabbed. She had tried sleeping directly on the deck instead, and had woken up with a mop in her face. "I don't like that we haven't got to know each other yet. There are girls I haven't even spoken to."

"We'll have plenty of time together over the next six months, why bother with it now?" asked Kate through the ribbon in her teeth as she finished plaiting her hair into its bedtime braid. They slept in their clothes— those were the rules, always keep your life vest at hand, never undress—but they allowed themselves the luxury of taking down their hair.

"I know, but . . ."

But they were all nervous. There had been an almost holiday air for the first week, with concerts every night, but once they entered the Bay of Biscay, the reality of the war slammed down upon them. No lights after dark. No music. No conversations. No cigarettes. All punishable on pain of arrest and a stint in a French prison. Maud and Liza appointed themselves guardians of the blackout and chased after men with radial watch dials, ordering them to cover their lights. Miss Cooper, Emmie had noticed, kept more and more to herself, writing letters to a friend at home, then crumpling them up again. One of the other women, Miss Patton, who had been a year ahead of Emmie at school, had a little silver flask she took out when she thought no one was looking and sometimes smelled of sherry when they all huddled together on the deck at night.

Mrs. Rutherford was nowhere to be found, closeted in her room with her plans and the doctors. There was no denying that an undertaking of such magnitude required a great deal of planning—Emmie had seen enough of her mother's grand endeavors to know the intricacies involved—but shouldn't she be paying a bit more attention to the women in her care?

Emmie managed to corner Mrs. Rutherford at

breakfast, drinking her coffee with one hand while taking notes with the other.

"Yes, Miss . . . Van Alden?" Their leader was, Emily noticed, writing in Greek letters. She rather hoped it was some sort of code and not because she was working on something to do with the ancients instead.

"I wonder," began Emmie, "if you might have noticed that everyone seems a bit . . . nervous."

"We are entering a war zone," said Mrs. Rutherford practically, with that disarming smile that made everything seem just as it ought. "We'd be fools not to be nervous."

"Well, yes, but . . . that is, I think we'd all feel better if . . . it would be such a *useful* thing to know what we're to do once we get there."

"But didn't I tell you already?" said Mrs. Rutherford, already half-distracted by whatever it was she was writing. Emmie shook her head as hard as she could. "I thought I had. Oh well, if you really think it would be an aid to morale . . ."

"Oh, I do," said Emmie fervently. "I really do."

Mrs. Rutherford called them together in the saloon the next day.

"Our voyage has almost ended," she announced. "And I must say, I'm very proud of how you all have conducted yourself. Just this morning, Dr. Van Dyke took me aside to tell me how fine he thinks you all are."

"Dr. Van Dyke?" Emmie murmured to Kate.

"The old goat with the beard and the monocle," Kate whispered back, and Emmie had to suppress a nervous giggle.

"You are just the right sort, he said, not neurasthenic enthusiasts, but with a natural dignity, and modesty without prudery."

"Neurasthenic?" wondered Liza.

"Barmy," Maud hissed back, not quite sotto voce.

Emmie did her best to look dignified and modest, but wondered just how Dr. Van Dyke would know. Or Mrs. Rutherford, for that matter. Hadn't they seen Miss Patton's sherry flask or Miss Cooper's hunched shoulders? Or maybe they were right and Emmie was wrong and this was all completely natural and normal when one was entering a war zone, and not the least—what had he called it?—neurasthenic.

"It has been brought to my attention that you might wish to have more information about our intentions." Mrs. Rutherford tapped the map spread out on a tea table, weighted down with books on four sides. "We shall make our home here, in the village of Grécourt. When the Germans retreated, they laid waste to the surrounding area—and then they sent the villagers home to live in it. Not all the villagers. The fit ones they took with them to Germany. The very young, the very old, the infant, and the infirm. Those are our charges."

"Pardon me." Maud was peering at the map over Mrs. Rutherford's shoulder. "Did you say we'd be *here*?"

She jabbed at the area with a finger.

"Yes," said Mrs. Rutherford. "That is why it is marked with an X."

"But—those lines over there—"

"Are the frontline trenches," said Mrs. Rutherford. She turned away from Maud. "Now, as I was saying . . ."

"But—we're practically in the trenches!"

"Actually," said Miss Dawlish helpfully, leaning so close to the map that her nose practically touched the print, "if you read the legend, it looks to be about ten miles away."

"Nine," corrected Mrs. Rutherford briskly. "Now—"

"Nine?" Maud appeared to be having difficulty speaking. "No one told us we'd be offering aid from the frontline trench!"

"We can hardly help villagers rebuild their lives from Paris, can we?" said Mrs. Rutherford in the same tones of exaggerated patience Emmie imagined

she used on students who mistranslated Homer. It
was a tone Emmie had heard frequently from her own
professors, in a variety of subjects. "Now, our entire
usefulness rests on our ability to travel between the
villages. Our first order of operation is to retrieve our
trucks. Our chauffeurs will go directly to Brest to fetch
the trucks." She consulted her notes. "Miss Shaw, Miss
Patton, Miss Cooper, you'll be in charge of the Ford
trucks. Miss Moran, Miss Englund, you will share responsibility for the White truck."

Kate sat very still, her face dangerously expressionless. "I've never driven a White truck. Only a Chalmers
touring car."

"And I've never driven a Ford," chimed in Liza. She
thought for a moment. "Or a White."

"You'll learn," said Mrs. Rutherford, obviously considering this an entirely irrelevant interruption. "As
for the rest of us, we shall be engaged in seeing to our
papers and securing the necessaries we need to bring to
Grécourt. We shall need upwards of sixty chickens and
at least four cows."

"Cows?" echoed Maud. "Did you say cows?"

"Or *vaches*, if one wants to get into the local spirit."
No one did.

Mrs. Rutherford sighed. "Cows have one great advantage, Miss Randolph. They create milk. We will

have eleven villages in our charge, with nearly two thousand souls relying upon us. There are babies without mothers; children wasting away from want of good, nourishing food. So we shall have cows."

"But . . . I've never had anything to do with cows."

Mrs. Rutherford squeezed Maud's shoulder, looking deep into her eyes. "You can do anything you set your mind to. Never let anyone tell you otherwise."

Maud's mouth opened and closed. She looked less like a cow and more like an outraged fish.

"I do have some books on animal husbandry for anyone who would like to do some reading. . . . Here is an excellent manual on the keeping of chickens. Miss Randolph, would you care to have it? I believe you will find it most informative."

"I'll take it," said Emmie quickly, since Maud looked about ready to lay an egg in rage.

"Excellent." Mrs. Rutherford turned the full force of her smile on her and Emmie felt her spirits, inexplicably, lifting. "You shall be in charge of our chickens, Miss . . . Van Alden, until our agriculturalist arrives. Now, is there anything else?"

No one dared venture anything else.

Mrs. Rutherford cast a benevolent smile in their general direction and drifted out, her ever-present notebook clasped to her side.

"I knew I'd be called on to do obstetrical work," commented Julia to no one in particular, "but I hadn't expected to turn veterinarian."

"That's Betsy for you," said Dr. Stringfellow with a certain grim satisfaction. She had, Emmie remembered being told, been Mrs. Rutherford's roommate at Smith, back in the nineties. "She'll have us all milking cows and liking it."

"Oh, not you," said Maud, too indignant to be politic. "You'll be too busy doctoring! But the rest of us . . ."

"I hope there aren't goats," said Miss Patton. Emmie could see her hand go to the pocket where the silver flask was kept, clutching it like a talisman. "I've never gotten on with goats. My grandmother kept goats. They were dreadful."

"I wonder if the children would like to help build chicken coops?" mused Miss Dawlish.

Maud glared at her. "Well, I think it's insane. Cows and chickens!"

"She does have a point about the milk," said Liza, and just as quickly subsided again.

"You milk the cows, then," said Maud crossly.

"I don't think she means us to milk them," said Emmie. "I think the villagers are meant to do that. We're simply to procure them and stable them. Does one stable a cow?"

No one knew.

"My uncle has a farm in Ohio," said Miss Englund. "But I grew up in Cleveland. Our milk came in glass bottles from a little wagon."

Kate laughed, a sharp, bitter laugh. "What a useless bunch we are."

Emmie smiled ruefully at her. "If there were a recital competition, I'm sure we'd be tops."

"Well, I don't think we're useless," said Maud. "I could be jolly well useful doing something that made any sense. The YMCA director says there's plenty of canteen work and loads that needs doing for the troops. And it has the benefit of not being in the firing line!"

"I wonder if she has any books on how to drive a Ford?" asked Liza as she followed her friend out of the saloon.

"It's going to be a disaster, isn't it?" said Kate.

Emmie tried to remember the way she had felt at the luncheon back in the spring, the luncheon where Mrs. Rutherford had first broached the notion of a Smith College Relief Unit; the way she had felt just a week ago when they had first been gathered together in this same saloon, the exultation, the certainty.

All her life, she had watched as her mother launched one grand scheme after another. Her mother was a born leader. Mrs. Livingston Van Alden was a founding member of the French Union for Women's Suffrage, despite the small impediment of not being French. But she hadn't let that stop her any more than she had let not being British stop her from chaining herself to the railings of Parliament with her great friend Emmeline Pankhurst. She had convinced Alva Vanderbilt to resume speaking to Mrs. Stuyvesant Fish for long enough to invite her to a suffrage conference at Marble House; she had given speeches and organized rallies all around the world, all while giving birth to seven children and seeing them raised along progressive educational lines.

Admittedly, this had been administered, in practice, by a series of nannies and governesses, but the theory of it had all come directly from Emmie's mother, who had mandated cold baths and Latin verbs with equal enthusiasm.

Emmie had been given the sort of education of which her mother had only dreamed—but she was not, her teachers said regretfully, academic by nature. Except when it came to poetry. She did like poetry. But Keats and Lord Tennyson weren't on her mother's list of Useful and Improving Topics. Emmie was meant to be studying the classics and absorbing rhetoric, but she found

Greek verbs impenetrable, and every time she got up on a podium, her tongue faltered (although she was rather good at draping bunting).

She was meant to be out there, rallying and marching, carrying the flag, motivating and inspiring, the very image of the New Woman. Well, her mother's image of the New Woman.

Instead, she had spent the last six years doing settlement house work, warming milk for babies, teaching children their ABCs, making sure the children of the Lower East Side had warm clothes for winter and that the library of the Girls' Club (for respectable young working women of the less-fortunate classes) was stocked with the sorts of books that might appeal to a twelve-year-old who had been put to work sewing shirtwaists at the age of eight.

Emmie wouldn't miss the chaos of the family brownstone on Thirty-Fourth Street—well, not much. But she did miss her girls. Some of them came to her so young—so young and so thin! And it was such joy to feed them up and teach them their letters if they didn't know them already and just give them a quiet, warm place where they could *be*. There weren't many places where one could just be.

It was all very useful work, and Emmie knew—at

least, she told herself—that it truly did make a difference to the recipients, but nothing to light up the world. Nothing to earn her mother's respect.

But here, here finally, was her chance to do something heroic.

If only it didn't all go wrong.

"It's this ship," Emmie said, desperately needing Kate to feel as she did, to believe as she did, because if Kate didn't believe, how were they to succeed? It was Kate who had got her through Smith, had kept her from failing her examinations. "It's the waiting that's so hard, being here and not being able to *do* anything yet."

"Yes, but what are we meant to do?" Kate asked practically. "Other than collect cows."

Offer hope to the hopeless, Emmie wanted to say, but somehow the words rolled off better from Mrs. Rutherford's tongue than hers.

"At least we have professional assurance that we're not neurasthenics!" When Kate looked at her skeptically, she added, "I'm sure it will all make sense once we get there. Everything will be better once we get to Paris."

Chapter Three

The Unit had an excellent time on the voyage. We had never all met until we embarked, but already we like and admire each other . . .

—Mrs. Ambrose Rutherford (née Betsy Hayes), '96, Director, to the members of the committee

Dear Beth,

I'm writing this on the train, so if my handwriting isn't up to form, you'll know why! I keep turning to speak to you and then remembering you aren't here after all, although I do understand why you couldn't come, with things as they are at home. Your replacement is a girl named Catharine Morran (?), class of '11. There are several other '11 girls, and some '09, and a great many older than that. They make me feel like an infant—although they're all very nice. Well, most of them.

They played us off the ship with "The Stars and Stripes Forever," which was very nice and very inspiring, but there's been some mix-up with our trucks, which haven't arrived yet or have arrived but aren't being released, it's not clear which, so now we're all on the way to Paris to find out what we're meant to do until we can get our trucks and get to where we're going. Everyone we see seems to be in uniform or in mourning. I've seen more widows' weeds in the past five hours than I have in all my life. Every woman we pass seems to be wearing black. As for the men—one of the girls said she feels strange having all her limbs, and that's just what it is. Every man on the train seems to be on crutches or wrapped in bandages, and we aren't even to Paris yet, much less the war zone.

I expect we'll feel better once we get to the hotel and have a good night's sleep. Can you believe? A Paris hotel! I feel better just writing it. A Paris hotel.

I wish you were here, Beth, I really do. It is so lonely without you. . . .

—Miss Margaret Cooper, '14, to
Miss Elizabeth Long, '14

August 1917
Hotel Voltaire, Paris

"**N**on," said Madame. "Twenty young girls? *Mais c'est impossible! Je ne peux prendre tout le monde!*"

"Fewer than that—and we're not that young," Kate countered.

She stood at the door of the hotel on the Quai Voltaire, the rest of the Unit behind her, rather the worse for wear after their long train ride from Bordeaux, disheveled and smoke-stained and weary. Their train hadn't come in until twenty past eight; it was full dark already, the streets sparsely lit, curtains pulled tight over windows to blot any light from within.

Mrs. Rutherford and Miss Ledbetter had taken on the task of attempting to find a cab for their baggage from the few ancient vehicles that still plied their trade at the station. It was clear that it would be miracle enough to find a taxi to carry their bags, much less any of them. Sore and tired, the rest of the Unit had gathered up such bits of baggage as they could carry and staggered forward on foot, along the night-dark Seine to the little hotel on the Left Bank where they had been promised that rooms had been reserved for them.

"Nine! Nine only I was told!" Madame protested.

"What is it?" asked Emmie, coming up behind Kate.

"There's no room at the inn—or, not enough room at the inn." Kate's throat was dry and scratchy after hours of coal smoke. Their landing—the playing of "The Stars and Stripes Forever" as they emerged from the boat; the excitement at being on dry land—all felt like years ago. "She says they can't possibly take us all, she has only two girls to help and there aren't enough rooms for all of us even if they had more people."

"But, then what . . ." Emmie glanced over her shoulder. Miss Cooper looked asleep on her feet. Miss Patton had dropped her bag and was sitting on it.

Kate could feel her lips set. "She says we'll have to find someplace else."

"But—our rooms were meant to be reserved." Emmie looked like a raccoon, her eyes ringed with purple. "Weren't they? Although our tags say Rue Scribe. Maybe we were meant to go there instead?"

Yes, it would be horrible if someone were to deliver their bodies to the wrong hotel.

Kate bit down the sarcastic words. She knew Emmie was as tired and drained as she was. Probably more. Kate had fewer compunctions about pulling her hat down over her eyes and pretending to be asleep when annoying people tried to talk to her.

"I'm quite sure Mrs. Rutherford said Quai Voltaire, not Rue Scribe. Please," said Kate to the proprietress. "Surely something can be arranged. We can share. We have cots—we will have cots, once our things are delivered. Do you have, perhaps, a room we might use as a dormitory? *Un dortoir—comme dans un pensionnat?*"

Madame considered. "There are the rooms already reserved. Five rooms. For nine girls. And an attic. But you cannot expect the laundry—and the meals—"

"We expect only a place to sleep. And we won't be here long. Just a week or so until we move on." Kate turned back to Emmie. "There's an attic."

"An attic?" Maud's hearing was remarkably acute when her comfort was at issue. "I'm not sleeping in an attic!"

"You can have one of the rooms." Kate was too tired to fight with anyone. "But don't expect anyone to make your bed for you."

"Liza and I will share," declared Maud in tones of great self-sacrifice.

"There is only one bed," Madame warned. At this point, she seemed to be rather enjoying herself.

"I don't mind lumping it, do you, Maud?" said Liza. "I promise not to hog the covers."

"I don't care where I sleep so long as no one starts

swabbing around me at three in the morning," said Miss Cooper bravely.

Behind them, a policeman wrestled with the gas jet of a streetlamp. The light went out, plunging the street into total darkness.

"Inside," said Madame with a sideways glance at the police officer. There had been signs all over the train station warning them to observe the blackout, to keep silent, to guard their words because the enemy might be listening. "Quick now. Who will have a room?"

"Mrs. Rutherford should have a room." Emmie immediately took on the role of hostess, working out the sleeping arrangements as though this were a party at the family cottage in Newport. She looked at her cousin. "And perhaps the doctors could share?"

It was just like Julia to get one of the rooms with a real bed, thought Kate. Although the thought of Julia having to share a bed with Dr. Stringfellow did rather lighten her mood somewhat. Maybe the doctor snored.

Kate was aware that this was not entirely the spirit of fellowship she ought to be cultivating.

"I'm for the attic," said Kate, not waiting to hear any more. "Who's with me?"

As attics went, it could have been worse. The room was a large one on the top floor, one side taken up by French windows that opened onto a long and narrow balcony edged with a decorative iron railing. It might even have been pretty—the windows looked out over the Seine, or would have, if it hadn't been too dark to see—but dark curtains had been hung haphazardly over the windows.

Madame wrenched them closed before lighting an oil lamp with an elaborate glass shade. "No light. It is not allow." She spoke in English for the benefit of the others but couldn't resist adding, "*Les boches.*"

In the lamplight, Kate could see a sewing machine, a dressmaker's dummy, and some rather battered side tables that appeared to have been exiled from the lower rooms. The one thing the room lacked was any sort of sleeping surface. The eight members of the Unit who had elected to share the garret stood there, in the center of the room, their coats still on, staring around them in despair. At least on the boat, the deck chairs had been broad enough to serve as beds.

Emmie bent over, shaking, weird snorting noises coming from between her fingers.

"Emmie?" Kate put a hand tentatively on her arm.

Emmie lifted her head, her eyes streaming, laughter coming out in great, undisciplined gasps. "Oh, Kate! A garret! What could possibly be more French than a garret! I feel like *La Dame aux Camélias* and Mimi and all the cast of *La Bohème* rolled into one!"

Kate grinned reluctantly. "This is far too nice a garret for that sort of thing. We need a few more holes in the roof, at least."

"A garret is a garret," said Emmie, wiping the tears of laughter from her eyes. "I refuse to be balked of my garret."

Miss Englund gave them a look of resigned toleration and began moving the furniture about to make room for pallets.

Unbuttoning her jacket, Kate went to help her. "Please promise me you won't start writing bad poetry and contract consumption?"

"I'm certainly not going to promise good poetry," said Emmie, joining Kate in shifting the dressmaker's dummy to a corner of the room. "What are we to sleep on until our cots arrive?"

"Our coats, I imagine," said Kate. "I'd try to cadge some pillows from Madame, but I'm not sure we can push her any further. She's already feeling ill-used."

Emmie carefully straightened the dummy, lowering her voice so only Kate could hear. "What were they thinking to only reserve for nine?"

"Perhaps they assumed that half of us would drown on the way over." At Emmie's expression of distress, Kate said, "Or it might be that Mrs. Rutherford only asked for the number of rooms she thought she could get and figured she would sort it out later."

That did seem to be the way their founder worked. Act first, sort out the details later. It seemed strange to Kate. Here was a woman of international reputation, the first woman to oversee a dig in Crete, ordering hundreds of workmen, responsible for an infinity of details—but from what Kate could see, her plans so far were sketchy in the extreme. She seemed to expect they would follow her blindly. Kate remembered the speech on the ship; how even she had, for that moment, been inclined to charge with Mrs. Rutherford into the breach or anywhere she chose to lead. Well, she could only hope that the hotel was an aberration and the rest of her arrangements were undertaken with more care.

Madame appeared at the door with an armful of blankets. Kate made a point of thanking her profusely, which mollified Madame not in the slightest.

Emmie pulled a wrinkled nightdress over her head. From inside the folds, she said, "I suppose we shouldn't tell her we'll also need a room for our baggage when it arrives."

Kate choked on a laugh. "Not tonight, no. I'm not sure Madame's nerves can take it."

Emmie dropped down on her pile of blankets,

smothering a yawn. "I don't care what we're sleeping on. I feel like I could sleep for a week. Good night, girls."

A chorus of "good night"s answered as, one by one, they changed into nightgowns and pajamas, relishing the sheer luxury of being out of their uniforms, of sleeping in a room, an actual room, with windows and a door.

With the blackout, it was dark, true dark, in a way it never had been in Brooklyn or Boston, where the streetlights glowed throughout the night. The dark wrapped Kate about, cushioning her, the tension of those last few days on the boat melting away. She hadn't even realized how terrified they had all been of torpedoes until the threat was gone. It was such a relief to be able to curl into a blanket, even a blanket on a floor, without having to use a life vest as a pillow or worry about awaking to water. . . .

Until someone awakened her by dropping a pile of pots. That's what it sounded like, metal pots, clanging, a cacophony of pots, all tumbling down, one on top of another. There was shouting and confusion, and for a horrible moment Kate was on the ship again and they were going down . . . down . . . down.

Kate opened her eyes but she couldn't see anything. She was blind. She was underwater. She was drowning, her limbs wrapped in seaweed, pinning her down, that complete darkness fearsome, pressing down around her, stopping her breath.

Until someone yelped, "Owwww! My foot!"

And she was in an attic in Paris, a very dark attic in Paris, surrounded by seven other members of the Smith Relief Unit, some already up and blundering about, trying to find the curtains. The noise, the awful noise, clanging and banging and blaring, was coming from outside.

"I think you just stepped on my spleen," said an aggrieved voice, thick with sleep. Kate thought it might be Miss Baldwin, but she wasn't sure.

"Sorry, sorry, I didn't see—what *is* that?" demanded Miss Englund's voice, rising over the din. "Ouch!"

"That was my arm," said Miss Patton plaintively.

"No, not that. The noise."

Miss Englund tripped over one of Kate's feet. Kate hastily scooted herself back as close to the wall as possible, wriggling to try to get free of the blanket, which seemed to have wrapped itself around her like the seaweed in her nightmare. Just a nightmare, she reminded herself, blinking away the sleep and the horror. Only a nightmare.

But the sirens were still sounding. There was some

sort of horror going on out there. Kate resisted the urge to wrap her blanket around her head and pretend she was back in Boston.

"I've got it!" called Miss Englund, achieving the wall of windows, having maimed roughly half her fellows in the process. She tugged one of the heavy curtains open, fumbling for the window latch. "Girls, girls, come out here! You must see this."

Kate stumbled to her feet, pulling the blanket around her shoulders like a shawl. Emmie was already there ahead of her, her angular form belted into a dressing gown.

"What is it, what is it?" asked Miss Cooper breathlessly, coming up behind Kate.

Together, they crowded onto the iron balcony, blinking at the cars racing down the street, dozens of them, hundreds of them, a multitude of them, horns blaring.

"Look up," said Miss Englund, and Kate did and saw the improbable sight of colored lights winking in the sky, red and green, attached to shadows like giant dragonflies, long wings stretched out on either side, swooping down, then up again, making the stars dim, blotting out the moon. Kate couldn't take her eyes away from it.

"It must be an air raid," said Emmie wonderingly. "I read about them, but . . ."

"But you don't understand it until you're in it," Miss Patton said, staring like the rest of them, all of them craning their necks to see the marvel above.

"Yes, that's it exactly," said Emmie. "It doesn't seem real somehow."

"Oh, it's real all right," said Miss Englund, rubbing her ear as another siren blared out.

"Do you think they mean to drop b-bombs on us?" Miss Cooper was shivering so hard she could hardly speak, even though the August night was warm. "Do we need to do something, do you think? Or g-go somewhere?"

Kate looked down at the street. "No one else seems to be going anywhere."

Of course, it was hard to tell. The lights were all dark in all the buildings. But no one seemed to be running for cellars.

"I think it would be zeppelins if they meant to bomb us," said Miss Englund briskly. "And those don't look like zeppelins. Well, if that's all, I'm for bed. I've some cotton if anyone wants some to stuff in their ears."

"Yes, please," said Miss Patton, drawing her dressing gown more tightly around her.

"Miss Cooper! Margaret! You're freezing!" Next to her, Emmie was clucking over Miss Cooper, chafing her cold hands. "Those pajamas feel like they're made of paper. Come inside. Kate?"

"In a moment." It was strangely beautiful up there, the signal lights winking red and green, some of the planes so close that she could hear the whirr of their wings on the wind, others far enough up in the sky that they looked like stars, shooting stars, bursting through the atmosphere. "I wonder which are ours and which are theirs."

"The ones not trying to drop things on us?" said Miss Patton with a nervous laugh.

Kate ignored her, watching the lights up in the sky, the wonder of it, that there were men up there in those contraptions, making them swoop and fly through the night sky.

It might be Nick up there.

Stupid, Kate told herself. Stupid to be thinking of Nick after all this time. He probably didn't even re- member her. There was no reason he should. He was probably too busy staying alive. They said the life span of an aviator was two months. Or was it two weeks?

She remembered Nick standing behind her, teach- ing her how to turn the crank to start the engine on that Chalmers touring car.

"Use that strong tennis arm," he had told her, and she had never had the nerve to tell him she didn't play tennis, that it wasn't something they had learned in Greenpoint, never realizing that he knew, that he'd always known she wasn't one of them.

Just another charity case. Another hanger-on.

It was, Kate had to admit, alarmingly comfortable to be with Emmie again, to fall into the old jokes, the old patterns. Or it would have been, if she could only have stopped herself from wondering if they were friends, if they'd ever truly been friends, or if she had only been one of Emmie's many projects. If she was still one of Emmie's projects.

In the street, another car raced past, bugle blaring the all clear. The lights had disappeared from the sky.

Quietly, trying not to wake anyone, Kate felt her way back into the room, drawing the curtain shut behind her. All of that was behind her, irrelevant. She was here to do a job—they were all here to do a job— and tomorrow, at last, they could start to do it.

Chapter Four

*You'll be surprised to get a letter from me
postmarked New York. Maud met a Montclair
boy who was sailing on Friday and said he would
take any mail we wanted, so it won't have to go
past the censors.*

*Paris is so much changed you would never know
it. The lights on the street go out at nine thirty
except for very small ones, and in the café where
Maud and I go for dinner (we don't dine with the
rest of the girls; we see enough of them anyway,
Maud says), if you dine after nine, all the lights go
out and you're left not being able to see your plate!*

*There is no white bread, not even those
delicious crescent rolls we used to have for
breakfast, and very little sugar. This morning, we*

*were waked at eight thirty by the maid with our
breakfast: a cup of poor coffee each and one slice
of dark war bread—no sugar, no butter! They call
the meatless days jours maigres (won't you be
amazed at how my French is improving! We've a
sort of French teacher woman with us who gave
lessons on the boat), and the jours maigres
certainly are meager. When we finish a meal, we
feel as if we'd just had the first course of a regular
meal and not a whole meal at all.*

 Please send DeWitt's crackers and Bailey's candy.
    — *Miss Liza Shaw, '09, to Mr.*
     and Mrs. Robert F. Shaw Jr.

August 1917
Paris, France

"There's been a delay," said Mrs. Rutherford.

"What sort of delay?" asked Emmie, trying hard not to yawn. She wondered if one became used to air raids with practice, or if one simply learned to use earplugs.

Unlike the rest of the bleary-eyed crew, Mrs. Rutherford was fizzing with energy. "Our trucks seem to have been mislaid. But never fear! We shan't let this discommode us. We shall simply bend like the reed, rather than breaking like the oak. Please pass the bread basket."

The bread basket was marooned in front of Maud, who was staring at it with horror. "Good heavens, what *is* this?"

"War bread, I think," said Emmie. She took an investigative bite. "It's not bad, really. Just a bit . . . grainy."

There was even butter, which Emmie hadn't expected. She could see Liza eyeing the butter dish and pushed it over to her with a smile.

Maud grimaced. "Is it meant to stiffen our spirits or our intestines?"

"Try it and see," suggested Julia. Sleeplessness emphasized her excellent cheekbones but did little for her mood. "In the interest of science."

Mrs. Rutherford, meanwhile, was eating her war bread with apparent relish with one hand and reading her correspondence with the other. "Exciting news! *Le Petit Journal, Le Petit Parisien,* and *Le Soir* all wish to send reporters to speak to us. Mr. Dewey of the *Saturday Evening Post* tells me that we are quite the best story of the war."

"Really? Us?" asked Emmie, feeling an entirely unworthy flare of excitement. Others adhered to the mantra that a woman ought only to appear in the papers three times: when she was born, when she married, and when she died, but her mother had made a practice of headlines. It wasn't self-aggrandizement if it was for a cause.

She wondered if her mother would see, if one of her many friends in France would send *Le Soir* back to her, with a picture of Emmie in it. A picture of all the Unit, of course. But it was hard not to daydream of being singled out for some striking stroke of heroism.

"But why?" asked Miss Englund practically. "There are other women in the war, surely?"

"Not like us," said Mrs. Rutherford. "We are not adding our efforts to someone else's work, to a man's work. We are, ourselves, complete and entire. *Les Collégiennes Américaines.*"

"*Les* what?" asked Liza, who hadn't benefited quite as much as she could from Kate's lessons on the boat, although she had certainly tried.

"The American College Women," translated Kate, without looking up from her bread. Kate was looking particularly white and pinched; Emmie wondered how long she had stayed out there on the balcony last night.

"A French title easily pronounced is absolutely necessary," said Mrs. Rutherford. "When I gave the list of all our names to the police, I wrote that above it. So as not to have any confusion about who and what we are."

"It sounds rather unpleasant, doesn't it?" said Miss Patton nervously, fiddling with the edge of the lace jabot she had added to her uniform shirtwaist. "Being registered with the police. As though we were felons."

"Or German spies," put in Maud. "I hear they're *everywhere.*"

This all seemed to be taking a rather dark tone, so Emmie decided it was time to intervene. "Would anyone else like some butter? I do think it's wonderful that we still have butter."

"Yes, just meatless Mondays and Tuesdays," said Maud, "and no hot water except on Saturday or Sunday. Do you think that really *is* the rule, or is Madame just trying to scare us away so she can have her boxroom back?"

"Madame is delighted to have us," said Mrs. Rutherford absently. "Do listen to this! Our agent has been busy on our behalf at Grécourt. La Baronne de Robecourt has agreed to let us stay in the château—such as it is. The army has inspected and cleaned the wells for us, and . . . the Ministry of the Interior has provided us with three barracks to house us!"

"Barracks? But . . . aren't we staying at the château?" Miss Patton glanced to Maud for support. "I thought you'd said there was a château."

"The château is not exactly habitable. Those days,

I fear, are gone. But wait! There's more. They've got plumbing for us! They've put in a small motor engine to pump water. It shows just how much they value our efforts. This region had the richest farmland in France—until the Germans came through. It is now in a state of almost total destruction. They are looking to us, ladies. To us."

"Not to till the fields, surely," said Maud darkly.

"It's the wrong season for that," said Mrs. Rutherford. "But we can provide the villagers with the proper seeds and the tools to do the tilling. We're not there to do their work for them, but to enable them to do it again for themselves. Let's see. . . . We'll have free transportation for our supplies to the nearest railway line—good news indeed!—and the Ministry of the Interior has arranged to requisition petrol, sugar, and coal for our use. We have everything we need."

"Except our trucks," pointed out Kate.

"And our medical supplies," put in Dr. Stringfellow. "We will need those, Betsy. All I have is what I carried with me in my bag."

"And our cots," added Miss Cooper timidly, stretching her aching shoulders.

"All in good time, ladies, all in good time." Mrs. Rutherford folded the letter and inserted it back in its envelope. "I mean to go to the American Relief

Clearing House and see what they can tell us about the whereabouts of our goods and chattels. Dr. Denison of Boston College believes he might have a way to expedite their arrival by having them taken to us by military train. War is a great game of waiting, ladies—but there are ways of bending events to one's will. The people of Grécourt need us and we *will* not disappoint them."

Maud's ears perked up. "Well, if we're simply waiting, I had some shopping—"

"Oh yes," said Mrs. Rutherford, willfully misunderstanding her. "There will be shopping in plenty! For all we've brought with us, there is more that is needed. Camp stoves and cots, rakes and plows . . . And the livestock, of course. I do hope you're getting on with the chickens, Miss Van Alden."

Emmie bit her lip. "I meant to read the manual on the train, but . . ."

But she had spent much of the time hearing all about Miss Patton's younger sister's wedding, with special attention to the bridesmaids' dresses and the details of the floral arrangements.

Mercifully, Mrs. Rutherford cut Emmie off before she could be forced to admit her continued ignorance regarding poultry. "Tomorrow, we will go see about securing our papers—there is a *carnet rouge* that is required for entry into the war zone, and, of course, the chauffeurs will need to acquire their permits. We are nothing without our chauffeurs."

"If we actually knew how to drive what we're supposed to drive," muttered Kate.

Emmie tried to make a joke of it. "I'll take the White truck if you'll take the chickens, Kate."

Kate grinned reluctantly. "At least the truck won't *cluck*."

"Dr. Pruyn and I will be touring the American Ambulance Hospital at Neuilly today," said Dr. Stringfellow, spreading butter sparingly on her war bread. She regarded it dubiously, shrugged, and then took a bite.

"Perhaps," said Mrs. Rutherford, looking up from her correspondence, "the whole Unit ought to go. I shall be busy making arrangements—but you might lead the group, Ava."

"It won't be pretty." Dr. Stringfellow frowned at her. "The discussion may become . . . technical."

"And what of it?" said Mrs. Rutherford. "It will be *instructive*."

Dr. Stringfellow looked hard at her old roommate. "It is not for the faint of heart."

Mrs. Rutherford gave her back stare for stare. "Neither is our work."

"Are you sure that will be wise, Betsy?"

"When did any venture ever succeed by being *wise*?"

Dr. Stringfellow raised her eyes to the heavens. "It's never any good to argue with you."

"Of course not," said Mrs. Rutherford, with a twinkle in her eyes. "You never win."

"Only because you refuse to admit defeat," said Dr. Stringfellow resignedly, and Emmie could imagine them in their room at Smith, in the pompadours and puffed sleeves of two decades ago, having the exact same argument. There was something terribly comforting about it, about the sameness of it. She and Kate used to bicker like that, years ago—back before they went their separate ways, with only the odd letter to mark the passage of the years. "On your head be it. We'll see what the hospital thinks when we show up with the whole lot of us rather than two."

"They will be charmed," said Mrs. Rutherford, and that was the end of that.

"What do you think she's up to that she doesn't want us around?" whispered Maud as they took the tram to Neuilly. She was wearing a crimson hat with her uniform, a determinedly Parisian hat, which Emmie found rather funny as all the Parisians they saw were wearing black. "Mrs. Rutherford, I mean. Did you hear all that at breakfast?"

"I think she wants us busy and occupied," said

Emmie, thinking about it. The Paris through which they were passing was a very different Paris from the one she had visited with her mother a mere five years before. This was a black-and-khaki Paris, populated by soldiers and widows. The busy traffic she remembered was gone, replaced by military vehicles and the odd taxi, too old and ancient to be of use in the war effort.

This wasn't a Paris for casual visitors; this was a Paris for those who had come to work. If one had to think about it too much, it would be, thought Emmie, terribly depressing. It made her fingers itch to be working at something, sewing a seam or knitting a fringe or writing a letter. Something. Anything.

"Are you sure that's all?" asked Maud ominously.

"We're almost to the hospital," Dr. Stringfellow said, effectively cutting off further speculation. "Do I need to straighten your hats and inspect your handkerchiefs, or can we simply proceed as a party of reasonable adults?"

Two by two, they filtered out after Dr. Stringfellow and Julia, the two doctors leading the way.

"We look like an American boarding school out for a walk," said Miss Patton, with a nervous giggle. She reached up to adjust her hat, of a rather violent purple. It was a brave hat, Emmie decided, even if it did make her complexion sallow.

"All we need are our field hockey sticks," agreed Miss Englund equably. "Is that the hospital? It looks more like a school."

"I believe it was a school initially," said Dr. Stringfellow. "Before."

There was something terribly ominous about that "before." Emmie couldn't stop staring. They were all staring. Emmie had been expecting—oh, not a tent, but something more makeshift. This was a grand edifice, immense beyond comprehending, wings stretching out behind wings, brick and stone and mansard roofs, more like a palace than a temporary medical facility. "It's enormous."

"And every inch of it in use," said Dr. Stringfellow grimly. "They tell me there's never enough room for all the *blessés*."

There were ambulances coming and going, soldiers everywhere. One wing seemed to be devoted entirely to garaging the ambulances. Uniforms of all varieties mixed and mingled. Emmie found herself craning her head from one side to the other as they walked through an enormous arch into a courtyard thick with windows. Windows upon windows, wings upon wings, all filled with wounded. *Les blessés.*

"There are a lot of them, aren't there?" Emmie swallowed hard. "It does seem like all the world has come to France, doesn't it? Do you see the Algerian soldiers in their red fez? Is it *fez* or *fezes*?"

"Or maybe it's something impossible like those Greek plurals you never see coming," suggested Miss Cooper, equally glad to seize on something silly. "Pais, paides. Fez, faides."

It was nerves, Emmie knew. Nerves made people act foolishly. She got silly when she was nervous, talking too much and telling endless stories and making horrible jokes. Kate, she remembered from college exams, got quiet and sharp. And Julia—Julia was always Julia.

Instinctively, they all huddled closer together as they entered the hospital, their noses stung by the strong scent of carbolic. There were *blessés* all about, *blessés* with faces wrapped in bandages, *blessés* standing on crutches, *blessés* waving greetings with the stumps where their hands used to be.

"They all seem so terribly glad to see us," murmured Miss Patton, waving back to a man without an arm.

"We're women," said Miss Englund bluntly. "And we're not here to stick needles into them."

"Dr. Stringfellow?" A woman in the traditional nurse's costume of white pinny over a voluminous gray dress came up to greet them. She had red hair tucked up beneath her cap and a dimple in one cheek. "I'm Nurse Fellowes. Welcome."

"How did you guess?" asked Dr. Stringfellow drily.

"We haven't many women doctors who call. You aren't all doctors, are you?" Nurse Fellowes turned to smile at the rest of the group, and Emmie had to press her lips tightly shut to stop her exclamation of alarm. A constellation of angry stars disfigured one side of her face, patches of shiny red scar tissue puckering the skin, all the way from her eyebrow to her chin.

"N-no," said Emmie, trying not to stare. "We're also with the Smith College Relief Unit."

"I'm Dr. Pruyn," said Julia, stepping to the front.

"Welcome to all of you, then," said Nurse Fellowes. Her voice wasn't English but it wasn't quite American either.

"Where are you from?" asked Emmie. It seemed a better idea than asking what had happened to her.

"Prince Edward Island," answered Nurse Fellowes as she turned to lead them down a long corridor. "Off the coast of Nova Scotia."

"Oh, Canada!" said Emmie brightly, feeling like an absolute idiot but unable to help herself.

"What happened to your foot?" blurted out Liza, and Emmie realized she had been so busy trying not to stare at Nurse Fellowes's face that she'd completely missed the strange shoe she was wearing and the lop-sided pattern of her gait.

"A shell," said Nurse Fellowes, smiling back at them with the dimpled side of her face. "I was very fortunate to have retained most of the foot."

The women all exchanged a look at that word, *fortunate.*

Miss Cooper took a long, deep breath. "Are you— are you a patient here?"

Nurse Fellowes shook her head. "Oh no. The work they do here is much more involved! Mine was a very simple injury. If you'll come with me?"

She led the group into a laboratory. After the bustle of the rest of the hospital, it seemed oddly quiet. The walls were lined with cupboards. The only furniture was a table, a chair, and an operating table, from which various restraints dangled.

"This is where we perform some of the more challenging reconstruction surgery." Nurse Fellowes opened a cupboard, taking out a pile of photographs. She set them out, one by one, on the table. "We've been learning as we go along, developing new techniques as the need arises. As you can see, some of these men came to us in a dreadful way."

"Dreadful," echoed Emmie. Her tongue felt unnaturally thick in her mouth. She had never, before, been aware of all the different features that went into a face until one looked, until one saw . . .

Nurse Fellowes went on laying out photographs on the table. "We've been experimenting, rather successfully, with facial reconstruction. In this case, you can see that the patient's upper lip and nose were largely destroyed."

The man didn't look like a man at all. There were bulbous blobs where his nose and upper lip had been, as if a child had tried to form a mask out of clay and got bored before smoothing out those final two features.

"In our first surgery, we concentrated on restoring his upper lip." Another photo. Then another. "Over the course of four surgeries and over a year, we were able to send him home like this."

The man's face was choppy, as though an artist had laid on paint too thick, but it was recognizably a man's face again, with a Roman arch of a nose and a discernible upper lip.

"That's incredible," said Kate quietly, touching the photograph, carefully, with one finger.

"You do it with skin grafts?" asked Julia, looking at the photos with a professional eye.

"Skin and bone grafts," said Nurse Fellowes, holding up another photo. Emmie took an inadvertent step back. If the last man had looked like clay, this one was all too clearly blood and bone. His face had a crater in it, a crater stretching from his cheek across his mouth, a gaping hole where the bottom half of his face had been, as though someone had smashed it like a pumpkin. "This was one of our more challenging cases. The man's cheek was entirely blown away. . . ."

Even in the black-and-white photograph, one could see the layers of muscle and tissue revealed.

How had he lived? How had he survived to come for treatment? How did one scream in pain if one had no mouth left with which to speak?

Miss Cooper made a gurgling noise. Emmie turned, glad for the chance to look away. Her colleague was a delicate shade of green.

Emmie didn't want to embarrass Miss Cooper by drawing attention to her, so she tried to turn the topic, seizing on a photo that wasn't like the others. It showed a nurse standing with a soldier on crutches, a dog sprawled in front. "Oh, how adorable! Whose dog is that? Miss Cooper, did you see this darling dog? I can't tell—is he a border collie?"

"An Airedale," said Nurse Fellowes. Her dimple deepened as she smiled at the photo. "I can't think how that photo got in there. It's a marvelous story. That's Private Thomas and his dog Snug. Snug dug him out after his trench collapsed. He saved his life. We were all rather fond of Snug. He was such a good dog."

"What happened to them?" asked Miss Cooper, a bit of color back in her cheeks.

"They went back to the front. Snug too." The smile was gone; the dimple too. Nurse Fellowes seized on another photo at random. "Look! We have had such success with the most remarkable bone regeneration from mere fragments. This poor chap lost all his teeth and some of his jaw, but you can see, in the progress of these pictures, the process of regrowth. . . . It's keeping them entirely still that's the hardest. Dr. Blake has devised the most ingenious variety of splints."

"Did I hear my name?" A slender man with a long, thin nose and a scrubbing brush of a mustache entered the room. "Ah, the lady doctors."

"Hello, Joseph," said Dr. Stringfellow. "It's an honor to be greeted by the great man himself."

"Still delivering babies in Philadelphia, Ava?"

"Among other things. I see you've been keeping busy."

"I try, I try. We're terribly proud of the work we do here. Has Nurse Fellowes been showing you our shop? We started out with 170 beds in '14. We're up to nearly a thousand. Some of our patients come through and leave; others are here for a year or more, for the more intricate work. Have you seen the fracture ward yet? We call it the machine shop."

"We've been hearing about your reconstruction work," said Julia. She held out a hand. "I'm Dr. Pruyn."

Dr. Blake nodded pleasantly, humoring her. "Pleased to make your acquaintance, Doctor. It seems a shame for a man to serve his country and come home a freak. So . . . here we are. Some of these men might have had no life at home at all, but for these surgeries. They don't always take, of course," he admitted. "But we do our best. As a last resort, we have the masks."

"Masks?" asked Emmie. Masks sounded like a safer topic than surgeries.

"Remarkable things. Made of tin. There's an American artist in the Latin Quarter who paints them. Matches 'em to what the man would have looked like before—well."

"These photos—they're remarkable," said Miss Englund.

Emmie nodded vigorously. *Remarkable* was one word for it. It seemed almost impossible to comprehend that a man could have suffered injuries such as the ones in the photographs and lived.

Dr. Blake put an avuncular hand on Julia's arm. Julia stiffened, her spine very straight. "We can do better than photos! I'll take you about to see some of our patients in a bit, but in the meantime, let's show you our collection of plaster casts." Dr. Blake nodded to Nurse

Fellowes, who obediently limped toward a cupboard. "We make molds before and after. It's useful to have a three-dimensional model."

Nurse Fellowes set two plaster casts down on the table. The second showed a normal sort of man, with a pronounced nose and a firm chin. The first—the nose was completely gone, leaving only a distorted hole. The mouth was drawn up on one side, a diagonal slash. One ear was half-gone. It had been painted, giving it a verisimilitude the gray-toned photos could never match.

"Oh Lord," murmured Miss Cooper. She took a half step back, her eyes glassy. Emmie could see the sheen of sweat on her forehead, the unhealthy pallor of her skin.

Her eyes rolled back in their sockets.

"Kate," said Emmie urgently. "Kate."

Chapter Five

*We went today to the big American Ambulance
Hospital at Neuilly and it was the most wonderful
and awful place I have ever seen. . . .*

*They are doing miraculous work restoring faces
that have been partly blown away. We saw plaster
casts of faces before and after and Margaret
Cooper (remember, the one who knows Gilbert's
cousin?) proceeded to faint on the spot.*

> — *Miss Alice Patton, '10, to
> her sister, Mrs. Gilbert
> Thomas (who did not
> attend Smith or even one
> of those other institutions
> that are not Smith)*

August 1917
Paris, France

They caught Miss Cooper just before she went over.
It was amazing just how heavy one slender woman could be in a dead faint. It didn't help that she was tall, thought Kate, who wasn't. She could only be grateful that Dr. Blake's back was to them as he attempted to explain something to do with bone grafts to Maud, who, for all her other sins, wasn't the least bit squeamish.

Julia looked back over her shoulder, frowning, and, for once, Kate couldn't blame her. She didn't want Dr. Blake to see one of their number fainting either.

Lady doctors indeed.

"We've got to get her out of here," she hissed to Emmie, who nodded faintly, her hair already coming out of its pins.

"You moved his leg to his face?" Maud's strident tones covered the sound of Miss Cooper's heels dragging across the floor. Kate could have kissed her.

"My dear girl, it doesn't work quite like that," said the doctor indulgently. "Now, if you'll see . . . A bit of bone from the shin, grafted to the chin . . ."

"I feel like Dr. Frankenstein, stealing bodies," muttered Kate as they maneuvered through the door. She could feel the sweat gathering under her arms and along the small of her back.

"I'm not sure they don't do that here," panted Emmie. Sometimes, Kate forgot the difference in their heights. Emmie tended to fold over onto herself, making herself smaller. But when it came to dragging a body between them, those eight inches mattered. Emmie was bent double trying to stay level with Kate, tripping over her own feet. "Do you think . . . we can set her down . . . here?"

Here was an abandoned office, a cubbyhole of an office, crammed with papers, maps and notices tacked to the walls. Kate was fairly sure it was a dreadful place to put a body. She was equally sure that if she tried to move Miss Cooper any farther, Miss Cooper wasn't going to be the only one in the infirmary.

"Yes," she said, resisting the urge to drop her side of the burden. "Together now."

Together they lowered Miss Cooper to the ground, her head and shoulders propped on Emmie's lap. She was breathing shallowly, her skin clammy with sweat. Emmie removed Miss Cooper's hat pin and smoothed the hair back from her brow.

Kate felt her wrist. "She has a pulse, at least." What

that pulse was, or what it was supposed to be, Kate had no idea.

Emmie looked up at Kate, her face distressed. "I knew I ought to have taken a nursing course."

"This place is teeming with nurses," said Kate roughly, because she felt just as useless. This did not bode well for their utility out in the ravaged French countryside. "She doesn't need a nurse, just a vial of smelling salts. Or a splash of cold water."

"Kate! It was awful, admit it. That last cast . . ."

Awful, yes. But also incredible, that the doctors could play with flesh like clay, could mold it back into shape. Or almost back into shape. Kate thought of her father, dead from a blow to the head from a horse's hoof. He hadn't died immediately. What might these doctors have done? Would they have reached into his very brain and brought him back?

"It's incredible what they do. Awe inspiring, even." Standing, Kate brushed her hands on her skirt. They were in a hospital, for goodness' sake. "*Someone* here must have smelling salts."

Emmie was squinting worriedly at Miss Cooper. "Do you think this is why Mrs. Rutherford wanted us here? To test us?"

"I don't know. Maybe." It was impossible to tell with Mrs. Rutherford how much was method and how much madness. If it was a test, Kate didn't like to think what it signified that they were already one down.

"But we're not going to work with wounded. Not these sort of wounded." Kate wished Emmie wouldn't look at her like that, as though she had the answers. None of them had any idea what the Germans had done to the villagers whose homes they had occupied. "It's meant to be social work. Visiting children and bringing them milk."

"Don't forget the chickens," said Kate.

Emmie smiled despite herself. "I've been doing my best to forget the chickens. I only volunteered to keep the peace. Although I imagine chickens could be rather sweet."

"Or rather smelly. Ouch!" Kate pulled back, rubbing her shoulder as a door banged open into her back.

"Dr. Blake? I need—" said a very clipped, very British voice. The man who went along with the voice stopped himself just short of tripping over Margaret's feet, which, admittedly, were stretched across most of the available floor space. "You're not Dr. Blake."

"Dr. Blake is busy," said Kate, her arm smarting. "Come back later."

"You don't work here," said the man. He was tall and thin, with dark hair clipped close to his head and a narrow mustache above his lips. He looked down his nose at them in a way that made Kate feel even shorter than her five foot one. "Do you?"

"We were touring the hospital and one of our friends was taken ill," said Emmie, automatically apologizing, as Emmie always did. "We know we probably shouldn't be in here, but we thought we ought to be out of the way. . . ."

"She saw the wounded and keeled over, did she?" said the man, who had, thought Kate, no business at all being so disagreeable.

She was about to tell him so, when Emmie lifted her chin and said, with great dignity, "Her breakfast disagreed with her. It's the sort of thing that could happen to anyone, really. It's the war bread, you see."

"You haven't any smelling salts, have you?" Kate asked before they could digress into the culinary.

The Englishman pulled on his gloves with sharp, jerky movements. "I didn't come equipped for swooning maidens. Now, if you'll excuse me—"

"Swooning maidens?" Emmie gave a gurgle of a laugh. "You make us sound like something out of a Gilbert and Sullivan operetta. You know, the bit where the pirate king starts shouting about maidens and they all run about—well, anyway. But we're not like that. We're . . . *les Collégiennes Américaines!*"

The Englishman stared at Emmie, and then said, "Three Little Maids from School, then."

"Seventeen, actually," said Emmie. "We'll be eighteen when our agriculturalist arrives. We're a relief unit sent by Smith College."

"Genius tutelary indeed. What are you meant to be relieving?"

"Eleven distressed villages in the area of Grécourt," said Kate sharply. "Look, are you going to help or not?"

"Grécourt?"

"Yes. You can find it on that map over there. Are those our lines?" Emmie added, her attention caught by the American flags stuck to the map on the wall.

"You aren't supposed to see that." The British officer stepped between her and the map, nearly trampling on Miss Cooper in the process. "You aren't supposed to be *here*."

"If we're that much in the way, we'll move," said Kate. She bent down next to Miss Cooper, prepared to lift her. "You needn't concern yourself."

"That's not what I meant." The British officer drew in a deep breath through his nose. There was rage in that voice, spilling out through the cultured vowels, the carefully controlled words. "This is no place for untrained amateurs. Not in this office, not in this hospital, and certainly not at Grécourt! Go see the Louvre. Walk along the Seine. But don't get in the way of the real business of the war. You have no idea what you're playing at."

Emmie peered up at the angry officer. Her eyes were a very light blue, as faded as her pale lashes. They always made her look nearsighted, even though she wasn't. "Were you a professional soldier before the war?"

The Brit checked, choking on his words. "Well, no—but that's different. It's not as though I had any choice in the matter."

Emmie sat back on her heels, politely curious. "Were you constrained to enlist?"

"Was I—no!" He looked like he'd been slapped. Then the mustache quirked. "I'd hardly admit it if I were. But no. I volunteered. More fool I."

"And so did we," said Emmie quietly. Her hands moved gently against Miss Cooper's hair. "We all do what we can. We know we haven't much experience, but we mean to learn."

He stared at her, wordlessly. Some of the tension seemed to drain away from his shoulders, leaving him looking gray and impossibly weary.

When he spoke, his voice was completely without

inflection. "France is a dangerous schoolroom. If you'd take my advice—go home. Go home now. And forget you ever saw any of this."

Emmie cocked her head at him. "It's not the sort of thing one can just forget, is it? And, having seen it, how can one go home and do nothing?"

He gave a sharp laugh. "Quite easily. You'd be surprised how little one can do when one sets one's mind to it."

On the floor, Miss Cooper stirred, making a faint noise.

The British officer nodded at her. "I'll send a nurse to you—for your fallen comrade."

And he was gone, his footsteps echoing along the hall.

Miss Cooper moaned. Emmie bent over her. "Miss Cooper? Margaret?" To Kate, she said, "I think we tell the others that—that we needed to answer a call of nature."

"Your friend is sending a nurse to us," Kate pointed out.

To her surprise, Emmie's cheeks turned a faint pink. "He's not my friend. Just a . . . helpful stranger."

"Helpful?" Kate had found him rude beyond bearing. "Or do all British men act like they own the earth?"

"Well, they do, don't they? Own it, I mean," said Emmie. Kate had forgotten Emmie's inability to recognize a rhetorical question. She always considered them solemnly, as though they were the prompt for writing a theme. "The pink bits of it, at least. Now, Margaret, don't fret, we'll just get you a bit of water and you'll feel right as rain in a minute. . . ."

Miss Cooper was still a bit gray about the gills when they made it back to the hotel on the Quai Voltaire.

"You shouldn't feel bad, you know," said Miss Englund quietly to Miss Cooper as they walked from the tram to the hotel, "about today. Every time I looked at those pictures, I saw my brother's face."

"Is he . . . here?" asked Emmie, trotting alongside with one arm protectively through Miss Cooper's, mothering with all her might.

"With the 11th Engineers." Miss Englund paused to let Maud and Liza brush past her. "Maybe we'll get lucky. Maybe it will be all over by the time our boys are moved to the front."

"Maybe," echoed Kate, glad she was behind them, glad Miss Englund couldn't see her face.

That map they'd seen, the map they weren't supposed to see. The American flags had been planted right behind the front lines. She was shamefully grateful that her own brothers were still too young to join up.

Her mother's real family.

"I, for one," said Maud loudly, turning back as she pushed open the door of the hotel, "think we ought to be doing something for our soldiers, not going off to milk cows for French peasants, don't you? And I mean to tell Mrs. Rutherford that. Oh! Mrs. Rutherford! I didn't see you there. . . ."

If Mrs. Rutherford heard what Maud said, she didn't let on. She did, however, sit them down and proceed to issue a series of rapid instructions. Their trucks would, at best, take another two weeks. In the meantime, there was work to be done and purchases to be made.

Emmie was put in charge of acquiring six cows, a bull, three pigs, one hundred chickens, eighteen pairs of rabbits, and, if time and budget permitted, possibly some goats.

"Barnum and Bailey travels with less!" exclaimed Maud, horrified. "People will think the circus has come to town."

"Ah, Miss Randolph—you can be in charge of buying yarns, cloth, and woolens. I would advise starting at La Samaritaine. You'll find it's rather like Gimbels."

"I don't shop at Gimbels," said Maud blankly.

"La Samaritaine," said Mrs. Rutherford, "is giving us a five percent discount."

And that was that.

Kate was rather less amused by Maud's discomfort when she herself was tasked with buying two hundred dollars' worth of agricultural tools. She refrained from pointing out that she wouldn't know a garden implement if it bit her; she suspected that Mrs. Rutherford would only inform her that there was no time like the present to learn.

At least it wasn't chickens.

While they were all in the midst of their orgy of shopping, Mrs. Rutherford was to tour the devastated areas; the doctors would visit hospitals. The rest of them, once they acquired their permits, would be loaned out to various organizations for the duration of their time in Paris, offered a choice of packing and unpacking supplies for the American Fund for French Wounded, rolling bandages for the Surgical Dressings Committee of the Red Cross, or manufacturing special splints for the wounded at the *Société pour les Blessés* in the Bois de Boulogne.

Kate had chosen the latter. She tried not to think what her mother would say about going all the way to Paris to engage in factory work, unpaid.

For that, she might have stayed in Brooklyn. And been paid for it.

The only saving grace was that their cots had arrived and were lined up in two rows in the attic like the beds for the seven little men in *Snow White.*

Kate crawled wearily into her cot, ridiculously grateful for something approximating a bed. It had been a long time since she had done anything more strenuous than write on a chalkboard. After carrying Margaret, her body felt as though someone had been at it with a hammer. And it was delicious to be on a mattress again, even only a sort of mattress, and not on a floor or deck. . . .

"Kate?" She heard the cot next to her creak as Emmie rolled in her direction. "Kate, are you awake?"

"Mmm?" She considered pretending to be asleep but couldn't quite make herself do it. "Yes?"

"I can't stop thinking about Nurse Fellowes."

"Nurse . . . oh." That morning felt like years ago already. It seemed absurd they'd only been in Paris for a day; it felt more like weeks. "The Canadian nurse with the red hair."

"I know. It's foolish of me." Kate could hear Emmie thrashing about in the bedclothes. "We didn't even *see* her foot. It wasn't like those pictures we saw of the men without noses or—oh, you know. And her face—I suppose it's the sort of thing that might happen if your hair caught fire on a candle, or you accidentally leaned too close to a fire, or goodness only knows what. Not necessarily a war injury. These sorts of things do happen. I met a woman at the settlement house who had lost both her eyebrows to a mistake with a gas jet."

Kate groaned and buried her face in her pillow. "Emmie. What are you talking about?"

"Nurse Fellowes. Every time I close my eyes, I keep seeing her face, with all those scars." Emmie sat up, swinging her legs over the side of the cot. Kate could see her in the darkness as a vague outline, long braid down over one shoulder. "It's just that one doesn't expect *nurses* to be hurt. Soldiers—they know they're going to be shot at. But nurses?"

Reluctantly, Kate propped herself up on one arm. "I don't imagine shells discriminate based on profession."

"It seems wrong somehow, to hurt someone who's trying to heal. War is war. I understand that. But— when someone is trying to do *good* . . ."

"I don't imagine they do it on purpose." It felt like being back at Smith again, whispering back and forth in the middle of the night. Although, admittedly, the subject matter had changed somewhat.

Kate had forgotten what it was to have a confidante, someone to talk to in the middle of the night. The last

six years had been solitary ones. She had gone skating a
time or two with her fellow teachers, and to the cinema
as opportunity offered, but the acquaintance had never
turned into friendship. The fault was hers, she knew.
She felt as though she were a fraud; that if anyone got
too close they would know her for what she was, not
Kate Moran, Smith graduate, but Katie Moranck,
whose mother scrubbed floors to keep a roof over their
heads.

It was only Emmie who had seemed not to care
about that, not to see her as less.

Until Julia had spoiled it all.

Emmie shivered and drew the blanket up around
her shoulders. "Someone—someone told me the Germans deliberately fire at the ambulances. I know I'm
not much to look at, but it's one thing to be plain with
the face one is born with and quite another thing to
be—to be disfigured. Does that make me a coward?"

"Emmie?" Kate struggled to a sitting position, peering at her friend's face in the darkness. "Is this because
of that horrible British officer?"

"He wasn't horrible. I don't think he was unkind
so much as sad. When you think about what he must
have seen . . . He looks as though he hasn't slept in a
month."

Kate muffled a yawn. "You aren't going to offer to

go plump his pillows, are you? That would be taking the angel-of-mercy act too far."

"I'm not trying to put on an act." The hurt in Emmie's voice was enough to kill any thought of falling asleep.

"I didn't mean that. I mean, I didn't mean it like that." Kate squeezed her eyes shut. They'd lost the habit of speaking to one another; it was like speaking a language at which she'd once been fluent and finding she was using all the wrong verbs. "It's been a long day. I hardly know what I'm saying. I guess I'm rattled too."

"I'm sorry," said Emmie, immediately all concern. "I should have thought . . ."

"Never mind," said Kate quickly. The last thing she needed was Emmie worrying over her; that would make her feel truly wormlike. "We won't be that near the front, you know. I doubt they'll think us worth shelling."

"And even if they did, it would be worth it, wouldn't it?" Emmie's voice was very small in the large room. Kate could hear Miss Patton snoring on the far side of the room. "For the children. I should be thinking of them, not us."

"Hmm," said Kate.

"It will all be better once we get there. It's the

waiting that's so hard," said Emmie, and Kate didn't point out that she had said the same thing on the boat, that it would all be better once they got to Paris. Well, here they were in Paris—and they did have cots, so she supposed that was better, by a certain value of better.

"Of course it will," said Kate, and hoped the woman who had once been her best friend wouldn't realize she was lying.

Chapter Six

Liza and I had a letter today from the YMCA director, inviting us to help them in their canteen. We wish we could—it's for our troops—but we know Mrs. R will never let us off. We are expected to love the cows and chickens. I personally consider her quite barmy. . . . Something will have to be done. I expect I'll have to do it, since no one else will bother.

> *—Miss Maud Randolph, '09,*
> *to her fiancé, Mr. Henry Craig*

August 1917
Paris, France

"There is a tavern way down in Brittany / Where weary soldiers take their liberty, / The keeper's daughter whose name is Madelon / Pours out the wine while they laugh and carry on . . ."

The troops crowded into the basement hall of the Gare du Nord banged on the tables, raising their glasses to the singer, who was belting out a popular ballad in both French and English. This was their last hurrah, one last bit of Paris to take away with them as they waited for the trains that would carry them back to the front.

Emmie hovered behind the soldiers, a tray of cigarettes in her hands, trying to figure out what she was meant to do.

"O Madelon you are the only one, / O Madelon for you we'll carry on . . ."

There had been a comedian on earlier. Emmie hadn't heard all the jokes—she'd been at the wrong end of the room for that—but from the way the men laughed, she'd suspected they might have been bawdy. Or maybe the men would have guffawed at anything just then.

But now the night had moved on, the wine had been poured and poured again, and the men were singing along, raggedly, singing to keep from crying.

"But Madelon she takes it all in fun, / She laughs and says, 'You see, it can't be done' . . ."

There was something so terribly lonesome in that

song. The room was crowded with men, hot with perspiration. Emmie wondered if each of them felt as alone as she did right now.

"You'll come with us to help out the Red Cross at the Gare du Nord, won't you?" Maud had asked, taking Emmie's agreement for granted, and Emmie had agreed, not so much because she wanted to, but because it was driving her half-mad, drifting along, waiting for their real work to begin.

It wasn't that she was idle. Seven hours a day, every day, Emmie sat in a temporary barrack in the Bois de Boulogne, making casts out of plaster of paris, ward boots, chin supports, splints. Maud and Liza had volunteered with the Red Cross; one of the other women, Miss Mills, had chosen to nurse at the Villier Fund hospital with another Smith classmate, not a member of the Unit. The doctors were away, touring hospitals in the war zone. But the rest of the Smith College Relief Unit went every day from the hotel on the Quai Voltaire to the workroom *pour les blessés* on the Bois du Boulogne.

The women chatted as they worked, sharing bits of themselves in the way one did when one's hands were occupied, speaking of their families, their lives, their work. Emmie learned about Miss Englund's brother, in the 11th Engineers, and her invalid mother, who was always having spasms; they heard a great deal about Miss Patton's younger sister and her new husband, who had been Miss Patton's beau first, or, at least, had seemed to be. Not that she said it in so many words, but it was clear all the same, at least to Emmie, who was used to receiving confidences and reading between the lines.

Except with Kate. The only one Emmie couldn't read these days was Kate.

No one could say Kate shirked, because she didn't. She turned out more splints than the rest of them put together. No one could call her unfriendly. She listened and commented and even joked, but she never, not once, shared anything about herself. Not even late at night in the quiet of the attic room. Not even to Emmie.

Emmie tried to make things better; she redoubled her attempts, falling over backward to try to show Kate how much she was still her friend, that it was all just the same as it had always been. But the more she tried to jolly her, the more Kate had withdrawn behind her eyes, faultlessly polite, the reserve that had always been part of her hardening into a wall, and Emmie hadn't the slightest idea how to make her come out of it again.

So when Maud asked Emmie to volunteer to help with the show the Red Cross put on at the Gare du Nord for departing soldiers, Emmie said yes, just to have something to do, someplace to go—and, maybe, just a bit, so it wouldn't look like she was quite so starved for companionship. She didn't particularly like Maud or Liza, but they were there.

Except, they weren't. They moved easily through the crowd, laughing and joking with the men, while Emmie stood in the back, feeling awkward and not quite sure what to do with herself. She had never been good at mixed social occasions, always too aware of her height, her protruding teeth, her fade-away lashes, all those things that made her, in a word, plain. She didn't have that facility for flirting that seemed to come naturally to Maud. With boys she'd known forever, she could be comfortable, but it was different with strangers. Aunt May had always been quite clear: there was only one reason any man would approach Emmie. Not her face, but her fortune.

Emmie was just considering, not very enthusiastically, the prospect of circulating around the room with her tray of cigarettes, when a soldier detached himself from a group and came up to her.

"Cigarette?" Emmie said brightly as a tall, thin man in a well-worn uniform approached.

"Do you think I deserve one?" asked a clipped, patrician voice.

Emmie's head snapped up. She was staring at a lean, tanned face, less haggard now than the last time she had seen it, but unmistakably the same. "You're the man from the hospital."

"I would understand if you would rather disavow the acquaintance." With an effort, he added, "I saw you here—and saw my chance to make good on my bad behavior of the other day. To put it bluntly, I owe you an apology."

He'd had a bath since she'd last seen him. Emmie could smell sandalwood soap, which made a rather nice contrast to some of the other smells in the room. He'd also shaved, but the mustache was still there, a thin dark line over his upper lip.

She probably shouldn't be staring at his lips, Emmie realized, and hastily began rearranging her tray of cigarettes. "There's no need for that. It wasn't your fault we were blocking Dr. Blake's office. I imagine it must be pretty maddening to be looking for someone and find three prone women instead. Are you *sure* I can't interest you in a cigarette?"

"Only one of you was prone. And it was my fault that I . . . took out my ill temper on you and your friend." There was something about his voice that demanded her attention. She could see the muscles in his throat work as he searched for the right words. "I was visiting a friend in the hospital. A man who ought to be at Oxford now, staring at bugs through a microscope and marveling at the miracle of wings, not blind in both eyes, staggering about on one leg."

She knew men like that. The US hadn't entered the war until the spring, but there had been Yale men who had felt strongly about protecting France any way they could, who had volunteered at the first word of war back in 1914, some in the air, some in the volunteer ambulance service, some in the French Foreign Legion. She could think of at least one cousin who ought to have been in New Haven right now, writing about the foreign policy of some long-ago King Louis, not buried in a graveyard somewhere in France.

But she couldn't explain all that, so she said only, "It's a horrible waste, isn't it?"

The Englishman looked down at her, and she knew he wasn't really seeing her at all. "We thought we'd blaze over here in a moment of glory, see off the Hun, and go home. We thought it was something like a holiday. And then to see you—more of you—going off, as we did . . ."

"Not in a blaze of glory, though," said Emmie. At the farewell luncheon, a poem had been read to them, comparing them to the heroes of the old sagas, now reborn in female form. It had been lovely and terribly inspiring, but even at the time, Emmie had rather doubted its applicability. "We're not looking for glory. Just to do something decent and worthwhile."

"Does that still exist in the world?"

"I should hope so. I think so. I don't know that we'll accomplish anything particularly heroic, but if we get milk to even a handful of children, that's something, isn't it? At least, it is to those children."

His dark eyes were fixed on her face, almost alarming in their intensity. At last he said, "Yes. It is."

It would have been nice to think he meant it. Emmie set her tray down on a table. "You think we're very naive, don't you?"

He reached into his jacket pocket for a cigarette case, his eyes never leaving hers. He drew it out, a silver one with a monogram on it. "Would you rather I called it idealistic?"

"I'd rather honesty than flattery." It was, she supposed, one of the benefits of being plain. One learned early on to discern flummery. She laughed at herself, her eyes crinkling. "You needn't sugarcoat it. Sugar's been rationed, and we've had our quota already."

She surprised him into a laugh. It was raw and hoarse, but quite definitely a laugh all the same. "So it has. All right, yes. I do think it naive. You haven't been to the front—you haven't seen—"

"What the Germans can do?" Here, Emmie felt on firmer footing. "I'm not a hothouse flower, you know. I've spent the last five years doing settlement house work. I've seen more than you think."

"Like the men at the American Ambulance Hospital?"

"No, nothing quite like that. At least, not on that sort of scale." How could she explain to him? She'd seen women with hands mangled from being drawn into machinery. She'd seen a pregnant woman so badly beaten by her husband that she'd lost the child, and yet still gone home to him after. She'd seen a child whose arm was a mass of scar tissue from having fallen—or been pushed—into a coal fire. She'd seen cruelty, but this was different somehow. It was the impersonal nature of it that made it so horrifying.

"That wasn't even the half of it. What you're letting yourself in for . . ."

Unthinkingly, Emmie put her hand on his arm, trying to reassure him. "It's kind of you to be concerned. We won't be working with the ambulances at the front. We'll be in a village well behind the lines. The conditions may be different from a city slum, but the needs are the same: shelter, clothing, food—affection. Those children need to know someone cares for them. The worse it is, the more that matters."

"And you have affection to spare?"

Her hand was still on his arm. Emmie snatched it away. "The last I looked, kindness wasn't rationed."

"Are you quite sure?" The officer inclined his head, saying formally, "I wish you well, Miss—"

"Van Alden." She had been rather enjoying the anonymity. People tended to react to the name Van Alden, because they were in awe of her lineage, offended by her mother, or, sometimes, both.

The British officer merely bowed over her hand. "Miss Van Alden."

He didn't seem to know who she was at all, and Emmie found that strangely wonderful. "Do you realize I don't even know your name?"

"Perhaps I prefer to dwell in mystery, like the Scarlet Pimpernel."

Emmie couldn't quite hide her delight. She adored that book, had read it at least a dozen times, possibly more, no matter how many times Kate had protested it was all entirely improbable and anyone would have known who he was inside five minutes. "Do I find myself addressing Sir Percy Blakeney, baronet?"

He smiled down at her, a little creakily. "You've discovered me, I see."

"Do those Frenchies seek you everywhere?"

He grimaced. "It's not much of a guess whether this is heaven or hell."

"'The mind is its own place,'" quoted Emmie, feeling a bit giddy, "'and in itself, can make a Heaven of Hell, a Hell of Heaven.'"

"When Milton wrote that," said the British officer wryly, "he'd clearly never been to the Somme. Besides, it's not fair switching authors. Next I'll trot out John Donne and then we'll be wallowing in Shakespeare before you know it."

"Would that be so terrible?" asked Emmie, enjoying herself tremendously and feeling vaguely guilty about it.

"It depends on whether you mean to quote *Much Ado* or *Titus Andronicus*."

"Possibly *Troilus and Cressida*," said Emmie determinedly, "but never *Titus*."

"'What plagues and what portents!'" he recited softly. "'What mutiny! . . . Frights, changes, horrors . . . enterprise is sick.' There's your *Troilus and Cressida* for you—and all too apt. Didn't I tell you we were in danger of Shakespeare once we started?"

"We could try Keats instead," suggested Emmie, wanting to shake that frozen look from his face.

"Beauty is truth? Maybe that means, then, that all this ugliness is nothing but a lie, an illusion—but it's a very solid one." He took her hand, his skin surprisingly warm through his gloves. "I would far rather stay and debate poets, but I have a rendezvous with a train."

It hit Emmie like a vat of cold water. "Wait, are you going back to—"

"To the front? Yes." Of course he was. That was why he was here. That was why they were all here.

In the delight of finding someone who spoke her language, even a slightly foreign dialect of it, she had allowed herself to forget, and the full horror of it rushed back upon her, choking her.

"I—I wish you well." What else did one say to a man heading to horrors unspeakable? "Good luck."

"And to you," he said solemnly. He raised his hat to her. "To decency and those who persist in practicing it."

With that he was gone, walking away, straight-backed. He hadn't, Emmie realized, ever told her his name.

"Who was that?" demanded Maud, arriving pink-cheeked with an empty basket.

Emmie looked after him, joining a group of men similarly garbed. "Sir Percy Blakeney. Baronet."

"Oh, is he a friend of your family?" Maud didn't wait for her to answer, setting down her empty basket on the table and adjusting her hat to a more becoming angle. "It's amazing the people one knows who one meets here. Liza and I just bumped right into the cousin of a friend of one of my parents' neighbors from Montclair—"

Emmie didn't even try to untangle the relationship. She let Maud ramble on while she looked again for the British officer, but there were too many khaki uniforms to find one specific one. It seemed unlikely she would ever see him again. Their discussion felt, already, vaguely unreal.

But she was glad, glad to have met him even for that moment. It had made her feel like herself again, for the first time in a very long time.

"—which is why what I wanted to talk to you about is so important."

"What you wanted—" Emmie blinked, trying to remember what Maud had been saying.

Maud sighed with exaggerated patience. "Yes, about our boys. I really think it's absurd that we're bothering with livestock and all that when we could be here, doing something for our boys."

Emmie looked out at the rows and rows of troops,

French and English and American. One could tell the Americans because they looked much better fed than their Continental counterparts, their uniforms fresher and cleaner. "But we are here, doing something for our boys."

"Yes, now. But what about when Mrs. Rutherford gets back? If she has her way, she'll drag us out to some godforsaken place to do goodness only knows what."

"But we do know what," said Emmie, feeling vaguely bewildered. "We're to offer aid to those in the devastated zone."

"You mean practically in the trenches," said Maud. "That might have made sense four months ago, but you must agree, now that the new offensive is on, it's perfectly insane to be even thinking of going anywhere near the front."

"There's a new offensive on?" That was one of the strangest things about being in Paris; they heard so much less about the war than they had in New York. The censors did their work well. But Maud appeared to have her ways, which, as far as Emmie could tell, consisted of dining out with a great many friends of friends and shamelessly interrogating all of them.

"Didn't you hear? They're clearing out all the Paris hospitals to make room for more wounded."

"No, I hadn't heard," admitted Emmie. She spared a thought for Julia and Dr. Stringfellow, touring hospitals, Mrs. Rutherford at Grécourt. "But surely the passes wouldn't have been issued if it were unsafe?"

"It's a war," said Maud, as though Emmie were particularly slow. "Everything is unsafe. But really, it's quite mad to make oneself even less safe—and to do it to play milkmaid for a bunch of French peasants!"

"But you knew what it was when you joined," said Emmie carefully. "It was always clear we were meant to be offering civilian relief. Mrs. Rutherford was quite specific about that."

She could still remember the way the room had stilled as Mrs. Rutherford spoke, back at the Smith College Club in Boston in April, telling of the evils she had seen in France, the good they could do, they, American college women, with their will and wit and resourcefulness, to comfort the forgotten and give shelter to the homeless.

"Mrs. Rutherford," retorted Maud, "is a ridiculous old pacifist. I pointed out to her what we could be doing for our troops, and do you know what she told me? She told me that men will always tear things up and it's our job to put things back together. As if we were on a different side from our own boys! It's absurd. Not to mention her obsession with farm animals. I think she's quite mad and I'm going to tell the committee so."

"You're going to tell the committee?"

"That a group of us agree, Mrs. Rutherford isn't fit to lead. We're just wasting their money on cows and plows and . . . and . . . chickens! And all this with the trucks! I'm sure we'd have had them ages ago if she hadn't annoyed everyone."

"I don't think that's really the problem," began Emmie, but Maud didn't seem to hear her.

"It would mean so much if you would lend your name to our appeal," Maud said, and Emmie could feel herself freezing. Oblivious, Maud went on. "Of course, we could very well do it on our own—and we will!— but your name would add it extra weight."

Not her, just her name.

It was always what they really wanted: not Emmie, who liked to read Tennyson and secretly enjoyed playing with children's cookery sets to make minia-ture pies, but Miss Van Alden of the Fifth Avenue Van Aldens, connected by blood or marriage to every Knickerbocker family of consequence, to all those Dutch and Huguenot and *Mayflower* descendants who had come to New York to trade in furs or silks and made themselves lords of the new land, in fact if not in name. They looked at her and saw not a tall, awkward girl with buck teeth and a long chin and flyaway hair but that long and silent procession of Van Aldens and Stuyvesants and Livingstons and Schuylers.

It was one of the reasons she had taken to Kate so quickly, all those years ago. Kate hadn't the first idea who any of those people were or why they mattered.

"Well, will you?" Maud asked impatiently. "We have it all written and ready to send off. Of course, it would also help if you would tell your mother—I'm sure people would listen to *her*—and then we could start doing the work that truly matters."

"No." The word was barely audible. Maud stared at her and Emmie tried again. "Our plans are already so well forward . . . it would be a waste at this point. . . ."

Maud waved her hand dismissively. "You mean because they put plumbing into a bunch of army barracks? I'm sure someone else can get some use out of it."

On the stage, the last song was drawing to a close. The men looked so sad, the last reprieve ending, the trains waiting.

To decency, the officer had said, *and those who persist in practicing it.*

She would persist. She would.

"It's not because of the plumbing," Emmie said earnestly, trying to make Maud understand, wanting

Maud to understand. "It's because there are women and children there waiting for us. They've been told we'll come. They're relying on us. It's summer now still—but what happens when winter comes? Could you live with yourself if a child died of exposure while we fed soup to the troops?"

"That's a bit melodramatic, isn't it?" protested Maud. "Like 'The Little Match Girl.' We don't know these children."

"We don't know these troops either." Emmie hurried on before Maud could explain exactly how she knew them and just who knew whom from Montclair. "If we hadn't committed to this, some other group might have come forward and done the work. But we *did*. Having done so . . . don't you think we owe it to them?"

"No," said Maud bluntly. "Now, about removing Mrs. Rutherford—"

So much for standing up for what she believed in. "Will you excuse me?" asked Emmie. "I believe some of those men might want some cigarettes before they go."

And she fled.

It was the next morning before Emmie had the opportunity to unburden herself to Kate. She'd wanted to tell Kate immediately, but Kate had been asleep already when she came back—and, besides, Emmie wasn't entirely sure Maud hadn't already suborned Miss Patton, who seemed pleasant enough but a bit nervous and changeable and not exactly steady of purpose. So she'd waited until after breakfast, when the others were getting ready to go, and made Kate stay with her downstairs in the breakfast room, pouring it all out in an anxious whisper with one eye on the door, just in case Maud or Liza might wander in in search of another piece of war bread.

"Do you think we ought to tell her—Mrs. Rutherford, I mean," Emmie asked breathlessly, "that Maud and Liza are . . ."

"Planning a coup?" Kate provided for her.

"Well . . . yes." It sounded rather melodramatic put that way. But that was what it was, wasn't it? A coup. "I think we ought, don't you?"

Kate was quiet for a long moment. "Would it be such a bad thing to stay in Paris?"

Emmie looked at her in dismay. "But that's not what we're here to do."

She couldn't explain it even to herself, but it mattered that they were going to Grécourt. It felt silly and self-important to describe it as a call, like Joan of Arc and her voices, but that was what it was. When she closed her eyes, she could see the boys and girls of Grécourt calling to her, needing her.

"You don't think they have a point, do you?"

"I think," said Kate carefully, and that very care was somehow alarming, because it meant that Kate was watching her words, was watching them with her, Emmie, "that we're more than qualified for canteen work, or even to go on with what we're doing now. I'm not sure we have the skills to reconstruct a destroyed village—much less eleven destroyed villages. Liza can barely speak French. And to call me a chauffeur is nothing short of absurd."

"You passed your test." Emmie felt a little clutch of panic in her chest.

"Only because the person just before me crashed into a camion and goodness only knows how many crates of apples. The street was impassable for nearly an hour."

"Aren't you underestimating yourself? And besides, you learned before—I remember you driving me down Thames Street in Newport without bashing into anything at all!"

"Yes, but that was six years ago," said Kate.

And there it was. Emmie could feel those six years sitting between them, weighing on them like lead. Six years of distance against four years of friendship.

"Has that much changed?" she asked, and she knew she wasn't just talking about driving. "You're still the same person you were."

"Yes, but the car isn't," said Kate, and Emmie felt like she'd been very neatly put off. Again. Some of her distress must have shown, because Kate leaned across the table and gave her cold hand a quick squeeze. "Emmie. Don't worry. I'm not part of Maud's cabal—I don't think she'd even think to ask me! I just wonder. That's all."

"I don't," said Emmie in a small voice, but she didn't know if Kate heard her because a horn was honking outside, gears grinding, people shouting, doors flinging open, footsteps running down the stairs.

"What on earth—" Kate ran to the window, Emmie bashing her shin against a chair as she followed, and there, in the middle of the street, was an army truck, cheerfully beeping its horn, and, on top of it, in full Unit uniform and an alarmingly large hat with a feather, sat Mrs. Rutherford.

"Well, that's an entrance for you," said Kate, looking at Emmie.

"Girls!" Mrs. Rutherford was calling as she waved farewell to her escort. "Girls!"

"We thought it was the Germans," said Maud crossly, coming downstairs with her hat in her hand.

"Not the Germans—the French. They were kind enough to give me a lift from the station," said Mrs. Rutherford, swinging her maltreated carpetbag to the ground. Her face looked thinner than it had two weeks ago, but it glowed with windburn and joy. "All is arranged for us! I've left them at Grécourt waiting for our arrival. I can't tell you how much they need us."

Emmie felt the tight knot in her chest relax a bit. "But our trucks . . ." she said hesitantly.

"Ha," said Mrs. Rutherford. "The people of Grécourt need us and they need us now. It's absurd to sit here waiting for our trucks any longer. If Mahomet won't come to the mountain . . ."

"Mahoment? Is he one of the Algerian soldiers?" asked Liza.

Mrs. Rutherford ignored her. "Miss Cooper, Miss Englund, Miss Moran, Miss Patton, Miss Shaw, make your excuses to your places of employment and pack your bags. If the trucks won't come to us, we must go to Saint-Nazaire and get them! If we leave tonight, we can be in Saint-Nazaire by morning. I've booked places for us on the train."

Liza cast an anxious look at Maud. "So fast?"

"It's actually a rather slow train," said Mrs. Rutherford, unpinning her hat and drawing off her gloves, "but it was the best one available. And I'm sure none of us minds a bit of discomfort in a good cause. We'll fetch our trucks and be off to Grécourt within the week."

"You see," murmured Kate as they went up the stairs to the attic. "You were worried for nothing."

"Ye-es," said Emmie. It was a relief that Mrs. Rutherford was here and that they might, just might, actually get started.

But she wasn't sure that Maud would give up so easily. And she couldn't quite forget that Kate hadn't wanted to go.

Chapter Seven

For two weeks and more we anxiously awaited the anticipated arrival of our trucks, which were meant to be forwarded by the YMCA from the port. When it became evident that they were too busy to attend to the matter, I decided to go myself with chauffeurs to bring the cars to Paris. . . . We at once located the crates containing the two Ford trucks and the White truck, also the sixty sections of the six portable houses, severally, some on a quay, some on a freight car, and some stacked in the freight yard. The cars had been exposed to sea air and were frightfully rusty.

To get the cases together, uncrate and put together the cars, and put them in running

condition took four days' very hard work. . . . Our
chauffeurs worked tirelessly and cheerfully.

Many more American uniforms are to be seen
in the streets than French. We were delighted to
see the "Sammies" and they to see us. Miss
Englund found a brother.

— Mrs. Ambrose Rutherford (née
Betsy Hayes), '96, Director, to
the members of the committee

September 1917
Saint-Nazaire, France

Liza stuck a grease-stained hand out from under
the truck. "Could anyone hand me that cup of
grease?"

"I'll get it." Kate set down her hammer, stretched
her sore muscles, and shoved a small cup of grease into
Liza's hand.

"Marvelous!" Hand and grease cup disappeared together under the truck, and Kate took a step back and
stared at their handiwork.

It looked like a truck.

Which was, in itself, nothing short of amazing. When
they'd gotten to Saint-Nazaire, woozy from sleeplessness after a night standing up on a packed train, they'd

found their trucks on the docks, not in one piece, but in boxes.

Kate hadn't even been aware trucks could come in boxes. She had assumed, if she had thought about it at all, that someone had driven the truck into the ship's hold and left it there. It had never occurred to her that it might have come from the factory in parts or that they would be expected to put it together.

"Well, of course you can," Mrs. Rutherford had said, and handed Kate a toolbox, no doubt cadged from their unsuspecting innkeeper, who had had no idea that his yard was about to turn into a garage. She had given Kate an encouraging pat on the shoulder. "It's hardly alchemy. You just follow the instructions and put the pieces together. If a man can do it, so can we."

By "we," she meant them. Kate had been left holding a hammer and wondering what on earth she was to do with it.

It was a commonplace at home that Kate was too educated to do anything useful. "Don't let Katie near the stove" was the family mantra. "She'll burn the bread while her nose is in a book."

Which was a little ridiculous given that her mother didn't bake her own bread; she bought it from Losher's bread factory, day old, at a discount.

Kate had always accepted that she was singularly

useless, accepted it because they all seemed to believe it—but now, three days later, she was standing here with a sore back and sore fingers and a truck that had a top because she had hammered it on. She'd screwed on the supports and hammered on the cab and realized it was backward and cursed and pried it all out again but she'd done it and no one had mocked her for slowness or made fun of her for hitting her own fingers.

Kate stretched her arms up over her head. Liza was still under the truck, applying grease—they'd all had way too much to do with grease over the past three days, and she'd probably still be sanding rust in her sleep for weeks to come—but it was only the finishing touches now. The truck was together. It was done. It might even go. She wished she could take a picture of it to send to her mother and stepfather and brothers to show them that this was something she had done with her own hands, something which had nothing to do with putting words on paper or being clever in an examination.

"Almost done!" came Liza's voice from under the cab.

Liza trailing around after Maud, Kate found deeply wearisome. Liza wearing an old slicker and squashy felt hat, covered with grease, was a surprisingly good companion, especially when one was flat on one's back under a car and not saying much more than "Could you pass that whatchamacallit, please?" Liza never seemed to tire and had a cheerful obliviousness to sarcasm, possibly as a defense against a decade of friendship with Maud. Whatever the cause, Kate found it strangely restful.

"No hurry," said Kate, and wandered over to see how Alice Patton and Frances Englund were getting on with the Ford truck.

That had been a revelation too. Not Fran Englund— she was just as she had always been, levelheaded and even-tempered and with a wonderfully dry sense of humor that came out under adversity—but Alice Patton, who, it turned out, beneath the flutters and the giggles and the doubtful taste in haberdashery, had a positive genius for anything mechanical.

Kate had been amazed to find herself—well, not enjoying herself precisely. Or maybe she was. It was good to be out in the early September air, in the sun and the wind and the salt of the sea, doing something with her hands and seeing it actually work, in the company of people who didn't ask more of her than to pass the nearest wrench.

Unlike Emmie, who was wonderful and good and kind, but always seemed to need something from Kate, if Kate could only figure out what it was, or if she had it to give.

"I can't believe that came out of all those boxes," Kate said, staring at the massively long Ford truck, off of which Alice Patton was sanding the final bits of rust.

"I do," said Fran Englund, wrestling with the crank. "I had to pry open every one of them and I'm not sure my back will ever forgive me. I think this crank is possessed. Or is, at the very least, a German agent. It just won't *go*."

"Have you tried putting more grease on it?"

"It's bathing in grease," said Fran.

"Elbow grease," said Alice with a giggle.

"I'm not sure my elbows have any left," said Fran, shaking out her wrists and examining the offending appendages.

"We'll grease them with a glass of burgundy at dinner tonight," suggested Kate.

"I'll drink to that." Fran came back around the car to stand next to Kate. "It does look impressive, doesn't it?"

"For something that came out of a box four days ago? Absolutely," agreed Kate.

"Now we actually have to drive them," said Alice, putting down her rag and coming to join them. "Who's the French saint for inexperienced drivers?"

"I thought you knew how to drive," said Kate, twisting her neck to look at her.

Alice fiddled with her earring. "Gil—I mean, my sister's husband, took me out a time or two and let me turn the wheel. I said I could drive so the Unit would take me. And I think I can. Maybe."

"I haven't driven for six years," confessed Kate.

"I'm a very good driver," said Fran Englund, and for some reason that struck them all as hysterically funny, and that was how Mrs. Rutherford found them, clinging to each other's shoulders, howling with laughter.

"Did I miss a joke?" Mrs. Rutherford asked.

Kate managed to choke in her breath, tears streaming down her cheeks. She wiped them back with a grease-stained hand.

"N-nothing worth noting," she managed, exchanging a glance with Alice Patton, who was choking into her own handkerchief.

"Well done, ladies! And ahead of schedule, no less," said Mrs. Rutherford. "No one would ever guess you aren't seasoned engineers."

That almost set them off again.

"I don't think she'll think we're quite so wondrous when we run her off the road," giggled Alice Patton.

"You'll be fine," said Fran Englund. "But I think I'll let you go ahead. . . ."

And they were fine. Mostly. One of the Fords was extra long, which was quite useful for piling on the giant pieces of prefabricated building materials that Mrs. Rutherford insisted would turn magically into living quarters and schoolhouses, but also meant that there was a great deal of truck they couldn't quite keep track of.

The man whose stall they knocked over was very nice about it, especially after they bought all his onions.

"What are we to do with these?" asked Alice Patton, holding up a string of onions and staring at it blankly. Fifteen similar strings adorned the cab behind her.

"Make soup?" suggested Kate, and ducked as Fran lobbed an onion at her.

They'd barely made it ten blocks, the long Ford seizing up and having to be re-cranked twice, before they got held up behind a series of very official-looking cars outside a large building flying an American flag. There was a group of soldiers milling about, very excited and surprised to see a convoy of American women driving three trucks.

One of the Sammies, a tall man with brown hair and

an open, windburned face, began waving frantically at them. "Fran!"

"Freddie! It's my brother—excuse me." Fran Englund slid down from the cab of the Ford.

Kate, who was sharing the White with Margaret Cooper, tried to remember how to put it into park.

"I think it's this lever," said Margaret, pulling it for her. Margaret, Kate had learned, was an excellent driver, although she said very little about it. She still apologized periodically for fainting on Kate, which Kate found awkward for both of them.

"Thanks," said Kate, and slid down from the truck, which wasn't white at all, but simply made by the White Motor Company.

They found themselves in a mob of American soldiers, all tremendously excited to find women who spoke English, ready to be friends with anyone who knew Fred Englund's sister, anxious for news from home, and all extremely disappointed that none of the women could tell them anything about the baseball season.

Margaret Cooper immediately found someone who had a sister who was her year at Smith. Kate was left to talk to two others and, in want of something to say, gestured to the house behind them, the one flying the American flag.

"That building—is it the American consulate?"

"It's—er, a sort of clubhouse," said one of the men, exchanging a look with another.

"They mean it's a bawdy house," said Fran Englund calmly as they went back to their abandoned trucks. She climbed back up into the Ford, sitting down on the board over the gasoline tank that served as a seat. "My brother told me. He said when our troops first landed there was a line that went down three blocks."

"That's dreadful. Don't their commanders *do* anything about it?" demanded Liza. Her eyes looked even more like glass dolls' eyes than usual, round as a cartoon in the Sunday papers.

"Sure they do," said Fran. "They demand the first spots in line."

Kate coughed to cover a snicker.

"It's not funny," said Liza earnestly, holding on to the side of the truck. "I've heard it's all a German plot. They're getting French loose women to seduce our troops to undermine the health of the American army."

"I'm sure our boys would never think of visiting a French bawdy house otherwise," said Fran, straight-faced.

Liza looked from Fran to Kate, wounded. "It's true! I heard it from a woman at the YMCA."

"Who I'm sure heard it from the Germans?" guessed Kate.

"Well, no—but someone reliable. Maud says it's dreadful and it's every American woman's job to keep our boys on the straight and narrow."

"Does Maud's fiancé know that?" whispered Fran to Kate as Kate passed by on her way back to the White truck.

"Maybe he's her own special reclamation project," Kate whispered back, and went to join Margaret Cooper in the White.

It was like college again—college with the threat of impending destruction, that was. She felt like she was playing a theatre role: college Kate, the Kate who bantered and laughed and pretended to be just like everyone else.

The difference was, in college, she had really thought she was just like everyone else, that being secretary of the literary society and volunteering with the dramatic society washed out all the differences, made her one of them. She'd always had an ear for languages; it had been easy to snuff out any lingering traces of a Brooklyn accent, until she didn't even have to think about it anymore, her voice had changed, just as she had changed.

It was so easy, with Fran and Alice, who didn't know her, who knew only that she was another Smith girl and a member of the Relief Unit, to pretend to be that person again. To actually be that person again. They didn't look at her and see a charity girl; they didn't know she was a charity girl. She was just Kate, who had done her fair share putting together the White truck.

But they were going back to Paris. Where Emmie never meant to make her feel less, but always did.

Not to mention that Julia would be sure to put her in her place given the chance.

No, it wouldn't do to get too comfortable. They'd only find her out eventually. Kate winced at the memory of Maud on the boat, assuming her mother was her nanny. She'd meant to tell her, she really had.

Or maybe she hadn't.

"Watch out for the—"

"Oh, bother." Kate bit her tongue hard as the truck hit a large pothole. "Would you like to drive for a bit, Margaret? You're better at it than I am."

The rain started just after lunch, hardening from a mist into a persistent drizzle, turning the roads to sucking pools of mud, soaking their hair under their hats, and dripping down the backs of their slickers.

The long Ford's crank seized; the White got a puncture. One minute it was rolling along—well,

maybe not precisely rolling. One minute it was slogging slowly but fairly steadily through the mud, and
the next it was listing to one side and Kate was clinging to the doorframe to keep from falling out and
Margaret was in her lap.

The extra-long Ford behind them skidded and fish-
tailed, but mercifully Fran was driving. She managed
merely to knock down part of a fence rather than hitting them, which Kate greatly appreciated.

Ahead of them, oblivious, the Ford jitney, holding
Liza and Mrs. Rutherford, grew smaller and smaller in
the distance through the gusting rain.

"Bother!" said Kate, slithering down. "Bother,
bother, bother. Can we patch it?"

It was sluicing down now; she had to shout to be
heard over the wind.

"Too far gone," said Fran, struggling over in her
slicker, her boots squelching in the dark mud. "We'll
need the spare."

Their cars were half-on, half-off the road. An army
truck, going just a bit too fast, honked angrily at them.

"Maybe one of these nice men will help us!" hollered
Liza, waving her arms over her head hopefully, but the
army truck blazed obliviously past, coating them with
mud in the process.

"They pr-probably don't r-realize we're female,"

gasped Alice, slipping in the mud and just managing not to fall. "Just l-look at us."

Fran spat mud. "What the fashionable chauffeur is wearing this season," she said, and got the jack out of the back of the White.

"Mmmph mmmph," said Alice, dancing around behind them. "Mmmph mmmpph mmpphh mmpph."

"WHAT?" screamed Kate.

"FIVE INCHES!" yelled Alice, who had read all the manuals. "You need to get it up five inches to get the wheel off!"

It might as well have been five feet. It took them an hour, working in pairs, to get the White up high enough to take off the wheel, and nearly as long to pump up the spare tire by hand and fasten it into place, which would have gone faster if their wet and muddy fingers hadn't kept slipping off the nut.

"We'll get better at it with practice," said Margaret Cooper, her hat dripping rain all around her face.

"I hope not," muttered Kate. "I'm not sure I could take any more practice."

Fran grinned wearily at her. "We'll all be strong like bulls by the time we're done."

"Or mad like bulls," offered Alice.

It was full dark by the time they made it as far as Nantes, having managed, in the course of a day, to go all of forty miles. They found the other Ford parked neatly in front of an inn and Mrs. Rutherford and Liza sitting down to soup and war bread.

"Only two hundred and sixty miles left to go," said Kate, slumping into a chair. They had paused only to scrub at the worst of the mud with the two inches of cold water allotted them by the innkeeper. The result was, at best, mixed. It was a blessing the lighting wasn't good; the mud just looked like shadows. It also disguised what was in the soup.

"It's going to take us a week to get back to Paris at this rate," said Alice, dragging her spoon through her soup.

"It's going to take a week to get to the next town at this rate," said Kate.

"I wonder why no one has invented puncture-free tires?" mused Liza, who hadn't spent the day wrestling with one.

"Because then the tire companies would be out of business," said Fran, dunking her war bread in her soup to soften it.

"Do you think they dropped the nails on the road?" asked Kate.

"No, that was probably the Germans," said Fran, straight-faced, and Liza nodded eagerly in reply.

"They think of everything," said Kate, and wasn't

sure whether to laugh or cry, so just gave up and ate soup instead.

It was only nine o'clock when they finished their meal, but it felt like midnight. Outside, the rain continued to sluice down. As she left the table, Kate found Mrs. Rutherford sitting in a tiny circle of light in the sitting room of the inn, surrounded by papers.

"I'm working out schedules," she said. "We've so much to do that we'll accomplish it best if we're all divided into committees."

"I had thought committees were a sure way to ensure nothing actually got done," said Kate, too tired to mind her words.

Mrs. Rutherford didn't look up from her charts. "That depends on the committee. Of bored society women, yes. Here, it simply means that those who can will. It's much more effective than one woman trying to oversee everything, especially when we're undertaking so much, so quickly."

There were six categories on the page: House, Social Services, Nursing, Supplies & Stores, Motor, Children.

"But none of us are nurses," Kate said. "How can we have a nursing committee?"

"None of you were trained mechanics either," said Mrs. Rutherford imperturbably. "And yet our trucks still run."

"When they run."

"A puncture is an act of God—or of the French roads, which is much the same thing," said Mrs. Rutherford, writing busily. "You can't blame yourself for it. You aren't responsible for everything, Miss Moran."

Based on the list, Kate wasn't responsible for much. She had been put down to serve on two committees: Motor and House. That was good, she told herself. She wouldn't know how to do any of the rest of it. She supposed she should count herself lucky there wasn't a separate category for instruction in the French language.

There also wasn't a category for farm labor. She thought of Emmie's earnest study of chickens. "But what about the farm animals? There's no category for agricultural endeavor."

"That comes under Supplies and Stores," said Mrs. Rutherford. "You didn't think we'd be caring for the animals ourselves, did you?"

"I'm not sure what we're meant to be doing," said Kate honestly. She wouldn't ordinarily have admitted as much, but she was so tired, and the little circle of lamplight felt like an island in the middle of stormy seas, a space out of time.

Mrs. Rutherford looked up from her work, surprised.

"I'd thought I'd explained. It's really very simple. What we're trying to do for them is give them the means to rebuild for themselves. We don't want to beggar them or make them feel the objects of charity. What we do is give them the materials to work: rags for braiding, yarn for knitting, straw for weaving. We'll run a store with food and supplies below cost—but not for free. Pride can be as important as bread. They've lost so much, these villagers. Many of them were once prosperous farmers, storekeepers, innkeepers, and now they're living in holes in the ground, sharing one sheet. We need to leave them their pride."

Pride. Kate remembered being six, and the well-meaning social worker who had singled her out at school. That had been during the lean years, when her mother had done her best, but that best hadn't extended to new coats or shoes. And Kate had grown so terribly fast.

"That poor child," the woman had said. "Doesn't her family *care*?"

She'd worn those new shoes, but she could feel them burning on her feet still. She would rather have gone bare.

It was odd to be on the other end of it. Playing Lady Bountiful, her mother called it. Good enough for some. "Won't they mind that we're selling below cost, then?"

Mrs. Rutherford smiled up at her. "No. They'll just feel glad they got a bargain. It's no shame to put one over on the Americans—they'll think we don't understand their money yet and enjoy shaking their heads over our naivete. Good night, Miss Moran."

"Good night," said Kate, and went slowly upstairs, feeling like Mrs. Rutherford's plans might be somewhat less mad than she had previously supposed.

The rain continued to persecute them. Margaret was right; they did get better at changing punctures, although it didn't get any more pleasant with practice. Whether it was the Germans or just French cart horses with loose shoes, the roads from Nantes to Paris appeared to be positively strewn with nails, all of which aimed straight at their tires. They ate their lunch as they went to save time, shoving down cheese and crackers and gulping coffee from a thermos, taking turns driving. Kate began to accept being wet through as an inevitable law of nature.

And then, just north of Chartres, the sun came out.

"What is that great yellow ball in the sky?" asked Fran.

"That's the sun," explained Liza helpfully.

Kate squinted up at the sky. "Unless we're hallucinating and it's just a mirage. It might be a mirage."

Fran put her hand up, palm out. "My hand is dry. It's real."

It was amazing what a difference a bit of sunshine made. They didn't even mind when they drove into Versailles, the home of kings, and promptly blew a tire right in front of the mayor's house, which looked like a miniature palace itself, and very French.

This time, they collected a crowd of interested citizens, all wanting to know who these shabby American women were and what they were doing charging about on three trucks loaded with building materials and the remains of fifteen strings of onions, now rather soggy.

While a few helpful soldiers debated the best way to jack the Ford (which apparently involved getting a petit blanc from the nearest café and discussing the meaning of life), an elderly woman in deep mourning, holding a little girl by the hand, approached Kate, wanting to know who they were and what they were doing.

"We're members of the Smith College Relief Unit—er, *Collégiennes Américaines.*" Kate's brain felt addled by days of driving. "We're here to offer aid to the former occupied zones near a town called Grécourt. Those are bits of houses we're bringing to build—for a *mairie* and a schoolhouse and whatever else is needed."

"Do you have relatives here?" the woman asked.

"None at all," said Kate, feeling a little silly. "I'm not even French. My family is mostly Irish."

No need to mention that her father was Bohemian. It was a little too close to German. To be Irish was bad enough, but at least not Boche.

To her surprise, the woman put a hand on her shoulder. "You are a good girl. One moment. Marie, wait with the lady."

Kate and the little girl were left regarding each other. The girl couldn't have been more than six, and Kate had no idea what to do with her.

"Do you live here?" asked Kate.

"Yes, now." The girl took her thumb from her mouth. "I used to live somewhere else, but then I came on a train with Madame Lepensier. How far away is America? Did you come on a train?"

Mercifully, at that point the grandmother returned, her arms laden with packages. "For you," she said, shoving half a chicken, a basket of peaches, and a whole cheese into Kate's arms.

Kate, surprised, grappled with it to keep it all from falling. "But this is—there was no need—"

The old woman rescued a peach and pushed it firmly

back into Kate's hands. "My granddaughter—she was evacuated from the occupied zone last year, when the Germans let some go. If she had stayed . . ." She shrugged, a Gallic gesture indicative of all manner of ills. "She was one of the lucky ones. What you do—it is good. *Que le Bon Dieu vous bénisse, maintenant et à l'avenir.*"

"What did she say?" Liza, drawn by the lure of food, came up as the woman was departing, leaving Kate, dazed, cradling a roast chicken, probably the woman's supper for the week.

"She said—" Kate's voice felt husky. She cleared it and tried again. "She said, may the good Lord bless you, now and in the future."

"That's so kind of her! Oh, is that cheese?"

While the soldiers debated the best methods of tire maintenance, the girls fell on the food, plunking down on the steps of the *mairie* and tearing into the chicken and cheese.

"My mother would be appalled." Alice Patton tried to wipe the chicken grease off her shirtfront. "She says a lady never eats in public."

"I don't care what anyone thinks as long as there's more of this cheese in the world," said Liza. "I'm surprised they're being so nice to us. Maud says the French are pretty down on us for not coming in before and feeding the Germans through neutrals. You can see how it would make them bitter to see all these strong men in new uniforms coming in tooting around in big cars all the time. Dr. Foster, you know the Red Cross man, said there was a pretty serious mutiny in the French army this spring, and that all that kept them from throwing the towel in was our coming in, but that we probably left it too late."

Fran grimaced at Kate behind Liza's back. Liza's news bulletins, they called her rambling digests of intelligence gleaned from Maud, some of which were contradictory and most of which had Germany victorious within the month.

Kate craned her head, looking back in the direction the woman had come. She wished she could thank her. She wished she could pay her. With rationing and meatless days, and the lean days of winter so close, that was a ridiculous amount of bounty to press on a stranger.

You are a good girl, the woman had said. And she'd given her chicken.

All because Kate had said they were bringing supplies to the formerly occupied zone.

"—that our troops won't be ready to go in until spring, and the French are just holding on by sheer *nerve*—"

"Excuse me," said Kate to the others, and pushed up off the steps, to where Mrs. Rutherford was sitting on the side of the Ford, meditatively munching a chicken wing.

"Why did she do that, that woman? Why did she give all this to us?"

"When the soldiers marched off to war," said Mrs. Rutherford, "the women lined the streets, handing out bread and wine. It didn't matter that they didn't have much to give."

"But we're not soldiers." Kate pressed her fingers to her temples. They smelled like ripe cheese. It made her feel vaguely queasy. "I don't understand. We haven't done anything yet."

"You're here," said Mrs. Rutherford. "That's doing something."

She said it so matter-of-factly.

Kate looked at her askance.

Mrs. Rutherford wiped her greasy fingers daintily on her handkerchief. "It is, you know. It's not all grand gestures. Just the fact that you came overseas."

On the steps of the *mairie*, the other members of the Motor Committee were merrily eating peaches and basking in the sunshine. Kate looked back at Mrs. Rutherford. "What if we make a mess of it? What if we leave them worse off than they were before?"

"I'm not sure that's possible," said Mrs. Rutherford. "Most of them are living in roofless cellars—and those are the lucky ones. But I tell you, to know you are there among them, living with them, bringing aid from a world they thought forgot them—that means almost as much as the physical goods we bring them. You don't need to do anything or even say anything. You just need to be *there*."

"But we are going to do something."

"Well, of course," said Mrs. Rutherford. She chomped down on a peach with obvious relish. "It would be madness to come all this way and just stand there."

Kate, contrary to instructions, just stood there.

She hadn't been entirely honest with Emmie back in Paris. Maud had tried to recruit her for the coup, not on her own behalf, but on Emmie's. "If you could use your influence with your friend . . ." had been the phrase used. Kate had disclaimed any influence and generally avoided committing herself.

Don't get involved, keep your head down. Those were the rules she had learned over the years.

The truth was, she hadn't been sure Maud was wrong. Now . . . she wondered if Emmie was right, if they ought to tell Mrs. Rutherford.

But what would be the point? They had their

trucks. All their plans were in hand. It would only be making trouble. It was probably all a tempest in a teapot. For all she knew, Maud had never even written those letters.

It is good, the old woman had told her. *You are a good girl.*

Mrs. Rutherford thrust a chicken leg into her hand.

"Here. Keep your strength up. Eat your chicken and let's get back on the road. If we make Paris tonight, we can collect the others, pack up our parcels, and be on our way to Grécourt by Monday."

Chapter Eight

*We made our long-overdue start for the country
on Tuesday, September 11. . . . The lateness of
our start made lunch an immediate concern, but
Miss Englund, who was driving the Ford truck,
insisted on a downgrade as a stopping place.
Apparently, the roads in France run remarkably
level. Cannibalism was staved off solely by the
discovery that someone had remembered to pack
a hamper with bread and cheese, which
prevented Miss Shaw from gnawing on the
nearest available arm, which, I fear, was mine.*

*If our women refrain from killing each other, I
believe we shall deal reasonably well together
(note the caveat). Betsy, as always, remains*

*entirely oblivious and is primarily concerned
about the conveyance of our cows.*

> — Dr. Ava Stringfellow, '96,
> to her husband, Dr. Lawrence
> Stringfellow

September 11, 1917
Paris, France

They left for Grécourt on Tuesday.

They'd meant to leave by ten, but noon saw the three trucks belonging to the Smith College Relief Unit still sitting stranded outside the hotel on the Quai Voltaire, occasioning a great deal of comment from passersby. It turned out that even when limited to one suitcase and one duffel bag apiece, there was a remarkable amount of luggage, particularly when one added in such sundries as rakes, hoes, crockery, portable stoves, eighteen cots, blankets, and all relevant bedding. Not to mention six loaves of war bread and one very precious tub of jam.

"Maybe if you put the *confiture* there . . ." suggested Alice, fluttering around, trying to rearrange packages and generally confusing matters.

"Where, on my head?" demanded Julia, who was wedged in between a spare tire and half a dozen folded cots. There were four of them in the White truck, crowded in among miscellaneous crates and packages, rakes sticking out the sides like pikes at the Battle of Agincourt, only with fewer men in doublets.

"It has to go somewhere," said Kate.

"I'll hold the jam," said Emmie, wondering if it was too late to suggest that Kate and Julia go in separate cars. She juggled the bucket of jam from one knee to the other, trying to find a comfortable spot. "Doesn't *confiture* sound much tastier than *jam*? Just like *framboise* sounds a million times more elegant than plain old *raspberry*."

"They're French raspberries; naturally, they're more elegant," said Kate, grinning back at her, and Emmie felt like old times, like setting off for a picnic on a borrowed sledge. "Can you grab the oil can, Alice?"

Alice Patton obediently clamped the oil can between her feet and Emmie shifted sideways to give her more room, eliciting a sharp cry of distress from Julia, who plunged forward to protect her medical bag, at the expense of her own kidneys, if necessary.

"Emmie! Watch your foot! If you squash my bag, we'll have no medicines at all."

The doctors had returned from their tour of hospitals only the night before and had been incensed to find that their medical supplies still hadn't been forwarded from the port—and that the chauffeurs hadn't thought to look for them.

"Sorry, I didn't mean to." Emmie tried to wedge her feet in between the oil can and the petrol crate. Her aunt May, Julia's mother, who had dainty, tiny doll feet, had always said Emmie's feet were too big. She could feel her cheeks flushing with old shame as she tried to hide her boatlike boots. "It's a tight fit."

"If the bag is so precious, hold it on your lap," said Kate from the front of the truck.

"If anyone had thought to *look* for our supplies—" said Julia.

"If anyone had bothered to *tell* us to look . . ."

"How far is it until Grécourt?" asked Alice, wiggling uncomfortably between the spare tire and the petrol crate.

"Eighty-five miles," said Kate. "But goodness only knows what the roads will be like once we get out of Paris."

"Are we ready to go? Once I start this, I'm not stopping it again until I find a hill pointing down," called out Fran Englund from the Ford truck. She and Margaret Cooper were driving the long truck, loaded with parts of portable houses and miscellaneous farm equipment. In front, leading the way, Liza had the jitney, with their duffel bags, suitcases, Mrs. Rutherford, Dr.

Stringfellow, Miss Dawlish, and Maud. Emmie wondered if Mrs. Rutherford was following the old adage
of keeping one's enemies close.

Three members had been left behind in Paris. Miss
Ledbetter, who wrote features for magazines, had
been detailed, on the strength of her journalistic cre-
dentials, to coordinate with the press. Miss Mills, who
had been working at the Villier hospital, was being allowed a week's rest before starting for Grécourt, which
Emmie really hoped wasn't code for her having picked
up something terribly contagious. Miss Baldwin, their
librarian, had stayed behind to try to beg, borrow, and
cadge books for the children.

Alice Patton turned the crank of the White and Kate
did something—Emmie supposed she really ought to
learn how it worked at some point, although she wasn't
sure it would be fair to inflict her lack of direction on
the world at large—and the truck started rolling forward, past the hotel, across a bridge, over the Seine.

They were on their way; they were truly on their
way. At last, at last.

The French sun shone down on them, blessing them
in their endeavors. Everyone waved to them as they
passed, old women in black veils, women in overalls
sweeping the streets, soldiers in gray and soldiers in
khaki, mothers wheeling babies in carriages and men

limping on crutches. It felt like a parade, like a festival day, like a Roman triumph, like Ivy Day at Smith.

"Fair is the earth today / Blooming over the lea, / And June is calling," Emmie sang, unable to contain herself.

It was their Ivy Day song, the one they'd sung together as they processed around the campus in their white dresses, escorted by the alumnae in their colored sashes, helping to launch them away into the world.

After a moment, Kate's careful contralto joined in, "Away! Ah, come away with me!"

Then Julia's trained soprano, carrying over them all, "Away, away! To the world so bright and free . . ."

Auntie May used to make Julia practice for hours with a voice teacher, then trot her out to sing at parties, posed with a harp. Julia had hated it and had staunchly refused to sing in any of the college musical societies, no matter how they'd begged. But she was singing now; they were all singing together, and it felt absolutely as it should be.

Emmie's spirit thrilled to the words. "We hear her magical call / And we follow the world around . . ."

Her voice wasn't beautiful, not like Julia's; she tended to slide between notes and she was often flat, but she felt like the words were drawn straight out of the very marrow of her bones. Away, away, the world around. She'd always wanted to go off on a quest like the knights in a romance, and here they were, here they were at last, even if it wasn't, as she'd told that British officer, anything heroic, only something practical and decent. But right here, right now, she felt like all the heroes of romance rolled together, armed with a rake instead of a sword and a bucket of jam in place of a buckler.

"Leave we our love behind / As the low winds softly croon . . ."

"Oh heavens, look at everyone stare," said Alice Patton, breaking off with a self-conscious duck of her purple hat as the White truck jolted down the Rue de Richelieu.

"There's the opera, maybe they want to recruit us," said Emmie giddily.

"Or run us out of town on a rail," said Kate, making a face but smiling all the same.

"I think I'm already sitting on one, thank you," said Julia smartly, trying to shift a rake handle from her posterior.

The truck went over a bump and Alice squealed as the crate of precious petrol bumped against her knees. "Oh no. That's left blue paint all over my skirt."

"At least it's French blue," offered Emmie, trying to hold on to the holiday mood.

From the wheel, Kate called, "Don't you dare drop the *essence*, Alice! It's a dollar the gallon; we'll never be able to afford more if it spills, and then where will we be?"

"Singing for our supper?" offered Emmie.

"Pushing the trucks, most likely," said Kate. "Uphill all the way."

Julia looked at Emmie sideways. "I'm sure Aunt Cora would stump up for gas money if you applied to her humbly."

Emmie could feel her cheeks flush. "I wouldn't want to—that is—"

She hated to be reminded of her mother's money. It made her feel as though she weren't really one of the group, but only included in the hopes that her mother might open her purse. And that wasn't the case, not this time. Her mother hadn't contributed, at least not more than anyone else.

Except for one thing. There was one thing Emmie had asked her mother for. But no one needed to know about that. It was quite beside the point.

Emmie fell back on generalities. "You know she thinks it's important we do this properly, through raising funds and all that sort of thing."

"Oh yes. It creates character, I gather." Julia's voice was drier than day-old war bread.

"I hear the New York committee has stumped up wonderfully," said Alice, and Emmie could have hugged her, if she hadn't been afraid of upsetting the petrol.

"My mother wrote me that they've all taken up knitting and have been making the most tremendous things for the children," said Emmie. "I've asked them to send chocolates for the children. They're so frightfully expensive here, and I want to make sure we have enough for everyone."

"I wouldn't mind a chocolate right about now," said Alice wistfully. "Do you think Fran will let us stop for lunch anytime soon? I could eat a cow."

"The cows are being sent separately," said Emmie, who had been responsible for buying them.

"And thank goodness for that," said Kate with feeling.

Emmie glanced back over her shoulder. She couldn't quite eat a cow—especially since they were rather depending on those cows for milk—but she wouldn't mind stopping for lunch sometime soon. The Ford truck was motoring steadily along behind them, clearing the road of taxis and pedestrians alike as it barreled forward. Miss Englund had both hands on the wheel and a look of extreme determination on her face. "Was Miss Englund serious about stopping only on a downgrade?"

Kate exchanged a look with Alice Patton. "Oh yes," she said.

Alice fiddled with the oil can. "Do you remember that time—"

"Outside Chartres?" said Kate.

"We had to pile all the pieces of the house back on," said Alice, grimacing. "Goodness, those were heavy."

"At least Fran didn't take off the fence that time."

"Or the onions! Remember the onions?"

Kate wrinkled her nose. "How could I forget? My uniform still reeks of them."

"They did make excellent soup, though," said Alice, "at that inn. You remember the one."

"Are you sure those were onions in the soup?" asked Kate, and they both laughed.

It was good that they were getting along so well, Emmie told herself. It was important for morale and camaraderie and all that sort of thing. It was very silly—no, not just silly. It was downright selfish to feel left out just because the chauffeurs had come back from their jaunt to Saint-Nazaire with not only the trucks but all sorts of shared jokes and experiences.

"Would anyone like some bread and cheese?" she asked.

They ate bread and cheese—even Julia unbent to

take a little, which meant she must have been very hungry, indeed—as the road wound through a forest, in all its leafy beauty. They were well out of Paris now, following the jitney through a landscape that felt like something out of Arthurian legend. It seemed impossible to believe, among these trees, that there was a war on. Until they got to the end of the forest and saw the first blasted village, houses crumbled in upon themselves, rubble upon rubble, like a block village after Emmie's little brothers had run amok. Except these hadn't been blocks; these had been buildings, real buildings, where people had lived and worked.

The trees here weren't leafy anymore; they were stunted, twisted things, the branches and bark blasted off by artillery, leaving only blackened stumps in their wake.

Along the bare horizon, Emmie could see tangles of barbed wire, long stretches of churned earth and abandoned encampments, and, in the midst of it all, the bright, incongruous red of flowers, like splashes of sealing wax.

Or the Scarlet Pimpernel, she thought, and wondered why she was thinking of that now, of the little red flower and the Englishman she had last seen at the Gare du Nord, headed back to the front.

Who might, even now, be food for flowers, another man lost in the trenches, his bones sunk deep in the mud of the Somme.

"The jitney's stopped," said Alice.

"I think that's a guard post up ahead," said Kate, slowing the White truck and just managing to pull around the jitney instead of bumping into it.

Mrs. Rutherford waved them forward. They climbed awkwardly down from the truck. Emmie was rather amazed that she could be so sore just from sitting; she hurt in places she hadn't been sure one could hurt.

"We're to show our *feuilles bleues*," said Mrs. Rutherford.

"Not our *carnets rouges*?" asked Alice, digging for her papers.

"I feel like a French lesson," whispered Emmie to Kate. "*Avez vous le carnet rouge de ma tante et la plume jaune de mon cousin? Oh, bonjour, monsieur.* Here's my *carnet*—I mean, my *feuille*. You know the one." Emmie smiled apologetically at the guard, feeling like an idiot, but it seemed her papers made more sense than she did, because he waved her forward.

She supposed she didn't look much like an enemy agent. As Auntie May liked to point out, she seldom looked like much of anything.

Kate's papers passed scrutiny, and then came Liza. And the whole procession stopped.

"This paper," said the guard, holding it up so they could see. "It is for Monsieur Shaw."

"But it can't be," said Liza blankly. "It's me. I mean, it's meant to be me. Er, for me."

"I assure you, *mademoiselle*, it is," said the guard, and he held it up. There it was, clear as day, on Liza's *feuille bleue*, "*M. Shaw*."

"Does she *look* like a man?" demanded Maud indignantly.

"That is the problem exactly," said the guard, not bothering to hide his boredom. "This paper permits *Monsieur* Shaw to enter the *zone des armées*. If *Mademoiselle* Shaw wishes to enter, she must go back to Paris and get another paper."

"It's a mistake," said Emmie, wondering how on earth none of them had seen it before. Of course, they didn't tend to go through each other's papers, and the writing on the safe conduct was next door to illegible, but even so. "You can see it's a mistake."

"I could drive her back in the jitney," said Margaret Cooper hesitantly. "Maybe we could fit everyone else in the White and the truck."

"Oh no," said Emmie. It wasn't just that they couldn't possibly fit everyone and everything into two of the cars. It was that they were meant to be a unit, and she had the oddest feeling that if anyone turned back now, that would be the end of it.

"I'll come too," said Maud quickly. "If everything else is this ill organized, I don't want any part of it."

"There's no need for that." It was Julia who had come forward, speaking in her perfect, beautiful, aristocratic French. Emmie always forgot that Aunt May's second husband had been a French count. He might even have been from somewhere not far from here; Emmie had never been entirely sure where the count's château was, only that it needed a new roof and her mother firmly refused to pay for it. "If you won't believe us, will you take the word of *Le Soir*?"

Julia held out a page cut neatly from a newspaper, folded so that the photo of the Smith College Relief Unit—all seventeen of them—was staring up at them.

Emmie waved enthusiastically at the photo. "You can see, that's us! And there's Mademoiselle Shaw, you see?" Liza obediently perked up, trying to look like her photo. "We're *les Collégiennes Américaines*!"

"*Les Collégiennes Américaines*, eh?" said the guard, studying the photo. In it, they were arrayed in two rows, Mrs. Rutherford and Dr. Stringfellow seated in the middle. Emmie wished she didn't look quite so tall looming in the back row. And that someone had told her that she needed to brush her hair. But the over-all composition seemed to be having its effect on the guard. "All the way from America?"

It was amazing, thought Emmie, that a newspaper could do what all their passports and *carnets* and *feuilles* hadn't. She was very impressed that Julia had thought of it. Although she did rather wonder why Julia had bothered to cut out the article at all. Julia wasn't the sort to keep a scrapbook of their adventures.

Which reminded Emmie that she really needed to start keeping a scrapbook of their adventures.

"Do you know," said Mrs. Rutherford cannily as the guard handed back the newspaper, "we never did have lunch. Would you care to share our bread and cheese with us? We might have a bit of jam put by as well. . . ."

The *confiture* clinched it. By the time the bread and jam had been eaten, they were all firm friends, and Monsieur Shaw had become a great joke, with Liza laughing hardest of all, even if her laughter did sound a bit forced.

It was just a little delay, and they would have been on their way at once—if their oil can hadn't rolled off and had to be retrieved.

"I do think if they didn't want oil cans to roll, they ought not to have made them round," contributed Alice.

"I wonder if the children might like to construct a square one?" mused Miss Dawlish.

Half an hour later, the oil can had been wrestled back into place. And the Ford refused to start.

"I *told* you we needed to stop on a downgrade," said Fran with grim satisfaction.

Another hour passed. With their new friend, the guard, working the crank and four of them taking it in turns to push, the Ford condescended to move again.

"It's past five," said Julia grimly. "We're barely halfway."

"At least we're not halfway back to Paris," said Emmie. "It was clever of you to think of the paper. I hadn't realized they'd printed an article about us already."

"Oh, several. This was the most fulsome." Julia looked sideways at Emmie. "I intend to send them all on to my mother."

"Oh, how nice," said Emmie, even though it wasn't really at all. It represented a declaration of war. Or, rather, the continuation of a war that had begun a long time ago, when Julia had announced her determination to go to Smith and Emmie's parents had agreed to pay her tuition and board.

"You can't mean to encourage Julia to become a spinster," Aunt May had raged at Emmie's parents, so loudly she'd heard it all the way through the oak doors of the drawing room and the marble entrance hall and into the music room.

Spinster. The word had a sting to it. But that was what they were, weren't they? The paper called them girls, or, rather, being French, *jeunes filles*, but the truth was that all of them, with the exception of Miss Cooper of the class of '14, were closer to thirty than they were to Ivy Day. Emmie generally tried not to think of that sort of thing, to tell herself that she was married to her good works, but there were times when the truth stared glaringly out at her, and she could hear Auntie May's voice, from long, long ago, saying, with shattering clarity, *It's a pity she looks so much like her mother*.

That hadn't stopped her mother from marrying, but her parents' marriage was something Emmie tried not to look at too closely. She liked to think that her handsome, dissolute father hadn't married her mother entirely for her money. She didn't think he had; her father respected her mother, she was sure he did. And they had liked each other enough to produce seven children.

But there was no denying she had no desire to re-create their circumstances. She didn't want to be married for her dowry and left to do good works while her husband spent his time drinking at the Union Club—or dining in the private rooms of Delmonico's with actresses young enough to be his daughter.

"Oh no," said Alice, and Emmie dragged herself out of her muddled thoughts. While she had woolgathered, they had bumped their way into the medieval town of Noyon, where they seemed to have stopped in the town square.

Emmie rubbed her eyes with the back of her hand. The dust of the road had got in them, making them water. "What's wrong?"

Alice pointed at the Ford, which had come to a complete stop in front of them. "That's not a down-grade," she said darkly.

The Ford, apparently, had stopped of its own accord. Something had gone wrong. Something mechanical. They gathered an interested crowd of townspeople and soldiers, all with opinions, none of them encouraging.

The sun set over the towers of the cathedral.

"If we were working for the Red Cross, this would never have happened," said Maud darkly.

"We'll have to stay the night," said Fran Englund, ignoring her. "There's no point pushing on to Grécourt now. We'll never find our way in the dark."

"No," said Julia with such force that they all stared. "I'm not staying."

Dr. Stringfellow stepped in. "We stayed in Noyon while we were touring hospitals—the only available room had a door leading to the main stair. We had soldiers passing through our room half the night. I wouldn't recommend it."

"After those air raids in Paris, I could sleep through a platoon," said Liza cheerfully.

"I couldn't," said Julia.

"Perhaps we could find someplace else?" Alice suggested, fiddling with her collar.

"Or we could just leave the truck," proposed Emmie, looking sideways at Julia, who was looking decidedly thin-lipped. "There's nothing on it we need tonight."

"Only our luggage," said Fran Englund.

"It makes more sense to stay here, rearrange the loads, and try to find our way in the morning," said Kate, siding with Fran. "It's taken us this long to get here; what does it matter if we arrive tonight or tomorrow? No one will be waiting up for us this late."

Everything she said made perfect sense, but Emmie felt, strongly, that it did make a difference. Certainly to Julia, who looked as though she wouldn't be dragged back into that inn for all the world. And to Emmie. Two days, the mechanic had said. Maybe three. To have made it this far and be stranded in Noyon seemed intolerable.

"Fran and I could stay with the truck," offered Margaret Cooper, "and the rest could go on."

"No need for that!" Mrs. Rutherford appeared from the scrum of French soldiers, dragging a thin man in a uniform with the three gold bars denoting a captain. "Look who I found! This is Captain Jaouen, currently of the French army, but previously a professor at the University of Michigan. He's offered us a replacement truck and the men to drive it."

"A temporary loan only," Captain Jaouen said quickly.

"The camion or the men?" Alice whispered with a giggle, and was hushed by Kate.

"So we can get on immediately," said Mrs. Rutherford. "Well, as soon as we transfer our load from the Ford to the camion. The captain has said he'll have his men get started right away—we'll be on our way within the hour."

"How does she do that?" asked Margaret Cooper, staring at Mrs. Rutherford as she marched off arm in arm with Captain Jaouen, discussing something that happened in Crete back in '98 or '99. "It's as though she snapped her fingers and conjured him out of thin air. Like—magic."

"She does seem to find a way to make things happen," said Kate cautiously.

"Magic," said Emmie. Four months ago, no one had even thought of such a thing as a Smith Unit, but one speech from Mrs. Rutherford and here they were, equipped and ready, mere hours from their post, all the intricate layers of army and civilian bureaucracy dealt with, all the red tape cut through. Mrs. Rutherford had done all that, and now she'd even conjured an army truck for them. "And just think, we'll be escorted by brave cavaliers all the way."

"Don't you mean *poilus*?" said Kate practically. *Poilus* were the rank and file of the French army. "I doubt any of them will be on horseback."

"I don't care who they are," said Fran Englund, "as long as they're the one hefting the trunks instead of me. I can't think how she got them to do it."

"Neither can I," said Maud darkly.

"Only Betsy," said Dr. Stringfellow, to no one in particular, and went to help direct the disposition of their belongings.

Chapter Nine

Our scrap of France must have once been lovely.
Down a long lane of poplars, half-felled by the
Germans, one passes through a massive iron gate,
beyond which you see the scarred, roofless walls of
a once grand château. In a bowl of green behind,
at the edge of a great wood, the army put our three
barracks, each with two rooms—each smaller than
our room in Northampton! I've bunked in with
two class of '11 girls, Emmie Van Alden and Kate
Moran. Emmie is a dear and very welcoming.
Kate is a little harder to know—but not unkind.
Just quiet. She's so efficient, it makes me feel all
arms and legs.

The handful of people left in Grécourt live in
the ruined stables, except for the gardener's wife,

*who has stubbornly remained in what is left of
her old cottage by the castle gate, with a canvas
awning in place of a roof. She is in possession of
the one stove in the village, so she once cooked
for the Germans and she now cooks for us—when
she has a mind to.*

*I can't tell you what a difference it makes to feel
we can finally do some good. Sitting around in
Paris, there were moments when I felt I wasn't
worth the food I was eating. I really do hope I can
do some good, Beth. I feel so useless so much of
the time. . . .*

*— Miss Margaret Cooper, '14,
to Miss Elizabeth Long, '14*

September 1917
Grécourt, France

There was a moat.

There was an actual moat, separating the castle from the chapel and outbuildings. Kate hadn't noticed the moat the night before. She hadn't noticed much of anything. It had been past midnight when they arrived, after an endless round of arguments with Julia, who insisted that they couldn't go wrong if they navigated by the North Star. Kate pointed out that the half-obliterated signposts might be a more reliable guide, since they were hardly the Three Wise Men. That, of course, led Emmie into entirely unhelpful musing about the nature of myrrh.

The soldiers in the camion had been no help. Either that, or they were too busy trying not to snicker to say anything.

When they finally arrived, all Kate had registered was looming gates that framed a darkness that seemed to swallow everything beyond. But behind the menacing bulk of the château were three small and very modern army barracks, with two rooms each, nothing more than plasterboard squares, but clean and new and built on a human scale.

Kate couldn't remember much beyond that, just kicking their cots into place and falling asleep wrapped in her coat, too tired to bother with bedding.

She had woken this morning to two coat-wrapped lumps: Emmie and Margaret, still fast asleep. It had been taken for granted that Emmie and Kate would room together, and Margaret had followed. Kate suppressed an unworthy thought that she would rather have had Fran. But Margaret had attached herself to Emmie like a stray cat.

Or like other charity cases of Emmie's acquaintance.

Kate had snuck out very quietly, so as not to wake

them, to take stock of their new world. It was . . . beautiful. She hadn't expected beauty. She had been braced for ugliness, for trenches and barbed wire and ruin. There was ruin here, but even the ruin looked picturesque, as though the manor house had crumbled into disrepair in centuries past, had sat here, like the Beast's garden, for a century or more, and not been deliberately bombed out by the Germans just this past spring.

It made her wary. The loveliness of the woods, the russet vines twining around a stone tower, the stolid redbrick facade of the village church, strangely unmarred by war. It felt like a trick, a way to lure them into a false sense of security.

Some wit had posted a sign over the green slime of the moat, saying *"Bonne à Boire"*: good to drink. Unless it wasn't a joke at all.

There was reality for her, Kate thought wryly. The Germans had poisoned the wells, Mrs. Rutherford had said. Perhaps the green water of the moat really was *bonne à boire* in comparison.

"Ah, another early riser." Mrs. Rutherford walked briskly toward her, coming from a dilapidated little house hard by the gates, just next to the bridge that led over the moat. "What do you think of our demesne?"

The archaic word just suited the scene. "I feel like

I've wandered into Sleeping Beauty's castle," said Kate. She looked at the jagged walls of the château. "After the moths got at it."

"Moths with teeth," said Mrs. Rutherford, staring at one of the medallions that graced the facade, the portrait of a long-gone Robecourt, now half-crumbled. "It was beautiful once."

There was a strange note to her voice. "Did you know this place? Before?"

"Briefly." Mrs. Rutherford didn't seem inclined to say more. After a moment, she said, "La Baronne de Robecourt relocated to a spa in Switzerland at the start of the war and left her people to fare as they would."

Kate wished she could say she was surprised, but she wasn't. The rich had always been good at protecting their own skins.

Mrs. Rutherford had used the feminine form of the title. "Is there no male article?" Kate asked.

Mrs. Rutherford began walking rapidly across the dew-slick grass, Kate trotting along behind. "The Baroness's husband died some years ago. The current holder of the title is only a boy. I suppose not such a boy anymore. He ought to be nearly twenty by now." They passed what had once been a greenhouse, reduced to twisted scraps of metal. "Madame la Baronne seems to have the strange notion that the war is a cross between a tennis match and a tea party. She wrote to the gardener's wife asking her to see that the garden was kept in order in her absence."

Kate looked at the great house, now missing several crucial details, like the entire third story. "Wouldn't a roof be more to the point?"

"She hasn't the faintest idea. She thinks she'll return to everything as it was and all her loyal retainers tugging their forelocks."

Kate looked down at her gray uniform skirt, more brown than gray with mud and dirt. "What does she have to say about our being here?"

Mrs. Rutherford's lip curled. "She's delighted to have a better class of women living in her cellars. She sent orders that the inhabitants—there are twenty-seven left in the village, just barely surviving—were to be turfed out in our favor. Let them eat cake. Or roots. When I came last month, they were terrified. They thought they were to be entirely homeless."

Mrs. Rutherford was, Kate realized, blazingly angry, the sort of anger that expressed itself by not expressing itself. "That's the very reverse of what we came here to do."

Mrs. Rutherford gave a curt nod. "I told them not

to be absurd, we'd do nothing of the kind. Of course, if we were being truly generous, we'd give them our barracks and sleep in the cellars."

"I'm not sure that's being generous." The barrack had a roof, but that was about all that could be said of it.

"You haven't seen the cellars yet." Mrs. Rutherford gave her head a little shake. "Come. I'll take you to see them—and to meet Madame la Maire. She's mostly to be found at the washhouse this time of day."

"Madame la Maire?" asked Kate, hurrying after her to a shack that lay to the right of the château, where a woman was making a vigorous job of scrubbing a woolen skirt.

"Most of the mayors in our villages are women—and doing a bang-up job of it too, with the resources they have. There's only one man left in the pack," said Mrs. Rutherford, "and no one likes him. They have their suspicions about how he avoided serving. But he knows too much about too many people, so they leave him be. Ah, Marie!"

The woman beating the clothes straightened.

Mrs. Rutherford hadn't mentioned that their mayor was also their laundress. "Madame la Maire, this is Miss Moran, one of our chauffeurs."

Marie nodded, started to speak, and then stopped,

dropping to the ground and pressing her ear to the earth. "Do you hear it? They're moving."

"The lines," said Mrs. Rutherford, as if this were all perfectly normal. "Marie's husband, the baroness's gardener, is at the front. She can hear which way the battle is moving from the trembling of the earth."

Kate could hear a distant rumble, but the earth appeared to be entirely stationary for the moment.

"Ça va," Marie said, and straightened, becoming immediately brisk and businesslike. "I take the dirty clothes on Monday. You will have them clean on Sunday. My boy will bring you hot water in the mornings for washing, one can per room, that is what we have arranged. I cooked for the Germans; I cook for you."

"I hope we're rather different from the Germans," said Kate, nonplussed.

Marie looked at her with a jaundiced eye. "They were men. They ate more."

The other girls were straggling out, blinking at the ruins. Kate was rather glad there wasn't a mirror in the barrack, because if she looked anything like they did, she didn't want to see it. Liza had a long crease down one cheek and Alice's hair was all squashed to one side, like a cake that had overflowed the pan. Emmie's hair was half-up, half-down, but that wasn't anything out of the usual; that was just Emmie.

More introductions were made before their mayor excused herself to put on coffee and finish the wash, which was conducted to a strict schedule.

"Well, *that* won't be the slightest bit awkward," said Maud, staring after her. "Madame la Maire, may I have my underthings, please?"

"Given that the alternative is doing your own laundry," said Mrs. Rutherford cheerfully, "I think you'll find that less difficult than you suppose. Unless you would like to take on the laundry for the Unit?"

Silence. Kate tried not to look at Fran. She knew she wouldn't be able to keep a straight face if she did.

"Now," said Mrs. Rutherford, with the air of a magician about to produce a rabbit, "come see the premises at our disposal! We're so very lucky to have a space like this, with a roof, that we can use for all sorts of purposes: a dispensary, a garage, a dining hall. Ladies, I give you . . . the Orangerie!"

Kate almost walked right past it at first. There were no oranges. More to the point, there was no glass left in any of the wide French windows. Every single window had been systematically smashed, leaving the building a mere shell of roof and pillars, more open to the air than not. Glass crunched underfoot as they approached. Inside, Kate could see debris, bird droppings, and yet more glass.

"It's . . . airy," said Emmie, trying to make the best of it.

"That's one way to put it," said Julia.

Kate caught her eye in agreement and then rapidly looked away, appalled to find herself in sympathy with Julia. She hurried after Mrs. Rutherford, hoping the soles of her boots would be up to the amount of glass underfoot. She did not want to have to go to the medical department to have shards drawn out.

Mrs. Rutherford was already inside, tramping blithely around through the wreckage. "We can garage the trucks here during bad weather—this opening should be just large enough to drive them through—and we can have the dispensary *here*. . . ."

"An open-air dispensary?" Dr. Stringfellow's eyebrows were even more ironical than usual. "That's well enough while the weather is fine, but I prefer not to give my patients frostbite."

"The French authorities have promised us some *poilus* to hang oilcloth in the windows," said Mrs. Rutherford airily. "They'll also clean up this mess and whitewash the walls for us. You'll see, we'll be right and tight as rain."

"Yes, with the rain coming in," said Maud, not even bothering to whisper.

"What about classes for the children?" asked Miss

Dawlish, looking concerned. "Are those to be in here too?"

"We're to have a portable house for that," said Mrs. Rutherford triumphantly. "Eventually. Eventually, we'll have portable houses set up in all the villages for schools and clubhouses. In the meantime—there's this lovely green field here. And on rainy days, they can come to the Orangerie."

"With the dispensary," said Dr. Stringfellow. "And the trucks."

"You won't have to hunt them down for medical care," said Mrs. Rutherford brightly. "Think of the time saved! Besides, the dispensary will only be at Grécourt at certain times. And the trucks will be out all hours, so it scarcely matters, does it? If you'll follow me through here—watch your step, Miss Cooper!— these are the old cellars. We can use them for storage."

"We do need storage space," said Kate, thinking of everything they had dragged along with them, all their plans for a store. Their barracks barely had room for them, much less all the various goods and chattels they intended to sell to the villagers.

Kate followed along after Emmie, her steps slowing as the smell struck her. Something had been rotting here. For a very long time.

Alice Patton held her handkerchief to her nose.

"Oh goodness," said Emmie, her voice very small. Kate couldn't bring herself to say anything at all; she was too busy trying not to gag. "What happened here?"

"Germans," said Mrs. Rutherford succinctly. Her hands were on her hips and she looked distinctly displeased. "Monsieur le Commandant Monin promised me this would all be cleaned up by the time we arrived. The Germans lodged here just before they retreated and made the most terrible mess."

Indoor latrines, from the look of it. Bunks made of chicken wire, padded with filthy straw, testified to just how many men had been crammed into the underground space. Someone had started a calendar, so many notches to the week. The walls were scrawled with slogans in German.

Miss Dawlish, who spoke the language, turned red and looked away.

"What does it say?" asked Liza.

"I don't think we want to know," said Fran Englund.

"I—I don't know most of the words," said Miss Dawlish. "I don't think I want to."

"They said two hundred men lodged down here," said Mrs. Rutherford, unperturbed. "Of course, it wasn't quite this bad before they dynamited the place and parts of the wall and the ceiling came down. It would have been watertight then, at least."

It certainly wasn't now. Damp dripped down the walls and seeped from the ceiling. It was cold, terribly, bone-chillingly cold.

"Didn't you say the villagers have been living in the cellars?" asked Kate incredulously. She supposed it was better than no roof at all, but these were conditions that made the miserable apartment she and her mother had once shared look like a rest cure.

"In the stable cellars, not these. I'll take you to them in a moment. In addition to being in our charge, they are an invaluable source of information about the other villages. Marie tells me there's a little Boche baby that was born in Canizy just last week, Ava," added Mrs. Rutherford as an aside to Dr. Stringfellow as they all struggled up out of the cellars, bumping into each other in their eagerness to get up into the clear air, away from the stench and despair. "You'll want to visit the mother and the child."

"A Boche baby?" asked Alice, trying to hold her skirt out of the muck.

"A German father," explained Mrs. Rutherford. "The mother is little more than a child—she was one of the spoils of war."

"A Boche baby sounds like it ought to be born with horns and a tail," mused Liza, tromping up the stairs behind.

"It's half-French," pointed out Kate with some asperity. She was a mutt herself and hadn't enjoyed hearing her stepfather's relations shaking their heads over her Bohemian blood, as if being her father's daughter made her somehow prone to fits or howling at the moon.

"Only the horns, then," said Fran, deadpan.

"Poor baby," said Emmie. "And that poor mother too. We must make sure we go to her straightaway."

"All of them need us straightaway. That's the challenge of it," said Mrs. Rutherford, waiting for everyone to join her by the ruined Orangerie that was to be their center of operations.

Once someone had swept it. And painted it. And put oilcloth on it.

The magnitude of it all pressed down upon Kate, and she found herself frustrated beyond measure by everyone and everything, by Mrs. Rutherford's blind optimism and Emmie's romanticism and those looks Maud kept giving Liza, those "I told you so" looks, all the more annoying because Kate tended to agree with her.

"Then we'll just have to be organized about it," said Kate sharply. "If we just run around scattershot, we'll never get anywhere. We'll need to go through the villages one by one and make lists of the people in them, who they are, and what they need from us in terms of supplies and medical care."

"Oh, is that all?" said Maud, rolling her eyes at Liza.

"That's a great deal," said Mrs. Rutherford soberly. "You have no idea what a very great deal."

Neither had Kate.

They set out after breakfast, two to a truck, taking with them piles of baby clothes and linens, what milk they had, and some small assorted medical supplies they'd been able to cobble together by going through their personal possessions for plasters and headache powders.

They visited with the villagers first, in the stable cellars, and no one made the obvious comments about mangers because the reality of it was too grim for joking. Twenty-three women, ranging in age from eighteen to eighty, one teenage boy, and three children, all living in the remains of a stable, water pooling in places on the floor.

Twenty-seven people grateful to have any roof at all, even a broken one.

Kate had a vague notion that things would get better the farther they got from Grécourt, that the more remote the hamlet, the more it might have been spared. They left Miss Dawlish behind to minister to the castle folk and set out to begin their inspections. The idea was that they would start with a social worker, a doctor, and a driver in each car, but they had three trucks and only two doctors, so Kate and Emmie made their way east on their own, across roads rutted by army trucks, bearing the scars of old military movements.

The first town they stopped at made Grécourt look like a thriving metropolis. There was only one house left standing; the rest had been deliberately destroyed.

Emmie consulted Mrs. Rutherford's list. "There are fifty children living here."

"Where?" asked Kate, looking around the ruins. The Germans had been thorough; she'd give them that. The houses were rubble, only bits of wall still standing.

"Wherever they can, I imagine. You'll take notes for me, won't you?" asked Emmie, wiggling down from the White.

"Of course." Kate guiltily swung her own legs over the side. No point in telling Emmie that she'd hoped her job ended with the driving. What was she to say to a French villager? I'm so sorry? The words stuck on her tongue.

"It makes it easier to talk if they don't see me writing things down," Emmie explained, as though she had done this a hundred times before. "It's easier if it's someone else taking notes. If I were by myself, I'd try to do it by memory, but since your French is better than mine anyway . . . *Bonjour! Madame? Nous sommes les Collégiennes Américaines. . . .*"

The first place they visited was a stable, although to call it that lent it a dignity it didn't have. It had been a distinctly one-horse shelter, roughly the size of Kate's boardinghouse room in Boston. Her despised room felt like a palace in comparison. Kate picked her way across the muddy dirt floor, weaving between wooden boards that had been laid on the ground in lieu of beds. A pallet in the corner was occupied by an old woman, snoring gently, her teeth in a cracked teacup beside her. A girl of about ten, with a dirty cap covering snarled hair, was cooking over a makeshift fire, ringed with stones.

A woman wearing a stained dress, a baby on her hip, came to greet them. Oh yes, she'd heard of them. The crazy ladies with the trucks. She didn't put it quite that way, but the inference was clear. Everyone seemed to have already heard about their driving around in circles three hundred yards from the castle.

"If you had only followed the signposts . . ." said their hostess helpfully, sticking her knuckle into the baby's mouth to suck to stop it crying. Kate added a note to get some pacifiers in. Also to strangle Julia.

Emmie made a comic tale of their misadventures,

and, in no time, the woman was telling them her story. The woman in the bed was her mother, who was ill; make no mistake, in full possession of her wits, just bedridden and cranky, it was the rheumatism, you know, which had been made worse by being evicted from their house, which had had four good bedrooms and silk paper on the wall of the dining room—"We'll send our doctors to look at her," Emmie promised. "Don't worry. They're good doctors"—her husband was away with the army; her oldest two sons, ages twelve and fourteen, had been taken away by *les boches* to a work camp in Germany, and no word had come since. Six other children, ranging in age from ten to two months (the baby wailed to confirm that he was, in fact, that young) shared the small room.

"We had a house once," the woman insisted. "A very nice house."

"And you will again," said Emmie with such assurance that Kate nearly believed it. "With silk paper on the walls of the dining room. We're waiting for our cows to be delivered, but once they come, we'll be able to start bringing milk. When was the last time you had milk for the children?"

It all seemed a bit haphazard, but as Emmie chatted and Kate scribbled as hard as she could, a very sizable dossier of information emerged: where the family had lived, who was missing, what they needed, information about the other inhabitants of the village.

It was the same everywhere they went. Too many people crammed into spaces with no roof, no proper floor. Emmie would produce a handful of candies for the children; hand out baby clothes and fine-tooth combs; elicit information about ailments and other pressing needs. And the missing. Every family had its tale of the missing, the children away *avec les boches*.

"She sounds lovely," Emmie would say as a beloved and tattered photo was shown or a bit of old embroidery displayed or a treasured teacup, that was the last possession of a daughter or sister lost to the *boches*. "Now, about your grandson, we mean to start holding classes for children. . . . May I put his name on the list?"

"We must bring a bathtub next time," Emmie said ruefully as they climbed back into the White, having made the rounds of all sixteen families eking out their existence in what had once been their home. "I've never seen so many lice. I'm itching. Are you itching?"

"I wasn't until you mentioned it," said Kate, not wanting to bring a bathtub, not wanting to come back ever again. *I'm just here to drive the truck*, she wanted to say, but of course, she wasn't, she couldn't; they were meant to all pitch in on everything. But she didn't know how Emmie did it, how she kept talking and talking when Kate felt frozen in the face of so much misery, so much grief.

I had a daughter once. . . . I had a house once. . . . I had a family once. . . . The catalogue of loss went on and on.

"Shall we go back and take stock?" Kate asked hopefully. "We can help sweep out the Orangerie."

"It's hours until sunset yet," said Emmie, spreading out the map. "Let's go to Canizy."

"It's after three already." It took a surprisingly long time, recording life histories. Kate had thought they would be in and out, checking boxes. "Canizy is the farthest of the villages."

"Yes, but I want to visit the Boche baby and make sure she's being properly cared for—if we leave by six, we should still be able to make it back before dark."

"Assuming we don't get a puncture. Oh, all right. Canizy it is."

Canizy wasn't even a ruin; it was a wreck. But the Boche baby was . . . a baby. A rather handsome baby at that, pink and crinkly-faced, folded in a dirty blanket, blinking its big, dark eyes at Kate in an unexpectedly endearing way.

Not that she'd expected horns. Not really. Or a miniature Prussian helmet.

"How perfectly beautiful," said Emmie, carefully taking the bundle-wrapped baby from its mother, who couldn't have been more than sixteen. Possibly younger still. It was hard to tell; dirt and worry added premature lines to the girl's face. Emmie began to unwrap the layers. "May I? He has the most expressive eyes—just like yours."

While Emmie was talking, she checked for sores and bruises, discretely testing the limbs, deftly changing out the stained swaddling cloth for a clean one they'd brought with them, all while keeping the mother engaged in a steady stream of gentle chatter.

Kate stood behind her, dutifully taking notes about the members of the household—one elderly woman whose mind was wandering, the young mother, the baby, all sharing the one room with another family— and making lists of imminent necessities, ranging from milk for the baby to shoes for the grandmother, who, it seemed, had a habit of wandering off and would come back with feet bare and bleeding.

"Georgette—that's the baby's mother—she's only just turned fifteen—says her grandmother used to be the heart of the village." Outside the hovel, Emmie's face seemed to age five years in as many seconds. She rubbed at her temples with her fingers. "Her grandmother was a figure of defiance throughout the first year of the war, Georgette says, a sort of Robin Hood in skirts stealing things back from the Germans and sharing them through the village and never getting caught. But then the *boches* took her husband, her son, and two daughters away with them into Germany and it broke something in her. Georgette says that they got word that her uncle—that's the son—died in a work camp in Germany, but no one will ever tell her grandmother that, so she keeps waiting for him to come home. I suppose that's kinder? And she doesn't seem to remember much from one moment to another, so it would be harder for her to have him die and die and die again."

"Are you hungry? We never did have lunch." It seemed obscene to eat after all that, but Kate's stomach wasn't aware of the proprieties and was beginning to growl quite obviously. And she didn't really want to discuss it anymore.

To die and die and die again . . .

Emmie shook her head. "Georgette told me there was a child hurt this morning, in the old brasserie next to the ruined town hall. I need to see if there's anything we can do. We can have lunch after," she offered, and Kate felt like the lowest worm who had ever crawled.

"Never mind lunch," she said. "Where's this brasserie of yours?"

If Kate had had lunch, she would have lost it. The child, a little boy of two, had sat down in a basin of boiling water, and his flesh looked like—Kate didn't want to think what it looked like. It seemed impossible he was still living, but he was, in a horrible, filthy room in the remains of what had once been a brasserie, with his nine brothers and sisters and another widowed mother with three other children. The din created by the thirteen children in that eerie, half-destroyed restaurant was unreal.

"We'll have to go back and see if we can fetch one of the doctors—" Kate began, raising her voice to be heard over the hubbub.

Emmie grabbed her arm. "This child needs help now. Ambrine—I think I have some ambrine. . . ." At the look on Kate's face, she said, "Don't worry. I've dealt with burns before. They're one of the more common injuries. There's a packet of paraffin in the car—could you get that? And some clean sheets? Don't worry, little one, we'll have you feeling much better in just a moment. And a candy? Two candies. I'll have candies for such a brave boy! Did I say it wrong? You'll have to help me with my French, won't you, little man? Kate, if you can heat this, and then if you just hold his arms—yes, like that—while I put this here. . . . I know! I know it hurts, poor little man. . . ."

Kate held his arms, despising herself for not wanting to look. But Emmie didn't seem to have any such qualms. She applied hot paraffin to the boy's scalded skin, wrapping it in yards and yards of clean linen. The boy's mother was instructed on wound care and promised a visit from the doctors the next day (Kate wondered how Julia was going to like that, although she suspected it didn't matter what Julia thought; Emmie would have her there one way or another) and a bed was made up out of a spare cot from the truck and clean linens, also from the truck.

Kate followed Emmie out, feeling thoroughly dazed and entirely useless. "I had no idea you knew how to do any of that."

"One learns," said Emmie. "I'm not a proper nurse, but you do pick up a bit over time. It's impossible not to. I couldn't imagine seeing a child in pain like that and standing there with my hands folded. It would be . . . immoral."

As Kate had been prepared to do. Well, not entirely. She had planned to send for the doctors. That was something, wasn't it?

"I don't know how you kept your head like that." Kate's hands were shaking. She stuffed them into her pockets to hide it. "I was ready to be ill."

"I can't say I've seen worse," said Emmie, tucking

the remains of their supplies carefully back in the truck, "but I've seen as bad."

"Was this what your settlement house work was like?" Kate had always assumed that Emmie's work was the merest hobby, flitting in and out of people's lives with books and baskets, like the do-gooders who came to Greenpoint to tsk over the poverty and filth of the immigrants and give them pamphlets on hygiene.

"It wasn't quite so open-air and there were more languages. You'd never imagine it, but I've picked up a smattering of the oddest dialects—German and Hungarian and Czech. Not much, but a few words, enough to help set people at ease and try to understand."

"You do a very good job understanding," said Kate soberly. There she had been, teaching French in an airy, well-appointed room to coiffed and gowned young ladies and thinking herself ill-used. She'd thought herself so superior to Emmie, just because she had to pay her own rent.

She wasn't fit for this. She hadn't the least idea what to do. She barely knew how to drive.

Yes, and she hadn't known how to construct a car either, and she'd done that. But that was different. That was mechanical. These were people, people who needed help and understanding, and Kate's very being quailed at the concept.

"They were being kind to us," said Emmie matter-of-factly. "It's often like that at first. They doubt what you can really do, but they're ready to give you a chance. We just need to prove to them we mean to stay. We need to find some way to bring everyone to us, to make them like us."

"Everyone does like you," said Kate ruefully. Emmie was inherently likable. Probably because she cared so much. It wasn't that she wore her heart on her sleeve; she carried it like a banner, waving in the air ahead of her.

"Mmm," said Emmie, ducking her head. "Oh dear, I'm losing my pins again. They're probably scattered from Grécourt to Canizy."

"Like bread crumbs, only less edible," said Kate. "Oh, stop, let me do that."

Emmie turned so Kate could repair her hair for her, as she had a thousand times before. "It will take us forever to get to know everyone at this rate. A whole day and we didn't even make it through two villages!"

"But they all know about the crazy ladies with the trucks," said Kate, jabbing in a pin hard enough that even Emmie would be hard-pressed to shed it.

"Yes, but is that how we want them to know us? I'd rather we be the crazy ladies with milk—or candy. We need to find a way to get everyone to us. . . ." Emmie turned, looking very un-Emmie-like with her hair neatly pinned away from her face. "We could hold a children's party on the grounds of the château—that might do it."

Kate thought of the old woman lying on a pallet in the mud; the Boche baby with its child mother. Of the baroness, living in comfort in Switzerland while her people huddled in the castle cellars. "I'm not sure a party is precisely what they need."

"People do like parties," said Emmie seriously. "Particularly when they haven't had anything to celebrate for a good long while. It's—it's the same way Mrs. Rutherford wants us to sell to them rather than give to them. It will make them feel like *people* again."

"It's charity," said Kate.

"Then we have to find a way to not make it feel like charity," said Emmie firmly, and got back in the truck.

Chapter Ten

On the twelfth, we called all day and didn't get home until past five. We were just sitting down to supper when a soldier rode up with a letter. It was from the commanding officer saying that six cows had arrived at the station at Nesle and must be removed immediately. After some confusion about where Nesle might be, two of our members set off with the soldier to secure our livestock while the rest of us practiced cantiques with the villagers in their stable for a religious celebration to be held here next week. With the arrival of the cows, the musical evening turned into a moonlit demonstration of best French milking techniques. Your Unit was enthusiastic. The cows were not—and I can't say I blame them. We must have seemed staggeringly inept.

*You can say one thing about life here: there's no
chance for ennui. It's a constant barrage of one
thing after another and I can't think of anything I
like better.*

*Do tell mother that Freddie and I are both well
and hearty. She's not to worry about us in the
least. If she's feeling fluttery, she should call Dr.
Sands, although I am quite certain there's nothing
wrong with her that a brisk walk and a good dose
of fresh air wouldn't cure.*

> *— Miss Frances Englund, '09, to
> her aunt Miss Millicent Rattner*

September 1917
Grécourt, France

It wasn't Emmie who found a way to bring the villagers to them. It was Julia.

They were at dinner in their tiny dining room in the first barrack, crammed around a makeshift table, eating lukewarm vegetable soup that Marie had carried over in a battered tureen from her tarpaulin-covered house, everyone talking over each other about their day.

"I don't see how we can do it all," Margaret said, poking at her soup. She had been part of the group detailed to go to three of the nearer villages with

Julia, serving double duty as driver and social worker. "There's just so *much*. We didn't get through even half of what we intended."

"Rome wasn't built in a day," said Mrs. Rutherford serenely.

"Before Rome can be built, it needs to be washed," said Dr. Stringfellow. "The levels of hygiene are appalling. We need well pumps and washtubs. By the dozen."

"Also fine-toothed combs," put in Emmie, trying not to scratch.

"Miss Randolph, will you add those to the list? Miss Randolph will be in charge of our store."

Emmie couldn't help but notice that Maud, beneath her aloof expression, seemed rather pleased with the appointment. "I'll need to go to Paris," Maud said importantly. "We can't rely on anything arriving unless we fetch it ourselves."

"Next week," said Mrs. Rutherford. "You can take the White."

"I can't drive," said Maud, looking at Mrs. Rutherford with barely contained contempt.

"Then you can take the train," said Mrs. Rutherford, "and someone will meet you at Amiens."

"With all the packages?" demanded Maud.

"You'll manage," said Mrs. Rutherford. "You

can collect our chickens while you're there. We're expecting—how many, Miss Van Alden?"

"Seventy-two," said Emmie.

"How am I meant to take seventy-two chickens on the train?"

"In crates, presumably," offered Fran Englund with a remarkably straight face.

"Oooh, goody," said Liza. "Could you add DeWitt's biscuits to the list? I've gone through all of mine."

"And candies—not for us, for the children," Emmie hastily amended.

"Oh, yes," agreed Anne Dawlish, looking up. "I went through my whole stock of Tootsie Rolls bribing the children to come see Dr. Stringfellow."

Dr. Stringfellow snorted. "I'm hardly *that* scary."

Emmie made the mistake of glancing at Kate, who had such a Kate-like expression of polite disbelief that Emmie had to take refuge in her napkin rather than disgrace herself by laughing out loud.

"But how do we ever get to them all?" Margaret was still worrying at her soup. "There are just so many. And they all need so much."

"Yes, like seventy-two chickens," muttered Maud.

Emmie leaned forward eagerly. "Kate and I were discussing this just earlier today, weren't we, Kate? Not the chickens, I mean, but how to let everyone know we're here. What we need is to bring the ones who can come this far here to us—to show them what we can do for them. We could have a party! A children's party. If we could get even some portion of them here . . ."

"How would they get there?" asked Fran, dunking a hunk of day-old war bread in her soup in an attempt to soften it. "Some of those villages are quite far."

"Oh, that's no matter," said Mrs. Rutherford, brushing that aside. "They'll find a way if they want to come—they walk the most tremendous distances. They might come for curiosity's sake, if nothing else. But we'll want to find something—"

"We should have a mass." Julia's crystalline voice cut through the group.

"A mass?"

"A church ceremony," said Julia impatiently. "The church is still standing, isn't it?"

"Yes." Mrs. Rutherford fixed Julia with a long, thoughtful look. "It was Bavarians quartered here, Marie says. Being Catholics themselves, they tend to be leery of blowing up churches. Of course, that didn't stop them from looting the church plate—scruples only go so far. But we can manage without, I imagine."

"The patron saint of the village is St. Matthew," piped up Anne Dawlish. "The villagers were telling me about it. His feast day is coming up quite soon—on the twenty-first, they said."

"That's it, then. Hold a mass for St. Matthew's Day." Julia looked up to find everyone was staring at her. Two bright spots of color showed in her cheeks. "Well, it's obvious. I spent several years in a village much like this one. They set their lives by the church calendar. There were processions for saints' days. . . . If we can find a priest to perform a mass for St. Matthew's Day, it will mean more to them than anything else we can do."

"You aren't *Catholic*, are you?" Maud was staring at Julia as though she'd grown an extra head.

Julia looked at her coolly. "My mother's second husband, the count, was. They all are here, in case you hadn't noticed. I spent two years in the tutelage of nuns—for which you'll be grateful if I ever have to sew you up."

"There must be a chaplain attached to one of the regiments in the neighborhood," mused Mrs. Rutherford. "I'm sure we can borrow someone to perform a service. It is an inspired notion, Dr. Pruyn. Well done."

Julia shrugged. "Anyone who's lived in France could tell you the same."

Emmie was full of chagrin that she hadn't thought of it herself. She plunged in as best she could, trying to make up for lost time. "It's brilliant! We can learn the prayers, so we can say them with them—it will make us seem less alien. Kate can help, can't you, Kate? You're Catholic. You can tell us what to do and what to sing. And then we can have all the children for a party afterward. . . ."

"I didn't know we had Catholic girls at Smith," said Liza in a loud whisper.

"There are a few," Maud said carelessly. "One doesn't generally meet them, though."

"You're determined to have that party, aren't you?" said Kate to Emmie, smiling, but her smile had a fixed quality to it.

"We don't have to have a party," said Emmie, floundering. She hadn't known it was a secret, that Kate was Catholic. It was just part of the Kate-ness of Kate, like her hair being brown. She hadn't meant to make things awkward. "Not if it wouldn't be appropriate. I don't know what one generally does after a mass. . . . It's supposed to be a cheerful thing, isn't it, a saint's day?"

"The 11th Engineers is stationed near here, aren't they?" asked Alice, mixing her pronouns with abandon in her nervousness. "There must be some Catholics among our boys who could help."

"Among the enlisted men, I would think," said Margaret unthinkingly, then looked at Kate and turned bright red.

"We should ask Madame la Maire." Kate held herself with white-lipped control. "About holding a mass. She'll be able to tell us what we ought to do."

"Of course," said Emmie a little too quickly. "I should have thought of that."

"*Allô?*" Someone rapped on the door of the barrack, making the whole wall shake. The door opened, and a man's head stuck through the opening, rather cautiously, as though he expected them to be in a state of undress. "Did somebody order a shipment of cows for Grécourt?"

"Cows? Oh. Goodness. Yes." Emmie half rose from the table, nearly oversetting her soup, incredibly relieved to have the excuse to go. "Those are my cows. I mean our cows. Do you have them with you?"

"The cows are in Nesle. In a boxcar," the man explained patiently, in very slow, simple French. "The station manager requests you come get them immediately."

"Nesle," said Emmie, not sure what to do first or how one was meant to convey cows or, for that matter, where she was meant to be going. She had a vague idea that Nesle was in Switzerland. She tried to picture the map in her head, but she'd never been much good with maps, or any sort of directions, really. She'd once got lost in Gramercy Park. Instinctively she looked to Kate. "Where is Nesle?"

"Six miles," said Mrs. Rutherford, unperturbed. "You'll need someone to drive you."

"And the cows, presumably," pointed out Julia.

"Oh goodness," said Emmie. "Will they fit in the White truck, do you think?"

"Take the jitney," suggested Mrs. Rutherford.

"We'll need somewhere to put them," said Fran Englund briskly, managing to push back her chair and rise without rattling so much as a single cup. "I'll see if any of the outbuildings are fit to hold them."

"I'll get my tools." Anne Dawlish sprang into action, glowing with the opportunity to put her hammer and nails to use. "We'll need to do some repairs."

"In the dark?" said Maud.

"You can hold the lantern," replied Fran, and Emmie, miserably, saw her exchange a small grin with Kate, and hated that Fran had been able to do what she hadn't, to make Kate feel like one of them again.

"You'll drive, won't you, Kate?" Emmie said, and felt about four again, tugging at her mother's skirt, begging her to look at her, to play with her, to be with her, feeling again that sensation of the fabric whisking away from her, her mother so impossibly far above her, always in motion, always moving away.

There was a small, awkward pause. Kate rose neatly from the table. "Of course."

The messenger had no time for any of it. He waved them anxiously forward. "The train needs to go. If you could come now?"

It was a bumpy six miles in the dark to Nesle, with the messenger, who had slung his bicycle in the back of the jitney, guiding them through the turnings just a moment too late, so that Kate had to wrench at the wheel. It made private conversation entirely impossible. Kate focused on the road with white-knuckled concentration and Emmie clutched the side of the truck and made bright observations on the weather to which no one at all responded.

She still didn't, quite entirely, understand what she had done wrong, only that she had, and she felt dreadful about it, with that creeping dread that comes when you know you've been in the wrong and have no idea how to make it right again, because you weren't aware of having done anything wrong in the first place.

It had all been for the villagers. She had only wanted to find a way to make them comfortable.

But she couldn't forget that horrible silence, that frozen look on Kate's face, the way everyone had stared at Kate as though she had suddenly grown horns.

But it was nothing to be ashamed of, surely? Not here in France.

One doesn't generally meet them, said Maud. And

it was true she couldn't think of any other Catholic girls their year. But that didn't mean there was anything wrong with it. Except for a thousand comments she vaguely recalled hearing, about the servants and their superstitions. Although no one had called it superstitious when Auntie May had married Monsieur le Comte de Talleygord. Then it had all been "terribly romantic" and "so very medieval" and Auntie May had proudly worn a pendant that was supposed to have been blessed by some famous saint or other, but the main point about it was that it had been in the family since the Crusades and boasted a very large cabochon sapphire.

The jitney bumped over a rail, and Emmie had to cling to the seat to keep from going headfirst over the side.

The stationmaster greeted them with something between amusement and pity. Once Emmie looked into the boxcar, she wasn't sure she blamed him. The cows looked like the beasts in the Bible who had been afflicted with pestilence, all skin and bone and covered with flies.

Kate joined her at the opening of the boxcar. "Are you sure these are the cows you intended to buy?"

"I—I took the best ones they had." They did look awfully bony. She could have sworn they hadn't looked this bony in Paris. Emmie bit her lip. "Maybe they're just tired from the journey?"

"I don't think they walked all the way." Kate's voice still had that dreadful flat note.

"Well, we can feed them up, and then—oh, I don't know." Emmie swallowed hard. They should have left this to someone better, someone more competent, someone who didn't muddle everything she touched. "Maybe they aren't as bad as they seem. I suppose we'll be able to get a better look once we get them out of the boxcar?"

"First we have to get them out of the boxcar," said Kate grimly.

Some helpful soul had inserted a plank into the opening, but the cows didn't seem inclined to go down it, huddling together in their sodden straw. Bending over, Emmie patted her hands against her knees and called, "Here, cows! Here, cowey cows!"

The cows flicked her looks of what Emmie could have sworn was bovine disdain. The men loading packages stopped to stare. One said something to another and they both snickered. A group of British soldiers climbing down from a train bumped into each other in their fascination.

"It—it worked on our old sheepdog." Emmie could feel tears prickling behind her eyes and hastily blinked them away. "What do cows like? Do they like grain? We could wave some grain in front of them. Or maybe a carrot. Like horses. They do use carrots to lure horses, don't they?"

Kate's face was a study in shadow in the torchlight. "Sugar," she said at last in an expressionless voice. "My father drove the wagon for a brewery. His pockets were always full of lumps of sugar to bribe the horse to go."

For a moment Emmie forgot the cows, forgot the soldiers on the siding. She'd never heard Kate speak of her real father before. She knew that Kate had a step-father and four half brothers—their overabundance of brothers and regrettable lack of sisters had been some-thing they had shared that first week at Smith—but all she knew of Kate's real father was that he had died.

Emmie put out a hand in the darkness, her fingers grazing Kate's sleeve. "Kate—I'm so sorry. About to-night. I never meant—"

Kate acted as though she hadn't heard. "Let's get these cows back. If you guide from the front, I'll push from the back."

"I don't mind pushing," Emmie said, but Kate had already clambered up the plank and disappeared behind the large, bony rump of a cow. Emmie took a deep breath, grasped the rope someone had considerately looped around the cow, and tugged as hard as she could.

The cow didn't budge.

It might have been bony, but it was still large. Large and determined. Emmie was also determined, but not nearly as large, and it didn't help that her feet kept sliding out from under her.

"Emmie!" came Kate's exasperated voice from behind the cow. "What are you doing?"

"Pulling! But this wretched beast just won't *go*." Emmie's voice broke shamefully. "Oh, heavens, and there are five more of them."

She wanted to sit down in the straw, pull her skirt over her head, and cry. How were they to move any of them? The stench was tremendous, even from outside the boxcar. Emmie couldn't think how Kate was bearing it from the cow's other end. She redoubled her efforts, ending up with rope burns on her palms and little else to show for it.

"I think it moved a little!" she called hopefully.

"Oh good," said Kate. "Another year should do it."

"Sugar! You said they like sugar!" Holding the rope with one hand, Emmie fumbled in her pocket and came up with a licorice twist, one of the sweets she'd brought for the children. The cow was unimpressed.

"There has to be another way," said Emmie as Kate straightened up, stretching out her back.

"We could hitch the boxcar to the jitney."

"I think it's designed to run on rails," said a crisp British voice behind them, and Emmie promptly lost her grip on the rope and did an impressive wobble on the plank that ended in a pair of hands grasping her neatly beneath the arms and setting her down firmly on her feet.

"Sir Percy," said Emmie, vaguely aware that she smelled like cow and that there was something unpleasant on the heel of her boot.

"Always happy to be of service." Having made sure she wasn't in imminent danger of keeling over, he stepped back. Emmie hoped it wasn't anything to do with what was on her shoe. "Miss Van Alden. And your friend."

"Katherine Moran," said Kate, making her way cautiously down the plank. "Sir Percy?"

"Blakeney. The Scarlet Pimpernel," explained Emmie helplessly. "They seek him here, they seek him—"

"Yes, I know that," said Kate. "Aren't you a century or so off?"

The captain rubbed his brow with his gloved knuckles. "Whenever England is in peril and all that. . . ."

"I thought that was King Arthur," ventured Emmie. "Sleeping under the hill."

The train did something unnerving, belching black

smoke. The captain winced as the whistle shrilled, jolting the dispirited cows into protest. One lowed. Another relieved herself. "Yes, if anyone could sleep through this racket. I take it these are your beasts?"

"They're cows," said Emmie.

"Are you quite sure?" asked the captain.

"These were the best that were to be had, I'm afraid." Emmie hurried on before anyone could disagree with her. "We need to get them to Grécourt. And feed them. Poor things, they look quite hungry."

"So you really are going on with your plans, then."

There was something in the way he said it that made Emmie duck her head, feeling awkward. "We're trying to. I'm afraid I've made a hash of this. We brought the jitney, you see, and I haven't the slightest idea of how to get the cows into it. . . ."

The captain turned to look at the jitney and broke out in a fit of violent coughing. "My dear girl, you can't mean to get those cows into that?"

"If Sir Percy Blakeney can get into the Bastille, I don't see why we can't get the cows into the jitney," said Kate acidly, moving to stand next to Emmie.

"It was the Temple prison," said the captain helpfully. "Not the Bastille. But even the Scarlet Pimpernel couldn't spirit those cows away in a Ford van. I think I might be able to help, though. If you'll pardon me?"

As he strode away, looking impossibly British, Kate turned to Emmie. "My dear girl?"

Emmie hunched her shoulders. "I don't think he meant it personally. It's just that he's English."

"Mmm," said Kate. "And a fictional character, apparently."

The fictional character was looking quite solid as he returned from the stationmaster's shanty.

"The stationmaster has a nephew who would be delighted to drive your cows to Grécourt for you."

"Tonight?" asked Kate skeptically.

"Tonight. He knows these roads and is well acquainted with cows—or was, before the war. Your cows should be delivered to you at some point no later than midnight."

"Goodness," said Emmie. "Thank you."

"You're both of you city-bred, aren't you?" said the captain, sounding deeply amused. He smiled at Emmie. "A word of advice: a good stationmaster knows everybody and can arrange anything."

"How much do we owe him?" asked Kate.

"Nothing," said the captain. "It's been taken care of."

"Oh, but we can pay! We do have funds. We're not nearly as destitute as we appear, are we, Kate?"

"Neither is the British Army, just yet." Someone called to him, and the captain raised a hand in response.

He bowed to Kate and Emmie, a neat inclination of the head. "Consider this payment for getting your cows off our railway line. Good night, ladies. Enjoy your livestock."

"I really should have insisted on paying him back, shouldn't I?" Emmie craned her head to try to catch a glimpse of him as she and Kate returned to the jitney. "Perhaps if we could find out how much he paid the stationmaster . . ."

"It was just what he said; he wanted to clear the line." Kate settled herself behind the wheel. "Let's hope I can remember the way back."

Emmie dug around on the floor for the map, losing another four pins in the process. "If he hadn't been here—"

"We would have thought of it ourselves." Kate backed the jitney up, inching past an army camion. "Eventually."

"I feel the worst sort of fool. I should have known we couldn't get six cows into the jitney." Or any cows. Now that she thought of it, it did seem insane. Emmie found herself truly, deeply hoping that their agriculturalist would arrive before she could make any other foolish mistakes. The captain was right; for all that her family spent a month every year in their camp in the Adirondacks, she was, fundamentally, city-bred. It would never have occurred to her to speak to the stationmaster. Or that a cow couldn't go in a jitney.

Kate shrugged. "No one else knew either. Mrs. Rutherford was the one who suggested it."

It made it even worse that Kate was being so nice about it all. "Yes, but if Mrs. Rutherford had been here, she would probably have persuaded those cows to march nicely up the plank and arrange themselves neatly on the bench like animals in a children's book. I couldn't even get them to come out of the boxcar."

"Yes, you did," said Kate reluctantly, and Emmie thought how like her it was to be fair even when she was furious. "Eventually. With a little help."

"Sir Percy Blakeney, baronet. Oh Lord. I forgot to ask him his name. Again. Do you think it's something deeply awful, like Algernon?"

"Or Cecil," said Kate, steering carefully around a very large pothole. "Either that or he's wanted by the police of multiple nations for crimes unspeakable."

"Don't say that in front of Maud," said Emmie, only half joking. "She thinks there are spies beneath every pillow."

"Not our pillows. They're far too thin," retorted Kate. After a moment she added, "We'll see if our cows make it all the way back to Grécourt or if your mystery man has a taste for roast beef. He might be making himself a feast in the forest."

"I don't think there's terribly much beef left on them to roast." It was such a relief to have Kate sounding like herself again, but Emmie knew she couldn't just leave it at that. "Kate. I really am sorry about what happened at dinner tonight. I never thought about your being Catholic—not as something that, well—when you think about it, absolutely everyone was before Henry the Eighth! Catholic, I mean. And he's not really a very good representation for the Reformation, is he?" She was aware she wasn't making much sense, but she couldn't seem to stop herself. "Of course, if I'd been alive then, I would have been Catholic too. In the time of Henry, I mean. Because everyone was. So it wasn't anything unusual at all."

"In the time of Henry."

Emmie nodded enthusiastically. "Can't you just picture Maud in a wimple?"

Kate choked on a laugh. "Strangely enough, yes. Probably as an abbess of a particularly exclusive convent. The sort of convent that wouldn't admit me."

"If Maud were abbess, I don't think she'd admit anyone," said Emmie. "I never meant to make you feel awkward. I just—I just thought you might help.

Because it was something you might know something about."

"I know." The jitney bumped along the road, broken tree stumps crouched on either side like the darker sort of fairy-tale creature. Emmie thought Kate meant to leave it at that, but after a very long while, she said, "It's . . . disquieting to have people look at you differently. You can be just like everyone else—and then, just like that, you're not. You're an imposter. An interloper."

"I don't think anyone thinks you're an interloper." Even as Emmie said it, she remembered the way they had all stared. "You're as much a Smith girl as any of the rest of us."

"Only until they learn that my father drove a delivery wagon," Kate said drily.

"My great-great-great-grandfather dealt in beaver pelts," offered Emmie. "That's how the family fortune began. They call him an entrepreneur, but that's just a fancy name for a man who skinned small animals for a living. He must have smelled dreadful."

"A few centuries take the pong off the pelt." The jitney bumped to a stop by the side of the road. "Would you mind taking a look at that signpost? I want to make sure I'm not driving us straight into the German lines."

"It's the sign for Grécourt," Emmie said. They'd passed it at least three times that day. "Didn't you recognize it?"

"Sorry," said Kate briskly. "I must be more tired than I thought. Now how do we explain to the others that we let a fictional character wander off with our cows?"

Chapter Eleven

You'll never believe what I've been doing! Dr. Pruyn, who was raised partly in a convent, had the idea that the peasants would like a mass, so Mrs. R (who I hope will not be long with us—but more on that later) dug up a soldier priest working with the Red Cross nearby. Our people here—the ones who live in our stables—swept the church and trimmed it with flowers, and I must say, it did look pretty and not at all gaudy. The Unit stood in the back and sang four French songs which Dr. Pruyn taught us, some of which were really quite patriotic and charming, although there was far too much about the nom du Sacré-Coeur for my liking. But the effect was very good and all the peasants seemed to enjoy it. They kept thanking us again and again until it was really quite embarrassing.

Afterward, we had 123 children here to play games on the lawn. I'd thought it would be the most frightful din, but they just trooped in and stood there, not making a mess or a noise—really quite good little creatures and so happy for anything. Their mothers said they hadn't played for three years, so they'd forgotten how. I'm not sure we ought to teach them again—they're so well behaved this way—but the others insist it's not the least bit normal and they ought to be taught to run around and scream.

If that's the way of American kindergartens, maybe we ought to send our children to school in France. . . .

> — Miss Maud Randolph, '09, to
> her fiancé, Mr. Henry Craig

September 1917
Grécourt, France

"Have you seen the skipping ropes? I could have sworn I took out the skipping ropes."

"Anne Dawlish took them." Kate dodged out of the way as Emmie staggered past, bearing an armload of hoops.

The mass was over and the Unit was attempting to marshal an alarming number of children on the lawn behind the château. Alice Patton and Margaret Cooper presided behind a long trestle table, doling out coffee for the adults—very watery coffee, but coffee all the same—and milk from their own cows for the children. The cows, contrary to all of Kate's expectations, had arrived as promised and had responded well to the enthusiastic, if untutored, ministrations of the members of the Smith College Relief Unit.

The cows weren't the only unexpected success. Kate looked around the lawn, at the members of the Unit rushing about being useful, at the villagers overflowing what had once been the baroness's private preserve, and had to admit that the mass had been . . . well, a smashing success.

Kate had been privately convinced that it would be a disaster. She'd been worried that no one would come or that the Unit would embarrass themselves. It would, thought Kate, be both the beginning and the end of their usefulness, when the French villagers saw seventeen American Protestants blundering their way through a mass, slaughtering the canticles and making inappropriate comments in carrying voices.

But Julia had led them in procession across the fields, and Julia had sung the canticles in her high, clear voice, and, somehow, with Julia in charge, it had all come out exactly right and even Maud had behaved herself, clothed in an odor of self-conscious sanctity. The inhabitants of villages from miles away had streamed into the small church, filling it to capacity and overflowing into the churchyard. Kate had stood in the back of the church with the rest of the Smith Unit as the priest in his scarlet vestments led the familiar Latin service, her lips moving to the long-known words, even as her gray uniform set apart her, set her with the other Smith women.

Domine, non sum dignus. . . .

Lord, I am not worthy.

Alice had looked around nervously and copied whatever Julia was doing, usually several seconds behind; Liza had bounced on the balls of her feet and made the wrong responses in the wrong places, but with vigor. Emmie, of course, sang loudest of all, and almost entirely out of tune. The French were very patient about it and complimented them all lavishly, and Kate had left feeling somehow—not cleansed, but with some unspoken fear unrealized.

Even the weather had cooperated. It was the most perfect sort of autumn day, the midday sun gilding the grass and the browning leaves, lighting the faces of the old Robecourts on the walls of the château. The mayor had cleaned all their uniforms for them and the gray with its touches of French blue looked wonderfully official as they all darted this way and that among the villagers, fetching milk, holding babies, explaining about the dispensary and the store.

The Unit was, Kate realized with a faint sense of disbelief, doing just exactly what it had set out to do. For all their differences, all their false starts, it was working. Over the past ten days, they had made a start, a true start. The social workers had been diligently making their rounds, bringing with them milk from their own cows. The villagers had begun to straggle into the makeshift clinic the doctors held at Grécourt in the mornings. Their traveling store was to begin the next day, the Ford truck loaded with the results of Maud's buying trip to Paris.

Maud had brought with her not just the chickens but three of the missing members of their Unit: Miss Baldwin, the librarian, who had arrived clutching an armload of French children's books she had begged, borrowed, or quite possibly stolen; Miss Mills, full of ideas about nursing picked up during her brief time at the Villier hospital (Kate foresaw trouble there with Julia, who had pointed out that Miss Mills hadn't actually trained as a nurse); and Miss Ledbetter, the journalist, who came armed with a legion of anecdotes about the history of Grécourt from the Merovingians to the present, almost undoubtedly apocryphal. They had all found themselves retiring very early from dinner the previous night under the onslaught of Miss Ledbetter's learned discourse.

Fran poked Kate in the arm. "Quick, the Ledbetter is heading our way. Time to get more sweets for the children."

"Do we have more sweets for the children?" Maud had bought what she could in Paris, but anything made with sugar cost the earth, and whatever packages had been sent them from home were all held up by the Red Cross Clearing House, distributed as it pleased them.

"Does it matter?" asked Fran.

"Fair point," said Kate. She'd been spending more and more time with Fran when not on her rounds, grateful for the other woman's easy company. Kate was, if she was being honest, avoiding Emmie, who kept trying to have discussions about their feelings. Kate didn't want to discuss her feelings. Much of the time she was so tired, she wasn't even sure she had feelings, and she was really quite happy with that. "Poor Alice. The Ledbetter's got her."

"I'm sure she'll be fascinated to hear all about Clovis's triumph at whatever it was," said Fran. Next to the refreshment table, Maud was whispering something to Liza, one eye on Mrs. Rutherford. "Maud's looking quite cat and canary."

"Have you heard she traveled first class on a third-class ticket?" Maud had only told them six times.

"No, did she?" With mock seriousness Fran said, "The real problem was that no one had thought to buy her a first-class ticket in the first place. This was only her way of putting the world back the way it ought to be."

"Like those people who insist that if they'd been born centuries ago, they'd have been nobles and not peasants."

"In a pointy hat," agreed Fran. "With a tame unicorn by her side. Don't mention it to Miss Ledbetter, though, or you'll hear more than you ever wanted about it, with excursions into *The Song of Roland* and the *Almanach de Gotha*."

"Were those at the same time?"

"I have no idea. I was always more interested in physics than history. We aren't planning on letting Miss Ledbetter loose on those poor children, are we?"

"Not the littler ones. That's Emmie and Anne Dawlish and Nell Baldwin. Emmie will recite lyric poetry at them, but I think they should be able to weather it." She was being catty about Emmie and she shouldn't be. The truth was, she was still annoyed at Emmie, even though she knew she shouldn't be. And she was still punishing Emmie in small ways, even though she knew she shouldn't be. It made Kate feel petty and horrible but she couldn't seem to stop herself. "Miss Ledbetter's supposed to be helping to teach the older children."

"You taught older girls, didn't you?"

"Yes, French. I don't think that would be much use here."

Fran raised a brow. "Still."

"I was a terrible teacher," Kate said firmly. It wasn't that she disliked children; she just had no talent for making them either love or mind her, not like Emmie, who collected small children like the Pied Piper. "I hated every minute of it and so did my unfortunate pupils. I refuse to inflict myself on these poor children."

Fran looked with concern at the group in front of them. "They're so quiet. Children that age—they should be making such a din we could scarcely hear ourselves think."

Miss Dawlish was working on getting a group of children to link hands and dance in a circle to "*Sur le Pont d'Avignon.*" She waved her arms about, bending exaggeratedly from the waist. "*Les beaux garçons font comme ça!*"

The *beaux garçons* hung their heads and looked uncertainly at the ground.

No one was running. No one was singing. No one was misbehaving. Emmie was running this way and that, with hoops and ropes, trying to coax children into activity, with distinctly limited success.

"I don't know much about children, but I do have four brothers. They used to tear through our house, screaming like banshees, chasing each other." It had driven Kate mad at the time, the constant din, the way they would fling themselves at each other and at her. Although they were rather sweet when they were snuggled up in her lap. For about five minutes.

"My brother and I were the same way. It gave my mother headaches." Fran thought for a moment. "To be fair, everything gave my mother headaches. But Freddie and I really were that awful."

"Do you think it's because they're undernourished?" asked Kate doubtfully, eyeing the subdued children. They were certainly thin, there was no denying that, their skin an unhealthy gray, but it was more than that.

"They haven't played for three years." Dr. Stringfellow came and stood beside them, her eyebrows, for once, at rest. "They don't remember how. Some of them have no memory of life being other than this. It's sickening."

"Is there anything we can do for them?"

"Not my department. I'll worm the ones who need worming, but there's no pill for having the childhood crushed out of you. If there were, I'd dispense it in bulk. And bill Kaiser Wilhelm."

Kate and Fran looked at each other as Dr. Stringfellow stalked away. "I think she's experiencing human emotion," said Fran.

"Does she have children?" asked Kate.

Fran shook her head. "There is a husband—I saw a letter addressed to him. But I have no idea other than that. She's very private."

"I'm not sure I blame her."

Fran cast her a sympathetic look. "It's not easy to be private here, is it? All of us crammed into those little rooms, living in each other's pockets. Poor Alice keeps trying to find a place to have a private cry but the best she can manage is under the covers when she thinks we're asleep. We shouldn't complain, I suppose. When you think of what we see in the villages . . ."

A little ahead of them, having failed with hoops and skipping ropes, Emmie was trying to coax a group of the children into a game of catch.

"Look, I'll show you," Emmie said encouragingly. "You just take the ball and throw it to a friend, like this—"

Emmie lobbed the ball, but the girl she'd chosen had turned away and didn't see the ball coming at her. It hit her in the shoulder. It wasn't a hard ball or a particularly hard throw, but the girl went rigid. For a moment the world stood frozen, Emmie and the children staring, and then the girl dropped to the ground, her arms over her head, screaming. Screaming in a way Kate had never heard before. Horrible, high-pitched, inhuman screams.

"I'm so sorry! I'm so sorry!" Emmie flung herself at the girl, trying to comfort her, but the girl just kept screaming and screaming, rolled into a ball in the dirt, kicking out when Emmie tried to touch her.

Kate hadn't even realized she'd moved, but there she was, on her knees in the dirt next to the girl, elbowing Emmie aside, because couldn't Emmie see she was making it worse, that the girl didn't want to be touched?

"Don't! Leave her," Kate snapped.

The girl's screams were beginning to turn into something like sobs; her wasted little body heaved and shook.

Emmie's face was ashen. She sat back on her heels, staring at the child in horror. "I had no idea—I never meant—oh goodness."

"Get her some milk," Kate said decisively, and Emmie stumbled to her feet, tripping over herself in her alarm.

The child was still shaking, her head hidden in her arms, curled up like a hedgehog.

"Hello," said Kate, not touching her, not moving. "We haven't been introduced yet. I'm Miss Moran."

A bit of tearstained face poked out. "Mademoiselle . . . *Marron*?"

The girl had turned Kate's name into the French word for *chestnut*. "Well, yes, I can be *Marron* if you like."

The girl lifted her head a bit more, sizing Kate up. She couldn't have been more than five, six at most. She wiped her nose with the back of one hand. Her voice trembled. "Your hair is the color of your name."

Kate instinctively put her hand to her hair, which had been braided and twisted back. The braiding was an ineffectual attempt to keep out insect invaders. "Chestnut? Yes, I suppose. I've only ever seen chestnuts after they were roasted."

The girl didn't move. "We have lots of them in the woods."

"Would you show me one of these days? I don't know anything about woods. I've only lived in towns."

Slowly, the girl uncurled, sitting back on her heels. "Like Amiens?"

"A bit like Amiens."

"But not as big," said the girl, taking for granted that Amiens was the extent of the metropolitan experience.

"But much bigger." The girl's eyes widened. "We have buildings taller than the highest church spire, and railways that run on tracks in the sky."

"You're making it up."

"I'm not, I swear." Kate struggled up from her knees and held out a hand. "Do you think you can get up now?"

The girl hesitated. There was dirt on her cheek where she'd buried her face in the ground. Kate resisted the urge to rub it away. The last thing the girl needed was fussing.

Kate kept her hand extended, not moving. "No one is going to throw anything at you again without warning, I promise."

"I know it was just a ball," the little girl said with dignity.

"All the same." Kate glanced around. Miss Dawlish had very determinedly got her group of children singing a round about a windmill and a fish. Emmie was waiting in line for milk, looking deeply distressed. But none of the Frenchwomen seemed to be headed their way. "Where is your mother?"

The girl's face closed. *"Avec les boches."*

Of course. She should have known better than to ask. "Mine is in America, all the way across the ocean, in a city called Brooklyn."

The girl looked interested, but Miss Baldwin came up, holding out a picture book. "Won't you read with me?"

The girl went with her, with a backward glance for Kate. Kate gave her a little wave, and then joined the group at the refreshment table.

"Does anyone know who that girl was?" she asked, breaking into a discussion about the best way to kill fleas. "The one who was screaming."

Emmie's face was gray. "I feel so awful. . . . I never meant . . ."

Alice Patton put down her coffeepot. "That's one of mine, from the *basse-cour*. She's called Zélie. It's a terrible story—well, they're all terrible stories, aren't they? Her whole family—mother, father, two older sisters—were all taken away by the Boche. Zélie and her brother were left with a neighbor. She's five, he was eight."

"Was?" Kate could feel her stomach doing something unpleasant.

"They were playing in a field, running about as children do—that's what the people there told me—and he stumbled across an unexploded shell."

She didn't need to say more. None of them did. Kate had to catch herself to keep from crossing herself. It wasn't something she'd done for years; she wasn't even sure where the impulse had come from.

"Oh my goodness," whispered Emmie, her eyes enormous in her stricken face, all bones and teeth. "Was he—?"

Alice fiddled with the handle of the coffeepot. "She saw it happen. There wasn't enough left of him to bury."

"So when I threw the ball . . ." Emmie clutched at her collar. "I have to make it up to her."

"Stop." Kate grabbed her arm before she could go. "Miss Baldwin's reading to her. Leave it be."

"I can at least give her an extra candy."

"And make her look like she needs special treatment? If you did that, it would be for your own sake, not hers." Emmie looked so stricken that Kate immediately felt guilty. "Emmie, I didn't mean—"

"You're right." Emmie ducked her head, blundering around the side of the refreshment table. "She's better this way. I'll—I'll just go help Margaret with the milk."

"It is a great success, isn't it?" said Alice uncertainly. "I mean, aside from poor Zélie. Look how many people came to us."

"And it will be even better when—" Liza began, but Maud elbowed her hard in the ribs.

"When we finally get some decent furniture in our barrack," said Maud decidedly. "And curtains. It's unthinkable to have the sun shining in your eyes first thing in the morning."

The general consensus was that the St. Matthew's Day celebration was a great triumph. When they met for breakfast the next morning, there was a festival air, everyone congratulating everyone else. Only Emmie seemed subdued; Kate had heard her thrashing about on her cot deep into the night.

"Well done, ladies." Mrs. Rutherford called them to order by tapping her coffee cup with her spoon. "Monsieur le Commandant was deeply impressed that we, foreigners, have a care not only for our people's bodies but for their souls. He says it is a sign that we understand this place and will do right by it—and anything we need from him, we need only ask."

"Medicine," said Dr. Stringfellow firmly. "Ask for medicine."

"And more books!" chimed in Miss Baldwin.

"Did you know," said Miss Ledbetter, "that the parish of Grécourt was founded on St. Matthew's Day in the year of our Lord 1235? Just think of it! Twenty years after Magna Carta, two hundred years before Agincourt, this little scrap of land—"

Everyone started talking at once, eager to avert further musings on the medieval. "That nurse told me we should go to Miss Morgan's place at Blérancourt—"

"That nice French officer said he has another cow for us, if we want it—"

"Could we add another village to our rounds?" Emmie's voice rose over the rest. "Someone was telling me about another village, just a little farther north, called Courcelles. It's in an awful way, they say. The Germans were stationed there during the early part of the war but there was a terrible fire and a German officer died and they retaliated rather horribly. The priest was telling me there are fifty children there and not one of them well. Couldn't we do something for them?"

"We've scarcely got the resources for the villages we already have," objected Kate, filled with a deep foreboding. "We're practically out of medicine— we're going to have to go get some from the hospital in Amiens. And wouldn't we have to clear it with the French authorities?"

"It was the French authorities who brought it up to me," said Emmie, looking around the table for support.

"Well—that nurse who was there with the priest. She said there's far too much for them to do. They would be delighted for us to take it on."

"I'm sure they would," said Fran drily.

Mrs. Rutherford tapped a finger thoughtfully against the side of her coffee cup. Kate was still having a hard time getting used to the cups; they were whimsical things, shaped like bowls with little wings to either side rather than a proper handle. "It's a sign of how word of our work is spreading. Monsieur le Commandant suggested we also add Bacquencourt and Eppeville."

"We can hardly take care of all of France!" Maud protested.

"No, but we can manage this bit of it," said Mrs. Rutherford, calmly applying jam to her bread. "In the little over a week that we've been here, Miss Van Alden alone has already made fifty-one calls on forty-two families."

Emmie blushed, looking modestly down.

Kate resisted the urge to point out that she had been there too.

"Multiply that number by the rest of the members of our social work department. We've distributed milk, bread, honey, and baby clothing in eleven villages. Miss Dawlish is organizing a weekly children's meeting. The medical department has seen—how many patients?"

"Nearly three hundred," said Dr. Stringfellow. "It would be more if the truck would stop breaking down."

Mrs. Rutherford made a note on her ever-present notepad. "Perhaps if we exchanged the tires on the White for hard rims . . . If we can do this much in ten days, how much can we accomplish in ten weeks? Or ten months? I believe we can fit an extra village into our schedule. You can go this morning after breakfast, survey the village, see if we might do something useful there."

Emmie glowed like a saint in a medieval painting.

Kate was feeling somewhat less sanguine. They already had more than two thousand souls in their care, a large number of them children. As Dr. Stringfellow kept reminding them, they were nearly out of medicine. They didn't have enough lumber to build houses, even if they had people who knew how to build them, which they didn't. Most of their villages lacked pumps for the wells; the Germans had broken them. Not to mention needing to dig new wells to replace the old ones, which had been poisoned. "And what if we decide it's too much for us? Won't we have raised expectations we can't meet?"

"Even if you only go today, that's something too.

Bring what you can, do what you can; you'll still leave them better off than they were."

"Any little bit is better than nothing?" Kate couldn't keep the skepticism out of her voice. "We're only seventeen women—I know, we'll be eighteen once Miss Lewes finally gets here, but that's hardly any difference at all."

"Our strength is as the strength of ten," murmured Mrs. Rutherford.

Kate decided not to get into a debate about pure hearts. Hers certainly wasn't. "We can count angels on the heads of pins all we like—or Smith girls on the backs of trucks—but we have all of three motors, three teachers, and two doctors. How can we sustain services for that many people in that many villages?"

"We don't," Mrs. Rutherford said, and smiled at her. "That's the whole point of it. They have their own teachers. Not as many as before . . . but some. Once we build their schoolhouses back up, once we give them the books they need, we'll leave them to it. Bit by bit, they'll need us less and less. We provide the foundation, and they'll do the rest."

"That's a lot of foundation," said Kate. An airplane droned overhead, a reminder that their time here might be limited.

Mrs. Rutherford patted her hand. "Day by day, Miss

Moran. Day by day. Ah, there's the post." Through the window, they could see a man cycling along one of the few surviving paths. "Shall we go meet him?"

There was a mad rush for the door of the barrack.

Kate held back, trailing along at the end of the group. There wouldn't, she knew, be anything for her. She'd written her mother with their forwarding address, but . . . But. Her mother was busy, she knew. Busy with the boys, busy with the house, busy with the large circle of family and friends she had acquired through her second marriage.

Kate had written, at first, that first year at Smith. But it had rapidly become clear that her letters only made things worse, that those things she had viewed as triumphs—being elected to a literary society, being chosen for a role in a play—seemed painfully trivial to her mother. Worse than trivial. Frivolous. And on her side, Kate had tried not to be hurt that her mother's letters seemed to be exclusively devoted to praising her brothers.

She had tried to go home again, briefly, after Newport. But her family hadn't known what to do with her; they had their patterns, which didn't include her. She didn't belong to Emmie's world, but she couldn't go back to her own either. She was lost, stranded, neither here nor there.

"Three for you, Maud! Lucky you!" said Liza, delving happily into the mailbag like a puppy digging for treats. "And I've got one from Harry too! Isn't he a darling to think of me. There's a thick stack for you, Mrs. Rutherford—and a telegram for you from the committee. You've got a telegram too, Fran."

"Is there anything for me?" Emmie asked hopefully.

"One from . . . Andover," said Liza, squinting at the stamps.

"Oh. That will be my brother. There's nothing from anyone else?"

"No, just the one," said Liza cheerfully, "but you know how these things are. Nothing for weeks and weeks and then you get fifteen all at once."

"Yes, that must be what it is," said Alice Patton, turning away from the pile, which contained nothing for her.

"Time to work, ladies!" Mrs. Rutherford crumpled the telegram and let it drop to the table. "We cannot rest on our laurels! This is a war zone. Time is of the essence. Miss Moran, Miss Van Alden—Courcelles. Miss Patton, Miss Mills, Dr. Pruyn—the dispensary, then take the jitney for visits. Miss Englund, Miss Cooper—the wheel has come off the White again. Miss Baldwin, Miss Dawlish, Miss Ledbetter—sewing and carpentry classes for the children of the nearer villages."

"What about us?" Maud asked. She was looking at Mrs. Rutherford and the crumpled telegram in a way Kate didn't quite like. Cat and canary, Fran had called it yesterday, and she wasn't wrong. If Maud had had whiskers, she would be licking them.

Mrs. Rutherford looked at Maud, her face seeming suddenly older. "Miss Randolph and Miss Shaw—load the Ford truck for the traveling store. Ava, if you could come with me for a moment?"

"Certainly," said Dr. Stringfellow, casting a quick, concerned glance at her old roommate.

"Onward!" said Mrs. Rutherford brightly, clapping her hands together, and whisked out of the room with more speed than grace.

Dr. Stringfellow followed Mrs. Rutherford through the connecting door from the dining room into their office, which was also their bedroom, and shut the door firmly behind her, leaving the rest of the Unit in the dining room, staring after them.

"I wonder what that was all about," murmured Kate to Fran, but Fran didn't answer. She was holding her telegram, her face frozen in an expression of disbelief. "Fran? Are you all right?"

Fran lifted her head, her eyes glazed. "It's my mother. She's dead."

Chapter Twelve

*I don't dare say much about the war. Somehow,
the actual horror never got hold of me while I was
at home, but here there is no escaping it. I can no
longer think in terms of flags and parades and
patriotism and glory. I just see mutilated bodies,
destroyed homes, and wretchedness.*

*— Miss Alice Patton, '10, to her
sister, Mrs. Gilbert Thomas*

September 1917
Grécourt, France

"Dead?" repeated Alice, horrified.
Fran turned the telegram around so they
could all see the stark block capitals.

MOTHER DEAD TUESDAY STOP RETURN
HOME SOONEST STOP AUNT M.

"That's . . . blunt," said Kate.

Fran gave a choked laugh. It was a horrible sound.
"Auntie Mill won't have wanted to spend the extra
money to say *passed away.*"

Marie stuck her head around the doorframe. "There
are children in the Orangerie," she said, much as she
might have said *mice.* "Many children."

"Oh dear," said Anne Dawlish. "That's my carpentry class. Fran—"

Fran gave a terse nod. "The children are waiting. Go."

Miss Baldwin followed, giving Fran's hand a quick
squeeze along the way.

Miss Ledbetter paused in the doorway. "When the
old lords passed away, their bodies would lie in state in
the castle chapel, all their loyal retainers passing by to
pay homage—"

Kate looked at her incredulously.

"The children are waiting, Miss Ledbetter." Anne
Dawlish grabbed the older woman by the arm and
tugged her away before she could start singing entirely
apocryphal medieval funeral songs.

"I think that's her way of showing sympathy," murmured Emmie.

"We have a cook and a scullery maid," said Fran unsteadily. "I don't think they'll be kneeling by my mother's corpse with candles. Corpse. Mother. I can't believe— She's been poorly for so long—we thought her illness was . . . a sort of hobby."

Kate and Emmie exchanged alarmed looks.

"Here." Emmie grabbed up Fran's coffee cup from the table. "Oh dear, I wish we had some sugar. Sugar is meant to be good for shock."

"Sherry," said Alice, turning with sudden decision for the door of the barrack. "What you need is sherry. I have some in my trunk. For medicinal purposes. If this isn't a medicinal purpose, I don't know what is."

"No—no—" Fran waved her arms futilely at them both. "The last thing I need is spirits at eight in the morning! Or your whole sugar ration. And aren't you supposed to be at the dispensary?"

Alice bit her lip, looking back over her shoulder as though unsure what to do. "Miss Mills and Dr. Pruyn have already gone. They won't miss me for a bit. They'll probably be glad I'm not there. I'm always dropping the bandages."

"What can we do?" Kate asked quietly.

Fran put her hands to her temples. "A train. I'll need to take the train to Paris. My aunt will need bucking up. They've kept house together since my father died. And there'll be practical matters to be dealt with. How long do you think it will take to get passage out?"

"I think you need to wait six weeks before they let you go," said Margaret Cooper. Emmie had forgotten she was there, she had been standing so quietly. "Someone mentioned it to me in Paris—I think it's so they can make sure you're not taking home unauthorized information from the war zone."

"Six weeks? But the funeral . . . Oh heavens, what am I saying? I'll miss the funeral either way. And Freddie—Freddie is over here too. Poor mother. We never imagined . . ."

"Maybe they'll let you go sooner since it's a bereavement," suggested Liza.

Fran shook her head. "I doubt it. And if so, they shouldn't. I could be faking it, for all they know. No, I'll wait my time. Maybe they'll let me see Freddie. . . ." She turned her head so they couldn't see her lip wobble, saying in a falsely energetic voice, "He's younger. He'll need me."

"Well, I think you should go at once," said Maud, even though no one had asked her. "Come along, Liza. We're meant to be stacking boxes."

"Do you think we ought to send flowers?" Emmie heard Liza whisper as she followed Maud out the door.

"Where would we send flowers? To the second barrack from the left?"

"I just thought that we ought to do something. . . ." The door thumped shut, cutting off their voices.

Fran buried her head in her hands, choking on a laugh. "I can't say I'll miss them, but I'll miss you. I'll miss all of you. I'll even miss that hideous Ford truck."

"Only on a downgrade." Kate reached out, not quite touching her. "I'm so sorry, Fran."

"It comes to us all, I suppose." Fran managed a crooked smile. "I'm sure my mother is feeling terribly vindicated."

"I can go up to Paris with you until you sail," offered Alice with sudden resolve. "I've got to run Dr. Pruyn and Miss Mills on their rounds, but then I'll come back and go with you. We can catch an afternoon train from Noyon."

"We'll be down two chauffeurs that way." Fran winced. "I mean, you'll be down two chauffeurs. Won't Mrs. Rutherford object?"

Alice hunched her shoulders. "You shouldn't have to be alone in Paris while you wait out your six weeks."

"Thank you. I won't say no to that." Fran blinked rapidly. "I need to tell Mrs. Rutherford. And I'll need to pack. . . ."

"I'll help you pack," Emmie said quickly, feeling like

she ought to do something. "You don't need to worry about a thing; just let the rest of us take care of you."

"I'm not an invalid," Fran protested. "Mother was the invalid."

"You're the least invalid-ish person I know," said Kate bracingly. To Emmie, she said, "We're meant to be going to Courcelles. Remember?"

"I suppose we could go to Courcelles another day?" Emmie hated the idea of giving up Courcelles, but they couldn't possibly leave Fran by herself, not after news like that.

"No," said Fran quickly. "No, don't put it off. The work is the important thing. I've held you up enough already—"

"I can go to Courcelles," offered Margaret tentatively. "I was supposed to be driving Dr. Stringfellow, but she's busy with Mrs. Rutherford."

"That's all right, then, isn't it?" said Alice as it belatedly occurred to Emmie that if Margaret could go to Courcelles, she could equally well have stayed with Fran, and that both Emmie and Margaret would probably have preferred that.

But it was too late now. Kate was giving Fran a quick hard hug and telling her how much she'd be missed, and Margaret was buttoning up her uniform jacket and grabbing her hat, and Alice flitted off to the dispensary, and Emmie was left pressing coffee on Fran, who didn't seem to want either coffee or sympathy, but only to be left alone.

Fran didn't need Emmie's help with packing. Alice's belongings were scattered all over the room, a small mirror hanging crookedly over a makeshift dressing table, hats in a drift on the floor, a shawl trailing over the end of a cot, but Fran's belongings were all neatly folded in her trunk in lieu of a wardrobe. It was the work of only a few moments to add her nightclothes and hairbrush.

"I'll leave my blankets," said Fran, looking around the room as though trying to memorize it. "I'm sure you can find a use for them."

"Are you sure you won't want them in Paris?" asked Emmie, and then realized how silly that sounded. "You'll be going back to the Quai Voltaire until you sail? At least you'll be able to get one of the rooms with a bed this time."

"Yes," said Fran bleakly. "Small blessings."

Emmie tried to make it better by bustling around, plumping pillows and rustling blankets. "Would you like to lie down? Can I get you a cold compress?"

"I've been bereaved; I haven't bumped my head. It's all right, you don't need to hold my hand. I have—I have some letters I should be writing."

"Are you sure? I could—" The look on Fran's face stopped her. It was a look of such uncomprehending misery that Emmie wanted to run to her and hug her, but that was clearly the last thing Fran wanted, so Emmie backed toward the door, saying, "I'll just go help Maud and Liza with the boxes, shall I? I'll be in the cellar if you need me. For anything. Anything at all."

"Thank you," said Fran distantly.

Through the bare windows, Emmie could see Fran sitting on her bed, not writing, not reading, not doing anything, just sitting. She looked the way Emmie's schoolchildren did when they fell in the play yard, when they realized they'd been hurt but hadn't quite started howling yet, that moment of stunned disbelief before the pain set in.

"Mademoiselle!" Emmie gave a guilty start as Marie bore down on her, launching into a detailed scold.

The other girls, they had been asking about their laundry. Did they not know that the laundry was available only on Sunday? Marie couldn't be expected to do all things. And why hadn't they finished the pot-au-feu she had made for them last night? Did they not appreciate her cooking? Did they know what it was to cook on a range beneath a canvas roof with such ingredients as she was given?

"I'm so sorry," said Emmie, when she could get a

word in edgewise. Marie had already threatened to quit twice in the ten days since they had arrived; the answer was usually to apologize and offer her more money, but Emmie was feeling too wretched to go through the regular routine. "Miss Englund—her mother just died. Everyone's terribly upset."

Marie was instantly in charge of the situation. A consommé, that was what was needed—she would wring the neck of a chicken at once.

"Oh, please don't," said Emmie, and immediately realized her mistake. "I'm sure it would be delicious, it's just that we need the eggs for the children, if they ever do start laying eggs. I do hope they start laying eggs soon. But perhaps some coffee? You do make the best coffee."

Maybe Fran might even want the coffee. Emmie wasn't sure what else to do for her.

It was only ten o'clock. It felt terribly strange to be left at Grécourt while the others were out. They had been here ten days now, and, except for the mass, Emmie had spent every day "visiting," making the rounds of villages with Kate, calling on each local mayor, looking in on families. Most days, they didn't even make it back for lunch, dining on bread and cheese as the White truck bounced between ruts.

She really should have just gone with Kate. Fran

didn't want her. But it was too late now, so she would just have to make the best of it and try to find something useful to do in between checking in on Fran.

Emmie hurried down to the cellar, where Maud and Liza were bumping boxes around, sorting out goods to put on the truck for the inaugural journey of their traveling store.

"—today?" Liza was asking, her voice muffled by a large pile of linens.

"I don't know. It depends what they—oh, Emmaline! We didn't see you there."

Maud made it sound like an accusation.

Emmie looked around the newly whitewashed room. The *poilus* had done a thorough job; she couldn't see where the chicken wire or the rude German inscriptions had once been. "Fran is writing letters, so I thought I'd come and see if I could help you down here."

"Yes, it's too terrible about her mother. But at least she gets to go back to Paris. You don't mind playing porter, do you? We're just about ready to haul everything up to the truck."

Emmie carried armloads of pots and kettles up the stairs to the truck, juggling rakes and scrubbing brushes, papers bristling with pins, spools of thread in serviceable blacks and browns, boxes of nails, shovels and trowels in all lengths and sizes, and even a consignment of axes, which Emmie held very, very carefully as she navigated the uneven treads.

"I never thought I'd turn peddler," said Maud. "Lord, what they'd say at home if they could see us now!"

The truck backfired and finally started. Emmie waved farewell to them, watching as Liza narrowly avoided smashing one of the gates on her way out. She could hear Maud's protest all the way over the moat.

Overhead, a plane wheezed by, and then another, circling each other, emitting puffs of smoke. Those little cotton-colored clouds looked so innocent until one remembered they were ammunition, meant to bring a plane down and end a man's life. Another plane joined in, way up in the clouds, puffing away like anything. Forty puffs, like candy floss, and the high, whining sound of the motors overhead.

Dr. Stringfellow stuck her head out of the room where she was in conference with Dr. Rutherford. "Where's Kate?"

"She went to Courcelles," said Emmie, surprised that Dr. Stringfellow had forgotten. "Is something wrong?"

The doctor didn't bother to answer. "When she gets back, send her in to us."

Dr. Stringfellow's head disappeared again before Emmie could ask why they wanted Kate. She hoped

Kate wasn't in trouble. She wasn't sure why Kate would be in trouble. Unless it was something to do with . . .

But no, as long as the money was being paid, it shouldn't matter where it was coming from.

They were laying the table for dinner, Emmie trying to remember not to set places for Fran and Alice, the table looking so much emptier with their chairs removed from it, when the White finally lurched over the moat.

Emmie left Anne Dawlish and Miss Baldwin laying out plates and ran out to greet them. "Oh, thank goodness you're back. Did you have a puncture? You've missed Alice and Fran. They left an hour ago."

"It's Margaret," Kate said without preamble, sliding down out of the White into a patch of mud. "She's not well."

Emmie hurried to the other side of the truck, where Margaret sat curled up on the bench, her elbows on her knees, her face in her hands, her thin back shaking.

Emmie looked back at Kate with concern. "Oh goodness, what happened? Is she ill? I can get the doctors—"

Kate lowered her voice, forcing Emmie to bend to hear her. "She's been like this since Courcelles. She had a fit of hysterics, and then threw up by the side of the road, and she hasn't spoken since."

"That pot-au-feu did taste a little off last night. . . . Poor thing, I think I have some bicarbonate left."

"It's not the food. I think she's having what the French would call a *crise de nerfs*."

"An anxiety attack?" It sounded so much better, so much more elegant, in French, but the result was the same in either language. "What happened?"

"Courcelles," said Kate simply.

"Miss Moran?" Dr. Stringfellow beckoned brusquely. "You're needed."

"They've been wanting to speak to you. I don't know what about," said Emmie. "You go. I'll manage. Margaret? Your poor cold hands! Let's get you inside and warmed up."

It was hard getting Margaret out of the truck. She did little to help herself; well, she couldn't, poor thing. She couldn't seem to stop shaking, and it took Emmie wrapping an arm around her waist and guiding her step by step to get her back to the barrack, tripping over things and slipping in the damp grass as they bumbled along together like the participants in a three-legged race—if one of the participants was shaking with fever, that was.

"It's all so useless." Margaret leaned heavily against Emmie as Emmie tried to maneuver her through the door of the barrack without tripping on her own skirt.

"What are we really doing here? We'll never really be able to do anything."

"Just one more step now—almost there." Margaret's arm around her neck was nearly choking her. "Let me feel your head—I don't think you're running a fever. You do seem awfully cold, though. Let's get you wrapped up in some blankets. Fran left hers. . . ."

"Lucky Fran," said Margaret violently, and Emmie stared at her in shock. Margaret made a quick, apologetic gesture. "I didn't mean that. Only I did. It's just— what are we *doing* here?"

"Why don't you sit down." Emmie guided Margaret to her cot. "Think how wonderful it was yesterday, all of us together and all the villagers so happy."

"Happy?" Margaret stared up at Emmie, her pupils dilated. "I can hear that girl screaming."

Emmie bit her lip. "I made a mistake. But the other children—"

"They weren't like children at all! They were like ghosts. They're all ghosts here. We're living with ghosts. No, not ghosts, monsters. It's hideous. It's all hideous. Why are we here? We didn't have to be here."

She was shaking so hard Emmie could hear her teeth chattering. "Coffee," said Emmie. "What you need is some hot coffee. . . ."

"No! I couldn't. I'll be ill."

"No coffee, then," said Emmie soothingly, wondering if she ought to try Alice's sherry or if that would only make Margaret feel worse.

Margaret was talking again, in a small, hoarse voice. "I thought if I could be busy and useful, then it might not be so awful, but it just gets worse and worse and worse. It was all Beth's idea, but then Beth didn't come. I never wanted to be here, I shouldn't be here. I'm not making anything better by being here, I'm just driving around in circles, recording horrors."

"Remember the singing?" asked Emmie desperately. "Remember the canticles? *Ils ne l'auront jamais, jamais, ce pays des preux, notre France.* Wasn't it tremendous? It made everyone feel so much better—"

"Did it?" Margaret made a choking sound. "We can't sing everything better. I thought we could—I thought we could do what Mrs. Rutherford said—we could bring them hope!—it all sounded so easy—but the boy I saw today—he wasn't *human* anymore. Do you know what they'd done to him? They took an explosive and made him hold it. And then they set it off. He lost his arm and half his face but he didn't die. That's the worst of it"—Margaret's voice rose to a painful pitch, on the edge of hysteria—"he didn't die."

Emmie's stomach twisted. "This was—this was in Courcelles?"

It was Emmie who had insisted they go to Courcelles. She should have been in Courcelles, not Margaret.

"I know it's a war. You don't need to tell me it's a war. But these aren't soldiers. These are just normal people. And there was no point to what they did to that poor boy. It wasn't a battle. It was just cruel. They maimed him for the fun of it."

"Maybe it was an accident. . . . Maybe they didn't mean for it to happen."

"They did," said Margaret sharply. "That was what the villagers said. You didn't see it. You didn't see him. It was inhuman, Emmie. It was evil. I don't want to be here. I don't—I don't want to be here anymore. I'm not cut out for it."

Emmie sank down on the bed next to her, feeling the cot sag under her weight. "You don't need to go back to Courcelles. You should never have been there. It was my idea. I'm sorry."

Margaret leaned into Emmie, burying her head in Emmie's chest. "If it were only Courcelles . . . It's all of this. Everything since we arrived, all the widows and the wounded and the air raids and the constant banging of the guns. I can't sleep at night without seeing those *faces*. Faces without noses, without chins, without ears—"

"You mean the ones in the hospital? But they're making them better, they're working wonders. . . ."

"Nightmares. They're making walking nightmares. And those are soldiers. This boy— Oh, Emmie!"

"Shhhh," said Emmie, cradling her as though she were one of Emmie's little brothers, having a nightmare.

Margaret pulled away from her, staring up at her with haunted eyes. "He was only *four* when they did this to him, Emmie. Four. I'll never be able to unsee that—I'll remember it when I sleep. I'll remember it when I die. Oh Lord, I'm going to be ill again."

"Let me get you some water." Emmie lurched to her feet.

Her hands were shaking as she poured water into a tumbler, slopping it over the sides. Only four. She remembered holding her brother Bobby at four. Bobby had always had nightmares and Nurse wasn't the coddling sort. So Emmie had gone. She could remember the feel of that little body, the smell of his head, the trust. Only four.

Making a decision, Emmie reached into the bag she took with her on her rounds, with its meager supply of ambrine, headache powders—and sleeping drafts. She took out a twist of white paper, emptying the powder into the glass.

"I thought I could bear it," Margaret said plaintively. "I really did."

"I know it's hard," said Emmie. She held out the

glass to Margaret, feeling like Lady Macbeth. But Macbeth murdered sleep and Emmie was trying to bring sleep, so it really wasn't at all the same. At least, she hoped not.

Water darkened the blanket as Margaret tried to take the cup. "If Beth had been here . . . At least you and Kate have each other. It makes it easier to have someone. You need someone here."

Emmie sat down next to Margaret, helping to guide the cup to her lips. "You'll feel better after a sleep."

"But I can't sleep. . . . If I dream . . ."

"I'll sit by you," promised Emmie, aware that it was so little, so painfully little. Courcelles had been her task, her responsibility. She'd just—she'd wanted to feel like she was doing something for Fran. It had been irredeemably selfish. "I'll sit by you, and if you feel a nightmare coming on, I'll be here with you."

"I wish—I wish I were brave . . . like you. . . ."

"You are brave," Emmie said, stroking Margaret's hair. "You're brave to have come here at all. You'll realize that. Once you've had a good sleep."

"—can't—sleep—" Margaret's shivers were subsiding, her body relaxing into sleep.

Emmie hoped she hadn't misjudged the dose. She hadn't realized how thin Margaret had become, much thinner than when they'd set sail on the *Rochambeau*.

She hadn't realized a lot of things. Gently, Emmie tucked an extra blanket over Margaret, one of Fran's blankets.

"She's sleeping," Emmie whispered as Kate came through the door. Not that she needed to whisper. With that much sedative, nothing short of a German invasion should wake Margaret now. "Are they waiting dinner for me? I don't want to leave Margaret. I promised I'd stay by her."

"No. They've all eaten." Kate's voice sounded funny. Emmie couldn't see her face properly. Darkness had fallen, and Emmie hadn't thought to light the lamp.

Emmie rose very carefully, trying not to jostle Margaret. "What is it? What's happened? Why did they want to see you?"

"Mrs. Rutherford is resigning as director."

Emmie caught her shin on the edge of her trunk, barely noticing the pain. "But . . . that's impossible. Mrs. Rutherford *is* the Unit."

"Not according to the committee." Kate kept her voice low, glancing back over her shoulder. The walls of the barrack weren't particularly thick. "Mrs. Rutherford is being forced to step down, effective immediately. They're going to put it about that she's resigning for health reasons."

"I don't understand." Emmie realized she had her

hand to her mouth, like the heroine in a melodrama. She forced herself to lower it. "I know Maud was trying—but why would the committee . . . ?"

Kate shook her head wearily. "Apparently there were some issues in the past—the committee wasn't sure Mrs. Rutherford was entirely stable. I don't know all of it. Dr. Stringfellow wasn't exactly forthcoming. She's the new director now."

"Oh." Dr. Stringfellow was certainly competent—frighteningly competent—but Mrs. Rutherford had a magic about her, a way of making things happen when you thought they could never happen at all. Passes, army camions . . . The Unit without Mrs. Rutherford was unthinkable. Emmie was suddenly, desperately afraid. "Is—is Mrs. Rutherford staying on at all?"

"She wanted to. But Dr. Stringfellow thought it would be too divisive. So she's going to go to Paris for a month in case we need her, and then back to the States to raise money for the Unit."

"But we do need her. We need her desperately." Emmie's mind was roiling. She could write her mother—her mother's name had authority, there was no denying it—although whether her mother would decide to help or not was entirely uncertain.

"Don't you think we can manage without her?" Kate's voice had a funny note to it.

"I don't *want* to manage without her." She sounded like a child. Emmie made a conscious effort to gather her wits about her. "Why were they asking for you? Are they telling us all one by one?"

"No." Kate sat down, very slowly, on her cot. "Mrs. Rutherford had certain conditions before she would agree to go."

"Conditions?" Margaret was snoring now, little snorts and hums.

"She wants me to take Dr. Stringfellow's place as assistant director."

"But—" But Kate hadn't even wanted to come. She had no background in social work. This hadn't been her project to begin with. Emmie looked over at Kate, looking so small, so braced for battle, and abandoned everything she had been about to say. "Congratulations. I'm sure you'll do a brilliant job."

"Mrs. Rutherford didn't ask me for my brilliance. She asked me because she thinks I can keep the accounts and keep the machinery she's set up running. She doesn't want the Unit broken up and sold for scrap to the Red Cross."

"Is that what she said?" Emmie wasn't sure whether to be relieved or offended on Kate's behalf.

"In that many words. Dr. Stringfellow is too busy with the medical end of things to manage everything that needs to be managed—so they need someone practical to run the day-to-day. That's all. I think she wants me because I *don't* have a vision of my own."

"Do you think we'll be able to go on without her?"

Kate rose, pressing the wrinkles out of her skirt with her hands. "I'll have to see that we do."

"We'll have to see that we do." Impulsively, Emmie reached out and took her hand. "We're all in this together."

Except for Fran, who had left. And Alice, who had gone with her. And Margaret—Emmie glanced down at her blanket-wrapped form. Hopefully Margaret would feel better in the morning, as long as the sleeping powder didn't give her a terrible headache.

Emmie decided not to mention any of that. "I'm sure you'll be a wonderful assistant director."

And she was. Mostly.

"Thank you." Kate let go of Emmie's hand. "We'll see how long I last. I'm sure Maud will waste no time writing the committee about me."

Chapter Thirteen

We have been driving and driving and driving. Liza and I have become milkmen as well as peddlers. We spend half the day taking milk to girls with Boche babies and the other half taking the doctors on their rounds. I can't tell you the misery of driving in the falling dark with the rain coming through the open truck and the wind howling like anything—and it's only October! I don't want to think what it will be like come Christmas. But maybe by then . . . we'll see.

There's no rest for anyone as we're a depleted group. Mrs. Rutherford is gone for good. One girl had to leave as her mother died and another went with her to keep her company. Another girl had a breakdown—a real breakdown—and had to go to

Paris for her nerves. The official line is that she'll
be back, but I wouldn't put money on it. And our
agriculturalist still hasn't arrived. It's really quite
dire. We've got seventy-two chickens and not a
one has laid an egg in the three weeks we've had
them. One of the girls—the one in charge of the
dairy!—mistook a cow for a bull simply because it
had a ring through its nose.

  I can't imagine why more farms aren't clamoring
for Smith graduates. . . .

  — Miss Maud Randolph, '09, to
  her fiancé, Mr. Henry Craig

October 1917
Grécourt, France

" **——A**nd they had a wonderful dinner for
us!" Alice said as the White bumped
back across the moat. "It wasn't a cakeless day, so we
reveled."

"That was kind of the Paris Committee." Kate
maneuvered around a rut masquerading as a swim-
ming pool. The rainy season was upon them, turning
everything to mud, mud up to their knees, mud that
tugged at the tires of the trucks and created hazards at
every turn. The Paris Committee had invited her—in

her new position as assistant director—but Kate had turned them down on the grounds of work. To take two days away, as things were, was impossible.

It had nothing at all to do with the fact that she was afraid of using the wrong fork.

"Well, we are something of a sensation now," said Alice frankly. "Mrs. Barrett was telling me there have been articles in the *Chicago Tribune* and *New York Globe*—they've been terribly complimentary, but they all include that same horrid photo of us together before we sailed. I do wish our uniforms were more becoming."

"They may not be glamorous," said Kate, drawing up by the Orangerie, "but no one can deny we're well supplied with pockets."

"Yes, because Mrs. R—" Alice looked at Kate, flushed, and broke off, looking guilty. Kate had never asked, but she strongly suspected that Alice had been part of Maud's cabal to oust Mrs. Rutherford, not out of any personal animus, but because Maud had asked and Alice wouldn't have liked to say no.

Kate wondered what they had been saying of her in Paris. She knew that Maud had been writing to the committee again, writing about her.

"Did you see Margaret in Paris?" asked Kate, swinging down from the truck.

"Only briefly." Alice stepped down somewhat more gingerly, wincing as her Paris boots sank ankle-deep in mud. "She didn't stay at the Quai Voltaire—I don't think she wanted to be around the Unit after—well, after whatever happened. I bumped into her once shopping, and she seemed awfully broken up about breaking her contract and leaving."

"Well, thank goodness you're back," said Kate honestly. "No one has a way with the motors like you do. We've been relying on the engineers to fix our engines, and they're not nearly as good at it as you are."

Alice's head popped up, a gratified expression on her face. "It's just a knack; I can't think where I got it. . . . Do you mean the 11th Engineers—the ones we met before I left?"

"Those are the ones. They've taken to inviting themselves over at odd hours, along with half the other men on the front. We've been overrun by American engineers and Canadian foresters—and even some Quakers. They've got a base near Ham."

Maud had tried to send the Quakers packing, on the grounds that they didn't want a pack of pacifists hanging about, but Kate had overruled her, on the grounds that whatever the Quakers' principles, they certainly had better carpentry skills than the Unit. Maud was still simmering over that.

"Goodness." Alice sat up straighter, unconsciously adjusting her hat to a more flattering angle. "I hadn't realized it would be so social."

"Neither did we," Kate said wryly. "We've had to ask them to confine their visits to weekends. The engineers had us to supper at their camp last weekend— which means we'll have to reciprocate at some point, although goodness only knows how. We haven't nearly enough cups and plates to go around."

Or enough food, or enough coal to cook with. The cold had set in with a vengeance, but the coal delivery they had been promised had yet to arrive.

Kate was finding it very hard to untangle Mrs. Rutherford's systems. Mrs. Rutherford had procured supplies from all sorts of places, getting the Unit classified as an infirmary so they could receive more than the usual ration of sugar, and as a military unit, so that they might qualify for an allowance of *essence*, but not everything had been properly recorded; some transactions were with the civil authorities, others with the military, and others still with the American aid organizations: the American Fund for French Wounded and the Red Cross. Mrs. Rutherford seemed to have managed almost entirely on force of personality. Lacking that kind of charisma, Kate would have been glad for some nice, plain record keeping.

Ledgers, for instance. Ledgers would have been marvelous. Not just piles of letters and receipts and carbons typed too thin to read.

It was all impossibly knotty and Kate never seemed to have enough time to tackle the paperwork to even try to untangle it. With only two drivers left at Grécourt, she spent her days in the White truck, driving the social workers and doctors from village to village. By the time Kate settled down with Mrs. Rutherford's records, it was usually past nine and freezing cold, and she was more likely to fall asleep on the papers than read them.

But now that Alice was back . . . she might just possibly be able to clear a day. Even a few hours would help.

"Alice!" Emmie was skimming and sliding through the mud, embracing Alice with a force that nearly sent them both flying. "Welcome back!"

Alice disappeared in a welter of greetings, Miss Ledbetter waxing poetic about returned warriors.

In the midst of the hubbub, Anne Dawlish quietly touched Kate's shoulder. "Kate. The coal came while you were away."

Kate let out a long breath. "Thank goodness. Dr. Stringfellow told me she has enough to do without tending to frostbite."

Two worried lines appeared between Anne's eyes. "You might want to come see it."

"Did I hear *coal*?" asked Liza, detaching herself from the scrum around Alice. "Oh, goody. I'm freezing. And we haven't been able to do any baking for *days*."

"I had them put it here," said Anne, pointing to a crate next to the barrack they used as their dining room. It was not a large crate.

"Is that for the week?" Kate had thought Mrs. Rutherford had arranged for monthly deliveries, but maybe . . .

Anne shook her head, looking like she was about to cry. "They said it's for the month."

"For the *month*?" Liza turned too fast and nearly landed on her bottom in the mud.

"I don't know how I'm meant to keep the children warm during lessons," said Anne, her voice scratchy. "I'd hoped they could at least be warm with us before they have to go home to the damp and the cold. And not a decent coat among them."

"We could burn wood," said Liza hopefully.

"No. Not if we want to try to provide any shelter for the villagers." The Germans had felled as much as they could, sending it back to Germany to fuel the German war effort. Wood was desperately needed, for rebuilding, for furniture, for heat. To burn it for themselves would be selfishness beyond countenancing. Although if it got much colder, Kate might just be willing to live with the guilt. "I hope you brought extra sweaters. And warm socks."

"We could, like the medieval peasants, burn the dung of the cow," offered Miss Ledbetter. "One takes the hardened pats and—"

"No," said Maud firmly. "I don't care what the peasants do, I'm not scenting my room with cow dung."

Liza looked thoughtfully toward the stables. "If it gets cold enough . . ."

"*No*," said Maud.

"We can keep warm by walking," interposed Kate. It was time to relay the rest of the bad news. "We'll have to walk anyway. We've run through most of our allowance of *essence*. We're going to have to start rationing it."

"Can't we get more?" asked Miss Mills, looking outraged. "Surely, given the importance of the services we're providing . . ."

"I tried," said Kate shortly. She'd written the French military authorities, the French civil authorities, the Red Cross, and the AFFW, all of whom had told her the same thing. "They can't conjure *essence* out of thin air. There's only so much to be had. We'll just have to be careful with what we have."

"Mrs. R—" began Emmie, and then stopped. But Kate knew what she had been thinking. That Mrs. Rutherford would have found a way. "That nice French officer who stopped by the other day offered to bring us a pony and trap. I could use that to get to Courcelles and Canizy."

"All that way by yourself?" It was far enough by car; by trap, on the rutted roads, it would be hours. "It's so far, Emmie."

"We could go in pairs," Emmie argued. She'd adopted Courcelles as her own since Margaret left, and had clashed with Kate more than once when Kate had vetoed extra trips on the grounds of saving their gas ration.

Kate wasn't convinced. "But how would a pony carry two of us? And supplies?"

"We're not that heavy," insisted Emmie.

"For a pony?"

"I had a pony once," said Liza. "Her name was Snowdrop."

"Not Snowdrop again." Rounding on Kate, Maud demanded, "What are we meant to do about the store? Unless you mean us to yoke ourselves to the truck like oxen and pull it all the way."

"No," said Kate reluctantly. The store had been a smashing success, thanks in no small part to Maud.

"You and Liza are working wonders with the store. We may have to hold more store hours here in the château, though. Anyone near enough to walk can come to us."

Maud folded her arms across her chest, narrowing her eyes at Kate. "Shouldn't Dr. Stringfellow be making these decisions? She is our director. Or had you forgotten?"

The others had stopped talking. They were all watching, with varying degrees of interest and discomfort.

"Dr. Stringfellow is seeing patients," said Kate neutrally.

"It's absurd having a doctor as director of the Unit," said Maud, addressing herself to the circle of women. "We need someone proper to manage us. Like Mrs. Barrett in Paris."

Kate didn't miss the way Alice began fiddling with the brooch on her coat. So that was it, then. Another coup. A coup against Dr. Stringfellow—which meant a coup against Kate, since Kate was the one actually running things. Kate had no illusions about the matter: she was the one Maud wanted out.

Kate didn't intend to oblige her. She might not have asked for this job, but now that she had it—she wasn't prepared to relinquish it.

"Mrs. Barrett," said Kate reasonably, "is in Paris.

Where her husband is. I doubt she'd be interested in relocating to Grécourt—even if we wanted her, which we don't."

"She sets a wonderful table," put in Alice unhelpfully. "She had the most wonderful dinner for Smith girls in Paris. And it wasn't a cakeless day."

"Mmm, cake," said Liza wistfully. "I do miss cake."

"Oh, look," said Maud, before Liza could wax rhapsodic about chestnut cream and almond paste. "Here comes our *director*."

Dr. Stringfellow ignored her, nodding briefly at Alice and then looking past her, at the bags in the White truck. "Welcome back. You brought our medical supplies?"

Alice picked at a clump of mud on one boot with the toe of the other. "I did try."

"When you say try . . ." Dr. Stringfellow made a visible effort to retain her patience. "Do you mean to tell me that our supplies are still in Bordeaux?"

"Well, no. Mrs. Barrett made inquiries on our behalf—and it seems that our medical supplies were distributed."

"Distributed?" Dr. Stringfellow's eyebrows were practically vertical. "Distributed to *whom*?"

"She's not quite sure. Hospitals most likely?" Avoiding Dr. Stringfellow's eyes, Alice added hastily, "You know the Red Cross is pooling all donations and giving them out as they're needed, so it probably made sense at the time, since we weren't there."

"Those weren't donations," Julia said, as though speaking to a toddler, all short words and simple sentence construction. "Those were our supplies, bought and paid for."

"Well, yes, but . . ."

"It's not her fault," said Kate, stepping in on Alice's behalf. Even if Alice was possibly plotting against her. "It wasn't her mistake."

Julia's blue eyes were practically black. "No, it was ours for not collecting them at the first opportunity. Instead of collecting trucks, we ought to have made sure of our medical supplies."

"Without the trucks, we wouldn't be here," pointed out Kate.

Julia looked at Kate, her lips a thin line. "We'll have to go to Amiens and beg. There's only so much we can do with bicarbonate of soda and prayer."

"I'm surprised you don't just go light a candle," said Maud, who had never forgiven Julia for making her participate in a Catholic mass.

"Yes, to the patron saint of small annoyances." Julia turned to Kate. "When can we go to Amiens? Or does our *essence* allowance not stretch to medical necessities?"

"I'll drive you to Amiens tomorrow." Never mind that she would rather do anything but. Kate raised her voice, trying to pretend that she was in control, that she wasn't failing miserably in her role as assistant director. "Shall we go in to dinner? We would have brought out the fatted calf for you, Alice, but Emmie refused to let us slaughter any of her cows."

"Some idiot's blocking our drive," said Julia.

The rain was sluicing down by ten the next morning, when Julia finished her morning shift in the dispensary and appeared beside the White truck—as though Kate were her chauffeur.

Which she was, Kate reminded herself.

"Is it Dave, the Red Cross driver?" Dave frequently landed in the ditch beside the gates. It happened with such regularity that they'd begun to suspect intent rather than incompetence.

"No. Some buffoon in a bow tie."

"Halloo? Anybody home?" The buffoon in a bow tie was slipping and sliding his way along the path around the château—or what had once been a path before it turned into a mud slick. "Is this the Château de Robecourt?"

"No. It's the Palace of Versailles," snapped Julia. "Your truck is blocking our gates."

The man's smile wobbled slightly. "Lowell Markham of the *Boston Commercial Advertiser*. I'm meant to be finding the Smith Social Service Unit?"

He sounded as though he rather hoped he'd landed in the wrong place. Gritting her teeth, Kate hopped off the running board and walked forward with hand extended. "Welcome. I'm Miss Moran, assistant director of the Smith College Relief Unit, and this is Dr. Pruyn, of our medical department."

"Doctor?" Mr. Lowell Markham regarded Julia with frank interest, examining her as though she were a zebra caught sunning itself in Central Park. "I didn't know you had lady doctors."

Kate cut in before Julia could say anything rude. "Dr. Pruyn is one of two doctors attached to the Unit, both graduates of Smith College. We were just leaving on urgent medical business. . . ."

The reporter's eyes lit up. He was going to ask to come with them, Kate could tell. They all did. He was the fourth reporter they'd had that month. It was all part of Mrs. Rutherford's plan to outwit the committee, to make the Unit such a media sensation that no one would think of disbanding it—which was all very well for Mrs. Rutherford in exile in Paris, but an absolute nuisance in Grécourt. They didn't have time to coddle self-important journalists who saw them as amusing curiosities. And they certainly didn't want to drag one to Amiens to watch them beg for supplies.

Kate spotted Emmie heading toward the *basse-cour*, head lowered against the rain, a roll of chicken wire clamped under her arm. "Do come meet the head of our social service department, Miss Emmaline Van Alden."

"Of the New York Van Aldens," said Julia, straight-faced. Kate frowned at her, knowing how much Emmie hated to be seen as an extension of her mother. But the reporter had already taken the bait.

"Any relation of Mrs. Livingston Van Alden?"

"Her daughter." It was for the Unit, Kate reminded herself. Emmie would understand that. "Emmie! Come meet Mr. Lowell Markham. . . ."

The last thing Kate heard as they made their escape was Emmie saying, "Do you know anything about chicken coops, Mr. Markham?"

As they pulled away in the White, she could see the bemused reporter tangled in chicken wire as Emmie explained something, her hands moving vigorously in illustration. Members of the *basse-cour* had come out to inspect and comment and three of the chickens appeared to have escaped and were pecking at Mr. Lowell Markham's good Boston shoes.

"That should hold him for a bit," said Kate neutrally.

"It had better," said Julia, inspecting the contents

of her medical bag. "If he interrupts Dr. Stringfellow's surgery, she'll go after him with her scalpel. Of course, they'll never find the body in this mud."

Kate looked sharply at Julia, but Julia's face, as always, betrayed nothing. It was a perfect blank, as serene as a statue of Diana getting ready to skewer some upstart huntsman. Just as she'd skewered Kate all those years ago.

Emmie's latest charity case.

"He won't be able to write the article if we bury the body," said Kate, more sharply than she'd intended.

"Are you so eager for publicity?" Julia made it sound distasteful. Something sordid and common. Like Kate.

Kate focused on the road. "I'm eager for donations."

"Socks knit by granny and lumpy aprons?"

Admittedly, Kate had just been complaining to Emmie about some of the boxes they'd been sent, which had been packed with more enthusiasm than consideration, but it still annoyed her to hear Julia say it.

"Money," she said distinctly. "Donations of money. Or is that too vulgar a topic for you?"

Julia gave a short bark of a laugh. "My dear, I root in people's entrails for entertainment. I'm hardly going to quail at a bit of filthy lucre."

Kate knew she shouldn't, but she couldn't help

herself. "Even if it's charity? You wouldn't want to have anything to do with charity."

That caught Julia's attention. She stared at Kate for a moment and then said, very slowly, "Not such a mouse, after all, are you? You do have teeth."

Kate wasn't sure why Julia should mind; it was Julia who had sneered at Kate for being a charity case all those years ago, not the other way around. But for whatever reason, Julia retreated into an offended silence. The silence continued all the way to Amiens, where Julia remained elegant and uncommunicative as Kate wrangled her way through the various levels of underlings to the commander's office.

"Do feel free to join in at any time," muttered Kate, who knew that her French, while good, was nowhere near as aristocratic as Julia's, and that these things did matter.

"You're the assistant director," said Julia blandly in English. "Do go on. . . ."

Monsieur le Commandant was more than willing to help them. And by help, he meant chat for longer than they could spare, offer a coffee they hadn't time to take, and direct them to the hospital with his compliments. He was, Kate knew, being exceptionally helpful and she was being exceptionally ungrateful. It was Julia's presence setting her on edge as Monsieur le Commandant escorted them to the hospital, making the necessary introductions, interspersed with compliments and small talk that strained Kate's French and her courtesy.

A nurse was sent to fetch a junior doctor, who, in turn, was sent to fetch a more senior physician.

"We only need to borrow supplies," said Kate in desperation. The rain was pouring and the clock was ticking.

"It is good to know one's colleagues," said the commandant, patting her arm in a fatherly way. "And everyone wants to know the so intrepid *dames Américaines.*"

"More muddy than intrepid right now," said Kate, and everyone laughed as though she'd said something very clever. Except Julia, of course. "Dr. Pruyn has prepared a list of the items we need most desperately. . . ."

"We must not have you reduced to desperation!"

Underlings were dispatched to fetch various items. More coffee was offered and refused. Kate suggested that she sign a receipt and felt that she had committed a faux pas.

"Ah, one of your countrymen!" The commandant waved at someone above Kate's head. "Dr. Stapleton! Dr. Stapleton is visiting from the hospital of the Red Cross in Nesle. Have you met *les dames Américaines?*"

They had, Kate noticed, gone from being *collégi-*

ennes to being *dames*. She wasn't sure whether that was a promotion or a demotion.

"Not in this country, I haven't," said an American voice. A man wearing a white medical coat walked up to them, stopping at the sight of Julia. "Julia. What brings you to this mud pit?"

"That's Dr. Pruyn." Julia's voice was as sharp-edged as ground glass.

"On such long acquaintance?" He began humming something. Kate recognized it immediately as "Auld Lang Syne." "Should old acquaintance be forgot . . ."

The song had the most remarkable effect on Julia. Her back tensed; her face was totally expressionless except for her eyes, which glittered in a most disconcerting way, like seeing the painted eyes in a portrait come alive.

Kate looked from one to the other. "I take it you know each other."

"Classmates," Julia bit out, her lips clamping down hard on the words. "At Johns Hopkins."

"And now colleagues." Dr. Stapleton held out his hand. Julia pointedly failed to take it. Dr. Stapleton shrugged, not visibly distressed. "I look forward to renewing our acquaintance."

"We're very busy," said Julia flatly. "Kate. We have everything?"

It was, thought Kate, the first time she had ever heard Julia use her name. "Yes, we should be getting back. I'd rather not drive after dark."

"No," agreed Dr. Stapleton, falling into step with them as they walked to the door. Julia made sure Kate was between them, but since Kate was considerably shorter than both, she proved a less-than-effective barrier. "It's dangerous out there for young ladies."

"Don't worry," said Julia, looking straight at him over Kate's head. "I have a revolver and I'm not afraid to use it."

"You don't really have a revolver, do you?" asked Kate as they loaded the parcels into the White truck.

"Why not?" Even in the grips of some strong emotion, Julia was careful with the precious parcels. She saw the last one secured and then looked defiantly at Kate. "Maybe, like Maud, I have an ambition to 'pot a German.'"

A German—or her old classmate? Julia, Kate remembered, had always been insanely competitive. She'd been first in their class at Smith and never let anyone forget it. Kate squinted at the road, or what had once been a road before the rains had got started on it. Army trucks had carved deep ruts in the mud. What had happened? Had Dr. Stapleton come out tops in an exam? It would be just like Julia to hold a grudge. Kate entertained herself thinking of various possibilities. A thwarted romance? A scholastic competition?

She couldn't resist needling Julia just a bit. "That Dr. Stapleton—do you think he'd help out with the infirmary once a week? If you went to school with him . . . We could use the extra pair of hands."

"We don't need the help," said Julia flatly.

"Oh, don't we?" One of Kate's innovations had been to have all the committees submit weekly reports. She knew exactly how many patients Julia and Dr. String-fellow had seen last week and how many remained to be seen. The numbers were staggering.

"Not *his* help," said Julia fiercely.

Kate looked at her askance. "Is he that bad a doctor?"

"That's what I should judge, isn't it?" There was a strange note to Julia's voice. She took a deep breath, choosing her words very carefully. "His value as a doctor. That's what matters. As to that . . . I don't know what kind of doctor he is now. He was an ambitious student. Whether that translates to success in practice, I can't tell you."

It was dusk already, a rainy-day dusk, casting Julia into shadow. But Kate could see Julia's hands clenched on the edge of the bench, as though holding on for dear life. Kate didn't think she was that bad a driver. They hadn't hit a pothole for at least a mile.

"I imagine any doctor is better than none," said Kate, looking sideways at Julia. "Out here."

"No." The word exploded from Julia. "You don't want him at Grécourt. He's a pig. A vile, rutting pig. He can't be trusted—"

Julia stopped, closing her lips on the words.

"All right," Kate said. "No dinner invitations."

They drove in silence, the dusk thick around them, the rain weeping down off the roof of the White. Kate concentrated on making her way past a cart that had stuck in the mud and been abandoned. A plane whined overhead, a noise so commonplace they barely noticed it now. The night was alive with the distant sound of the guns at the front.

Next to her, Julia was very still. It was a brittle, haunted silence. Like a mouse in a hole, although it was really absurd to think of Julia in those terms. There was no one less mouse-like than Julia. But there it was. Not hauteur. Wariness. Worse than wariness. Fear.

Kate thought of the way Julia had looked when Dr. Stapleton had hummed "Auld Lang Syne." He had made it seem a joke. But Julia had looked—terrified. Sick. She'd never seen Julia look like that before.

Or had she? Uncomfortably, Kate remembered the way Julia had stiffened when the doctor in Paris had patted her arm, her insistence on not spending the night where men might walk through her room in Noyon, the way she had frozen when Dr. Stapleton approached them. As if trying to decide whether to fight or run.

But this was *Julia*. It wasn't that Kate hadn't heard of such things—especially here, where Dr. Stringfellow had delivered at least five Boche babies already. But Julia was one of the golden ones. It was the unprotected women who got taken advantage of. The maids and the shopgirls. Not the Julias of the world.

It was probably just an academic rivalry, Kate told herself. She'd probably got the wrong end of the stick. Julia would laugh at her. No, Julia would be offended. And then she would laugh at her.

"You don't need a revolver," Kate said before she could think better of it. "Not if you know where to hit. The best place to strike a man is the nose. He won't expect it, and if you hit hard with the palm of your hand, you can break it fast. Nails to the eyes also work."

Julia's head jerked toward Kate. "Were you also—"

"No." The single syllable felt like a betrayal. She hadn't really thought—but there it was. That word *also*. Everything she hadn't believed could happen to Julia. Kate swallowed hard. "My stepfather taught me. Just in case. He felt it was something I ought to know."

Julia was silent for a moment. Then she said, "Would you teach me?"

She was dead serious. Kate tried to make light of it. "Perhaps we should organize a boxing class for the Unit."

"Not boxing," Julia said passionately. "No Queensberry rules. They don't abide by them. Why should we?"

Tentatively, feeling on very uncertain ground, Kate asked, "Did you tell anyone—about Dr. Stapleton?"

"Are you mad? They would have said I invited it. Bad enough to have women in medical school. Worse to have them distracting the real doctors. I would have been out on my ear." Julia flexed her gloved hands. "I started carrying a knife in my pocket. I told him if he did it again, I'd gut him and stand in the dock with pleasure."

Her voice resonated with emotion, so much emotion, more emotion than Kate would have thought Julia was capable of feeling.

Kate said the only thing she could think to say. "Maybe we'll get lucky. Maybe he'll be hit by a shell."

Julia gave a guttural laugh. "I'm not sure I want to rely on the intervention of Providence."

"We can just tell Maud he's a German spy and let her at him," Kate offered.

"That might be punishment enough." Julia cast Kate a long, sideways look. "You won't say anything to Emmie?"

Kate had never expected to feel sorry for Julia. Or to feel kinship with Julia. "No."

Julia stared straight ahead, at the raindrops glinting in the light of the lamps. "I was such a little fool. I thought we were colleagues. Equals. When he said he wanted to exchange notes, I actually thought he wanted to exchange notes."

Kate winced as the White slid a little too far to the right, fighting to keep the truck on the road. "He ought to have. You were always at the top of our class at Smith."

"That was only because I worked extra hard to stay ahead of you." Julia turned away before Kate could see her face, pointing at the signpost. "There's the turnoff for Grécourt. Do you think that reporter's still infesting the place?"

Chapter Fourteen

In addition to running our own classes, we are making an effort to supply the schools with everything the state gave them before the war, so the education of the children won't suffer any more than it already has. You can imagine our joy when the Inspector of Education in Amiens told us there were some old school benches in the attic of the National School—there are scarcely any benches or desks and no wood to make any, which has been a great trial in trying to restore school hours to what they were. He said he had been trying for four months to send them to a certain sector, but there was no way to get them to the station (!!). We asked him if we could have them if we could move them. He said yes, only it couldn't

*be done, and anyway, it would require the
permission of some other official, and what about
the other people to whom he'd promised the
benches. We told him we would wait while he got
the proper papers. He shook his head and said
something about Americans. The poor man stayed
over his lunch hour before he knew it, and I don't
think he will ever quite recover.*

*But we have our benches! I know how deeply
you concern yourself with education and
particularly the education of young women, so
thought you might like to hear of this small victory
in the grand battle for universal education. . . .*

> *— Miss Emmaline Van Alden, '11,
> to her mother, Mrs. Livingston
> Van Alden*

November 1917
Grécourt, France

"'In the midst of a vast desolation close to the front, seventeen American college girls are carrying the kindly spirit of the new world to martyred peasantry. . . .'"

"Martyred peasantry?" Nell Baldwin choked on her war bread. "That sounds a little too Golgotha for me."

"Joan of Arc would be more appropriate, I should think," offered Kate, sounding more relaxed than Emmie had heard her in ages.

A holiday air prevailed at the breakfast table, where the Smith Unit was partaking of an unusually late repast, not because it was a Sunday, but because the engineers were coming for luncheon. It had been decided that there would be hardly enough time to do their morning rounds and prepare for guests. So here they were in their dining/sitting room, with Nell toasting her feet on the fender and Alice reading aloud from a crumpled piece of newspaper that had just been forwarded to them via the Paris Committee. Even Dr. Stringfellow had closed the dispensary for the morning and was eating bread and jam quite like a normal person.

It was cold in their makeshift dining room, but the cold didn't bother Emmie as it had in New York. Maybe it was because here they were always doing, always busy, always moving. There was always a visit to make or animals to feed or something to be repaired or crates to be stacked or beds to be delivered to villagers. They could do duty as furniture movers when this was all done, Maud complained, but Emmie loved the feeling of her muscles stretching, of walking distances she never would have contemplated at home, of being able to be really, truly useful.

Even if she did worry, sometimes, that her use was limited to fetching and hauling and bandaging scraped knees, the sort of thing anyone could do. She didn't have Julia's medical training or Kate's grim determination; she couldn't even drive the cars. When it came to bullying bureaucrats, she was, Emmie had found, rather ineffectual.

Yesterday in Amiens, for example. They'd got word of some school benches, stored away in an attic somewhere, a find so rare that Kate had agreed to take the jitney and drive Emmie up. But after ten minutes of the official from the department of education telling them how sad it was the benches were just sitting there and how impossible it was for them to be moved, Kate had taken over. The benches couldn't be moved? Why not? They had been promised to four other villages? Well, clearly, they were going to none of those, so why not the Smith Unit? Haulage? They would deal with haulage. Really, they were doing the department a favor, taking these benches off their hands.

There was something about the way Kate spoke that made Emmie think of building blocks: each phrase a stone in an indestructible wall. The poor Inspector of Education had been so cowed, he'd not only promised them the school benches; he'd stayed past his lunch hour. They'd left him muttering something about "*les*

Américaines," looking thoroughly unnerved by the whole experience.

But they'd got the benches. Glorious, glorious benches, which would furnish the schools at Hombleux and Canizy and, most particularly, Courcelles, Emmie's own special village. Kate had promised she'd have first pick of the benches for Courcelles. Emmie had already wrangled a temporary building that they could use as school and town hall, over the objections of Miss Mills, who had protested that the nearer and larger villages ought to be served first. But the nearer and larger villages hadn't been so thoroughly decimated as Courcelles, and Emmie was determined, determined, that her people there, her fifty children, none of them well, would get their due in buildings and benches, tools and schoolbooks.

She couldn't wait to tell them. Wednesday, perhaps. Her visits to Courcelles were limited by the number of cars in service at any given time, and right now the White was in Paris having hard rims put on and the old Ford truck was sounding decidedly rheumy, leaving only the jitney. Sometimes, Emmie rode with Maud and Liza and the store, but they never stayed quite long enough for Emmie to visit all of her families, not properly. With the cars constantly out of commission, it was a struggle to find someone who would take her. Even the doctors were doing their rounds on foot, hiking miles across muddy fields with their medical bags strapped to their backs.

So she supposed she shouldn't complain, not really. It was just that the need in Courcelles was so great. . . .

"What on earth is this rubbish?" Kate took the paper from Alice. "Ah. This must be that pest who came the day we went to get medicine, Julia. 'I would have turned back, thinking I had mistaken the way, had I not then perceived two female figures in black oilskins and rubber boots. Their quick muscular movements left no doubt these were Americans.'"

Alice looked down at her arm, in its rather ragged gray wool casing. "I wouldn't say we were *muscular*, would you? It just sounds so . . . mannish."

"At least the engineers don't seem to mind," said Liza cheerfully through a mouthful of war bread.

"Yes, because we're the only women for fifty miles," said Nell. "Unless you count the French."

Kate flapped the paper to get their attention, and Emmie couldn't help noticing how naturally she took charge. "There's a bit about you and the chicken coop, Emmie—'the noble descendant of one of our first families, not too proud to wrestle with menial tasks in the thick mud of the Somme.'"

"I suppose it's a good thing I'm muscular, then,"

said Emmie, feeling a bit as though she'd been reduced to the role of cart horse. They'd had such a conversation, she and that reporter, all about the children and their needs and the work they were doing—but all he remembered was the hammer and the mud.

Not that there was anything wrong with good, honest labor. But it made her feel as oversize and awkward as the time Auntie May had pretended to mistake one of her dancing slippers for a boat.

"Anne got a look-in too," said Kate. "You waxed eloquent about the children not knowing how to play anymore."

"Did I?" asked Anne, and Emmie bit her tongue to keep from pointing out it hadn't been Anne; it had been Emmie. It shouldn't matter, of course. What mattered was that it had been said. "I mostly remember swatting him out while I was trying to teach the five-to-eights."

Kate raised her voice to be heard over the commentary. "'Far from resenting the advice of *ces dames Américaines*, the people have already come to love them and look to them for guidance of every sort. After three years of bitter loneliness, suffering, and oppression at last someone is really taking a personal interest in them. No wonder they are grateful.'"

There was a moment of quiet as the words resonated around them.

"Mawkish rubbish," said Julia, breaking the silence. "Did they pair it with a drawing of a draggle-haired infant?"

"Three draggle-haired children," corrected Kate.

"Oh, don't," said Emmie, feeling a rush of guilt for her pettiness. What did it matter who did what, when this was the result? What if she was muscular? "I think it's—he understood exactly. Everyone else just sees these poor people as being in the way of the war. But we're here for *them*. Whatever we do or don't do, that's something, isn't it?"

Kate set down the paper. "Yes," she said, and for once, Emmie felt as though she understood, really, truly understood. They might have had different ways of getting at it, but Kate felt it too, why they were here. "More than something."

"I should say so!" said Maud indignantly. "When I think of waking at six thirty to load up that blasted truck and getting soaked to the skin driving about in all weathers, I should think they should jolly well give us a medal!"

"Or at least some rain hats," said Nell, grinning. "Mine's got more holes in it than a cheese grater. It doesn't so much keep the rain out as gently disperse it."

"Just think of it as a hair wash," said Kate, pushing back her chair, which heralded a general folding of napkins and brushing off of crumbs. "It saves time."

"I'll just tuck some soap underneath next time," said Nell. "We can patent it when we get home and call it a time-saving device. What do you think, girls? Nature's own shower."

"Yes, with all funds to go to the Unit," said Emmie gamely, trying to get in on the joke.

Maud rolled her eyes. "You're all mad. I'm going to go set the tables in the Orangerie. *Someone* has to prepare for our guests."

"I," said Kate, "am going to tackle the Unit's official correspondence. I'm weeks behind."

"*Weeks* behind?" Maud looked pointedly at Kate. "That's a fine face the Unit is putting to the world."

"If you'd like to answer all the correspondence, be my guest," said Kate, dropping her napkin onto the table. "You can tell Mrs. Patterson from Sheboygan why we haven't received her parcel of twenty-five hand-knitted mufflers—and put in all the paperwork for renewing our permits with five separate agencies, none of which use the same form."

"Don't they?" asked Anne Dawlish with genuine interest. "Someone ought to suggest it to them."

Maud folded her arms across her chest, staring at

Kate. "We need a director who can properly represent the Unit—not someone who lets letters sit for a month."

But she hadn't, Emmie wanted to say. Night after night, after a full day of driving the truck, Kate sat hunched next to their tiny stove, trying to thaw out her hands and the ink, scratching out replies by the meager light of one lamp. Sometimes, Emmie would wake in the morning to find Kate with ink on her cheek, having fallen asleep on the letter she was trying to write.

"If Mrs. Rutherford were here," said Kate, staring at Maud with palpable dislike, "she would handle all of this. But she's not."

And they all knew why.

Anne Dawlish checked the watch pinned to her breast. "Goodness, is that the time?"

"Tooth mugs!" sang out Nell, clunking dirty dishes together with reckless enthusiasm. "Everyone bring me your tooth mugs! We haven't nearly enough bowls for the pumpkin soup, so we're going to have to slop it into the mugs, and so much for style."

"I'll fetch ours," Alice said to Maud and Liza. To Kate, she added, "I've put the accounts on your bed."

"The accounts?" Emmie realized she was holding a stack of plates and put them down very, very carefully, lingering as the others jostled out. "I'd forgotten that Alice is treasurer."

Kate grimaced. "Just what I was wanting. More paper. Alice is really quite brilliant with numbers, so at least I won't have to go and fix all her figures. I just— it's just so *much*. I'd like to see Maud handle half of it," she added viciously.

"Would you like me to go through them for you?" Emmie asked tentatively. She could almost convince herself that she was offering just to help, just because Kate was overwhelmed, and not because she wanted to see those numbers before Kate did. Just in case. "I know I'm not as good as you are with numbers, but I can make sure the columns tally. It would be one less thing for you to do."

Kate blinked, hard, and, in a rare gesture of affection, put her hand on Emmie's arm. "Thank you. I appreciate it, I really do. Especially since I know just how much you hate arithmetic."

Emmie felt like the lowest sort of crawling creature. "It was all the fault of that governess of mine, rapping my hand whenever I got a sum wrong—which was pretty much every single time. I still cringe whenever I see a row of figures." She was, Emmie realized, hardly helping her own case. "But I don't mind, really."

"Bless you," said Kate, giving Emmie's arm a squeeze. "But even the Smith Unit hardly demands that sort of sacrifice. If you're determined to beard dragons, could you go see Marie? You know she likes you better than the rest of us. She said something about digging up some extra dishes for us. . . ."

It appeared that *digging* was the operative term.

"The Germans never found them," said Marie proudly, holding up a dirt-encrusted dinner plate in the canvas-roofed kitchen of the old gatekeeper's house, where Marie cooked for them on the one working range left in the whole village. "Idiot Boche."

"They're beautiful," said Emmie, yanking her mind away from Kate and those accounts. Through the clinging earth, Emmie could just make out a red-and-white design. "What a lovely pattern. And how clever of you to hide them."

"I wasn't going to let those swine eat off them." Marie clutched the dish in both hands, her face contorted with anger and grief. "They were my wedding dishes."

"Oh," said Emmie. She took the plate from Marie, holding it very, very carefully. Her wedding dishes, symbol of her life with a husband who was away now, off at the front, his prospect of coming home slim. "You're so kind to let us use them."

Marie thrust a trowel at Emmie. "Here. I've marked the spot by the moat. See you don't break any."

Emmie set the plate tenderly down on the ground. It was really a rather ugly plate. But to Marie—did she look at it and wonder if her husband would ever come home to eat off that plate again?

One could argue that it might have been worse: Marie's husband hadn't been shot outright or shipped off by the Boche; he was fighting and free—but, still, how awful, to be constantly wondering, with every German plane overhead, if this, this was the bomb that would end it all, with every tremble of the earth if this was the sapper who would make her a widow.

It made Emmie feel very small. No matter how hard they tried to help, they were just passing through. This wasn't their tragedy. It was the Maries who were suffering, who had had their lives upended, who had buried their china so the Boche wouldn't eat off it. It seemed almost wrong to be digging it up so that a group of American officers could be served roast beef and cauliflower au gratin. Never mind that those American officers were fighting to free France. It still made Emmie feel that they were imposing.

Kate would tell her that she felt too much, that she shouldn't give way to every stray emotion.

What would Kate feel when she found those accounts Alice had left for her?

They mightn't be that detailed. It would just be numbers. It wasn't necessarily all itemized—at least Emmie hoped it wouldn't be. Maybe there would just be one lump sum for payments from all Unit members instead of individual ones. Emmie dug her spade deep into the damp earth. She was probably worrying about nothing. These weren't real worries, not like Marie's. And if Kate did find it—well, it had been such a little lie. Not even a lie, really. More of an omission.

Next to her, the bridge over the moat quivered on its supports as it always did when a car approached. And this was the very crème de la crème of cars, as long as a boat and as shiny as anything could be in the mud of the Somme.

Emmie wiped her hands hastily on her skirt before staggering to her feet, her thighs aching. She couldn't possibly have been digging that long. The engineers weren't meant to be there until one, and it couldn't be much past eleven. Could it?

The big, black car rumbled to a stop, and the door opened, followed by a pair of long legs in tall black boots.

"It's an odd season to be gardening," said the British captain as the rest of him emerged from the car. "You're not burying the body, are you?"

"I'm digging for dishes," said Emmie brightly, and immediately wished she hadn't.

"Digging for—" He peered narrowly at the patch of disturbed dirt and the small pile of plates next to it.

"You do realize that transferware doesn't grow underground like potatoes?"

"Don't be silly. Everyone knows plates grow on trees." He looked as though he couldn't tell whether or not she was serious. Flushing, Emmie launched into an explanation. "These are Marie's wedding dishes. Our housekeeper. She buried them to keep them from the Germans. We've twelve officers from the American engineers coming for luncheon today, you see."

"And I've gate-crashed it? Don't worry, I won't impose on your hospitality. Thirteen's an unlucky number."

"Doesn't that depend on who you ask? Besides, we'll be twenty-five if you count the Unit. Twenty-six, with you. We do mean to wash the dishes first," Emmie added hastily.

"I don't know," said the captain. "A meal of good, honest dirt makes a nice change from bully beef. I should imagine it would taste better too. But I didn't come by to beg a meal. I found more of your property left lying about at the station, so I thought I'd bring it round."

The passenger door edged open, and a rather squashed brown felt hat poked out the side. "Hullo? Is this the place?"

"Miss Lewes!" The Unit's agriculturalist was still in civilian clothes, but Emmie recognized her from the luncheon, a comfortably rounded woman of less than medium height, who looked more like a children's book illustration of Old Mother Hubbard than a woman who could hobble cows or whatever else it was that agriculturalists were meant to do. "We didn't think we'd have you until next week!"

Ignoring the captain's offered hand, Miss Lewes rolled out of the car. "Neither did I, but my pass came through—so here I am! I'm afraid I've a good deal of gear with me—everyone was pressing parcels on me for the Unit."

"Oh goodness, what a time you must have had, getting this all down to us!" The back of the big car looked like a jumble sale, filled with crates and brown paper parcels, some rather the worse for wear. One of the cases appeared to be moving of its own accord.

"I can tell you, I wasn't looking forward to trekking all the way here with my poor little bunnies." Miss Lewes burrowed in among the parcels, lifting the burlap over a large cage. "They've been jostled enough, poor dears. But Captain DeWitt was kind enough to give me a lift from the station."

"DeWitt?" Emmie looked over her at the captain. "So it's not Blakeney, then."

"No," said Captain DeWitt shortly.

"DeWitt—like the biscuits?" The captain stood like patience on a monument, if patience had a thin mustache and a decidedly frozen expression. Emmie recognized that freeze. It was the same way she froze when anyone mentioned her mother. "Oh goodness, you are the biscuits, aren't you?"

"That, I am afraid," said Captain DeWitt politely, "would be anatomically impossible."

"My father sent a box but we've run through them already. There's fierce competition for them. They're really quite our favorites." Emmie was babbling, she knew, but she felt as if she had to make up for mentioning it, for making him feel awkward. "You've the endorsement of the Smith Unit, for what that's worth."

"Thank you. I'm sure they'll put it on the advertisements going forward." Captain DeWitt sounded very, very British.

"We won't even charge you for the use of our photo." Captain DeWitt was not amused. Emmie locked her hands together at her waist, saying more formally, "Thank you for bringing Miss Lewes to us. You can't imagine the trouble I've been having with my chickens."

"Can't I?" Captain DeWitt relaxed into a smile. It worked wonders for his thin face. "You do have the most curious notions of agriculture. Digging for dishes and all that."

"Now you're making fun," said Emmie with relief. "I'll have you know that our crop of porcelain is second to none. We're thinking of going into business."

"Crop?" Miss Lewes emerged, rear end first, pulling her case of rabbits along with her. "I hadn't thought you'd begun—"

"Oh no," said Emmie hastily. "It was just a joke. I'll show you to your room, shall I? And by your room, I mean our room, Kate's and mine—Kate Moran, that is. You wouldn't have met her at the luncheon. She's our assistant director since Mrs. Rutherford left."

"I'll help with the bags," said the captain, once Emmie had run out of breath.

"There's no need, really. We're used to hauling things. We're all terribly muscular, apparently. At least, according to the Boston papers." Why, oh why, had she felt the need to tell him that? Emmie took refuge in peering into the back of the car. "What is all this, Miss Lewes?"

Miss Lewes began hauling bags from the back of the car. "The carpetbags, the rabbits, and the seeds are mine—the rest are all bundles from the Paris Committee. They've sent Christmas stockings and presents for the children—there's even some chocolate."

"How thoughtful of them." It couldn't possibly

be that close to Christmas already, could it? Emmie couldn't decide whether they'd been at Grécourt for a week or a year; time blurred here. It had begun raining again, the steady drip they'd all come to dread. "Don't tell the others about the chocolate or it might not last until tomorrow, much less Christmas."

"Would you like the British Army to guard it for you?" offered Captain DeWitt.

"If by guard, you mean eat, then no," said Emmie, softening the words with a smile. "It's for the children, you see."

Ignoring her instructions, he efficiently stowed a parcel under each arm and a bag in each hand. "How many do you have in your care?"

Since it didn't seem worth arguing with him, Emmie started walking, leading the way down the path that branched out to the right from the moat, past Marie's house and the old stables. "Altogether, counting all of our villages? Roughly two thousand. Here at Grécourt we have twenty-seven, but there are always more coming in from the nearer villages. We have the children in for games and sewing and carpentry classes here in the Orangerie on Thursdays. Oh, do let me help you with that, Miss Lewes."

"What about the animal population?" asked Miss Lewes as they rounded the side of the old château.

"We've eight cows now. Our people in the *basse-cour*—that's the cellars of the old stables—take care of them for us and do the milking."

"Have they recovered from their ordeal in the boxcar?" inquired Captain DeWitt.

"The more apt question is, have we! Captain DeWitt helped us get the cows home," Emmie explained to Miss Lewes. "We did appreciate your assistance, you know. They might still be there at the train station at Nesle but for you."

"They'd have been steaks long since," said Captain DeWitt cynically.

"Oh, don't say that! They're now quite wonderful milkers—we've so much milk that we've not only enough for our children but to spare. It's a wonderful feeling being able to give a child a pail of milk and not have to ration it! Especially when they haven't had any for so long. . . ."

"I can imagine it must be," said Captain DeWitt quietly, looking at her with a strange expression on his face.

She was going on again, wasn't she? Boring on, Auntie May would say.

Emmie determinedly turned her attention back to their agriculturalist. "But you wanted to know about the animals, Miss Lewes. We're waiting for a delivery of pigs and also some goats, which we mean to sell on to the countryfolk. We also keep hens, although our hens have been rather a worry, since they're not great layers. . . . Well, to be honest, they haven't laid anything so far. We can't think why. And here we are! Watch your step. It can be a bit tricky over here."

The path between the barracks was knee-deep in mud. In desperation, they'd laid some duckwalk left by the Germans, but the knobby concoction of twigs and wire was treacherous at best, apt to trip the unwary. Emmie had landed flat on her backside more than once and Miss Ledbetter had a bruised hip and had spent a week ostentatiously hobbling with a cane.

Captain DeWitt nudged the duckwalk with one booted toe. "What is this?"

Emmie looked up at him in surprise. "Duckwalk. Isn't that what you use in the trenches to keep your feet dry?"

"By a certain definition of *dry*." The Captain detoured around the duckwalk. "That isn't duckwalk."

"The Germans said it was," said Emmie, stepping blithely onto the duckwalk and tripping over a protruding twig.

Captain DeWitt grabbed her arm before she could go over. "It was clearly a mistranslation. Or a booby trap. You'll break your neck on that if you're not careful."

"We're careful," Emmie promised, just as Liza

came running from the Orangerie, launched herself onto the duckwalk, and went into a long skid that had her arms waving like propellers. Miraculously, she managed to right herself and scramble through the door of her barrack.

Captain DeWitt raised an eyebrow at Emmie.

"Mostly careful," amended Emmie, smiling helplessly at Captain DeWitt. She felt strangely giddy, as if that smile had taken over her whole head, turning it into a sort of balloon. She could just float up and away—only her legs were quite firmly planted in mud up to the middle of her rubber boots and her hem was so sodden she couldn't float anywhere.

"Forgot my tooth mug!" Liza panted, waving it at them from the door of the barrack. "Who's this? You're not the engineers, are you?"

Emmie made a note to herself to take Liza aside at some future point and gently suggest it wouldn't be such a dreadful thing to wear her spectacles. "Miss Lewes has arrived! And this is Captain DeWitt."

"Oh, like the biscuits?" Her face lighting up, Liza started forward, tripped over the edge of the duckwalk, executed a complicated sort of flip, and landed hard on one shoulder. "Oooooph."

"Liza!" Dropping Miss Lewes's parcels, Emmie flopped down on her knees in the mud beside her.

"Don't worry—I'm fine—" Liza made an attempt to lever herself up, turned an alarming color of gray, and collapsed back down.

"No, you're not." Captain DeWitt was on Liza's other side. "Can you move your arm?"

Liza tried, and immediately turned gray again.

"If I may?" Captain DeWitt rapidly and impersonally examined Liza's arm and shoulder. In an undertone, he said to Emmie, "It's not the arm. I think it's the collarbone. You have a doctor on-site?"

"Yes, two of them."

Miss Lewes elbowed Captain DeWitt. "Let me take a look. I've set a few broken hocks."

"Hocks? Like ham?" Liza made another attempt to sit, and rapidly subsided.

"That's terribly kind of you," said Emmie to Miss Lewes, "but would you mind getting Dr. Stringfellow? She should be at the dispensary. It's the little temporary house next to the Orangerie. Down that path that way. It would be a great help."

For a moment she thought Miss Lewes might protest, but she evidently saw the wisdom of it, because she sprang to her feet and slogged off through the mud, largely in the right direction.

"Well done," said Captain DeWitt quietly, and Emmie decided not to remind him that she wasn't one of his soldiers. "We need to get her out of this mud—and get that bone set. Do you think you can bear it if we lift you?"

Liza started to nod, and then stopped abruptly, her lips an alarming bluish white.

"It's a good thing we haven't far to go," said Emmie cheerfully. "We'll have you in your own bed in just a tick."

"On the count of three," said Captain DeWitt. He took one side while Emmie took the other, sliding their hands into the mud under Liza's back and knees. "This *is* going to hurt."

His eyes met Emmie's across Liza's prone form, and she could read what he was thinking as loudly as if he had said it. There was no room for error. No slipping in the mud, no losing their grip or their balance. This had to be done quickly and cleanly.

Emmie gave a short, firm nod.

"Three," said the captain, and together they rose to their feet, as smoothly as they could, which wasn't very smoothly at all. Liza made a gurgling noise, her face going very white and her eyes rolling back in her head. "Together now."

Together, they carried her through the open door of the barrack. Emmie thought vaguely that the first time she had seen the captain had been just after Margaret had keeled over. It was much easier carrying Liza with the captain than it had been carrying Margaret with Kate—she and the captain were nearly of a height; there was no need to stoop or jostle. They moved together as one.

"Bed?" asked the captain.

"The one with the bear on it."

They lowered Liza gently onto her bed, which was covered with a steamer rug, a sleeping bag, four blankets, and one slightly battered teddy bear.

"We need to get her out of those wet things," said Emmie worriedly. "She's soaked through with mud. She doesn't need a chill on top of an injury."

The captain didn't waste any time on false modesty. "We'd best cut her jacket off. Getting those sleeves off will only hurt her."

"But her uniform—" Emmie shook her head. "Never mind. You're right."

She'd never realized before just how durable wet wool could be. After what seemed an eternity, they had Liza out of her wet skirt and jacket, covered with three blankets filched from Maud's bed, the covers carefully tucked just so, so they wouldn't put pressure on her left side.

Kneeling by the side of the cot, Emmie checked Liza's pulse. It was slow but regular. Captain DeWitt, she realized, had risen to his feet and was standing just behind her.

Looking up at him, Emmie said quietly, "Thank you."

He held out a hand to help her to her feet. "All in a day's work."

"Rescuing fallen damsels?"

"I warned you that duckwalk was a German trap."

"So you did." In her thick rubber boots, she was only an inch or two shorter than Captain DeWitt. They stood eye to eye. His, Emmie noticed, were a rather pleasant shade of hazel, all greeny brown like the sort of stream one stumbled on in the Adirondacks in summer, green leaves and brown silt and quiet contentment.

"Where's my patient?" Dr. Stringfellow stalked into the room, followed by Miss Lewes.

"Over here," said Emmie, dropping Captain De-Witt's hand. Or maybe he dropped hers. She wasn't quite sure. "She's insensible, poor thing."

"Lucky thing, you mean," said Dr. Stringfellow. "We haven't enough morphia to spare. The less she feels, the better."

"I'd be happy to examine—" Miss Lewes began.

"When I have a lamb that needs looking at, I'll call you." Dr. Stringfellow leaned over Liza's recumbent form. "It's her collarbone. No heavy lifting for her for quite some time, I'd say. You. Captain. Do you have any experience setting bones?"

"I've some experience with field dressings."

"Good. I need to put that arm in a sling—we'll immobilize it and hope for the best. You can lift while I wrap."

"Doctor," said Captain DeWitt gravely, and saluted.

Dr. Stringfellow snorted. "Less nonsense, more lifting. Save your flirting for the young fry."

Emmie was feeling decidedly *de trop*. "I'd best tell Kate."

"Better you than me," said Dr. Stringfellow without looking away from her patient. "Let her know she's down a driver."

"I'll get my things," said Miss Lewes.

"Oh goodness," Emmie said guiltily. She had forgotten all about their new member. "What a welcome for you. I wish I could say it was out of the ordinary, but I'm afraid it's always something around here—although not always something like that. Poor Liza."

Miss Lewes's carpetbags had been left just outside, half-off the duckwalk, cheerfully soaking up mud.

"No matter," said Miss Lewes, picking up one bag and giving it a brisk pat. "There's nothing wrong with a bit of dirt."

"Except that it leaves the most dreadful stains," said

Emmie, struggling to extract the other bag from the mud, which appeared to have gotten hold of it and didn't want to let go. "Marie, our mayor and general factotum, does the laundry for us—she starts on Monday and we get our clothes back on Sunday, although not always the same ones we started with."

"Washing is highly overrated," said Miss Lewes cheerfully. "There's nothing like a good layer of dirt for keeping the warmth in."

"Well, we've certainly plenty of that. . . . Dirt, I mean, not warmth. We're two barracks down, that one, over there."

As she struggled along the duckwalk that led between the barracks, Emmie wondered how she was going to break it to Kate that they were a driver down. That meant Kate taking more shifts in the truck . . . and Kate was doing too much already.

"Kate?" Emmie called as she opened the barrack door. "Kate?"

Her roommate was sitting on her bed, surrounded by a welter of papers, a portable writing desk sitting on the coverlet beside her. But she wasn't writing. She was just sitting there, her head bent.

"Emmie." Kate's voice sounded rusty. "Emmie, there's something—I have to ask you—about these accounts—"

Emmie felt the world lurch around her as her stomach dropped down into her boots. She'd forgotten. With the captain and Miss Lewes and Liza, she'd forgotten about Kate and the accounts. About what Kate might find in the accounts.

"Kate, Miss Lewes is here!" Emmie dropped Miss Lewes's carpetbag with a thud, effectively cutting off what Kate was about to say. They would talk later, Emmie promised herself. She would explain. She would. Somehow. And once she explained, Kate would understand it was all for the best. "I've told her she can room with us, since we've an extra bed since Margaret left. . . ."

Chapter Fifteen

We had thought we worked hard the rest of the week, but Sunday has become our most hectic day, because that's the day when every man in the neighborhood comes to call. Last Sunday we had more than twenty men over for tea—French, British, and American, Quakers, engineers, cavalry, aviators, and civilians! This Sunday it was luncheon for twelve officers of the American engineers (roast beef, cauliflower cheese, and chocolate rice pudding—if you think it sounds good, it was) and a British Captain who wandered in for some reason or other and turned out to be the DeWitt of DeWitt's biscuits! Our guest book is absolutely killing! You'd never believe the signatures we've collected. . . .

— Miss Alice Patton, '10, to her
sister, Mrs. Gilbert Thomas

November 1917
Grécourt, France

"Miss Lewes?" Kate's muscles moved without conscious direction from her brain. Setting aside the paper she'd been holding, she rose from the bed, saying automatically, "Welcome to Grécourt. We didn't expect you so soon."

"My pass came through, so here I am! Is this my bed? Lovely."

Emmie had fallen back behind the other woman, trying to make herself as small as possible.

A fund, Emmie had told her. A fund set up to pay living expenses and fees. Some of the girls were volunteering to pay their own way, to save the Unit expenses, but the money was there, part of the plan.

Not charity, Emmie had sworn. Impersonal funding donated by scores of Smith alumnae who wanted to do their bit but couldn't go themselves. Money available to anyone.

A lie. All a lie. There was no fund. Everyone was paying her own way.

Everyone except Kate.

"That's your washstand, Miss Lewes." Kate felt thoroughly distracted, but the amenities had to be observed. Her voice sounded like it was coming from someone else, calm and normal, when she wanted to scream and howl. "The water tends to freeze overnight, but Marie's son Yves brings us two cans of hot water every morning for washing."

"Sounds like luxury," said Miss Lewes, carpetbags underneath her cot. "Where can I keep my rabbits?"

"In the *basse-cour*, I would think. That's where we keep our cows. Kate—" Emmie was wringing her hands like Lady Macbeth after a hard night of regicide, wringing and wringing them until Kate wanted to reach out and make her stop, just stop. "Kate, you should know—"

"Yes?" Every muscle in Kate's body tensed. She both wanted to hear what Emmie had to say and was dreading it.

"Liza broke her collarbone," Emmie blurted out.

"Her collarbone."

"On the duckwalk, although Captain DeWitt says it isn't really proper duckwalk, so maybe that's why . . ."

Liza, duckwalk, broken bones—Kate's brain felt like it had been stuffed with wool; nothing made any sense. "Captain DeWitt?"

"That Englishman we met at the hospital. He just happened to be passing by and gave Miss Lewes a lift." Emmie was backing away, toward the door of the barrack. "Welcome again, Miss Lewes! I'll tell the people in the Orangerie to ladle out an extra tooth mug of pumpkin soup for you. Unless you can have Liza's— I'm not sure if she'll be up to lunching. I'll just go and check on her, shall I?"

With that, Emmie fled, letting the door bang shut behind her.

"A bit nervy, that one, isn't she?" said Miss Lewes, looking after Emmie with interest from her perch on the cot. "Her eyes roll just like a colt I once knew."

"Not usually," said Kate shortly. If Emmie was nervy it was because she'd been caught out. "It's been a trying day, I gather. Will you excuse me for a moment?"

Maybe there was an explanation. Maybe she'd misunderstood. Maybe the accounting was wrong.

Either way, Kate needed to know. She needed to hear it from Emmie's own lips.

But by the time she found Emmie, diligently scrubbing plates, the engineers had come roaring in, and Kate found herself pressed into service with a ladle, dishing out pumpkin soup into tooth mugs. And then it was a regular melee as everyone rushed about collecting the tooth mugs to be rewashed for the chocolate pudding, setting out platters of cauliflower cheese and roast beef, parrying the banter of the engineers, who were in roaringly high spirits.

All the while, Kate couldn't help looking around the

table at her sisters in arms, seeing them as if for the first time, all of them with their own quirks, their capable hands and determined faces, Alice's lacy jabot contrasting with her grimy uniform, Maud ostentatiously waving her engagement ring and speaking loudly of Henry, Liza trussed up in bandages from the waist up but pink cheeked and happy as could be with two engineers to help her manage her cutlery and grab her the best pieces of beef.

They all looked so sure of themselves, despite their ragged uniforms that could never be made entirely clean, no matter how Marie scrubbed them. It was an assurance that couldn't be taught, an assurance that came of always having had a cook and housemaid, of knowing that Daddy was a lawyer or a professor or a banker. It sat on them like polish.

Kate, wearing the same uniform, no more ragged than the rest, felt, nonetheless, very small and shabby, as if they could see in her bones she was different, that she wasn't pulling her weight. Her head ached with the din of all those voices, all those strident, confident, honking voices.

One of the engineers was asking her about her people, and Kate smiled and responded vaguely. It didn't matter—he mostly wanted to talk about himself, anyway, but Kate felt naked, naked and a fraud. Only

Julia sat silent, with Dr. Stringfellow on one side and Emmie's British captain on the other.

Charity case, Julia had called Kate all those years ago, and Kate had burned at it, at the indignity of it, when she had never accepted a penny from Emmie, when she had been so very, very careful not to ever take anything from Emmie. But now—now she was what Julia had called her and worse.

Kate looked around the table, wondering what this made her. Not a proper member of the Unit, a member of their fellowship, but a sort of paid companion, only there due to the munificence of—what had that loathsome reporter called her? The noble descendant of one of our first families.

Emmie's charity case.

Would this lunch never end?

Finally, finally, the tooth mugs were cleared a second time, sounds of repletion made, napkins dropped. Finally, finally, they could disperse and Kate wouldn't have to keep smiling in a way that made her face hurt.

But then the engineers produced, with a great air of triumph, a Victrola.

"A dance!" cried Nell, hiking up her skirt and hopping out of her chair. "Huzzah!"

There was no hope for it after that. The tables were pushed aside, the dishes stacked haphazardly to await

cleaning later; Marie was miraculously induced to produce coffee, and the luncheon turned into a dance, engineers and Smithies galloping around the makeshift
dance floor in their rubber boots.

Julia, Kate noticed, had disappeared, and she was
deeply tempted to do the same, but there were more
men than women and she found herself yanked into first
one dance and then another, dancing with a sameness
of pink-cheeked, clean-shaven men who all seemed to
have a first cousin once removed who was engaged to
this or that Smith girl, and, say, wasn't it a bully thing
they were doing here.

Emmie's Brit had been attached by Alice, who was
attempting to lead him in a Viennese waltz, swirling
and dipping with anxious gaiety.

Emmie, meanwhile, had busied herself quietly collecting plates, as if trying to make herself as small as
she could. For a moment, their eyes met, and Kate saw
pure misery, misery and guilt, before Emmie ducked
her head and began stacking plates with renewed vigor.
Kate tried to make her way across the room to her—
this was absurd, they needed to talk about this, they
couldn't just go on being miserable at one another—but
she was plucked off by an engineer in want of a dancing partner and neatly suborned into another dance.

Waltzing past her, Kate heard Maud's voice, too

loud as always. "Look at Emmie Van Alden sulking! She shouldn't think she can monopolize DeWitt's Biscuits just because she saw him first. Did no one ever teach her to share?"

Share? Kate wanted to kick Maud's booted legs out from under her. Emmie was the most generous person Kate knew.

Which was, of course, just the problem.

Kate's head ached with thinking about it. She'd pay it back, of course. She wasn't sure how, but she would. But it ate at her all the same that all this time, from the very beginning, Emmie had been lying to her.

The engineers stayed. And stayed. When they finally took their leave, with promises of return engagements, there was Miss Lewes in their room, and Kate could have screamed in frustration.

"Emmie?" she tried whispering, once Miss Lewes had subsided into snoring slumber on the third cot, but Miss Lewes murmured and turned and Kate had to retreat beneath the pillow.

It wasn't until after breakfast the next day that Kate finally caught Emmie at the chicken coop, draped over the chicken wire, looking mournfully at her poultry.

As impossible as it was, the mud seemed even thicker here. Kate sank to the tops of her boots with every step. "Emmie?"

Emmie looked up at her, her eyes glassy with unshed tears. "My hens are roosters."

"What?"

"My hens." Emmie sniffed, scrubbing her nose with a large, monogrammed handkerchief. "Miss Lewes just told me. The reason none of my hens are laying is that they're all roosters. I bought seventy-two roosters instead of seventy-two hens. What are we to do with seventy-two roosters?"

"Make stew?" It would be so easy just to let herself be drawn back into the day-to-day, to let it all go. But she couldn't. And Kate minded terribly that Emmie was making her feel sorry for her just when she wanted to be angry at her.

"They didn't have big combs, so I thought . . . But apparently, not all French roosters do."

"Yes, things aren't always what they appear, are they?"

Emmie bit her lip. "Kate—"

"You told me the Unit was paying for travel and living expenses."

Emmie ducked her head, looking down at her chickens. "I told you that alumnae were donating money."

"And you're an alumna? That's pure sophistry, Emmie, and you know it." There was a world of difference between being bankrolled by an anonymous group of donors and having her expenses paid by someone she knew. "Why did you assume I couldn't pay? I'm not a pauper, Emmie. My family aren't paupers."

"I know that," said Emmie, a little too quickly.

"We're not poor, Emmie," Kate said fiercely. But of course they were to Emmie, with her Fifth Avenue mansion and her camp in the Adirondacks and her "cottage" in Newport that was bigger than most apartment buildings. It didn't mean anything to Emmie that Kate's stepfather, the police officer, could put meat on the table or lace curtains on the windows; those were inconsequentialities to Emmie, these things that to Kate and her mother had seemed so monumental and miraculous. "I have a job. I had a job."

Emmie looked at Kate with wide, childlike blue eyes. "Yes, but why shouldn't my mother pay our way? The cost wasn't anything to her—she spends more than that each week on stamps!"

"No. It's not anything to her." The air stank of chicken excrement; Kate's boots were sticky with mud and feathers.

Emmie mistook Kate's words for agreement. "And you know she's always liked you, Kate. She wanted you to be her secretary. . . ."

"And I said no."

Emmie's forehead wrinkled. "I never blamed you for that. I know my mother can be a bit . . ."

"It wasn't because of your mother." Kate rather liked Emmie's mother; there was something about her drive that spoke to Kate. She would have loved to be Mrs. Van Alden's secretary, to travel with her around the world, helping her to write strongly worded letters to the editors of all the major papers. "I said no because I didn't want to be beholden. I was your friend, Emmie. Not your project." There was a horrible moment where Emmie was silent, the only sounds the clucking of the chickens. "Wasn't I?"

"Of course! You know I would never have got through Smith without you. That's why I wanted you here so badly. I knew I couldn't do this without you. And I knew that you—well, you might not have the money to spare, so I thought—I thought that if it were all paid already . . ."

"You shouldn't have assumed—"

"Maybe I shouldn't have, but when I started to tell you about the Unit, you looked so skeptical, and I knew you were going to say no. . . ."

And there had been that room. That depressing, cabbage-scented room with its paper shades and fraying coverlet. The very picture of poverty.

Kate pressed her eyes shut, fighting hard to keep her composure. "You might have given me the choice."

In a very small voice, Emmie said, "I was afraid if I did you wouldn't come."

She seemed so small—which was ridiculous, since Emmie was a full head taller than Kate. But she did. She seemed so small and so vulnerable. Kate's heart twisted.

But then Emmie ruined it all by saying, "And you did have a choice, didn't you? You had the choice to come or not come. I just didn't want—I didn't want the money to be a factor. I just—I knew that you'd be brilliant at it. And the truth is . . . I didn't know if I could do this without you, Kate. You—you make everything *manageable*. Even algebra."

But it wasn't a choice, not a true choice.

Kate's throat locked. She struggled to find the words to explain, but Emmie was still talking, faster now, as if determined to get it all over with.

"I know it was wrong to lie to you, Kate. I do. It was just . . . I needed you so badly." Emmie looked at her appealingly. Kate knew that expression so well. It was Emmie's hapless face, the one that got people to do things for her. She didn't do it on purpose. It was just part of who she was. "You're not sorry you're here, are you?"

Constantly wet and freezing. Never enough sleep, never enough time. All those different personalities to manage. The challenge of it, never the same from day to day, always a new obstacle to be surmounted, a new battle to be won, a broken truck to be fixed, a reluctant bureaucrat to bully . . .

It was alarming to realize how much she'd come to love it, this strange life here. One could say many things about it, but it was never dull. Kate never felt, as she had in Boston, that she was wasting her time and her energies. It was maddening and rewarding and it suited her as nothing else had.

"No," said Kate slowly. "I'm not sorry."

"I was so worried at first that you were miserable and I'd done something terrible by bringing you here, but then . . . you seemed so happy. You don't dislike it here, do you?"

Kate's lips felt numb. "No, I don't dislike it."

On the contrary, she was terrified of losing it. Of Maud finding out and deciding she was hardly a real member of the Unit at all. When had she come to love it so?

"Just think what you would have missed if you'd never come!" Emmie leaned forward earnestly. "And you wouldn't have come if you had had to pay, would you?"

Kate could feel her stomach drop, but she couldn't make herself lie. "No."

Emmie's face lit up like a thousand candles on a Christmas tree. She clapped her hands together, bouncing on the balls of her boots. "You see? Oh, Kate. Surely you must see how much the Unit needs you—how much you've done. And you seemed so unhappy at that school in Boston. . . . So it all turned out for the best."

"But that's not—" Kate's throat felt scratchy with frustration and chicken feathers. "You can't just sweep in and decide you know what's best for me! I'm not one of your settlement house girls, Emmie."

Emmie grabbed Kate's hands in hers, squeezing them affectionately. "But it was what was best for you, wasn't it? And for the Unit. They've made you assistant director! That says something, doesn't it? What does it matter who paid for what? You're here and that's all that matters."

Kate stood frozen, her hands caught in Emmie's, feeling like she'd never known Emmie—or that Emmie had never known her. "No. It's not. You've made me into your debtor—your hireling. You've made me beholden."

Kate saw relief in Emmie's face and knew she'd entirely misunderstood. "Is that all? You don't need to pay it back—I never wanted you to pay it back. It really doesn't matter, Kate. Can't we just forget it? You can pay your own way going forward if it makes you more comfortable."

"Thanks," said Kate flatly. "How big of you."

Emmie looked at her in confusion, like a kicked puppy, and Kate felt a moment of guilt. But this was *her* life Emmie was playing with.

This was the job she'd given up and the trip she'd taken overseas and working in a war zone, all under false pretenses. Emmie had blatantly, openly lied to her. Because she knew Kate would mind. But she'd gone ahead and done it anyway. And kept on lying.

Kate couldn't quite get her head around it, the selfishness of it. "Did you never stop and think of how this might make me feel?"

Emmie twisted her hands together. "I was hoping—I was hoping you would never find out. And then it would all be all right."

"Mademoiselle Marron!" Zélie came running up, breathless, barreling between them. She stopped in front of Kate, too full of her news to notice the tension in the air. "*Deux camions . . . anglais . . .* And a *billet* for Mademoiselle Aimée."

Zélie glanced a little nervously at Emmie—she was still wary of Emmie after that incident with the ball back in September. She was Kate's own special assistant and it was foolish and childish to be grateful she was here now, as a sort of shield.

"Thank you, Zélie," said Kate, taking the note from

her and handing it to Emmie, holding it out from the edge so that their fingers wouldn't touch. Emmie took it, casting a long, searching glance at Kate before dropping her head to the paper.

"It's from Captain DeWitt." Emmie looked up, her whole face lighting. "He's sent us two loads of duckwalk—proper duckwalk—and eight Tommies to set it out for us. He says he'll come by later to see that they've put it down properly."

"The Tommies," said Zélie, "the Tommies, they ask that you tell them where the walk is to go."

"You'd best go, then. Or we'll have those camions blocking our drive all day. Liza can't drive, so I need to take Dr. Stringfellow out. Some of us need to earn our keep. Apparently." Realizing she was being horrible, Kate added stiffly, "Please give Captain DeWitt the thanks of the Unit."

"I will. And Kate?" Emmie paused and turned back, clutching the note like a holy relic. "I'm sorry I didn't tell you sooner—but I'm glad you're here."

"Mademoiselle Marron?" Zélie was tugging at Kate's arm. "Mademoiselle Marron? Is there anything else I can do?"

"No." *I'm sorry I didn't tell you sooner?* That wasn't an apology at all. Because Emmie didn't think she needed to apologize. Kate felt sick with anger and grief.

It had all worked out as Emmie wanted it to work out and therefore it didn't matter that she'd done violence to Kate's deepest sensibilities. Maybe she thought Kate didn't have any sensibilities. What was pride to the poor?

"Mademoiselle Marron?"

Kate looked down at Zélie with regret. "I'm sorry, Zélie. My mind was elsewhere. *J'étais distrait.*" The girl looked so disappointed that Kate added, "I have to drive to Hombleux today. Would you like to ride along with me and the doctors?"

It was some distraction, listening to Zélie talk about life before the war—but never her brother, she never talked of her brother, who had been killed by a mine in a field, and Kate was very careful never to ask—and to watch her wonderment as they detoured to Noyon, which Zélie swore was so big it must be bigger than Paris. They let her help hold the bandages and she felt very grown-up and important indeed, and Kate took a moment from seething to be soothed by the thought that at least she had made someone happy. At least someone saw her as a person and not a project or a pawn.

Not that Emmie really saw her as either of those things, Kate knew, not consciously. But she couldn't get past it, that Emmie believed she'd done nothing wrong—nothing other than being found out, that was. Emmie had wanted her here and so Emmie had arranged it, and never mind how Kate might feel about it.

And what if Kate had been miserable in Boston? It was her right to be miserable in Boston. Yes, she was happy here, but not at the cost of her self-respect. She hated that she'd been the recipient of Emmie's largesse. It didn't matter that she hadn't known about it; she ought to have known about it; she ought to have known Emmie well enough to guess. Maybe she had guessed, on some level, and had chosen not to know, which made it worse, because then she was complicit in her own beggaring.

They didn't want to pauperize the French villagers, Mrs. Rutherford had insisted. They were to sell, not give. But that was just what Emmie had done to Kate. She'd forced her charity on her. And maybe, just maybe, Kate might have forgiven her if she'd been properly horrified. If she'd broken down and apologized and acknowledged she was wrong. But to stand there and insist it was for the *best*—

It made Kate furious just thinking of it.

The rain, the endless rain, dripped down. Even the mud was covered with mud. Nothing was ever dry. The best they could hope for was an acceptable level of dampness. The green twigs they poked into their stoves popped and smoldered. The Canadians explained to them that they were meant to dry the wood on the top half of the stove and then burn it, but there was never enough time, and so their meager fires smoked and never gave off near enough heat to dry their stockings, much less anything else. Tempers ran short, particularly Kate's.

It didn't help that Emmie watched her, constantly, darting anxious glances at her, as if trying to make sure she was enjoying herself. It soured everything. It made every triumph, every moment of joy or even mere content feel like an admission.

And she wouldn't, couldn't admit that Emmie had been right. Because she wasn't. Not about what mattered.

When the Canadian foresters invited the Unit to their camp for Thanksgiving, Kate would have much preferred to beg off, but she was, still, despite it all, assistant director of the Unit, and her presence would be expected. If it hadn't been for the Canadians dropping off loads of wood for the Unit, they would have frozen long since. Or chopped off a few stray limbs trying to chop their own wood. They couldn't afford to offend them.

So, grudgingly, Kate put on her cleanest and driest shirtwaist and got back into her despised rubber boots. It was an eerie trip through barren fields marked with barbed wire and desolate forest with the mist rising from the ground. Like something out of a fairy tale, Kate thought, and almost said as much to Emmie before remembering she wasn't speaking to Emmie. She saw Emmie glance at her and looked away, turning to determinedly chat with Miss Ledbetter, who only wanted to tell her all about the history of the forest and the château at which the Canadians were quartered.

Because it was a castle, a proper castle with a moat around it, not in ruins like Grécourt, but an uncannily preserved remnant of an earlier time. Beauty and the Beast, Kate thought—she and Emmie had read Mme Leprince de Beaumont's fairy tales together at Smith. But there were no beasts here, only good, honest Canadians, who served them an incongruous supper of lobster and apple pie in a gray-paneled salon trimmed with holly and mistletoe.

Kate made an effort to chat cheerfully—they'd gone to such an effort, these Canadians. They'd even made menu cards for each place, decorated with a jaunty American flag. But she felt tired and lonely—all the more lonely in the midst of a crowd—and her hand hurt. She'd scraped it a week ago, trying to fix the Ford truck when it had broken down on them outside Canizy, and, despite cleaning and wrapping, it still felt as raw as it had that first day. Worse even.

"Don't forget your dance card," the man next to Kate reminded her when she rose from the table. He flipped the menu over to reveal a dance card. "We're starting with a Virginia reel!"

"I'm afraid you'll have to roll me through the reel after all that pie," said Kate, and escaped as they began pushing the tables to the sides and sprinkling the old parquet floor with boracic acid for dancing.

She couldn't leave until the others did—the truck was waiting to bring them back—but the candles were burning her eyes, the noise too loud. She wondered if she might not be a little feverish. Possibly. Or maybe it was just the exhaustion of being angry all the time, of going and going and going, because if she stopped, she would have to accept that Emmie was never going to understand why she was upset. And if she couldn't, what did it mean for their friendship? Or had they ever really been friends?

Kate wove her way across the room, passing Maud, who was holding forth to a group of five foresters. "Our doctors may be all right delivering babies, but as general practitioners, you're better off with a medieval barber-surgeon! Liza and I got into their records, and, can you believe, for a case of cancer of the stomach they prescribed soda mints? I ask you!"

"If that's doctoring, I have a degree too," one of the men said with a grin.

Kate paused. She had been there that day. She knew the woman Maud was talking about. Turning, she said, "They gave her soda mints because she was too far gone to do anything else."

There was awkward silence and shuffling of feet. Kate felt like an utter heel, but she couldn't have just left it. It wasn't right. It wasn't fair. Dr. Stringfellow and Julia were doing their best.

"Well, I wouldn't want them to doctor me," said Maud loudly, and turned back to her audience. The conversation resumed, with Kate on the outside of it.

A wave of bone-deep fatigue hit her, making her sway on her feet. Usually, Kate enjoyed the rest of the Unit. Even Maud's antics were entertaining in their own twisted way. But tonight, she had no energy for any of it. She just wanted somewhere dark and quiet. It was so hot in the gray salon, with all the bodies, people galloping up and down the dance floor, a fire blaring in the great hearth. The foresters had no shortage of wood at their disposal, it seemed.

Kate escaped through a lightly gilded door into a room that seemed, mercifully, unoccupied. As her eyes adjusted to the gloom, she could just make out the shape of furniture, and golden lyres molded onto the panels of the wall. Her hand was throbbing terribly. Kate peeled back the bandage, wincing as the scab stuck to the linen.

"What's wrong with your hand?" demanded a voice out of the darkness. A shadow detached itself from one of the settees.

"Julia." Kate clutched at the bandage. "What are you doing out here?"

"I don't like dancing." Julia hadn't danced at the luncheon for the engineers either, Kate remembered. She'd disappeared as soon as the music started. "Show me that hand."

Kate put her hand behind her back. "It's just a scrape."

Julia leaned against the carved back of the settee. "It's festering, isn't it?"

"I cleaned it."

"It's something in the soil. Cuts don't heal properly. The soldiers call it *Boche button*. Don't ask me why. Come to the dispensary tomorrow and I'll dress it for you."

"There's no need."

"There is if you want to keep your hand." Without changing tone, Julia asked, "Why aren't you and Emmie speaking?"

Kate stared at her, startled. "We're speaking."

They sometimes exchanged as many as two sentences in a row.

Julia let out a short, harsh laugh. "I went to Miss Porter's for two years. I know not speaking when I see it."

"We've had . . . a disagreement."

Julia raised her eyes to the ornate ceiling. "Because no one has ever had one of those before."

"Never mind," said Kate, turning to go, but her knees felt like rubber and she had to grab the edge of the settee to steady herself.

"No. Wait." Julia wiggled herself up straight, her voice changing, becoming almost serious. "Emmie is the nearest thing I have to family. As opposed to her usual air of sickening cheer, she currently exudes misery. I want to know why."

As Julia sat up, Kate caught a strong whiff of spirits. "Did you get into Alice's sherry?"

"That rubbish?" Julia raised a silver flask. Even in the gloom, Kate could see that it had a coat of arms on it, old and elaborate. "This is brandy, my child. Want a slug?"

"I'll pass," said Kate drily. No need for Julia to know that she already felt dizzy and that a sip of brandy might put her under entirely.

"Suit yourself." Julia waited a moment and then asked, "What happened?"

It was too much trouble keeping it to herself. And it was dark and the thump of feet and tinny din of music echoed from the next room, adding to the general feeling of unreality.

Kate lowered herself onto the other end of the settee, folding her hands carefully in her lap. Her fingers felt as though they didn't belong to her. "Emmie's been paying my board without telling me."

"Is that all?"

Kate's head felt very heavy. She lifted it just enough to glower in Julia's general direction. "What do you mean, is that all? She had no right—"

Julia shrugged. "She likes to do things for people."

Kate shifted against the surprisingly lumpy cushion. "What if people don't want them done? I know you think I'm Emmie's charity case, but—"

Julia lowered her flask. "Emmie's what?"

"Charity case," said Kate tightly. "Those were your own words. That's what you said. To Nick Penniston. In Newport. You called me Emmie's latest charity."

"Oh, yes," said Julia after a long moment. "I'd forgotten that."

"I hadn't," said Kate bitterly. It felt very real, just then, that long-ago moment, coming down the stairs to find those two golden heads together. "Why did you hate me so much? Was it because you thought I was sponging off Emmie? I wasn't, you know. I never took a penny from her, not then, anyway. Or"—it was something she had always wondered, deep down—"was it because of Nick?"

Next door, they were playing "Blue Danube." The sickeningly romantic strains floated through the room as Julia spluttered on her brandy. "Nick? You thought I was jealous because of Nick?"

"Why not? Or was I not important enough to be a threat?" Just another Bridget: Irish and poor.

"Good Lord, Nick," said Julia reminiscently. "He was a decent enough specimen of his kind, as male creatures go. Utterly spineless. Pleasant, but spineless. No, I didn't hate you because of Nick," said Julia in a detached, cool tone. "I hated you because I was jealous of you."

She said it so matter-of-factly, as if it ought to have been blindingly obvious. "What on earth could I possibly have that you don't?"

Julia sat up straighter. "The right to earn your own living. A scholarship, a proper scholarship, free and clear."

"That's just because my family didn't have the money to send me." Kate had been so grateful for that scholarship and worked so hard to justify it. *Free and clear* were never words she would have used to describe it.

"Did you think mine had?" demanded Julia. "Do you know what I had to do to go to Smith? Beg. You want to talk about charity cases? You're looking at one."

Kate blinked at Julia, trying to make the world stand still again. "But you—your family—"

"Doesn't have two beans to rub together," said Julia with a certain grim satisfaction. "My father lost it all on the stock market in '93, poor sap. Then he killed himself. They put it about that it was a hunting accident, but it wasn't really. He just didn't have the nerve to face my mother. I don't blame him. Well, I do, really. But I can understand why he'd rather face a bullet than my esteemed mater."

"But wasn't your mother married to a French count?" It had been mentioned a time or two. Or ten.

"Oh, yes. This was his—pretty, isn't it?" Julia waved her flask, the silver glinting in the sparse moonlight. "He thought he was getting a rich American. My mother thought she was going to be Marie Antoinette without the whole guillotine bit. Both of them utterly washed-up. He was a wonderful old wastrel. He didn't have a sou, but that didn't stop him from buying me rafts of toys—and then tearing up the bills," she finished cynically. "He had a theory that aristocrats shouldn't have to pay. Unfortunately for him, that was a little too *ancien régime* for these democratic times. His creditors caught up with him eventually."

"I don't think we ever bought anything we couldn't pay for," said Kate wonderingly. Even when they were terribly, terribly poor. Her mother had a horror of credit, and of the pawnshop. "We went without when we couldn't afford it."

"That, my dear, is because you are poor but honest," said Julia mockingly, but Kate knew, somehow, in this strange half-dream state, that the mockery wasn't for her. "Not a washed-up aristocrat with delusions of grandeur. I refer, as you may have gathered, to my stepfather. My mother hasn't delusions. She's just a venal witch."

Kate thought of her own mother, her work-worn hands turning the pages of a library book as she read to Kate. She must have been so tired—that was before her stepfather, back when her mother was scrubbing houses to keep them fed—but she had always taken the time to read to her.

"That seems a bit hard," she said cautiously.

"Does it?" Julia gave a humorless laugh. "She tried to sell me off. They tart it up by calling it marriage and making it sound honorable, but my debut was really just another sort of auction. I was meant to be the last great hope, snag someone suitably plump in the pocket, and rescue my mother from the indignity of paste jewels. My mother was *furious* when Aunt Cora agreed to pay my tuition and board at Smith. But she couldn't do anything about it—darling Auntie Cora holds *all* the purse strings—so she just had to wait and bide her time. Every moment I was at Smith I knew I was on borrowed time. You want to know why I hated you? I hated you because you were so *free.* There you were, off to do whatever you wanted to do—"

This was not the way Kate remembered it. She felt as though she was being told an entirely different version of her past. "Teach French to spoiled society girls?"

Julia shrugged. "*Chacun à son goût.* Maybe you liked it. Whatever it was, you didn't have someone on at you about how you *owed* it to her to marry the first wealthy bore who crossed your path." In her usual bored drawl, she added, "Apparently she gave up her figure for me, and that means I'm meant to keep her in Paris frocks for the rest of her life."

Kate said the first thing that came to her head. "Wouldn't a strong corset be more to the point?"

Julia raised her flask to her. "Touché. In any event, that summer I was hanging about because I needed to persuade Aunt Cora to front me the money for medical school. Horrible old fraud. Big ideas, big plans, big speeches, but I don't think she'd know a good deed if it bit her. She gives speeches about women's education, but when it comes down to it—it's like squeezing blood from a stone."

"But a scholarship—"

"Do you think anyone was going to give me a scholarship? You must be joking. The worthy poor, yes"— Julia gestured elaborately in Kate's direction—"but never Livingston Van Alden's niece."

"Oh, thanks a lot."

"I would trade in a heartbeat." With a shock, Kate realized she meant it. "I had to beg for the money to go to Smith. The only reason my uncle gave it—and it was he, not Aunt Cora—was because he wanted to annoy my mother. They've always hated each other, my mother and my uncle. Since they were children. It's because they're too much alike. And because my uncle actually managed to marry money and my mother will never forgive him for it."

All the feuds were making Kate's head spin. Whatever her own family was, however apart from them she felt, they all liked each other. They might not always understand each other, but they liked each other. And they meant well. "You make me feel like my own family is relatively uncomplicated."

"Everyone's family is complicated. But some of them are nicer than others. My family are vipers. Emmie excepted. But that's probably why she's quite so holy. It had to balance out somehow. I'm a viper. I've had to be. It's bite or be bitten."

"I always thought you had the world handed to you."

"That's what everyone thinks. That's what they're meant to think. It's miserable being proud. We're all rotten with it, though."

"Even Emmie?"

"In her own sweet way. In her case, it takes the form of noble self-abnegation. Emmie's odor of sanctity always makes me feel like a louse," added Julia frankly. "But she does mean it, you know. It's not a put-on, like Aunt Cora."

"I know." That was what was so miserable about it. When Emmie said she meant it for the best, she did. She genuinely felt she was helping Kate. But what if Kate didn't want to be helped?

As if she could read what Kate was thinking, Julia said, "She can't help herself, you know. She just likes to give things to people. She thinks it will make them like her."

"I wish she wouldn't."

Julia turned her flask this way and that, admiring

the sheen. "Maybe that's why she likes you. Because you're not looking for anything from her."

But she'd been given it all the same. "All right. How would you feel if you found out someone was paying your way?"

"You dear, innocent child. How did you think I got here? My mother disowned me. I'm a medical student. It's all I can do to keep myself in stockings and shirtwaists."

Kate sat up a little straighter, feeling her head throb with the movement. "Is Emmie paying for you too?"

"No. Dr. Stringfellow is. One Smith doctor to another."

"And you don't mind?"

"I'm here, aren't I?" There was silence for a moment, as laughter and music filtered from the next room. Kate could barely hear Julia's voice when she spoke. "Do you know what I've learned? You take what you can get and you don't ask too many questions. Scruples are for people who can afford them. When you want something, you do what you have to do."

"You mean like ask your aunt for money?" asked Kate skeptically.

"Do you know how I paid for medical school when Aunt Cora said no? I sold my pearls. My mother raised the biggest fit, but there was nothing she could do. Other than disown me, that was. Best day of my life. I took that money and I paid my tuition and I worked hard, so hard. I lived on bread and milk. I studied harder than any of the boys. But none of them will ever, ever admit that I might be a real doctor."

Our doctors may be all right delivering babies . . .

"I'm sure they don't all think that," Kate said, because it was the sort of thing one said.

"When we went to the hospital at Neuilly, Dr. Blake stroked my arm," said Julia flatly. "They all think that way, all of them. To them, I'm just a piece of flesh. Because an educated woman must be a whore—just a whore they don't have to pay for."

Kate felt very cold all of a sudden. She'd been so wrapped up in her own misery, she'd forgotten about that day in Amiens, Dr. Stapleton and "Auld Lang Syne."

"Not all of them are Dr. Stapleton," said Kate quietly. "There are some decent men out there."

Her stepfather, for one. He'd tried so hard with her. It wasn't his fault that she'd never forgiven him for not being her father. It must, she realized, have been as hard for him as for her, having a sullen eight-year-old on his hands. But he'd tried. And he'd never called her anything but daughter.

"I'll believe it when—how does the line go? When

they make men of some other matter than earth." In the voice of one determined to be fair, Julia added, "Nick was a good one, as they went. He was sweet on you, you know."

Kate's eyes were burning. Her voice came out in a hoarse whisper. "He was?"

"I don't know if he'd have had the guts to do anything about it—his mother slept with the Social Register under her pillow. But he was sweet on you." Julia gazed into the unlit fireplace, her voice sounding very far away. "He died, you know. About a month ago. He was shot down."

"No, I didn't know." Kate was shivering. She couldn't seem to stop shivering. The chills racked her body. "Sometimes, I'd look into the sky and wonder . . ."

"Kate?" Julia swung her feet to the ground, her voice changing. She sounded, suddenly, remarkably sober. Kate felt the back of Julia's hand against her forehead. "You're burning up."

"I thought—" Kate's teeth were chattering and her head felt like there was a vise around it. "I thought it was just hot in here."

"Idiot," said Julia. "Come on. I'm looking at that hand whether you like it or not."

Chapter Sixteen

The history of Courcelles is one well known within the annals of chivalry. Across these fields the Merovingian kings fought their battles. From this castle did the Lord of Courcelles sally forth on Crusade with his retinue of knights. And it was here, as legend has it, that the Demoiselle of Courcelles, the first of that name, Lady Melisande, brought the blessed Dame of Orleans, none other than Jeanne d'Arc, and besought her lord to follow the saint into battle for the glory of France.

Today, the proud banner of Courcelles no longer flies from that storied castle. It is well known that in these recent hostilities, the present holder of that title, unwilling to bow to the yoke of the German invader, consigned himself and his

castle to the flames, bringing to their deaths a
number of German officers, in the finest tradition
of his house. . . . The German repercussions were
swift and sure. Nothing now remains of the noble
château or its accompanying village but the saddest of ruins. . . .

> — *From* A Château in Picardy:
> Sketches of France at War, *by*
> *Miss Ethel Ledbetter*

December 1917
Grécourt, France

Mme Lepinasse's hand was limp and cold in
Emmie's.

"Madame? Mme Lepinasse?" Emmie tried to rise
up on her knees, to look at the woman's face, but
she had been kneeling by the cot for so long that she
couldn't feel her feet anymore. Dusk had fallen, leaving
the sad room in shadows. "Madame?"

No answer.

Outside, through the great hole in the wall left by
German explosives, indifferent snowflakes drifted by
against a charcoal sky. The little fire, no use against the
bitter winter cold, cracked and spluttered.

"Madame, wake up, it's me, *la dame Américaine*."

The cat crouching on top of the potbellied stove gave an unearthly yowl and jumped down to stalk over to her mistress, butting her head against her mistress's limp hand.

Mon seul souvenir, Mme Lepinasse had called that cat. The one thing left to her after the Germans had departed.

Emmie felt the tears start to her eyes and blinked hard.

It was important to stay strong, they had all agreed. It was important that the villagers see them competent and cheerful. But Emmie couldn't help it. There was no one here but the cat, just the cat, and the shadows of all the people who weren't anymore, dim daguerreotypes of a husband shot by the Boches, children gone away no one knew where, all gone gone gone, and Mme Lepinasse—always so full of life, full of stories told in so thick a Picard dialect that sometimes Emmie could hardly understand her—gone too.

Emmie lowered her face to the older woman's cold hand, pressing it to her forehead in apology and shame. She hadn't even known Mme Lepinasse was ill. It had been nearly a month since Emmie had made her appointed rounds in Courcelles.

A month.

Oh, there had been reasons. First there had been

Miss Lewes, who needed to be shown all the animals and who had been terribly nice about it and tried not to tell Emmie she had done everything all wrong, but had cheerfully gone about fixing everything. The roosters, the useless roosters, had been distributed at a cut-rate price to the people of the villages and had been replaced with actual chickens, who didn't look all that different as far as Emmie could tell, but that was just the problem, wasn't it? She hadn't been able to tell, so she had wasted the Unit's funds and cheated her villagers of the fresh eggs they might have been eating all this time.

Miss Lewes's hens laid beautifully. The villagers had not only eggs but also three goats, who provided both milk and entertainment. Kate's Zélie had become unofficial goat girl and could usually be seen trotting about running errands, followed closely by Minerva, the smallest of the goats, who seemed to be under the misapprehension that she was actually a dog.

Then there had been Liza. It wasn't clear whether it was something wrong with the way the break in her collarbone had been set—as Maud loudly claimed—or if the fault was with Liza for refusing to follow Dr. Stringfellow's orders and stay still—as Julia countered—but Liza's collarbone just wouldn't heal. In the end, there was nothing for it but to send Liza off to Paris for surgery. Maud, of course, had gone with her.

So Emmie had volunteered to take over the store. She was half-mad with anxiety at that point. It wasn't that Kate wasn't speaking to her. She was speaking to her. She just wasn't saying anything that mattered, and all of Emmie's attempts to broach the topic, to talk it out, only seemed to make matters worse. Everyone else seemed so busy and useful: Anne Dawlish had her carpentry classes, Nell Baldwin was starting a lending library, and Ethel Ledbetter had the older students in hand—which left very little for Emmie to do. Emmie organized games on the lawn once a week, but the children of the *basse-cour* and the neighboring villages didn't need that anymore, not as they had. They were playing on their own now, playing like children again, and it filled Emmie's heart with joy, but also made her feel decidedly out of it.

But the store had been an unmitigated disaster. Maud, it seemed, had had a talent for convincing people that what the store had was what they wanted. The wrong sort of *sabots*? But these *sabots* were so much better. And she would sell whatever it was and go away with an empty truck and the people would walk away feeling as though they'd got a bargain.

Emmie, on the other hand, would apologize profusely, take copious notes about the right thing (often entirely contradictory), and then give them the offending item as a gift to make up for it. By the end of the first week, the store was deep in arrears and running days behind schedule. They were supposed to have been to Courcelles by then, but Emmie had made it to only eight villages in five days, not the eighteen they were scheduled to serve.

"We need you on the Christmas party committee," Alice had told her, but what it really meant was that they wanted her away from the store.

So Ethel Ledbetter had taken over the store, and Emmie had been sent down to the cellars to sort out Christmas presents for the women and children: a new suit of clothes, candy, and a toy for each child, and a practical present and candy for every adult.

It would all be fine, Emmie told herself as she stood in the freezing cellar, digging through boxes, checking her lists and matching up gifts with names, if only they had their trucks again. Then she could do what she was really here to do: social service work with the outlying villages. But the White truck was still in Paris, waiting for a hard rim to be put on, a simple job that was meant to take a week and seemed to be taking a month. The Ford truck had given up the ghost and was in Noyon for parts. Only the jitney still worked, and that sporadically, when coaxed.

The *sous-préfet* at Nesle, feeling sorry for them,

had loaned them a horse and cart, but Tambour, the horse, had been around since roughly the days of Miss Ledbetter's beloved Merovingians and deeply resented being asked to cart around muscular Americans. It took two of them to move him, one to drive and one to poke him with a stick. He moved at a rate of two miles an hour, when he deigned to move at all.

Kate, undaunted, had worked out a schedule, allocating use of the jitney and Tambour between the store, the doctors, and the social service department, with trips doubled up whenever possible, even though the doctors complained about riding with the store, with the rakes and hoes poking them in the posterior, and Miss Ledbetter complained that all those passengers were taking up room needed for goods.

"What about Courcelles?" Emmie had asked that morning, coming up to Kate after the others had gone, grumbling, on their way. "You don't have Courcelles on the schedule."

"Yes, I do," said Kate, looking harried. A giant shipment had just arrived from the Red Cross, everything from rice to mattresses to women's winter coats, and needed to be signed for and sorted. "It's there for the week after next."

"But—that's not for ages." Emmie stared at Kate in dismay, wondering if this was because of their fight, if Kate would have found a way if they hadn't argued. Which was silly, she knew. Kate wouldn't be so petty. At least, she didn't think Kate would be so petty. Then, she also hadn't thought Kate would mind so terribly about having her board paid.

"I can't conjure trucks out of thin air, Emmie." Kate had always been slight, but since her bout of fever she looked like an ivory carving, all thin lines and hollows, burning up from within. As if trying to make up for it, she added, "There's an English Ford for sale in Amiens. I'm going to try to get it for us."

"How long will that take?"

Kate grimaced. "How long does anything take here? I'll do my best."

"I know you're doing all you can." Emmie hurried away before either of them could say anything more, anything they might regret.

It had been like that ever since Thanksgiving: there were days when they would seem almost normal again, if somewhat wary of each other, and then Emmie would say something, something entirely innocuous, and Kate would close up, and they'd be back to the beginning again, with Emmie in the wrong and still not entirely sure why.

Kate wasn't the only one being paid for by someone else. Maud was funding Liza; Nell Baldwin's bills were paid by an aunt. It didn't make them any less members of the Unit. But when Emmie had tried to point that out to Kate, Kate would only say it wasn't the same.

She was so *good* at all this, Kate. Emmie just wished she could make her see it, how much she was needed, how much she was valued, what a very good thing it was she was here, no matter how she'd got here.

Emmie only wished she could be half as useful.

On her way to the cellar, Emmie passed Dave, the Red Cross driver—disastrous Dave, Nell called him, or Dave-in-the-Ditch, for his habit of crashing his truck against their gates—finishing unloading the last of the bags of rice. And that was when she had her grand idea.

"Do you think you could give me a lift to Courcelles?" she asked. "I need to do my rounds and we haven't any cars."

She paused only long enough to stuff a few supplies in her haversack and scribble a note for Kate.

Gone to Courcelles with Red Cross Dave. Back by supper.

It was heaven getting away from Grécourt, away from the cold water dripping down the cellar walls, the stench of the animals in their little farm. The sky was an opaque gray that signaled snow, but it wasn't snowing yet and the clear, crisp air felt glorious against Emmie's cheeks after weeks of rain. The ruined houses and barbed wire had become just part of the landscape now; she was used to them. Army camions rumbled past them on the road, taking a convoy of French soldiers to the front. They waved their caps at her and Emmie waved back.

"Mademoiselle Aimée! Mademoiselle Aimée!" The children had come running out before the truck even stopped in Courcelles, in what had once been the village square before the Germans had got to it. Little hands waved up at her, grabbing at her hands, her skirt. Emmie sank down into the fray, delighted.

Miss Ledbetter, much more efficient than Emmie, had made it to Courcelles once a week with the store, but when asked if Pauline had had her baby yet or if little Leon's cough was better, Miss Ledbetter waxed poetic about the Merovingians and went off on tangents about the Crusades.

But here she was herself, with Leon's mittened hand—she'd brought the mittens last month, donated by members of the Chicago Smith Club—in hers, tugging her to see the new school building, which now had benches and five books, five whole books, and wouldn't she like to see them?

Why, yes. Yes, she would. And she needed to see Blondine's missing tooth, proudly displayed with a hideous pulling back of gums, and the new mattresses that had been delivered by the Red Cross man, the one who didn't speak any French.

"Wait, wait," said Emmie, laughing, as her arm was half tugged off in one direction by a six-year-old, her skirt pulled by a toddler. "I've treats for you all. Let me just get to my haversack."

Monsieur le Commandant had slipped them seven hundred francs for *bêtises*, as he called it. Get yourself some scented soap, he'd said, some fresh hair ribbons. So Emmie and Nell had gone to Amiens and indulged in an orgy of shopping: picture books for the lending library, whatever chocolates could be had, dolls and tops and hobby horses.

"This one is for you." Emmie dug in her haversack and produced a doll, a real doll with a porcelain head, for Blondine. "Mind you don't let your little brother get at it."

It was such joy to make her rounds and see everyone—well, not well settled, but better settled. There was canvas stretched over gaps in the masonry; new mattresses donated by the Red Cross and distributed by the Unit; little potbellied stoves replacing open fires. It was cold, bitter cold, but the children all had warm coats and mittens and mufflers, admittedly a somewhat motley collection, knitted by eager if not always expert alumnae, but warm, all warm.

The milk had been delivered, Emmie was assured. The new storekeeper—she liked her history, eh? They'd made up stories for her and sent her away satisfied.

What made up? contested Blondine's grandmother from her habitual mattress. It was all true.

Pauline, whose baby still hadn't come, rolled her eyes at Emmie.

Emmie promised Pauline she'd see the doctors visited within the week, not that there should be any trouble, this was Pauline's sixth, but all the same.

Family by family, Emmie made her rounds, checking off names, taking notes, making lists of items still needed.

She saved Mme Lepinasse for the very last. Although the older woman was a gregarious soul, she lived away from the rest, up the hill in the ruins of the castle. She'd started as scullery maid and risen to cook in the castle; she'd lived there most of her life and she'd not be leaving it now, she'd told Emmie, when Emmie had urged her to move down to the valley, to live with her cousins in the village. She had her cat for company and her memories, and that was enough.

It was starting to snow as Emmie trekked up the steep path to the castle, thick, beautiful flakes like something out of a Hans Christian Andersen story.

Her haversack was lighter now, most of her gifts

distributed, save for a packet of tea and some precious DeWitt's biscuits for Mme Lepinasse, who did so love to put the kettle on and have a good gossip, telling stories of the glory days of the castle, of Count Sigismund, who sounded like a lovable old autocrat, and his daughter, Aurélie, filching food from the German invaders to feed the village, like a French Robin Hood.

Mme Lepinasse never spoke of the deformed fingers of her left hand, broken, one by one, when the Germans had questioned her about the whereabouts of Aurélie de Courcelles, who had escaped during the great fire that consumed the castle. Or of the husband who had been shot by the Germans in retaliation. It was only the happy stories she told.

"Madame?" Emmie was out of breath by the time she reached the summit. This was why no one from the village ever visited. The hill was steep, the path treacherous, the road that had led from village to castle purposefully destroyed by the Germans.

The castle was beautiful from below, less so at close range. Even two years on, one could smell the soot from the fire that had consumed a thousand years of history in one go. Mme Lepinasse lived in what had once been a guard room, a stone box with narrow windows, which had the benefit of retaining most of its roof, a luxury most of the houses in the village didn't boast.

Madame's cat met Emmie at the canvas flap that served as a door, bumping the backs of her legs to push her inside. The stove was cold; the room was freezing. Usually, the stove would be crackling, a rushlight lit, Mme Lepinasse sitting in her chair sewing. As her eyes adjusted to the gloom, Emmie finally spotted her on her mattress in the corner of the room, huddled under a blanket.

"Mme Lepinasse!" Emmie rushed to her side, grasping her cold hand.

Mme Lepinasse tried to sit up, which was a mistake. She fell back against the pillows, coughing and coughing, a cough that shook her whole frame.

"Hush, hush, don't trouble yourself, here, let me get you some water. I'll make you a cup of tea, you'll feel better after a cup of tea. . . ." Emmie tried to pretend she hadn't heard the dreadful rattle in Mme Lepinasse's throat, the rattle that meant pneumonia.

How long had she been sick, how long had she been here like this? A day? A week? Had Ethel even known to come up this way? Probably not. It was Emmie's own fault. She ought to have told her. She ought to have been here herself.

"Don't worry, I'll have you warm and comfortable in no time." Murmuring useless nothings, Emmie tucked the blanket around the other woman and poked at the stove, which had gone out entirely. There was an old-fashioned flint sitting next to the stove. Emmie hadn't the faintest idea how to use it.

With a surge of relief, Emmie remembered the matches in her haversack. Emmie made a fire as Mrs. Rutherford had taught them, sticks layered, little spills of paper to catch the flames, struck a match, and set it alight.

The kettle was bone-dry. So was the ewer. There was no water in the house. After checking on her patient, who called her Aurélie and grabbed at her hand, Emmie extracted herself and found the castle well. The Germans hadn't bothered to poison it; it was too far away from the village. She held a cup of water to Mme Lepinasse's lips, got her to drink a few sips, wiped away the spill.

By the time she had made the tea, in the broken Limoges teapot Mme Lepinasse had salvaged from the wreckage, Mme Lepinasse had lapsed into unconsciousness, her chest rising and falling with difficulty, her breath still showing in the air. Emmie stoked the stove, throwing in whatever she could find.

The snow fell harder and harder, drifting through the makeshift doorway. Emmie tried to pin the canvas down with a stone, but the wind howled through the edges. On her thin mattress, Mme Lepinasse stirred and whimpered, calling for Vincent, for Aurélie.

"I'm here, I'm here," Emmie told her, kneeling by the cot, and Mme Lepinasse seemed comforted, at least a little. Emmie stayed by her, frozen in place. She tried to pray, bits and pieces floating through her head. *Yea, though I walk through the valley of the shadow of death . . .* It was dreadfully shadowy here. *He maketh me to lie beside green pastures.* There had been green pastures here once. It was horrible to think what had been done, all the waste of it, so much lost, and why? She couldn't even remember why anymore, only that here was a woman who had once had a home, a family, and lived now in a ruin with only a cat and a stranger to hold her hand, to sit by her in the valley of death.

Emmie didn't know what time it was or how long she had been there. There was no way to measure time in that little room, with the old wooden shutters barred, the canvas pinned down, the only light the feeble glare of the stove.

"Mme Lepinasse?" Emmie whispered, but the only sound was the stove, and the hand in hers had gone limp. "Madame, wake up, it's me, *la dame Américaine.*"

She wasn't going to wake up, not ever, and Emmie knew it, had known it as soon as she had walked through that door and seen her lying there in that icebox of a room, forgotten, abandoned.

Emmie lowered her face to the dead woman's hand

and cried hopeless tears as the cat licked the salt from her cheeks.

Why hadn't she thought to ask Dave before? Why hadn't she taken Tambour? Why hadn't she done *something*?

"I'm so sorry," she apologized, but the other woman didn't answer, couldn't answer. She had survived the Germans, had survived torture, and succumbed to winter, to a cough. "If I had been here . . ."

If she had been here, she could have—what would she have done? Tried to shore up Mme Lepinasse's poor little hut to keep the heat in better. Boiled up one of those blasted roosters to make her soup. Done *something*. Never mind that they lost more people to pneumonia than anything else. They shouldn't. That was what they were there for.

It was winter, it was cold; it had been Emmie's responsibility to look in on Mme Lepinasse, to look after her. It had all seemed so reasonable at the time; they hadn't the trucks, everyone was taking turns. But in the meantime, Mme Lepinasse had been here, alone, sick.

Outside, the sky had darkened from silver to charcoal. Dusk. Emmie's limbs felt stiff; she struggled through the snowdrifts down the hill, slipping and sliding, her skirt dragging at her legs, bumping into fallen stones obscured by the snow, too cold and numb to feel the pain, although she knew she'd have a nice set of bruises later.

The mayor received her with surprise, a baby on one hip and a toddler holding on to her skirt, in the half-destroyed stable she called home. Yes, they would see to the funeral arrangements when they could, but the snow—and it was dark already—and the way up to the castle treacherous. . . .

"Can't anything be done for her?"

If it were summer . . . The mayor shrugged. In the cold, she would keep.

And Mme Lepinasse hadn't been of the village. She had risked her life during the occupation to help smuggle food to the village, but she wasn't one of their own, not really.

The mayor had children of her own; of course she wasn't going up to the castle in the dead of night. And who else would go? Emmie knew the census of Courcelles by heart. The elderly, the infirm, children.

"Someone needs to feed her cat," said Emmie helplessly, knowing that no one was going up there after a cat, not now. It was full dark and still snowing, light, indifferent flurries that didn't care whether they fell on the living or the dead.

A broad swath of light suddenly swept the square.

Emmie turned and squinted into the glare, which resolved itself into a Ford jitney, which groaned and rumbled its way through the snow, stopping in front of what had once been the town hall.

A small, well-wrapped figure swung down from the truck.

"There you are," said Kate with relief. "We found your note when you didn't come in for supper. What were you thinking, Emmie?"

"Kate." Emmie clutched her friend's gloved hand. "We need to bury Mme Lepinasse."

"Madame—"

"Lepinasse. She's all alone up in the castle and she—she was sick and alone and I thought with a little warmth and hot tea—but she's dead, Kate. She's dead and we can't just leave her there. Do you have a shovel?"

Chapter Seventeen

We've had our first taste of real winter weather
here—and I don't mean just the water freezing in
our pails. We're used to that by now. We had our
first snow this week and it took us all by surprise.
The inhabitants say they've never known it to
start so early and they hadn't thought they'd see
us again until spring. But nothing stops these
women from their appointed rounds. Nell
Baldwin staggered off to Esmery-Hallon and
came back just before supper looking like a
walking icicle. Our assistant director had to take
our one working truck and go off after the Van
Alden girl, who had, it appeared, spent all day in
a miserable hut to make a dying woman as
comfortable as possible (pneumonia, in case you

were wondering—we have a great deal of
pneumonia here).

    As for yours truly, this morning, Dr. Pruyn and
I arose at five thirty and started for Hombleux
with the horse and cart (I use the term horse
broadly) lent us by the sous-préfet. We got a little
more than halfway and found the snow in such
drifts that we had to abandon the cart entirely and
walk the beast the rest of the way to Hombleux. I
think it expected us to carry it, but we were
already carrying half a medicine chest on our
backs and had to decline.

    If the snow keeps up, we are going to be in a
very bad way indeed. Our villages cover such a
large territory. . . .

> *— Dr. Ava Stringfellow, '96, to*
> *her husband, Dr. Lawrence*
> *Stringfellow*

December 1917
Grécourt, France

"Emmie." Sick with relief at finding her, Kate grabbed Emmie before she could go haring off for a shovel. "We can't just bury this—whoever it is. She'll need the last rites. We'll tell the commandant.

He'll send a priest. When the snow lets up," she added with a grimace at the road, which wasn't much of a road at the moment.

Emmie looked down at Kate with stricken eyes, making it impossible to be upset with her. "But we can't just leave her! Her cat will eat her."

Kate wasn't quite sure cats ate people like that, but she knew that once Emmie got an idea in her head, there was no budging it. "Which one is the mayor?" she asked resignedly.

The mayor, unfortunately, was no more excited than Kate by the idea of hiking up the snow-covered hill to fetch a body. Also, Kate was interfering with her children's bedtime and letting the cold air in.

Five minutes later, Kate returned to Emmie with the best compromise she could broker. "She says the Germans used the old bathhouse as a morgue. If we get Mme Lepinasse down, we can put her there."

And that was how Kate found herself, in the dark, the ruins of a medieval castle looming over her, carrying a body down a hill, with Mme Lepinasse's cat hissing and spitting irritably from the depths of Emmie's haversack. She was also liberally coated with snow from having fallen while carrying said corpse.

"I f-feel like Victor Frankenstein," commented Emmie, her teeth chattering uncontrollably.

"Remind me not to consider a career in body snatching," panted Kate as Emmie edged backward ahead of her, holding the corpse's feet while Kate grasped the body awkwardly beneath the arms, the head bumping disconcertingly against her chest.

"Do you think we've become hard?" Emmie asked anxiously.

They were carrying a woman's body down a snow-covered slope in pitch darkness so her cat wouldn't eat her. The idea of Emmie becoming hard would have made Kate laugh if she'd had the energy to laugh. "No. Can we keep moving, please? I can't feel my feet."

Finally, finally, Mme Lepinasse was safely stowed in the makeshift morgue and her cat with the mayor, whose toddler had been delighted and immediately tried to pull its tail.

Emmie looked anxiously over her shoulder as she climbed into the jitney. "D-do you think we should try to go straight to Amiens to get them to s-send a p-priest?"

"Wrap yourself up in that lap rug," ordered Kate as she vigorously turned the crank, her breath steaming in the cold air. "And no. No one will come tonight. We'd best get back to Grécourt and send word in the morning. If the roads are clear enough."

They weren't clear now. The lamps of the jitney

glinted off an entirely unrecognizable landscape, softened by snow, the barbed wire and broken buildings all turned into something pure and lovely.

"It looks like gingerbread," said Emmie dreamily. In the light of the car lamps, her lips were a distinct blue. Kate could practically see the veins through her skin. "A gingerbread world, all frosted with sugar."

"When's the last time you ate?" Kate asked.

"Breakfast?" Emmie stirred a little, pulling herself upright. "I guess that would explain why I've been feeling so light-headed."

"Yes," said Kate resignedly. "Yes, it would."

This was the problem of trying to be angry with Emmie. One just couldn't, not for extended periods of time. Emmie was so busy giving and giving and giving that she never thought to care for herself, so that, inevitably, someone—that someone being Kate—had to step in and do it for her, and you just couldn't stay angry at someone who didn't even remember to eat.

Emmie fingered her haversack. "I've some DeWitt's in my satchel. I brought them for Mme Lepinasse."

And that was just like Emmie too. She'd set the biscuits on the woman's grave as funeral offerings rather than eat them herself. As gently as she could, Kate said, "I'm sure she wouldn't begrudge them to you."

"No, she wouldn't—she liked feeding people. She'd

been a cook, you know. Up at the castle. And then, during the war—she helped feed the village." Emmie clutched her haversack with both hands. "She wasn't even that old. About the same age as my mother. In her fifties, maybe. I keep thinking, if only I had come sooner . . ."

Kate felt a brief stab of guilt. She'd made out the rota for truck use as fairly as she could. And Courcelles was so far, on the outer edges of their rounds. It used up so much *essence* and *essence* was in such short supply. "You weren't to know."

"But I should have known. If I had been doing my job . . ." Emmie squirmed on the bench seat. "She had no one, Kate. Just us."

More sharply than she intended, Kate said, "There are two thousand people here who need us. Many of them have no one. You can't let yourself get too attached."

"Too attached?" Emmie stared at her in horror. "They're *people*, Kate."

"So are we." Kate's shoulders tensed as the jitney wobbled in the deep tracks left by some larger, heavier vehicle. She had never been so aware of her own frailty, her own limitations. Just flesh and blood and force of will. "We're only people, Emmie. We can't be in fifty places at once."

"If we changed the schedule—" Emmie began.

"How?" They'd come to a crossroads. Kate swung the truck east, toward Grécourt. "There are only fifteen of us—thirteen now, with Maud and Liza in Paris. I wish we could do more. I wish we had trucks that worked, Emmie, and people to drive them, but there's only so much we can do with what we have."

"What if I learned how to drive? If we had another driver—"

The thought of Emmie at the wheel was so horrifying that Kate turned her head for a moment to look at Emmie. A mistake. Ahead of them on the road, a dark shape loomed up, large as a woolly mammoth. Breathing in sharply, thinking all the words her mother had told her never to say, Kate braked hard, feeling a sickening lurch as the truck swayed and spun.

For a moment, she thought she could feel Nick Penniston's hands on her shoulders, hear his confident voice saying, "If you lose control of the machine, drive into the spin."

Blindly, Kate turned the wheel in the direction of the skid, feeling the truck finally, mercifully, stop, just short of a snow-covered hedge.

She sat there, breathing hard, a cold sweat prickling beneath the linen and wool of her uniform.

"Well," said Emmie weakly, picking herself gingerly up from the floor of the truck. She rolled one shoulder, wincing. "If that's how you feel about my driving . . ."

Kate pointed a shaking finger. "That's how I feel about *their* driving." Blocking the road was an overturned army camion. A slow anger churned in her stomach. "The idiots. They could have at least pushed it to the side of the road. If we'd hit that—"

"But we didn't." Emmie bumped her shoulder against Kate's in a quick gesture of affection, and Kate felt her chest tighten, because it was so like Emmie, always these fleeting touches, as if she were afraid she'd be pushed away. "Thank goodness you're such a smashing driver."

"I'm trying not to smash, thank you very much." Kate drew in a deep, cleansing breath, feeling the cold scouring the back of her throat. She'd have had no idea what to do but for Nick—had Nick taught her that? She didn't remember it. Her memory was of endless sunshine along Bellevue Avenue. But he must have. Otherwise how would she have known? "Nick Penniston showed me what to do."

"Well, thank goodness for Nick, then," said Emmie with feeling, and Kate tried not to glance around her shoulder for the shade of a man in goggles and scarf.

The dark and cold were making her fanciful. "How can we get around them?"

"We can't." Forcing herself to focus, Kate took a deep breath, flexed her shoulders, and readjusted her grip on the wheel. "I'm going to back up until we can turn. We'll have to find another way. Get that map out, will you?"

Very, very carefully they backed up, retracing their own tire tracks. But the snow had knocked down rotten signposts, and those that were still standing were so blurred they were hardly legible. They backed up and turned and turned again, burning match after match from Emmie's haversack trying to read the tiny print on the map.

"Cookie?" offered Emmie as they came to yet another illegible signpost.

Kate shook her head. "We'd best ration them. We might need them later." If the cold didn't kill them first. "I haven't the faintest idea where we are."

Emmie peered at the sky, which still had that overcast aura, as though it were contemplating snowing again. "Could we navigate by the stars?"

"Like Vasco da Gama?" Kate didn't know whether to laugh or cry.

Emmie contemplated. "I think he used an astrolabe."

"Yes, well, we don't have one of those either," said

Kate. They had two choices, both unpalatable. They could go on, and risk going the wrong way, getting farther and farther from Grécourt, possibly even blundering into hostilities. Or they could stop for the night. "I'd say we should stop for the night and reconnoiter in the morning, but if we do, we might freeze."

"I'm in favor of not freezing," said Emmie. With the echo of her old optimism, she added, "Surely we'll find *someone* sooner or later."

So they went on, on roads eerie in their emptiness. Usually, the night was the safest time for troops to travel; the roads were generally thick with army camions, with French or English troops on the move, supply trucks, ambulance drivers going back and forth from the front, the air lit by the flashing lights of airplanes overhead. But tonight, with the storm, the roads were abandoned, unrecognizable. Even the planes weren't flying.

Kate began to go from annoyed to afraid, genuinely afraid, afraid that their petrol would run out, afraid that they wouldn't find shelter before the cold claimed them. She drove on, grimly, wondering how long it would be before they would have to stop and rinse their feet in snow water to ward off frostbite. Her toes were dangerously numb.

Emmie was buried so deep in her muffler that Kate could hardly see her. In a very small voice, she said, "Thank you for coming to get me."

"I was hardly going to leave you roaming a war zone." It sounded so grudging put that way. Kate tried again. "You know I wouldn't leave you there."

"You've been so upset—" Emmie's voice changed; she jerked upright. "Kate! Kate! Over there! To the left—I mean, the right—do you see the light? Is that—"

"It's a house." Kate felt light-headed with relief. "A house! And an army camion in front of it—no, two camions. Maybe they can tell us where we are."

Emmie was already straightening up, adjusting her coat, fussing with her mittens. "I was afraid we were going to run out of *essence*," she admitted. "And freeze."

"I'm sure it wouldn't come to that," said Kate, even though she had been thinking the exact same thing. She spotted a man detaching himself from the side of one of the camions, a cigarette tip glowing red in the darkness. "Look, there's a soldier guarding the camions. We can ask him where we are."

The soldier pitched his cigarette to the ground, grinding out the stub. *"Qui va là?"*

"*Les dames Américaines,*" said Emmie eagerly, half falling out of the truck. "Sorry, we're a bit frozen. We've lost our way. We're trying to get back to Grécourt, but we haven't the faintest idea where we are."

The soldier looked at the jitney and then back at them. "All by yourselves?"

There was something about the way he said it that Kate didn't quite like. "If you could just show us on the map," she said coolly, "we'll be on our way."

He could do better than that, the soldier said, suddenly very helpful. He could escort them as far as Ham, if they were willing to wait an hour. He and his comrades in arms were just having a bit of supper. Would *les dames Américaines*—he essayed an exaggerated bow—care to share their repast?

"Oh, yes, please!" exclaimed Emmie, before Kate could decline on their behalf. "How kind of you. Isn't it terribly kind?"

"Ye-es," said Kate, wondering if the cold had just addled her brain. Here they were, looking for shelter, and they'd found it. But there was something making her uneasy. "I'm not sure, though—"

Emmie jostled her with her elbow. "Food! And heat! My fingers are icicles. Either that or my icicles are fingers. I can't tell which."

"Welcome," said the soldier, throwing open the door

and speaking in rapid French to the people inside. Kate caught the words *women* and *alone*.

"Oh, lovely!" said Emmie, and plunged inside, Kate following more slowly.

After the outdoors, the room was smotheringly hot, the air shimmering with steam coming off an iron range, a pot bubbling on the top. Some seven or eight French *poilus* were sitting around a table in their shirtsleeves and braces, being served bowls of soup and thick slices of black bread by a woman who seemed to have forgotten to do up all the ties of her blouse. Another woman sat on the lap of a soldier, removing herself, none too speedily, as they came inside.

Behind them, the door slammed shut. Kate turned, frowning, and the guard made little swooshing gestures, urging them forward. He was grinning in a way she didn't at all like, showing teeth stained by cigarettes.

"Goodness, it's lovely and warm in here!" exclaimed Emmie, happily oblivious, as the woman at the stove surreptitiously did up a button. "I can't tell you how grateful we are to have found you."

Seven men stared at her. One of them, with black hair slicked back and his sleeves rolled to the elbows, pushed back his chair and stood. "But who are you?" He looked to the guard. "Pierre?"

Pierre shrugged. "They just drove up. In a truck."

One of the men gave a guttural chuckle. "One doesn't look at the bridle of a gift horse."

"No, just the legs," retorted another, and they stared at Kate and Emmie in a way that made Kate put her hands on her collar, even though it was already buttoned as high as it would go. Emmie, whose French wasn't nearly as colloquial, smiled uncertainly at them, aware that there was a joke, but not sure what it was.

Kate didn't at all like the way the men were smiling. "We," she said crisply, "are with the American Red Cross."

These men might not have heard of the Smith Unit, but everyone knew the Red Cross. And Americans.

"Red Cross, eh?" The men all exchanged glances. The leader, the one with the black hair, smiled back at them, showing too many teeth. "We love the Red Cross."

"We do what we can," said Emmie, pleased. "We're so happy to be here to help."

"Oh, I have some ideas for how you can help," called out one of the men.

"Really? We're always looking for ways to improve our services," said Emmie gamely, and looked confused when that raised a great laugh.

Kate edged closer to her. "Emmie, I don't think—"

But Emmie was resolved to be pleasant. "We can't tell you how much we appreciate your hospitality." Kate could see her determinedly ignoring their discarded jackets and the fact that they made no effort to put them back on. "What regiment are you with?"

There was a sudden, charged silence. The woman at the stove concentrated hard on her soup pot.

"Oh, you wouldn't have heard," said the black-haired man smoothly.

"I told them," said the guard standing behind Kate, "that we can take them as far as Ham. After we have our supper."

"Ah, yes. After supper." The black-haired man banged the table. "Two more bowls of soup! Come, sit, eat."

"No, thank you," said Kate, grabbing Emmie's sleeve to keep her from going to the table. There was something about the way the man had said "after supper" that raised her hackles. She thought, without being sure why, of Julia, and the man who just wanted to share his notes. Until he didn't. "We just need someone to show us where we are on the map. And then we'll be on our way."

"But Kate . . . there's *soup*." Emmie had eyes only for the tureen. "Besides, it would be so rude to say no now that they've invited us. And I've only just started to feel my toes. It's already so late, surely another hour won't make any difference."

The serving woman slammed two bowls down on the table, slopping soup over the sides.

Kate didn't like the way the men were looking at them; she didn't like the way the guard was standing between them and the door. "I don't think we should stay, Emmie."

"Why are you standing there?" The black-haired man came around the table. Sizing them up, he slung an arm companionably around Emmie's shoulders. "Come, sit, take off your coat."

"Er, um, thank you," Emmie said breathlessly as the man's hands went to the buttons of her coat. "That's very kind of you."

"Oh, we are all very kind," said the man, showing too many teeth, as he propelled Emmie toward the table.

Emmie grimaced at Kate over her shoulder, more bemused than alarmed. Kate felt frozen, terrified and helpless.

Pausing, one hand on Emmie's shoulder, the black-haired man said quietly to the serving woman, "The room upstairs, it is free, yes?"

Kate's paralysis broke. She grabbed Emmie's hand, pulling hard. "Emmie, we're going *now*."

The man grabbed Emmie's shoulder, equally hard. "Oh, no," he said, and he wasn't smiling anymore. "I think she stays."

Kate didn't waste any more time. She hit him, right in the nose, with the full force of her five foot one inches and one hundred and two pounds.

She did it the way her stepfather had taught her: striking up with the flat of her palm. Her hand hit his nose with a sickening crunch, sending him reeling backward into the table, men yelping, chairs toppling, soup and bread crashing down. Blood spurted through the man's fingers as he sprawled on the table.

He stared at it with disbelief, and then he lifted his head and Kate saw murder in his eyes.

"Quick!" Grabbing Emmie by the hand, Kate ran for the kitchen door, not looking back, ignoring the angry cries behind them, her fingers fumbling on the door handle, knowing every second counted, every second gave them a chance.

Kate was never quite sure how after, but somehow she got Emmie through that door and into the jitney, turning and turning the crank with all her might, praying it wouldn't break down, praying the men wouldn't catch them before they could start, knowing that she'd be no use against all of them. Any one of them could break her arm with one hand tied behind his back. She wished she had a gun like Maud, a knife like Julia, anything.

"Go, go, go," Kate muttered to the jitney, and nearly sobbed with relief when the engine caught. Every instinct screamed speed, but she forced herself to go carefully; if the truck broke down, they'd have no escape and the retaliation would be dreadful.

Light arced across the snow as the kitchen door swung open. The motor hiccupped and Kate nearly cried, but then it caught again, the truck jerking backward, out of the clearing, as the man in the doorway shouted curses, his shirt stained with blood and soup.

Kate swung the truck. The road was dreadful, rutted and icy, but she clung grimly to the wheel and kept going, away, away, just away. She had no idea where they were; the only important thing was to put as much distance as possible between them and those men.

"But—what—" Emmie was twisting back, staring over her shoulder. "You hit him."

"Not nearly hard enough." The full realization of what had almost happened swept over her. A room upstairs—be kind—alone—

Emmie's voice seemed to come from very far away. "Do you think—do you think we ought to pay for the damage?"

The truck bounced over a pothole. Kate was shaking so hard she could barely hold the wheel. "The what?"

Emmie was twisting and twisting her fingers. She was missing her gloves, Kate noticed, probably dropped in their flight. "The damage. To that inn."

"Pay for the damage?" Kate knew she sounded hysterical. She couldn't help it.

"Well, yes," said Emmie, sounding mildly bewildered, and Kate nearly ran the truck into a ditch. "We did make rather a mess."

Through determined effort, Kate wrenched the car back onto the road, managing not to kill either of them. "You do realize what they meant to do, don't you?"

"Give us soup and take us to Ham?" said Emmie wistfully.

"Do you really believe that?" Kate wasn't sure whether Emmie was being willfully obtuse or whether she was really that naive. Or maybe it was just that Kate had gone mad. But she didn't think so. She remembered the way that man had looked. She remembered Julia. "They were never going to take us to Ham. Didn't you hear that man asking about a room? They were going to take us upstairs. He was unbuttoning your coat."

"It was warm in there," said Emmie, but she didn't sound entirely certain. "I think he was just trying to be . . . helpful."

"Helpful?" Kate's voice went up. "They meant to rape us, Emmie!"

It felt very strange to say it.

There was a moment of silence as the trunk bumped along. And then Emmie said, "You mean like the Sabine women."

As if rape were something that happened only in ancient Rome. Kate found it entirely infuriating. "Like all those women with Boche babies. How do you think that happened? It certainly wasn't out of pure and lasting affection."

"But those were Germans," said Emmie, as if that made all the difference. "These were Frenchmen. They're our allies."

"They're men," said Kate, thinking of Julia and that doctor. He was meant to be her colleague, and look how he'd behaved. "I'm pretty sure these were deserters. Didn't you see how they looked when you asked after their regiment? They were men with nothing left to lose. And we're women, alone, in a war zone, in the middle of the night."

"But—" She could see Emmie struggling with it, fighting it, and wanted to shake her. "Everyone's been so helpful."

"Yes! To the Smith Unit! But tonight we weren't the Smith Unit; we were just two women alone—you can't just assume that every man you meet is going to help you."

But Emmie did assume that. In Emmie's world, everyone was there to help. And why wouldn't they? She was Emmie Van Alden. Doors magically opened for her and courtiers threw down their cloaks in the mud. It was like being Queen of England without the responsibilities.

The engine gave a strange hiccup, but Kate barely noticed. She was too busy being upset. "We should never have been there in the first place! But no, you had to up and go to Courcelles by yourself in the middle of a snowstorm!"

Emmie curled herself into a pretzel on the bench. "It wasn't snowing when I left."

It wasn't snowing. That was all she had to say?

They were in a war zone in the middle of the night. She had no idea where they were or how much *essence* they had left, and somewhere was a group of French deserters—Kate was reasonably sure they were deserters—who wanted them dead. And all Emmie could say was that she hadn't known it would snow.

"Do you ever think of anyone but yourself?" Kate demanded. "I *told* you we'd have a new truck soon—"

She broke off as the engine made a strange sputtering sound and then went alarmingly quiet. Kate managed to turn the wheel, steering the truck to the side of the road, before the jitney stalled out entirely.

Emmie's voice was full of trepidation. "What happened?"

"We're out of *essence*." There ought to have been another can in the truck, but there wasn't, because she hadn't bothered to check before she went running off after Emmie, convinced Emmie was lying dead in a ditch somewhere between Grécourt and Courcelles. "We could try to walk, but I have no idea where we are. We're going to have to camp here until morning."

Here being the side of a road, which could, in the snow, be just about anywhere. They were surrounded by barbed wire, stunted trees, and the ruined remains of houses, which could have been anywhere between the Somme and Switzerland. With the headlamps of the jitney dead, it was pitch-black, the true darkness of the more horrifying sort of fairy tale. And it was cold, bitter, wretched cold.

In the darkness, Kate heard Emmie fumbling with her haversack. A hand emerged right in front of Kate's face and a small voice said, "Biscuit?"

Kate thought about saying no, on principle, but she was hungry. Without a word, she took the biscuit from Emmie.

They crunched in silence for a moment, and then

Emmie said, "I am sorry." When Kate didn't answer, she went on, stumbling over her words, "I meant to leave Courcelles by two at the latest, but then Mme Lepinasse was so ill, and I couldn't leave her—"

"So, really, it's not your fault at all," said Kate, knowing she was being unfair, but unable to help herself, because she was cold and scared and really not at all looking forward to freezing to death. "Nothing is ever your fault. It's always Saint Emmaline off to save the world, and never mind who gets hurt along the way, because you always *mean* well."

"But—I don't know what else I could have done," said Emmie helplessly.

"You could have not been there! We should never have taken Courcelles in the first place—but that was another one of your impulses. You had to have Courcelles, and then poor Margaret had a nervous breakdown."

Admittedly, Margaret would probably have had a nervous breakdown anyway, but Kate was in no mood to be reasonable. Being reasonable didn't seem to have gotten her anywhere. She had tried to be reasonable, but Emmie had gone running off on her own, and here they were.

"And never mind that we have a schedule—a schedule designed to keep everything running properly and everyone safe—you have to go running off to the edge of beyond!"

She could feel Emmie stiffening on the bench next to her. "There was nothing for me to do at Grécourt. . . ."

"There's always something to do! There were parcels to sort and children to teach and letters to write—you could have found something. You could have helped Florence with the animals or Nell with sorting books. You just didn't want to because it's so much more fun playing Lady Bountiful among the peasantry!"

Kate hadn't meant to say it. She hadn't even known she was thinking it. But there it was. The words hung in the cold air, ugly, between them.

"I'm not—I don't—" In a very small voice, Emmie said, "I was just trying to help."

"I know." Kate could feel the cold seeping into her bones, the cold and the weariness. She should have felt vindicated, but instead she just felt drained. Because Emmie *was* trying to help. "You can't just do whatever you want whenever you want to. You've been so sheltered—you have no idea what's out there."

"Like those men tonight?" There was a moment of silence, and then Emmie asked, "Do you really think they meant to force themselves on us?"

"Yes." And if they were deserters, possibly also kill them, but Emmie sounded upset enough that Kate decided not to mention that. "Emmie—I know you didn't know."

"But that's no excuse, is it?" Emmie sounded frantic. "You're right. I got us both into this. I made you come here. If you hadn't hit that man—"

"Thank my stepfather for that. He taught me. I never thought I'd use it, though." Next to her on the bench, Kate could feel Emmie shivering, and not just from cold. Feeling thoroughly chastened, Kate scooted a little closer, until they were side to side. "We'll get out of this, Emmie. We will."

They sat in the dark, huddled together for warmth, listening to the tree branches crackle in the wind.

"Do you know what time it is?" asked Emmie.

They used one of Emmie's precious matches to check the watch pinned to Kate's jacket.

"Nine thirty," said Kate, wanting to cry. She'd thought it was well past midnight. It would only get colder throughout the night. Their hands and feet were already dangerously numb. At least nine hours to get through before it would be light enough to venture on.

"We could do calisthenics to keep warm," suggested Emmie.

"Or we could sit as still as possible so we don't attract wolves."

"Are there wolves?"

"I don't know," admitted Kate. "But I feel as if there ought to be—what was that?"

"It sounded like hooves." Emmie clutched Kate's hand. Or maybe Kate clutched Emmie's hand.

And a voice, in English, called out, "Halloo? Anyone there?"

"Americans?" asked Kate in a high-pitched voice she hardly recognized as her own.

"Even better, Canadians!" the voice responded, and the clopping noise resolved itself into two sets of horses' hooves. Kate shielded her eyes as an Eveready flashlight blazed in her face. "Sorry about that—Miss Moran?"

"And Miss Van Alden." Now her eyes had recovered, Kate could see them properly, two Canadians with the distinctive badge on their hats showing a beaver and two crossed axes. "You're the foresters!"

"Guilty as charged. What are you doing all the way out here?"

"We got lost in the snow and then—" Emmie broke off, looking at Kate uncertainly.

"We had a spot of trouble with our truck," said Kate briefly. It seemed best not to go into the rest of it. "We were visiting one of our villages, got turned around in the snow, and stalled out here."

Fortunately, they seemed to think that an entirely

sensible story. There was a murmured conversation between the two Canadians.

"You'd best come back with us. We've our housekeeper there as chaperone," added the shorter of the two men hastily, turning a little pink about the ears. "She can give you assurance as to our honorable intentions."

"We never doubted them," said Kate gravely. They had no idea. "Thank you. We appreciate your hospitality."

"Oh, it's nothing, nothing at all. Happy to share the old château. Can you ride pillion? It's too far to walk. We'll send someone to fetch your car in the morning."

"Poor old jitney," murmured Emmie, patting the truck's side. "Do you really think you can fix her?"

"She looks like she's had a time of it," said the shorter Canadian cheerfully. Kate thought she might have sat next to him at Thanksgiving, but she wasn't entirely sure; she'd been too loopy with fever to pay much attention. "But we'll do our best. At least we can offer you a warm fire and some hot soup."

It would be soup, thought Kate madly. But these weren't French deserters. These were their Canadian friends. They were back through the other side of the looking glass, the one where everyone was a friend. They were the women of the Smith College Relief

Unit, due every courtesy—not just women, alone. Easy prey.

"Soup would be lovely," she managed.

Emmie made a choking noise, covering her face with her hands.

The Canadians clearly thought that was a perfectly reasonable reaction to being lost in the cold.

"You look done in," the taller one said sympathetically. "If I can get Bucephalus here close enough, d'you think you could use the running board as a mounting block?"

Chapter Eighteen

Merry Christmas to all at home! Your very own Smith Unit is exhausted with merrymaking. I never thought I'd be sick of parties, but you try having ten of them and see how you feel. Think about having two Sunday-school parties a day for five days and that's about the shape of it. We started out with our own private party for the Unit, then one for the Unit's friends—aviators and Quakers and engineers and foresters and doctors and even a few odd Brits. The only one who didn't make it was the partridge in the pear tree. Some of those men came four hours to spend thirty minutes eating plum pudding with us! But they said it was worth it. (Probably more for the plum pudding than our dubious charms—most of us

haven't had a proper wash in weeks. Florence
Lewes claims the dirt keeps the warmth in.)

Then it was back to work with parties for all our
villages. Just imagine the mercury well below zero
and all the roads clogged with snow and us in our
little trucks, with Ethel Ledbetter dressed up as
Père Noël in a red bathrobe. Then back to Grécourt
to pack more presents and do it all again—and
again—the next day. We're all terribly grateful that
Christmas comes only once a year, even in the
Somme, where terrible things happen all the time.

It was so cold in those military barracks we're
using as village halls that one little girl froze her
toes and had to stick her feet through a hole in the
wall to be washed with snow! We had to organize
a running-around game to keep everyone from
frostbite, which got rather more exciting than
planned when two stray dogs decided to join in the
fun and bit Ethel, who promptly fainted and had
to be revived with—you guessed it—more snow.
Don't you see the fun you're missing?

But it was really touching to see how happy
they all were, the old people as much as the
children. . . .

— Miss Eleanor ("Nell")
Baldwin, '14, to her family

December 1917
Grécourt, France

The Canadians were true to their word and perfectly lovely in every way.

Their housekeeper, in a flannel wrapper and long gray braid, came out to make hot soup and sent Emmie and Kate off to bed in her own room with blankets that smelled of lavender and a hot water bottle tucked in by their feet.

But Emmie kept thinking back to that other room, the man with his arm around her shoulders, unbuttoning her coat for her.

"Don't say anything to anyone about this, will you?" Kate murmured as they snuggled down into their borrowed bed, their borrowed chaperone on guard in the next room. "About those men, I mean. If anyone asks, say just what we told the foresters. We got lost in the snow and the jitney broke down on us."

"But why? If they're deserters, shouldn't someone be told? Unless you don't want them to get into trouble. . . ."

"I don't want *us* to get into trouble." The bed dipped as Kate rolled onto her side. "We can't let anyone see us as a liability. If they think we're weak, that we need defending—our position here might be compromised."

"You didn't need defending. You defended both of

us." Emmie hated how useless she had been, how entirely ignorant.

"I got lucky. Another time . . ." Kate lowered her voice. "It's not common knowledge yet, but there's a rumor our sector might be transferred over to the Brits. If it is—they don't like women in their war zone. They'll seize on any excuse to see us out."

"But they've been so helpful."

"You mean Captain DeWitt has been so helpful?" said Kate with some amusement. "We don't need the authorities being reminded that we're female. Right now they're charmed by the idea of us, and they like what we're doing, and everyone is only too happy to help, but that's only so long as we pull our own weight and don't cause anyone any trouble. No one wants to have to shoot a soldier over us. Or deal with the flurry in the American press if American women are—well, hurt."

"If you and I had been . . . hurt tonight, what would have happened?"

Kate thought for a moment. Emmie could hear the old building creaking around them. "They would want to keep it quiet, I imagine. It would be very embarrassing to both governments. And that would be it for the Unit. They wouldn't want us here after that—or anyone like us."

Emmie had never thought that she might be endangering not only herself but the future of the Unit.

"But nothing happened," said Kate firmly. "We're both fine, and the Canadians are pleased as punch with having rescued us. It will make a good story, we'll both be teased for getting lost, and no one ever needs to know the rest of it."

But Emmie knew. Yes, they were in danger here, she'd always known that, but it had been an impersonal sort of danger, the same sort of dangers that threatened the foresters or their Quaker friends over at Ham: shells, Germans, frostbite. The usual dangers of war and weather.

Emmie felt terribly naive. Sheltered, Kate had called her. She'd never thought of herself as sheltered. She'd thought her settlement house work had made her terribly worldly, but—she had always known herself to be safe. These sorts of things happened. But they happened to other people. They happened to factory workers and French villagers, not girls like them, not Smith women. Not to a Van Alden.

For the first time, Emmie noticed the safeguards built into Kate's schedules. She'd assumed, if she'd thought about it, that they went places in pairs because they needed to maximize their few forms of transportation, or because it made sense for a doctor to visit alongside a social worker, or for a social worker or doctor to ride along with the store. But what it really meant was that no one was ever out on her own.

Because it was a war zone, and there were desperate men about.

It was hard to remember that when everything went on as usual, when there were engineers and aviators for tea on a Sunday, French *poilus*—such nice, friendly *poilus*—helping to put up temporary houses, and Canadian foresters visiting with loads of firewood and greenery, decking the Orangerie with wreaths and garlands as their own particular Christmas gift to the Unit. Everyone was so *kind*.

But out there, beyond the gates of Grécourt, were places where a woman wasn't safe, and not just because there was a war on.

The idea that anyone would hurt them—Emmie just couldn't quite wrap her mind around it. To be sure, there had been a French soldier who had made an inappropriate comment to Alice in Paris, but he had apologized profusely once she had identified herself as American, and they had all thought it was a great joke.

Except it wasn't a great joke to the Frenchwomen, was it? Or to women who weren't them.

The one positive bit was that Kate didn't seem to be

angry with her anymore. Emmie told herself that was a good thing, at least. They were friends again. Mostly.

Without saying anything about it, Kate quietly changed the schedules, assigning Emmie to the villagers in the *basse-cour*, on the pretense that Alice was too busy with the trucks to do social service work as well. Emmie appreciated it, she did, but it was hard knowing that it was charity of sorts—giving her something to do where she could be close at hand.

Playing Lady Bountiful, Kate had called it. It wasn't, Emmie realized, terribly much fun being on the other end of it, knowing that your life was being managed for you—for your own good, but even so. Because you couldn't be trusted to do it yourself.

She would do better from now on, Emmie promised herself, and redoubled her efforts on the Christmas planning: caroling on Christmas Eve, the Unit's own Christmas party on Christmas morning, a party for all their officer friends Christmas Day, parties for all the villages at the rate of two a day thereafter, with a personally chosen present for every single adult and child in their domain. The plans grew more and more elaborate: a fishing game for the children, with gifts attached to hooks behind a screen. Matching gifts to ages. Praying the packages from America would arrive and going on an emergency buying trip when they didn't.

Hours in the frozen cellar, sorting and packaging and attaching fiddly little hooks to fishing line.

It was a blow when all plans were canceled Christmas Eve. It was a beautiful moonlit night, like an illustration out of a book of carols, snow like frosting on the old stone church—and the authorities, speeding through in their cars, warning everyone that there would be air raids, that mass was canceled.

"But we knew our French carols so well," Emmie mourned. "Even the descants!"

"We'll still have our parties. Those are during the daytime," Kate consoled her, but it seemed like a very inauspicious start. When Kate planned things, they stayed planned.

"Maybe you should have had someone else in charge of Christmas," said Emmie glumly.

"You can't control the weather—or the German planes," Kate said sleepily, but Emmie wasn't mollified.

It helped to wake up on Christmas morning and see the sun shining on the snow, and the delight of the other girls when they stumbled into breakfast to be greeted by Captain Linoleum, a six-foot-tall roll of linoleum with a face chalked by Nell, a khaki cap, stick arms holding a Smith Unit "comfort bag" with a generous check from the class of 1904, and a ribbon-decked wastebasket at his feet (Kate's, borrowed and bedecked) holding a pile of presents.

"Captain Linoleum offers his Christmas greetings to the Unit and will soon unroll himself on the barrack floor to warm our feet," said Emmie breathlessly, distributing such luxuries as hot water bottles, briquettes, and all-weather socks amid cries of delight, while Marie's contribution, coffee, real coffee with real cream from their own cows, steamed on the table in their red-and-white cups that looked more like bowls.

"New phonograph records! Thank goodness! I thought if I had to hear Alice playing Caruso's 'O Sole Mio' one more time, I was going to scream!"

"Oh, look, this one's a fox-trot. We can dance it with the boys tonight."

"In our hobnailed boots?"

"Better than our rubber rain boots."

"I knew I forgot to pack my dancing slippers."

"Socks! Socks without holes! I may avoid frostbite yet."

"And cream for chilblains!" Emmie said happily. They all had chilblains, and nasty things they were. "That nice doctor in the hospital in Nesle told me what to get—he says it's a sovereign remedy."

"Dr. Stapleton?" said Kate, glancing at Julia.

"Make sure it doesn't have arsenic in it," commented Julia shortly.

"Didn't people used to use arsenic for their complexions?" asked Alice. "Or was that belladonna?"

"Hand it here," said Dr. Stringfellow, and sniffed. "Well, it won't kill you, at least."

"I don't care if it kills me," said Nell fervently. "I'm putting it on *now*."

There were parcels from home as well, parcels and mail. Emmie's mother had sent a letter and Emmie's heart lifted as she opened it, only to plunge again when she saw it was only a series of clippings, press related to the passing of the suffrage act in New York last month, her mother holding a banner.

The good work continues—first the state, then the country! her mother had scrawled along the top.

Underneath was a bank draft, with the scribbled injunction: *For your village schools.*

She hadn't expected anything, not really. Emmie had arranged for presents for the boys before she left in August, knowing her parents would never remember: a new phonograph for Jack, a camera for Nat, a glass case for George to house his rock collection, a phenakistoscope for Bobby. They would have been put under the tree by the housekeeper.

Kate had cut the strings on a brown paper parcel. "It's

a present from my parents and brothers. New boots. My mother says—" Her voice caught. "My mother says the saleswoman at Gimbels told her these are the very best for keeping the damp out. She must have bought these and had them sent right after we left."

"My mother sends Christmas greetings and wishes us all well," Emmie lied. It wasn't entirely a lie. She was sure her mother did wish them all well. When she remembered. Her mother had always liked Kate. "What are those?"

In the middle of the table was a pile of paper scrolls tied up in ribbon.

"A surprise for you," said Dr. Stringfellow complacently. "Santa made it through last night and left a note for each of you."

"Santa's handwriting looks strangely familiar," said Julia.

"I have no idea what you're talking about. You're meant to read them aloud and guess who they're for," Dr. Stringfellow added helpfully. "Go on now, children."

"I think I've found Emmie's," said Anne, unrolling the first scroll. "'*Our angel of the barrack, she tramps both near and far / Through snow and mud and dark of night, not waiting for a car. Although she may not be able to tell a rooster from a hen / When it comes to building chicken coops / Her strength is the strength of ten.*'"

Emmie winced. "No one will ever let me forget those roosters, will they?"

"They made very tasty soup," said Alice, trying to make her feel better.

Liza put the next scroll right up to her nose, squinting at it. "This one's cheating—there's a name in it. '*Though small of stature she may be / Her heart is undismayed / By broken trucks and missing coal / And shipments all delayed. / Our patient Kate, our canny Kate—*' Couldn't we be trusted to guess?"

Dr. Stringfellow shrugged. "Literary license."

"'*She keeps us all on time / She bosses and she wheedles / And finds in every haystack / A regular crop of needles. Our stalwart assistant director / She keeps us all on time / And so it fits her schedule / I'll promptly end this rhyme.*'"

"Can you really call that a rhyme?" asked Maud, shuddering delicately.

"A rhyme, certainly," said Ethel Ledbetter, "but is a rhyme necessarily a *poem*? The troubadours of old—"

"I'm a doctor, not a poet," retorted Dr. Stringfellow, cutting Ethel off before she could get started on *chansons de* something or other. "You try making fourteen doggerel verses all by yourself."

Nell's poem was about her library; Anne Dawlish

had an elaborate conceit about their savior being a carpenter; Alice worked wonders with their cars.

Liza blushed at "'*She always wants to lend a hand, despite a broken arm / Canadian, Ami, Engineer / Alike have felt her charms.*'"

And while Maud tossed her head at "'*No peddler sells better / Than she who runs our store / She sells them soap and sabots / And aprons by the score,*'" Emmie could tell she was pleased.

"Have we had any outbreaks of lice since I sold everyone soap? I thought not," Maud said haughtily. "And there were washtubs too, I'll have you know."

"I think all the lice just died of cold," said Alice, shivering.

"If you wore more wool and less lace—" began Gwen Mills in her patronizing way.

"Then how would we keep up the elegant reputation of the Unit?" drawled Julia, who was perfectly happy to defend Alice if it meant squashing Gwen.

Emmie watched them all bickering and thought how very odd it was that six months ago most of them hadn't known each other at all, and here they were, with a very clear idea of each other's strengths and foibles. They might mock Alice's lace collars, but they all knew that Alice could fix any truck that had a bit of life left in it. And Gwen Mills might be an utter pill, but if you were sick in the middle of the night, she'd be there with a washbasin, holding back your hair. Even Maud. She complained, but she was out there in that truck in all weathers, peddling with all her might. They might not all love each other, but, by a strange alchemy, they all worked together.

Even if Emmie wished that someone would remember her for something other than chickens.

"These are lovely," Emmie said, to make up for feeling ungrateful. "How did you ever do it all?"

"Don't you mean Santa? I do pay attention, you know," said Dr. Stringfellow, looking pleased. "I'm not one for speeches, but what you're doing here—what we're all doing here—is something worth doing, and I think you all, every single one, should be proud of yourselves. Those poems may not be much in terms of meter, but they're a tribute to each and every one of you and all you do."

"There you go, rhyming again," pointed out Florence Lewes cheerfully.

"Thank you," said Dr. Stringfellow. "I'll try to keep this bit in prose, shall I? I wanted to do something for all of you before I go—I'll be leaving in January. It's been an honor and I'll dine out on tales of the Unit for the next decade, but my own work and family are waiting for me in Philadelphia."

"She has a family?" whispered Alice, on Kate's other side.

"I heard that, Miss Patton. And yes, I do. You'll be getting a new director and a new doctor—but not until January! You're stuck with me until then, and I warn you, I mean to eat my share of the Christmas chocolates."

"Must you go?" asked Emmie. Dr. Stringfellow was brusque, impatient, and frankly uninterested in administration, but there was something terribly reassuring about her.

"Bless you, child. I never wanted or asked to be director—and I only hope you're better served by the next one. I only agreed to be assistant director because Betsy promised me I'd never actually have to do anything about it."

For a moment, the ghost of Mrs. Rutherford was there with them. If a living person could be a ghost, thought Emmie. It seemed wrong that they should be celebrating all this here without her, when all of it was, one way or another, her doing, from the design of the uniform to the purchase of the chickens.

Dr. Stringfellow cleared her throat. "Let's give thanks where thanks is due—to our assistant director, who did all the real directing so I could go on doing the job I actually know how to do. Kate, the first chocolate is for you."

There was hugging and exclaiming and ironic comments from Maud and general pandemonium and Emmie watched her friend surrounded by the Unit, her thin face glowing, and thought how long ago August felt, and how wonderful it was how Kate had come into her own, and how she wished, just once, she could be more like Kate, confident like Kate, strong like Kate, organized like Kate.

"It's no more than anyone would do," said Kate, once the last strains of "For She's a Jolly Good Fellow" had died down.

"Oh, it is," said Dr. Stringfellow frankly. "And I hope our new director realizes how lucky she is to have you."

"Who will the new director be?" asked Alice, putting into words what they were all wondering.

"You all know her already—Mrs. Barrett of the Paris Committee. And the new doctor, not that you asked, will be Dr. Clare of the class of '92. Here." Dr. Stringfellow rooted around under her chair and produced a large box of chocolates. "Mrs. Barrett sent this as an earnest of her good intentions—and it's an earnest of my good intentions that I didn't eat it all myself and hide the note."

"Shouldn't we save it for the children?" suggested Emmie, and was promptly booed down.

"Hush, angel of the barrack," said Nell. "Christmas won't be Christmas without scarfing down all the chocolates and feeling sick after."

"If you do," said Dr. Stringfellow, "don't come to me. I'm strictly off duty today and mean to be as much of a glutton as the rest of you. All dyspeptics report to Dr. Pruyn. Now let's make sure we're ready to receive our guests, shall we? Everyone to their stations! And that's as much directing as I intend to do."

"Did you know?" Emmie asked Kate as they heaved their stove out of their barrack to carry to the Orangerie. The Orangerie was to be their ballroom for the day, and with all the stoves burning at once, plus a rusty old iron range Emmie had found in the cellars on which they were going to cook creamed potatoes for their seventy-five guests, they thought they could just about keep it above freezing. "About Dr. Stringfellow leaving?"

"Yes." Kate adjusted her grip on the stove, head down. "But not about the new director."

Emmie backed down the path, bent nearly double to stay level with Kate. "She seems very capable."

"I know. Alice says she serves a good dinner." They staggered through one of the doors of the Orangerie, setting down the stove. Kate straightened, flexing her gloved hands. "Maud's been wanting her here for a long time."

Emmie glanced over her shoulder. "That doesn't

mean—well, what it might mean. We're here now, and there are so many projects in hand—they're not likely to move the Unit back to Paris now or put us into canteen work."

"I hope not. With the Brits coming—we'll see what happens. You did do a lovely job with the Christmas parties, Emmie. Captain Linoleum was an inspiration."

"That was really Nell's idea." Emmie didn't mention that Nell had wanted to call him Captain Duckwalk and provide him with a British flag. "I just found the linoleum roll."

"And presents for everyone." Someone was calling Kate. She paused a moment to add, "I know you've worked so hard on this. Thank you."

That was very much the assistant director speaking, not her old friend Kate. It felt like a consolation prize. She might have messed up everything else, but at least she planned a good party.

Emmie pushed the thought away. It was a good party. It was an excellent party, really. The old Orangerie had been made beautiful by the foresters, who had decked it with all the greenery they could find, nestling candles amid sprigs of holly, stringing boughs and garlands everywhere. The meal was a simple one: cold ham and turkey, hot creamed potatoes in massive piles, bread and real butter, and even plum pudding with brandy butter. They'd learned their lesson after the debacle of the tooth mugs. No soups, no multiple courses, nothing fancy, just a good, hearty buffet.

Alice brought her Victrola out and cranked it up—not, Emmie noticed, Caruso this time, but popular songs, songs that people sang along to. People raised their voices to talk over the music, adding to the holiday air.

Kate and Julia were in the center of a group of aviators, one of whom was a distant cousin of sorts—Emmie vaguely remembered Julia terrifying him when they were children. The engineers, who had seen some rough action at Cambrai the month before, were being made much of by Liza and Alice. Anne was discussing woodworking with a Canadian forester, and Ethel was expounding on medieval heresies to the Quakers.

Dr. Stringfellow was in the midst of a loud but largely amicable debate with a doctor from the hospital at Amiens (for some reason, Kate had requested they not invite the hospital staff from Nesle, and Emmie had been mystified but complied), and Alfalfa Bill, one of the Red Cross drivers, had just produced a mandolin, when one of the canvas flaps they were using for doors opened and in walked the Brits.

"The redcoats are coming!" called Red Cross Dave, and promptly fell backward off his chair.

They weren't red; they were khaki. There was a senior-looking sort of man, with a great many medals and an extremely ferocious mustache, and a younger man, with very carefully arranged hair. And then there was Captain DeWitt.

Who was promptly pigeonholed by Maud. "You didn't tell us you were a lord. My friend says—"

The Victrola hiccupped. Captain DeWitt looked at Emmie over Maud's head, telegraphing extreme distress. Suddenly the lights seemed much brighter, the room warmer, the music louder. Everything resumed at double the speed.

"If you'll excuse me," Emmie said to the Canadian she'd been speaking to. "Nell—is it time to send out the goat?"

With a nod, Nell whisked outside and reappeared with Zélie, who looked like an illustration from a children's book in tiered skirts and ruffled pantalets, her goat following along behind her on a beribboned leash. They'd decked Zélie's pet goat, Minerva, with white panniers with big red bows, filled with Ramses cigarettes, a surprise treat for their guests.

There was a mad dash for the goat, everyone exclaiming over the cigarettes, and Emmie seized the opportunity to rescue Captain DeWitt from Maud. "Cigarette? I'm afraid these are ill come by. We had a parcel misdelivered to us and couldn't figure out who they were meant to be for, so we decided we'd just distribute them broadly and make up for it that way."

"Robin Hood with tobacco?" suggested Captain DeWitt, raising a brow. He seemed particularly tall and thin and British in his dress uniform, looking as though he'd stepped out of a bandbox rather than comfortably splattered with mud and herding cows.

"I can't say whom we robbed, since we don't know," admitted Emmie. "But enough of our parcels have gone missing that we felt it was really more of a trade than anything else. I had no idea you were a peer of the realm."

"I'm not. My father is. And he hardly counts." Captain DeWitt cast a wary glance behind him. "It's a bit stifling—do you mind if we step out for a moment?"

It was all of fifty degrees inside, but something about the press of bodies made it seem warmer than it was. Maud was fighting with Alice over the choice of music for the phonograph, and the goat was trying to eat someone's uniform.

"Yes, let's," said Emmie, and quelled the thought that Kate probably wouldn't approve. Kate was deep in conversation with Captain DeWitt's commanding officer, the one with the bushy mustache. "I can't promise the air will be much clearer out here, but at least it will be quieter."

She led Captain DeWitt out of the Orangerie, to a makeshift bench overlooking the green water of the moat, with its well-worn placard reading "*Bonne à Boire.*"

They sat down on the bench, the air crisp on Emmie's flushed cheeks, the bare trees rustling around them.

She'd sat out dances before, in ballrooms in New York, decked in satin and gauze, pearls at her neck and ears, hothouse flowers blooming. She'd sat with any number of eligible bachelors, Yale men and Harvard men, old money and somewhat less old money; she'd sat on narrow gold benches in dresses that bared her neck and shoulders, her legs clad in whisper-thin silk stockings and heeled slippers instead of heavy lisle and hobnail boots.

And yet she'd never felt so bare, so aware of the wind finding the naked spaces between her collar and her chignon, the backs of her ears, the nape of her neck. She could feel the plank bend as Captain DeWitt sat next to her, painfully aware of every movement, every creak of the wood, as the plank dipped, tilting them closer. She could smell soap and wool—this must be his best uniform, the one that got saved, that didn't get drenched in trench mud.

Emmie remembered, uncomfortably, that her own uniform had been rather spottily laundered and was badly patched in several places, and that those brave touches of French blue were now a rather dirty gray.

"How is one partly a peer?" Emmie asked, just to have something to say. "I thought you either were or weren't."

"That depends on who you ask," said Captain DeWitt. He turned slightly toward her, his eyes green and brown like the moat. "My father is what they call a soap-and-pickle peer—still with the stink of the shop about him."

"What's wrong with soap and pickles?"

Captain DeWitt looked at her quizzically, as if trying to figure out if she really meant it. "They're common. Trade. When I was at Harrow, it was considered a great joke to try to brand me with a burning biscuit."

Emmie sat up straight, making the bench bounce. "That's ridiculous! Think of the joy you've brought to people with your biscuits. What have any of them ever done for anyone?"

Captain DeWitt smiled wryly. "Bunk with William the Conqueror? Affright the French at Agincourt?"

"You're allies with the French now, so that's not much use, is it? Affrighting the French, I mean. I'd far rather have tea biscuits." Struck by a sudden thought, she tilted her head up at him, studying his face. "Is that why you were masquerading as the Scarlet Pimpernel? I thought you wouldn't tell me your name because it was something awful—like Algernon."

"There's that too. And no," he added, with the hint of a smile, like sunlight on the moat, "it's not Algernon."

"It can't be more awful than mine. Imagine going through your life named Emmaline. I tried to get my governess to call me Lily, but my mother found out and put a stop to it."

"Why Lily?" He rested the flat of his hand against the seat of the bench, his arm brushing the back of Emmie's jacket.

"Well, you know, flowers and all that." Emmie hunched her shoulders, looking away, feeling all the old awkwardness descend on her. She had thought it sounded delicate and feminine, the name of someone who floated rather than clomped and didn't wear dancing slippers the size of boats. But she didn't want to admit to any of that.

"The lilies of the field that toil not?" offered Captain DeWitt.

"Oh, do we toil," said Emmie with feeling, trying to make a joke of it. "I've spent the week in the freezing cellar stringing gifts on bits of fishing line for the children."

"Why fishing line?"

"Because we didn't have yarn to waste. We wanted to make it all more special for them, not just handing each child a gift, but making, well, a bit of a production of it. We've made a sort of screen and labeled the gifts according to age, and each one will get a go with the fishing rod—"

Captain DeWitt was listening to her ramble on, listening as if every word meant something, and Emmie realized how silly it must all sound. The ruins of the outbuilding reproached her, falling ceilings and missing walls. There were men dying only a few miles away. And here she was, going on about toys and fishing line.

She looked hopelessly at him. "It all sounds very trivial, doesn't it, in the midst of all this? But we just wanted to give them, oh, I don't know. Something to make up for all those years without. Something . . . wonderful."

"I think it sounds wonderful." He was looking at her in a way that made her feel like she'd just come out of the gloom into strong sunlight. "I think you're wonderful."

"No, I'm not—oh goodness, you have no idea. I wish—" Emmie had to clamp her lips shut to keep it from all pouring out, Margaret and Courcelles and the snowstorm. All the mistakes she'd made, all the dangers she'd brought on them.

Very gently, Captain DeWitt asked, "Is something the matter?"

Any excuse, Kate had said. The British would take any excuse to evict them from the war zone.

Emmie blurted out, "Is it true that you're taking over our zone from the French?"

Captain DeWitt sat back. She could feel him move away from her, sitting very still and straight. "Where did you hear that?"

"Here and there," said Emmie vaguely, wishing she hadn't said anything, that they could go back to talking about fishing line and how wonderful she was.

Captain DeWitt leaned his head back, staring up at the hard silver sky. "So much for secrecy. I'm sure the kaiser has it down on his calendar already."

"Does that mean yes?"

"Possibly."

That meant yes. Emmie stared down, folding and refolding her hands in her lap. She couldn't seem to figure out what to do with her thumbs, of which she suddenly had ten. "They say you don't believe in women in the war zone. The lot of you, I mean. Not you personally."

Captain DeWitt waited a moment before speaking; she could feel him weighing his response. "As a rule, yes. If we have to rally around and protect you, we lose valuable time and resources."

Which was just what Kate had been saying. Emmie looked at him with alarm. "But we don't need you to rally around and protect us. We're not those sort of women. Really, we're not."

Captain DeWitt raised a brow. "What sort of women are you?"

"Smith women," said Emmie firmly. When that didn't seem to make the desired impression, she translated for him, "We're rather like Oxford women, I suppose, only without the accents."

"Oxford has women's colleges, yes," Captain DeWitt said slowly. "My sister is in her final year at Somerville. But the university doesn't award degrees to them."

Emmie was horrified. "That's barbaric! It's positively medieval!"

That surprised Captain DeWitt into a laugh, a rich chuckle that cleared the shadows from his eyes and made him look years younger. "Says the colonial."

"We haven't thrown tea in the harbor for ages—but I have my degree and I have the right to vote. In New York, at least," Emmie amended.

"That's all very well," said Captain DeWitt, laugh lines fanning out around his eyes as he looked down at her. "But not precisely applicable here. You can't vote away an invading German army."

Emmie perked up, struck by the idea. "Wouldn't it

be nice if one could? If we could just vote them away? If all the women of the world could vote, we'd have far fewer wars."

"I'm not sure Madame Defarge would agree with that," said Captain DeWitt drily. "Or Milady de Winter. I can't tell you anything about what will happen here when the shift occurs—mostly because I don't know."

She noticed that he said *when*, not *if*. "Do you think we'll be allowed to stay?"

"You know I can't comment on that."

Emmie looked up at him, her eyes meeting his. "That won't stop me asking."

"Do you mean to wear me down?" he asked, and somehow, he was holding both her hands in his.

"Could I?" asked Emmie, with great interest.

"Yes," he said, and Emmie noticed that his eyes had little golden flecks in them, and that the braid on his uniform was scratchy beneath her palms. "I rather think you could."

Chapter Nineteen

We're a depleted unit—the doctor and three of our number have left, and the replacements are in Paris, waiting for passes. With the change of regime, no one knows how long that might take. Last week, the French moved out and the English moved in. It was rather like a parade, great guns being tugged along, cavalry on horseback, camion after camion. One day, a Scotch regiment came through with their bright plaid skirts, and all the children ran out to hear the bagpipers play.

Our agriculturalist has us bending all our efforts to the spring planting, which means less time for the children. I am particularly disappointed not to have a house to devote to the children's work, as we'd originally planned. Our classes are held either in the cold of the Orangerie, in between our machines, or at the feet of the cook, who has things to say about our being underfoot. But we've been promised faithfully that there will be improvements as soon as the planting is done—if we're allowed to stay, that is.

> *— Miss Anne Dawlish, '07,*
> *to fellow Sloyd teacher Miss*
> *Ruth Minster*

January 1918
Grécourt, France

"How many plows do you need?" asked Kate, scribbling busily in her notebook.

"Ten," said Florence firmly. "And a man to help and at least one caravan. Has there been any word on the seeds?"

"The Paris Committee says they're getting together the seeds we've asked for." Ever since they'd finished their grueling rounds of Christmas parties, they'd been setting their minds to the spring planting, busily canvassing all the villagers as to exactly what sort of crops they'd had before the war; what they needed for their kitchen gardens; and exactly what they meant when they said *"chicorée,"* which apparently had multiple varietals about which their villagers felt very strongly, some lobbying for *frisée*, and some for *non-frisée*. "They're to be sent down with Mrs. Barrett."

"We can't start too soon," said Florence. "The sooner we plant, the more chance we have of growing enough to sustain these poor souls through next winter."

Would they still be there next winter? Their six-month contracts were up; some, like Dr. Stringfellow, had left. Others, like Florence, had signed back on for another six months. Inch by inch, Kate reminded herself. Everything had to be undertaken in the expectation they would be there to finish it, but with the assumption that everything could change in a moment.

Especially if the Brits had their way.

"I'll contact Monsieur le Commandant Monin," said Kate, making another note to herself. "I'm sure he'll be able to scrounge some plows for us."

"Whole ones," Florence reminded her. The Germans had made a good job of smashing whatever had been here before. The plows they'd been offered for sale thus far had all been incomplete in some way or another, the sellers the picture of innocence when it was pointed out to them that the plow couldn't exactly plow. "Oh, and we need more chickens. Buff Orpingtons, by choice."

Contact Mr. Orpington re chickens, Kate wrote on her list. "Where can I find Mr. Orpington?"

"Mr.—" Florence's craggy face broke into a broad smile. "Kate. They're a kind of chicken."

"And this is why we have you—yes, Alice?"

Alice had stuck her head through the door. She looked dreadful, her eyes pink and her chignon lopsided. She hadn't even bothered to put on her lace jabot, and her uniform looked strangely incomplete without it. "There's a camion stuck in the mud by the gates. Would you come see to it?"

"I'll be right there." But Alice was already gone. She'd been like this for days now. Kate wondered if it was something at home—they'd had mail last week, and Alice had been like a week of wet Sundays ever since. Even their new aviator friends flying by to do stunts and drop them messages attached to long ribbon streamers hadn't cheered her up.

Emmie would know; Emmie usually did. Kate made a note to ask her.

Reassuring Florence that the planting would start—soon!—Kate made her way down to the gate, her feet warm and dry in her Christmas boots. The ground made a happy squelching sound around her toes. Marie had sworn the weather they were having was only a false spring and there would be more snow to come, but it was heaven to be able to walk about without being muffled from head to toe. The sky had gone from the flat silver of impending snow to actual blue, with fluffy little clouds in it. The snow had melted, leaving behind the smell of good, damp earth, and birds chirped on the bare branches of the trees.

And mud, of course. Acres of mud, and a flood in the cellar of the château that had ruined a good half of their supplies.

But it still felt heavenly being not cold. After the deep freeze just before New Year, hauling from village to village in the bitter cold, forty-five degrees felt semitropical. Everyone was flinging off their coats and dashing about with renewed energy.

They'd seen Dr. Stringfellow off two days ago, with a cake made from all of their sugar rations put together.

"Don't like the new doctor better than you like me," she'd told them gruffly. "Marjorie Clare is a decent doctor but she plays terrible pinochle."

Liza, Maud, and Ethel had taken the train with Dr. Stringfellow, to Paris, Ethel to wait out her mandatory six weeks before sailing to the States and embarking on a lecture tour, Liza and Maud to canteen work.

"I can come back for a few months if you need me," Liza had offered, and Kate had been reminded of how much she liked Liza when she wasn't with Maud. "It's just that the Salvation Army really does need every American woman helping. You wouldn't believe the state of our poor boys, all alone over here, tempted by wine and Frenchwomen. It's just dreadful for them."

"But now they'll have you to keep them on the straight and narrow," Kate had promised, trying not to laugh as she'd hugged Liza goodbye. "We've got four new girls waiting for their passes in Paris—if we need you to come train them in our ways, we'll let you know."

She was only half joking. It was a little disconcerting to think of so many of their original number departing, with their new director due to arrive this week. It wasn't just the weather that was changing. It was everything.

The French army had clamped down on the distribution of *essence*, saving it for the February push. The White truck, now with hard tires and a repaired engine, had been shipped down to them by train to save the gasoline and was currently sitting, useless, in the Orangerie, with their other trucks. For the very first time since they had arrived in September, they hadn't been able to buy any gasoline at all, not even when Anne had taken the train down to Amiens and wheedled every official she could think to wheedle.

But it was the sort of day on which it was easy to see

silver linings. To save on *essence*, they were spending the whole week at home at Grécourt, engaging in Herculean housekeeping efforts before the arrival of the new people. The Augean stables had nothing on it. The flooded cellar had to be emptied, the goods sorted to see what was soaked beyond repair and what could be dried out and salvaged. Rooms had to be cleaned and reassigned. Kate's makeshift desk was covered with maps of their villages, fields marked out for plowing—once they managed to wrangle some plows. And horses. And men.

Bit by bit, though, it was all coming together. As Kate rounded the side of the château, she could see a buzz of activity near the ruined stables. Families were moving their possessions out of the cellars where they'd lived since the German retreat and into the temporary houses the Unit had built for them. The temporary houses might not be much, but they had walls and roofs and could be heated in a way the broken old cellars just couldn't. Kate waved to Zélie, who had, of course, declared herself Kate's deputy and was directing everyone, her pet goat tagging along after her.

Their next task would be to move the supplies from the flooded castle cellars to the newly emptied stables . . . and then . . .

Kate's head was full of plans.

They had schools up and running now in most of the villages, led by schoolteachers who had weathered the German occupation or managed to return, which meant that the Unit's classes were purely extras, freeing up the women to concentrate on spring planting and building infrastructure. Anne had an idea about starting clubhouses; Nell wanted a traveling lending library.

Someone would have to take over the store now that Liza and Maud were gone. Not Emmie. Nell, perhaps? She could combine the store with the library, with Alice to drive . . .

If they stayed. If they were allowed to stay.

For the past two weeks, the roads had been bright with French blue as the French army moved out of the region. There were days the Unit couldn't get their trucks through at all, the roads were so thick with soldiers. And then, just like that, the *poilus* were gone, and the Tommies were slogging through, drab in their khaki, the officers at their head strolling along with lordly unconcern, as if they were just out for a spot of a walk, what? The Unit had already been visited by a rather grim British major, who had poked around every corner of their camp, as if searching for hidden Germans.

It hadn't helped that Maud, being Maud, had put on a fake German accent and tried to convince their British guests that they were all spies.

But for the moment, the women were still here. And they intended to stay.

"Kate!" Emmie hailed her from just outside the gates, where a truck was stuck in the ditch, a morose French driver smoking a nasty-smelling cigarette standing by. "It's Dr. Clare's trunks. Eight of them—and he says there are three loads equally big in Noyon, but it's not worth the trouble to his truck coming all the way out here."

"Better give him double the usual tip," said Kate in English, before turning to the driver and thanking him in her by now nearly local French.

Triple the usual tip persuaded him to help them unload the trunks and several duffel bags containing Dr. Clare's personal effects, which included a load of bricks—or possibly medical reference works.

The driver took the trunks over the moat. It was left to Emmie and Kate to manhandle the baggage under shelter in the Orangerie.

"There can't really be more, can there?" Kate collapsed onto a trunk, stretching her sore arms. "Three more loads! I can't even imagine. Did she bring her whole house with her? Good thing we've got the *basse-cour* cellars now. I've asked Anne to give them a whitewash and then we can move all this in there."

Emmie nudged a duffel with her toe. "The driver said it was Hague trunks full of relief supplies—twenty-seven of them."

"Hague trunks?" That was enough to give Kate the energy to lift her head. This was proper aid, under the aegis of the Hague Convention, not the usual amateur rubbish. "Glory be. We can replace what's been soaked in the cellars. Thank heavens it's Hague supplies and not more parcels from the Bangor Committee."

An alumna from Maine had posted a doggerel verse in the alumnae magazine, urging everyone to empty their attics for the Smith Unit, and since then they'd been inundated with moth-eaten fur stoles, calico bonnets, and other items both unsuitable and unusable. Some of it, Anne had managed to convert to rags for the growing rag-rug industry she was fostering among the villagers, but much of it was simply absurd. Who needed someone's great-grandmother's nubia? Kate wasn't even sure what a nubia was—whatever it was, her great-grandmothers hadn't owned one. She'd had Alice sorting through the rubbish.

Which reminded her . . . Kate looked up at Emmie, who was trying to drag Dr. Clare's duffels into a neat line where they wouldn't impede Anne's classes. "Do you know what's bothering Alice? She looks like she's been crying."

"She's missing Liza and Maud, I think," said Emmie carefully, not meeting Kate's eyes. "They're the closest she had to friends here. And there's the shelling. The shelling is getting on everyone's nerves."

"Except Florence," said Kate, wondering what it was Emmie wasn't telling her. "As far as I can tell, she's completely nerveless. She even slept through that bombardment last night. Are you sure that's all that's wrong with Alice?"

Emmie considered for a moment. "Don't say that I said anything, but she's had some news from home."

"No one's died, have they?" Kate asked, alarmed. With Liza gone, they were down to two drivers, at least until the new girls arrived.

"No." Emmie shook out her skirts, trying to decide how much to say. "Her sister is having a baby."

"But isn't that good news? I would think that was good news."

Emmie sank down on the trunk next to Kate. "It would be, but Alice's sister's husband used to be Alice's beau, and Alice feels it rather. She wants to be happy for them, but it's hard. And now, with the baby—well, you see. It makes it all feel so much more final."

Kate would have thought it would have been final from the moment of "I do" but refrained from pointing that out.

"She's not thinking of leaving, is she?" If Alice left—they'd have to take Liza up on her offer to put off her canteen work and come back and drive for them.

"No, quite the contrary. She can't bear to go home. I think that's why she joined in the first place," Emmie added, lowering her voice and looking over her shoulder, just in case Alice might enter. "So they wouldn't know she minded."

"We'll just have to keep her too busy to fret. That shouldn't be a problem once we finally get some essence—we'll be short-handed until the new people finally get here." Anne, Gwen Mills, Nell, Florence, Alice, and Julia had all signed back on; Kate had their contracts on her desk. "Oh, that reminds me. I need your contract."

"About that . . ." Emmie traced circles in the dirt on the floor of the Orangerie with the toe of her boot. "I've been thinking and thinking and thinking about it, and I'm not sure I should."

"Should what?" Kate was mentally shuffling schedules, only half listening.

"Renew my contract." As Kate stared at her, Emmie said diffidently, "I've been thinking—maybe I should join the others in Paris. Maybe I would be more use doing canteen work."

"But you would hate canteen work." Kate couldn't get her head around the idea of Emmie not renewing, couldn't think why Emmie was even talking about it. "You've always said that wasn't the point of the Unit."

"It's not the point of the Unit"—Emmie was twisting and twisting her hands—"but there's nothing that says I need to stay with the Unit. The Unit can go on being the Unit, and I can go . . . serve soup."

"But why on earth— This isn't anything to do with Captain DeWitt, is it?"

Kate had seen them coming into the Orangerie together at the Christmas party, Emmie all pink-cheeked. Emmie had entirely refused to be drawn on the topic, not even when letters started arriving from Captain DeWitt on a practically daily basis.

"Why would he have anything to do with it?" asked Emmie, genuinely confused.

Kate wasn't entirely sure herself, other than that it was something Emmie had been keeping to herself, and it was killing Kate that Emmie wasn't talking about it. After all, who knew what Captain DeWitt's intentions were? And Emmie could be so credulous. "All those letters he's been sending you—he didn't say anything about our position here, or the war . . . ?"

"You know all the letters are censored. So no one can say anything, really."

"He sends awfully thick letters for someone who can't say anything." Kate wished she hadn't said that; she'd meant to pretend she hadn't noticed. But she couldn't help seeing how thick they were, those missives.

Emmie didn't seem to notice her blunder. "We write about books. And poetry. Just not Shakespeare. We haven't descended to Shakespeare." Emmie shook her head, as if trying to clear it. "It's nothing to do with any of this."

"Then why? I don't understand." The idea of Emmie's leaving the Unit was unthinkable. Emmie had been there from the beginning; she was the Unit.

"Do you remember Dr. Stringfellow's Santa notes?" When Kate looked at her blankly, Emmie went on determinedly, "Everyone else had something good that they did—Nell had her books and Anne had her carpentry and Maud had the store, and, oh, you know. But the only things there were to say about me were the things I got wrong—picking the wrong chickens and getting lost in the snow. . . ."

"But those were meant to be a joke." Kate could barely remember now what had been said; it was all a blur of laughter and good fellowship. She did remember Nell making fun after. . . . "Didn't she call you the angel of the barrack?"

"She had to say something—and that was only because you've all decided I'm the one who can get around Marie." Emmie was, Kate realized, on the verge of tears. "And you only say that because you need to give me *something*. I'm not, really. I'm not an asset at anything."

"Emmie." Kate turned, Dr. Clare's trunk creaking ominously. She'd never imagined that Emmie felt this way; she always seemed so happily impervious, as if mishaps just slid off her. But here she was, her face splotchy, talking about being useless. "You planned ten Christmas parties for over two thousand people. You made sure two thousand children and adults had gifts. And yes, you may have bought roosters instead of chickens, but how were you to know? You'd never seen a French chicken before."

"Yes, but you'd never seen a White truck before and you managed! You didn't break it on the first go."

"You didn't break anything. . . ."

"I nearly broke the Unit—you said so."

Kate felt sick. "Do you mean that night in the snow? But that was over a month ago! And, Emmie, I scarcely knew what I was saying. I was so cold and scared—you can't have thought—"

"But you were right," Emmie said doggedly. "You were right about all of it. What good do I do, really? I may not want to do canteen work, but at least I can't hurt anyone there."

"They might burn their tongues," said Kate huskily.

Emmie wasn't amused. "I put you into danger."

"We're in danger simply by virtue of being here," said Kate desperately. "We all knew that when we signed up."

"Yes, but I didn't need to make it *worse*. Every time I've tried to do something for the Unit, it's gone so horribly wrong. Maybe if I knew how to drive—but I don't. I can't even do that."

"The children—" Kate began.

Emmie shook her head hopelessly. "Zélie still won't even look at me. Our very first event and I scared a child into hysterics. And then I sent Margaret into a nervous breakdown—"

"Margaret sent Margaret into a nervous breakdown," said Kate harshly. "She was miserable from the moment we got there. Remember how we had to haul her out of that hospital room?"

"And met Captain DeWitt." Emmie's face softened for a moment, but then she remembered herself, looking down at her clasped hands. "It's no good, Kate. I'm no good."

"You're—how can you say that? You're nothing but good. Everyone loves you." Yes, Kate had said those things, but she hadn't meant them, not really. All right, maybe a little bit, but not like this. "Do you think Alice would have told me about her sister? Not in a million years. You're our conscience, Emmie. You're our heart. We need you."

"To be angel of the barrack? I don't even know what that means. You don't need to worry I'll abandon the Unit. I'll—I'll tell everyone about the wonderful work you're doing and get them to send money. . . . Real money, not someone's grandmother's shawl."

She can't help herself, you know, Julia had said. *She just likes to give things to people. She thinks it will make them like her.*

"Please," said Kate, wanting to take it all back, make it all go away. "Don't make any decisions right now. Not because of ridiculous things I said in the snow weeks and weeks ago."

"Kate? There you are! I've been looking everywhere." Nell hurried into the Orangerie, tripping over one of Dr. Clare's duffels. "Ouch! You'll never imagine— Mrs. Barrett's here—and she's brought a house! Well, bits of it."

"But she's not supposed to be here until tomorrow!" Kate was on her feet before she knew it, reaching automatically to check that her hair was straight. "Did you say a house?"

Nell gestured wildly with her hands. "Didn't you hear the truck? She's brought it in pieces. She's got some Red Cross men measuring for it behind the château. They're to put down the foundation tomorrow. It's to be a *mairie-école* when we leave, but a house for us and a place to hold our classes in the meantime."

"That will make Anne happy," said Emmie in a slightly wobbly voice. "She's so wanted a better place for her classes."

"I'd best go see—" Kate paused, looking anxiously at Emmie. She couldn't just leave things like this. Not when she'd made Emmie feel horrible and hadn't even realized it.

Or maybe she had. Maybe she'd wanted to punish Emmie for paying her way and not telling her.

"Go on." Emmie smiled at her, the sort of smile that didn't reach her eyes, which were still terribly, heart-breakingly sad. "You're the assistant director. They need you there. I'll go help Alice with sorting what's left in the cellar."

It was hard to go greet Mrs. Barrett with the requisite enthusiasm, Mrs. Barrett in her sparkling new uniform that was the color their uniforms used to be, which Kate had nearly forgotten. Mrs. Barrett with her chestnut hair beautifully dressed under a Paris hat and a deep dimple on the left side of her mouth. She put her bags in Dr. Stringfellow's room and assured Kate and Nell with a twinkle and a flash of that dimple that these accommodations were only temporary—had they seen the house going up?

They held a Unit meeting after supper, in a dining room that seemed much smaller and shabbier with Mrs. Barrett in it.

She'd brought fresh uniforms for everyone.

"I guessed at your sizes based on the pictures," she said, heaping fabric into their arms. "You can't uphold the honor of Smith looking like you've come out of the rag bag."

"Is this what a garment looks like when it hasn't been bathed in mud?" said Nell wonderingly, holding up the gray expanse of a skirt.

"Or pounded for three days straight by Marie?" added Alice, trying to get into the spirit of it.

"Thank you," said Gwen seriously, upholding the honor of the Unit, which couldn't be trusted to behave itself.

"About that Marie . . ." said Mrs. Barrett, settling herself comfortably back in her chair. "It's absurd you've had to manage with just Marie for so long. I've engaged Madame Gouge as a cook and housekeeper for us and arranged for two of the local girls as *bonnes*. You'll have better meals and cleaner clothes and won't have to worry yourself about the housekeeping."

"Ought we to be wasting the money on ourselves?" Kate asked, holding her new uniform. "We've been fine so far."

"My dear, it's not waste if it gives you the freedom to do the work you're here to do. You'll do more better housed and better fed, and our people will be grateful for it."

"You'll have to break it to Marie, Emmie," said Nell.

"I'll do my best," said Emmie in a muted voice. "Although I'm not sure she'll give up the laundry that easily."

"I won't know what it is to wear a garment that hasn't been first battered and then frozen stiff," said Nell cheerfully. "I may have to jump up and down on them myself just to make them feel right."

Mrs. Barrett smiled indulgently at her. "You really have had a time of it, haven't you? Trust me, I don't intend to take away all your creature discomforts"— there was an obedient titter of laughter—"just ease the edges a bit. We'll still be working just as hard, doing just as much, and getting our uniforms quite as muddy."

It was very hard to imagine Mrs. Barrett getting muddy. But maybe Kate was being unfair. In fact, Kate was rather sure she was being unfair. Mrs. Barrett, class of '02, had been a stalwart supporter of the Unit from the first, had tirelessly raised funds, coordinated with the American committees and the various Smith clubs, wrangled favors on their behalf via her husband's position, and provided a standing invitation to dinner for any Smith Unit girls in Paris.

In short, she'd done everything she could to be helpful, and it wasn't her fault at all that she was poised and polished and out of place.

"I have some very exciting news to share—the Red Cross has agreed to take us on! As of the end of February, once our affiliation with the AFFW runs out, we will be officially a unit of the American Red Cross."

"Is that—is that really what's best for the Unit?" asked Kate hesitantly, since no one else seemed to be saying anything. "We've prided ourselves on making our own way. What if the Red Cross decided to divert our funding or to break up the Unit entirely?"

"They have promised we'll keep our name," said Mrs. Barrett. "You know that Mrs. Rutherford originally sought affiliation with the Red Cross, and they sent her away. They wanted us to prove ourselves first. We've proven ourselves, girls, and in spades. Do you know what Mr. Folks of the Red Cross said to me when I spoke to him in Paris yesterday? He said that taking over the SCRU will be a boon to the Red Cross—because we get so much more publicity than they do."

That was all very well, but not exactly an answer. "Can they offer us any assurances that we'll be allowed to go on with our own work in our own way?"

"There are still details to be worked out, but there's really no choice in the matter," said Mrs. Barrett firmly. "The Red Cross is consolidating all the aid organizations. Either we affiliate with them, or we won't be able to work here at all. And there are benefits to it! Mr. Jackson, the Red Cross delegate, has been very helpful. He's told us once we're officially under their umbrella, they'll be able to provide all sorts of things. I've been going over the reports you submitted to Dr. Stringfellow, with your lists of requests—"

"Champagne with supper and pâté for breakfast?" suggested Nell.

"I was thinking more of"—Mrs. Barrett consulted the list by her side—"a village pump, a *chaudière*, two horses and a plow, and beds for forty-seven children for Courcelles. Mr. Jackson says we can have the pump and the *chaudière* and roughly half that number of beds by the end of the week."

"Really?" Emmie lit up like a Christmas tree. Kate didn't see how Emmie could be thinking of leaving the Unit when anyone could tell how much she cared. "I can't tell you what a difference that pump will make. . . ."

"You don't have to," said Mrs. Barrett, laughing. "You identify the need and the Red Cross will take care of the details for us. They've also promised us *essence*, immediately. I've been going over the schedules, and I can see ways we can manage our time more efficiently—not that you haven't been doing wonderfully," Mrs. Barrett added, "with all the breakdowns and having to scramble and muddle along and do the best you can."

She made it sound like it was their fault, that they'd just been running around like headless chickens. Kate glanced at Emmie, feeling dreadful. Maybe chickens weren't the best metaphor.

"In the Somme," said Kate, her voice very dry, "the best-laid plans have a way of going agley."

"Yes," said Alice, rousing herself out of her doldrums. "You never do wind up doing what you were meant to be doing. Something always seems to come up."

A loud crash made the china on the table rattle.

"Like that," said Nell cheerfully. "Do you think it's Ham again?"

The Germans had been pounding their Quaker friends at Ham. One of their villagers in a neighboring village had died of a heart attack last week from the shock of the noise.

"Or Cambrai?" Florence tilted her head, listening.

"Wrong direction," said Alice. They'd all become experts on determining the direction and distance of artillery.

"You scarcely notice it after a while," Emmie said helpfully to Mrs. Barrett. "And we've got earplugs for at night."

"I've brought mine with me from Paris," said Mrs. Barrett, smiling at Emmie. Of course she loved Emmie. Everyone loved Emmie. Kate didn't understand how Emmie didn't see that. "Back to business. . . . We're doing all we can to press the authorities for passes so our girls can get here from Paris."

"Is there any word on when Dr. Clare will arrive?" asked Julia.

"Her trunks came today," Emmie offered. "Eight of them. And a folding dispensary table."

"Dr. Clare is still waiting for her pass, but we expect her momentarily. In the meantime . . ." Mrs. Barrett looked very pleased with herself. "I've arranged for a doctor from the Red Cross hospital in Nesle to visit three times a week to see patients. Dr. Stapleton of Johns Hopkins."

Julia's face was roughly the color of the whitewash Anne had been using on the cellar walls.

"There's no need for that," said Kate, and was aware of just how harsh and ugly her voice sounded, how rude and ungrateful. "Dr. Pruyn can manage. Dr. Pruyn *has* been managing. Brilliantly."

Mrs. Barrett regarded Kate tolerantly. "Miss Moran, the point is not to manage. The point is to make everything go as smoothly as possible, with as little difficulty as possible. Dr. Pruyn shouldn't have to manage."

She had no idea, thought Kate wildly. She just thought Kate was being difficult. And maybe Kate was being difficult, but there were reasons, if only Mrs. Barrett had bothered to stop and ask. She'd read the reports and spoken to the members who had visited in Paris and thought she knew all there was to know, but that wasn't the half of it.

Mrs. Barrett smiled at Julia, clearly misinterpreting Julia's white lips and set face. "It's no reflection on your skill, Dr. Pruyn. There's far too much work here for one doctor. The Unit was always meant to have at least two doctors on staff."

Julia pushed up from her chair. "I need to go back to the infirmary."

Straight-backed, Julia stalked out of the barrack, letting the wind slam the door shut behind her.

Mrs. Barrett watched her go with concern. "And that's just the problem. You've all been working yourselves sick. Don't think I don't appreciate it—or how necessary it was! But now you've laid the groundwork, we can all learn from what you've already done, and make improvements going forward. You were the pioneers—but now we've entered a new stage of our grand project. We don't have to create anymore, but refine."

"I need to go refine the mess in the cellar," said Nell, hopping up from her chair. "Are you coming, Alice?"

"I'll go too," said Emmie, not looking at Kate.

Kate would have followed, but Mrs. Barrett forestalled her. "Miss Moran? May I speak with you for a moment?"

"Of course." She was worried about Julia. She was worried about Emmie. But she couldn't say no. "I didn't mean to be difficult during the meeting. It's just that we've been here some time and we've developed habits and ways of doing things."

"You've all worked wonders," said Mrs. Barrett, "and particularly you. I've seen your system of reports. It's a thing of beauty."

"Er, thank you?" said Kate, taken off guard.

"You've been a tower of strength. To take on the running of the Unit like that—it was unconscionable that it was all simply dropped on you like that."

"Dr. Stringfellow did her bit."

The corners of Mrs. Barrett's eyes crinkled. "Ava Stringfellow is a brilliant doctor and an absolutely ruthless pinochle player but she had no business being director. And you needn't jump to her defense! I'm repeating exactly what she told me. She was insistent that the Unit only survived—and thrived!—these past four months because you took on more than any human being could be expected to accomplish."

"Oh," said Kate. She'd been expecting to be admonished, not praised. "It wasn't just me. We all did our bit."

"You did your bit and about ten other people's," said Mrs. Barrett, and Kate felt the full force of her charm. "Which is why I wanted to ask . . ."

The table shook again, a coffee cup overturning. Kate caught it just in time. "Yes?"

Mrs. Barrett winced. "I do wish they wouldn't do that. Now, what was I saying? Oh yes, I wanted to ask . . . my dear, when was the last time you took a few days away?"

"I haven't," said Kate dumbly. She thought about it. "That is, I went to Amiens for a bath and shampoo two weeks ago. Or maybe it was three weeks ago."

Mrs. Barrett looked at her closely. Something about her expression reminded Kate, strongly, of her mother. "And you did the Unit's shopping while you were there, didn't you? And were still back before supper."

"Just after," said Kate, feeling like she'd lost control of the situation somehow.

Mrs. Barrett nodded. "As your director, I direct you to take two weeks in Paris. And to spend at least two days doing nothing at all."

Kate stared at her in mute horror. But there was the planting, and Julia, and Emmie—

She cleared her throat. "There's really no need—"

"Make that three days doing nothing," said Mrs. Barrett firmly.

Chapter Twenty

*Miss Moran has organized the work in a
wonderful way and her system of reports is a thing
to be proud of, but I feel strongly that the Unit
needs a director who is not a specialist in any one
thing, neither a doctor nor a social worker nor a
chauffeur, but only there to direct. . . . The Unit
has been like Topsy to this point, growing at an
astonishing pace, but I feel like something more
systematic can now be worked out.*

*I wanted to get a "taste" of the work, as you
might say, so I went out with the girls on my
second day here. The weather turned, bucketing
down snow, but twenty-one blankets had been
promised to Sancourt, and those girls were
determined to get the blankets through. You*

wouldn't believe the adventures we had going all of twelve kilometers: the machine stalled, we couldn't see the road for the drifts, the tires burst, and one of the girls had to stop and rub snow on her feet to prevent frostbite. But we got those blankets through and made it home by dark. The peasants of Sancourt slept warm that night, even if the girls at Grécourt didn't.

It's grueling work, but they take it on without a grumble. By the following day, the roads were too thick with snow for the machines to get through, and you would have thought that would be that, but our lady doctor (Julia Pruyn, '11) slung her supplies over her back and our social worker (Eleanor Baldwin, '14) grabbed up a valise of milk bottles—four gallons' worth!—and a massive bottle of malted milk to boot and they hauled it all two miles through the snow on foot. The kiddies of Canizy had to have their milk, you see—and there were some sick children too—and since the cars couldn't go, they walked. As simple as that. And nobody thought it was anything out of the ordinary. It's just what they do.

I only hope I can be worthy of them. They resist utterly having money spent on them, because the more they spend on themselves, the less they

have for the people. But I'm working hard to bring
them a few comforts—whether they like it or not!
— *Mrs. James R. Barrett (née*
Ruth Irwin), '02, Director, to
the Paris Committee

February 1918
Grécourt, France

"I've made you sandwiches for the train." Emmie pressed a waxed-paper packet into Kate's hands. "And for Julia too."

Kate blindly accepted the packet. "It's ridiculous to be taking a vacation when there are only eight of us left."

"Nine if you count Mrs. Barrett," pointed out Emmie. "Don't squish the sandwiches—you'll want them later."

"Mrs. Barrett doesn't count," said Kate, tucking the sandwiches into her carpetbag. Both Kate and the carpetbag were meant to be in the Red Cross truck already, on their way to the train, but Emmie couldn't seem to get her out the door of the barrack. "It's not as though she's in the fields with the plows."

"I'm sure if we needed the extra pair of hands, she could muck in sorting seeds," said Emmie consolingly.

"Hmmm," said Kate, which was the noise Kate always made when she didn't want to disagree, but did.

Emmie knew exactly what she meant. Mrs. Barrett was a brilliant director, but being a director was very different from being a member of the Unit. Which was exactly why the committee had chosen her, of course, so that she could direct without being distracted by daily duties. But it was different from what they were used to. It was all different.

Emmie knew Kate hated it. Kate hated leaving, hated going to Paris, hated giving up the reins of command to Mrs. Barrett. Kate hated the new house that had been put up behind the château, furnished with a rug—a real rug, not a rag rug—donated by Mrs. Morrow of the Paris Committee, a piano that Mrs. Barrett had wrangled goodness only knew where, and a framed copy of the Stuart portrait of George Washington, so that their first president eyed them beadily at all their meetings.

The entire tone of the enterprise had changed. They still trekked out to their villages in all weathers, but there was now a housekeeper to cook their meals and maids to clean their rooms while they were out doing their rounds. It made the hardscrabble months feel a bit like children playing house, as though a grown-up had arrived and replaced their tent of tree branches and twine with a proper one, store-made.

"It's only two weeks," said Emmie. She wasn't sure whether she minded Kate leaving or was relieved by it. "Two weeks in a real bed will do you a world of good."

It had been horrible seeing the bruised look in Kate's eyes when Mrs. Barrett had handed out their new schedules, or when Mrs. Barrett had spoken to someone who had spoken to someone who had miraculously produced enough *essence* to keep their trucks running for the next month. Kate was still, officially, assistant director, but Mrs. Barrett had made it very clear that the weight of the work wasn't on her shoulders any longer. They had a director now, a proper one, and Kate could get on with the regular work of the Unit, with driving and social work, and not bother herself with larger issues.

Emmie had never seen Kate look so lost, not even that first week at Smith when they'd all been wandering wide-eyed around Northampton.

"Yes, but we've got so much to *do*," said Kate, worrying at the handle of her carpetbag. "Mrs. Barrett just doesn't understand. We're short-handed already. Dr. Clare still doesn't have her pass, and with Julia coming to Paris . . ."

"Gwen Mills is itching to take over the dispensary," said Emmie cheerfully. "She can't wait to have full sway over the bottles and bandages."

"Gwen isn't a doctor," said Kate sharply.

"No," said Emmie soothingly, "but poor Julia does look done in—and we have that nice Dr. Stapleton from Nesle three times a week."

Kate bit down hard on her lower lip. "Yes, about that . . ."

Emmie chivvied Kate toward the door. "I know it's not a replacement for having a doctor of our own—we were spoiled with Dr. Stringfellow!—but the rest of us can deal with the minor cuts and scrapes and fevers. I do worry about Julia. If you won't go for yourself, go to keep an eye on her. She needs the rest and you're the only one she'll listen to. If I say anything, she just tells me to stop fussing."

"I don't think it's overwork," said Kate guardedly. "If Mrs. Barrett had only left well enough alone . . ."

"You're as bad as Julia," Emmie said firmly, maneuvering Kate out the door. "Anyway, it's decided. There's no getting around it. Mrs. Barrett says everyone needs to get away at least once every six weeks, and you're first because you've been working hardest."

Although Emmie did wonder whether it was really because Kate had been working hardest or more because Mrs. Barrett desperately wanted to be left to get on with it in her own way and not have Kate just *looking* at her every time she suggested something new.

"And you know that Florence can't get away because of the planting but she desperately needs someone to get her more chickens. You will get Florence her chickens, won't you?" Nothing made Kate feel better than a bit of responsibility.

"Yes, she's given me very specific instructions. No roosters this time." Kate looked horror-struck. "I didn't mean—"

Emmie felt the familiar lump form at the back of her throat. This kept happening. Everything would be normal and then suddenly they'd hit on that sore spot again, like biting down on a rotten tooth. "I know you didn't. It's all right."

"But it's not, is it? I never should have said what I said to you. I was angry about your paying my way— my pride was hurt. But that was no excuse for lashing out at you."

"It doesn't matter." Emmie's head hurt thinking about it. Kate had been on her about it ever since she'd mentioned the prospect of leaving. For once, it was Kate who wanted to talk, and Emmie who wanted to be left alone.

"But it does." Kate glowered at the new house, where Mrs. Barrett lived and worked. "I hate that she's making me go just now—"

"You'd hate it a week or a month from now too,"

said Emmie, propelling Kate down the path. "If you're going, you'd best go. What was it that Lady Macbeth said? If it were done, it were best done quickly? Not that you're planning to commit regicide or anything like that, but I imagine the same principle applies. Look, there's Julia in the machine already. You'd best get it over with so you can come back sooner."

Kate gave her a quick, fierce hug, a gesture that so surprised Emmie that she completely failed to hug her back.

"You won't make any decisions while I'm away?"

"I won't," promised Emmie. "I promise I won't say anything to Mrs. Barrett until you come back from Paris. Other than the usual sorts of things like hello and good morning and please pass the toast."

Julia gave her a brief, ironic wave, and they were off, bumping along in the Red Cross truck with Dave, while Marie came out of her cottage to watch and comment acerbically that it would be a wonder if That Man didn't kill her young ladies.

Emmie watched them go, wondering how two people who meant so well could hurt each other so badly, and how one could get past the tangle of who'd done what and who'd been right and who'd been wrong and whether it mattered anyway.

Because no matter what Kate said now, it didn't

change the fact that Emmie had walked them into an impossible situation that night in the snow.

Or that she'd brought Kate into the Unit under false pretenses.

She'd promised Kate she wouldn't go until the new people came, and that was something of a relief, at least, because it meant she wouldn't have to think about it until then. But she did think about it anyway. She thought about all she'd meant to do and all she hadn't. Or all she'd done but done wrong.

When Emmie had joined the Unit, she'd had such grand ideas of bringing people together, of doing something wonderful and heroic. But in the end, that had been Kate's destiny, not hers. Maybe her mother was right, Emmie thought resignedly, as she went to join Alice in the cellar. Maybe she had a small mind, suited only to small things: to wrapping presents and planning parties and putting thousands of seeds into tiny little packets.

Or ladling soup into bowls for soldiers in a canteen somewhere in Paris.

It might not be their decision in the end, Emmie reminded herself. The British might make it for them. They'd had word—not from Captain DeWitt, whom Emmie hadn't seen in person since Christmas, who wrote of cabbages and kings but never of the war—that all women in British-run aid organizations had been ordered out already.

"Hullo? Alice?" The days were starting to get longer, but it was still winter dark and winter cold in the castle cellar. Emmie heard a scrabbling and a sniffling and saw Alice stumbling to her feet, wiping her eyes on the back of her sleeve.

"I was just . . . getting the seeds," said Alice, belatedly shoveling a bunch of seed packets into a basket.

"The air down here is dreadful, isn't it? It always makes my nose run," said Emmie, giving Alice a chance to collect herself. "Would you like my spare handkerchief? I always bring an extra for cellar work."

"Thanks," said Alice thickly, and blew her nose with a honk of despair.

"I've just seen Julia and Kate off." Emmie concentrated on putting the seeds into piles, so many of cabbage, so many of lettuce. "Dave is driving them to the train at Amiens."

"It's so strange with everyone gone," said Alice, putting seeds into the wrong piles. "All the original crew. It makes me feel ancient."

"We should have the new people soon."

"Yes, and they'll probably be all young and cheerful and not have any idea how anything is done and they'll make fun of us for being so shabby. . . . And goodness knows it's crowded enough here as it is. There's never any place to *think*, even if we could hear ourselves think with all the shelling," added Alice resentfully. Of all of them, Alice minded the raids the most. "There's not even any place to have a good cry without someone asking you what you're sniffling about. And then they just try to *jolly* you. . . ."

Emmie's head popped up. "Have I been jollying you?"

"What? Oh, not you. It's Nell, mostly. And Anne. They're both so relentlessly *cheerful*," said Alice despairingly.

Emmie wasn't quite sure she would have put it exactly that way. Anne was actually something of a worrier, she worried away at things, single-mindedly, until she got them done. Nell was full of a coiled sort of tension that might be mistaken for gaiety, but wasn't really. Emmie had been determinedly cheerful enough herself to realize the sort of insecurities it might hide. "They probably have their own demons. Everyone does."

"Do they? They both have such—such a sense of purpose. I can't imagine there's anything that bothers Anne that she couldn't just hammer away. She's got those boys making shelves for their new social center, and all the girls sewing curtains. . . ."

"Yes, and you have three trucks that you somehow

keep running. Alice?" Emmie wasn't sure where the idea came from; it just sprang on her out of nowhere. "There's been something I've been wanting to ask you. . . ."

Alice paused in her seed sorting, looking deeply wary. "Yes?"

"Would you be willing to teach me how to drive?" The second she said it, Emmie knew it was an awful idea, but she plowed on regardless. "You're our best driver—and I'm afraid the others would make fun. I'm horrible at anything mechanical. And you know when someone says go right, I always go left. Never mind. Maybe I shouldn't try. We don't have enough trucks to be worth risking my wrecking one."

"No, no," said Alice, setting down her seed packets. "You can't possibly do any worse than Red Cross Dave. And why should it matter about your right and your left? I'll tell you what to do, and we'll just follow the road—but not near the ditch."

"Are you sure? I really don't want to be a bother. . . . And we do have so many seeds to deliver. . . ."

Alice straightened, adjusting her collar. "Yes, I'm sure. We can start now."

"Now?" asked Emmie apprehensively. "Now as in now?"

"We won't waste any extra *essence* that way," said

Alice, suddenly brisk. "I'll show you what everything is and what you do, and then when we find a straight stretch of road on our way to drop off the seeds, we'll swap."

Emmie wasn't entirely sure that her definition of a straight stretch of road and Alice's coincided, but if Emmie stalled the truck three times on the first attempt, at least she could tell herself it was all in aid of making Alice feel better. Alice was endlessly patient, explaining the same things over and over, without reproach. This was a very different Alice, an assured, confident Alice, not the Alice who simpered and tittered and always chose the absolute worst sort of hat.

"You're really very good at this," said Emmie as Alice directed her around a pothole.

"My father always said that I was the son he never had," said Alice. She grimaced. "My mother said that if I wasn't pretty, at least I could be useful. Not like my sister. . . . Look, Emmie! You're driving!"

"Wait, I'm—what?" Emmie turned, forgetting that she was holding the wheel. The wheel turned with her. So did the truck.

"*Not* the ditch." Alice lunged over her to grab the wheel, wrestling them back onto the road. "But there, you see? You did it! You weren't even thinking about it and you drove the truck a good half mile."

"I drove the truck?" She knew she'd been sitting there, holding the wheel, but she hadn't quite equated that with the magical act of mechanics that the other girls were capable of accomplishing.

"Yes," said Alice, beaming at her. "You drove the truck. Now do it again. It's just repetition—like sewing. The more you do it, the less you have to think about it."

"A friend offered to teach me once, in Newport," Emmie confided to Alice, "but I was afraid I would take the car over a cliff."

"Well, there aren't any cliffs here," said Alice. "Now I'll show you how to back her up. . . ."

The fence, Alice assured her, had been rotten and on the verge of falling over anyway. And the Tommy she nearly hit was very nice about it and didn't even bother to check her pass, even though he was standing there as part of a checkpoint. In fact, he seemed very eager to see them on their way.

"Oh no," said Alice, when Emmie suggested that maybe that was a sign she shouldn't be driving after all. "If that were the case, no one would let Red Cross Dave behind the wheel. Or Alfalfa Bill."

Alfalfa Bill had spent two days living in the *basse-cour*, doing odd jobs for the Unit, after ditching his truck in the mud by the gate and declaring himself incapable of getting it out again.

"Yes, but do you think they're really that bad at driving, or they just want Madame Gouge's coffee?" Emmie asked seriously.

Alice shrugged. "Either way, by the end of the week, you'll be a better driver than either of them, I promise."

Emmie wasn't sure about that, but Alice was relentless. Emmie drove on every straight stretch. She drove when they took out the store on Monday and Wednesday, distributing milk and seeds and selling the usual selection of aprons and *sabots* and kitchen implements. She drove when they took Nell to Canizy and Anne to Verlaines, where both were working on outfitting social centers for the villagers. She'd thought they might be nervous at driving with her, but they weren't; they were too taken up with talking about the social centers and the various classes they intended to hold.

"I'm fitting up a corner as a dispensary," said Nell, who had raided the Hague trunks for first-aid supplies. "Don't you think that will be a huge help? Then the doctors don't have to carry everything with them when they make their rounds. We can start working out of the villages instead of carrying everything on our backs like a snail. Or do I mean a turtle?"

That afternoon, Emmie managed to drive the truck

through the gates and over the bridge, a feat that Dave and Bill had yet to master.

Alice gave her an approving nod. "You see? You should get Mrs. Barrett to add you to the chauffeur list."

The chauffeur list. They depended on their chauffeurs like nothing else. The idea that she could climb into a truck and take them where they needed to go, without asking Kate or someone else to drive . . . according to Mrs. Barrett's schedule, of course. "Won't I need a driving license?"

"It wasn't very hard to get one—when Kate and Julia come back, you could go to Paris and take the test. It would make such a difference having another driver."

Emmie climbed down, lingering by the side of the truck. "Aren't two of the new girls meant to drive? Williams and White?"

"Yes, but we can always use more. We started out with Fran and Margaret and Liza as well as me and Kate—and now look. We're down to two of five. It really wouldn't hurt to have an extra."

If she left . . . but that didn't really matter, Emmie told herself. She'd promised Kate she'd stay at least until the new people got here, and the new people showed no signs of getting here. They were all still in Paris, waiting for the British authorities to issue passes. Given the way the British felt about women in their war zone, that might be quite some time.

Florence knew how to drive, but Florence was fully occupied with the spring planting, moving from village to village on a two-day schedule to make sure the crops were put in properly with a combination of community and government effort.

The store needed to be taken out at least two times a week; the doctors needed to be driven (or would, once they had doctors again); the social workers could walk to the nearer villages, but not the farther ones, not the ones that needed help the most. And it really wouldn't be fair leaving Alice and Kate doing all of that on their own.

She would go see Mrs. Barrett before she lost her resolve.

Unlike Kate, who was generally fifteen places at once, one always knew where to find Mrs. Barrett. She ran the Unit from the living room of the new building, which doubled as both the Unit meeting room and the director's office.

"Mrs. Barrett?"

It wasn't until she was inside that Emmie realized they had visitors. A coffeepot and three cups sat on the table that held the framed portrait of George Washington. Mrs. Barrett, in a spotless uniform, sat across from the British colonel with the exceedingly bushy mustache who had attended their Christmas party. And behind him stood Captain DeWitt.

"You remember Miss Van Alden, Colonel?" said Mrs. Barrett.

Chapter Twenty-One

Over the months of January and February, the social service department reports the distribution of more than 800 articles to 165 families in 12 villages. Among the articles distributed were: 72 beds, 8 mattresses, 16 armoires, 9 tables, 60 chairs, 28 buffets, 238 sheets, 138 blankets, 91 quilts, 10 stoves, and 118 articles of clothing. These distributions are relief work unrelated to supplies sold from the store. The sale of supplies in January and February amounted to $3,264, approximately 2/3 the cost of the articles to the Unit. Under the guidance of Miss Dawlish, 40 women in our villages were given material to make 986 garments, which they sold to the Unit for $714.45. More material has been purchased.

Miss Baldwin reports that the library contains more than 700 volumes, and now includes books for adults. An effort is being made to find the right person in each village to take charge of their circulation, most likely through the schools. At Grécourt, a house will shortly be opened at specified hours for a reading room, lending library, game room, and center for sewing classes, children's classes, and mothers' meetings. Another house is to be fitted as a workshop for the boys. A portable cinema machine has been purchased for the instruction and amusement of the children, who walk miles to see these pictures. An average of 320 children are being reached weekly through these channels, not counting the children reached through the creation of similar social centers in the villages of Canizy, Courcelles, and Verlaines.

When reading the medical report, it should be remembered that since January 24, there has been only one junior doctor at Grécourt, so the medical work has been greatly limited. Over the past month, with the assistance of one nurse (Miss Mills), Dr. Pruyn has made 364 house visits and received 160 patients in the dispensary for a total of 524. In the absence of our doctors, in serious cases we have the assistance of Dr. Stapleton of the

American Red Cross hospital at Nesle, who holds
dispensary at Grécourt three times a week, and
also of Dr. Cooney of the AEF. Getting the proper
pass from the British authorities for Dr. Clare and
renewing the pass for Dr. Pruyn is of the highest
priority for the ongoing success of the Unit's
mission. . . .

> — From a report by Miss
> Katherine Moran, '11,
> Assistant Director, to the Paris
> Committee, February 1918

February 1918
Paris, France

"I would like to see the general," said Kate, for approximately the twenty-third time.

"*Ce n'est pas possible*," said the very minor official to whom Kate had progressed via a series of other minor officials. "Monsieur le General only grants audiences on Saturday afternoons from half past three until five and on Wednesday mornings from nine until half past ten."

It was Wednesday afternoon. The clock on the official's desk read three thirty.

"I was here at nine in the morning," said Kate, channeling her fury into withering politeness. "I was here *before* nine in the morning. I was told I needed a pass to enter the building. I went to another office and acquired the pass. Then I was told I needed another pass to proceed up the stairs. That was ten thirty. It has taken me six and a half hours to get to this office and I. Am. Not. Leaving."

She spoke very slowly and clearly, just to make sure he understood.

He didn't. "It is not the time at which Monsieur le General receives visitors."

"Well, he'll receive me," said Kate firmly. She fumbled in her pocket. "Look. This is a letter of introduction from the Marquise de Noailles. Tell Monsieur le General that the assistant director of *les Collégiennes Américaines* is here to see him at the express request of the Marquise de Noailles."

"Ah, *les Collégiennes Américaines.*" He looked at her as though it explained a great deal, not necessarily in a good way, more in the way of suddenly being confronted with a zoo animal who might or might not bite. "One moment."

Kate didn't wonder he looked at her strangely; she probably looked like a madwoman. She was wearing her uniform, the new one that Mrs. Barrett had brought for her, but it was slightly too large and already stained. Her red rubber boots, *de rigueur* for the mud of Grécourt, were entirely out of place on the streets of Paris and even more out of place on the elegant marble floor of the ministry. After six months of boots, it had never occurred to her to bring shoes. She'd practically forgotten what they were. Or what it was to walk on solid flagstones instead of sinking knee-deep in mud.

There was a chair in the anteroom, a spindly gilded thing, so different from the stout wooden ones they'd been distributing to their villagers. Kate had been standing all day in one way or another, standing in line to get passes, standing in line to be admitted to the building, standing in line to be admitted to this office. She should sit, she knew, and muster her strength, but she was fizzing with nervous energy.

It had been nearly a week since she'd been in Paris, and she hadn't accomplished a single thing she'd set out to do.

It had been an unnerving and largely silent train ride with Julia, who was officially in Paris to get her pass renewed. When Kate had delicately tried to broach the question of whether the presence of Dr. Stapleton at Grécourt might have something to do with her sudden desire to go to Paris, Julia had simply looked at her— one of her Medusa looks, designed to turn the unlucky into stone—and looked away again.

It was a moot point anyway, Kate had told herself

as they sat in stony silence for the rest of the journey, Julia's gigantic duffel bag wedged on the seat between them. As soon as Dr. Clare got her pass, they'd have no need for Dr. Stapleton and therefore no need to discuss it.

She and Julia had gone straight from the train to the hotel on the Quai Voltaire, which had become a sort of dormitory for the Smith Unit in Paris. They'd found the new girls there. They looked disconcertingly clean. Clean and pressed and entirely unprepared. Had she looked like that once? Kate supposed she had, but it was hard to remember. Their nails were smooth and white, not jagged with the stains of earth under them that never quite came out. They wore clothes that hadn't been pounded by Marie, and their faces had a city smoothness to them, not windburn from months spent riding in an open truck with the wind and rain and snow howling through.

They were, as Kate and the others had, volunteering with various charities while waiting for their passes to come through, making prosthetics and special shoes, both awed and alarmed by the proximity of Grécourt to the war zone, full of questions about what had been done and what they were meant to do.

"Is it true that you walked through a blizzard carrying four gallons of wine?" asked Miss Williams.

"It wasn't wine," said Kate wearily. "It was milk. Milk from our cows. Milk needs to be delivered, even in the snow."

"Thank goodness it's spring now," said Miss White, huddling into the shawl she had wrapped around her uniform jacket. "I can't bear the cold."

"The weather has been much better." No need to tell them it was like Greenland at night, even in springtime. "And we've got plenty of blankets."

"Were we ever that frivolous?" she asked Julia. They were sharing a room, a proper room. The dormitory, where Kate had stayed that first month, was being used for storage, bristling with things the various local Smith clubs had sent to the Unit, waiting to be sorted.

"They'll learn," said Julia, and put her pillow over her head to discourage further communication.

It felt odd to be sleeping in a proper bed, rather than a cot made of springs and sharp edges. Kate missed the slump and creak of it. She woke half a dozen times in the night at familiar but forgotten noises, the thrum of traffic, the sound of male voices. It was even worse leaving the hotel to run her errands. There were just so many people. The air felt different, warmer, stuffier, sootier. It felt wrong to be walking on pavement again instead of slogging through mud. The soot-stained buildings pressed too close around her; the air stank of assembled humanity instead of cows.

Kate had never thought she would miss the cows.

"Kate!" A large woman in a brown suit flung herself at Kate, nearly knocking her down.

"Liza!" Kate couldn't believe how glad she was to see the other women, even though it was odd to see her with her hair washed and done up properly, in a suit that was very much the wrong color for her complexion. "I hardly recognized you in civvies!"

Liza plucked at her suit. "I hardly recognize me," she admitted. "I never thought I'd miss the old uniform— but it does feel odd being out of it."

"What are you doing in town?" Maud joined them, dressed to the nines in the best the Paris shops could offer, looking Kate up and down in a way that Kate remembered well, as though she were sniffing out potential weaknesses.

"Reports and errands." Kate couldn't bring herself to say that Mrs. Barrett had mandated that she take a rest. "I've promised fruit trees and chickens for Florence and I want to see what I can do about getting Dr. Clare's pass expedited."

"Well, do try to enjoy yourself while you're here," said Maud patronizingly. "Before you have to go back to the wilds."

"I do miss the cream from our cows," said Liza wistfully. "In Paris, you can only get milk with a doctor's prescription. I've had to take my coffee black."

"Yes, but you can get tickets to the opera," said Maud. She eyed Kate's headgear. "And hats that haven't been gnawed by a goat."

Kate grinned. "Minerva sends you her love too."

"Her love? She owes me a lace collar and two hats," said Maud indignantly.

"Bill it to the Unit." Kate couldn't resist adding, "You'd never know the place now. We're drowning in luxuries. Mrs. Barrett even found us a piano."

They parted with insincere expressions of goodwill, but Kate found the meeting acted on her like a tonic. No matter how annoying Maud might be, she was somehow Kate's now, like a horrible cousin one couldn't disown. She didn't miss her precisely, but she was strangely glad to see her. And be annoyed by her again.

Liza paused halfway down the block, said something to Maud, and came hurrying back. "I just wanted to say . . . if you need me, I can come back, you know. I had to get my pass renewed that time—remember how they had the wrong name for me? So I did it when I was here getting my collarbone fixed and the new one is good until April."

"Are you sure?" asked Kate, touched despite herself. "You were so looking forward to canteen work."

Liza looked back over her shoulder at Maud, dropping her voice so she wouldn't be heard. "I miss Grécourt. I even miss the mud. It's dreadful being cooped up in a canteen instead of out there, getting about."

"What about our boys?" Kate asked. They'd heard a lot about Our Boys before Liza and Maud had left.

"We're doing our best for them, but they don't seem to want awfully to be saved from temptation." Liza sounded genuinely bewildered. "Oh dear— that's Maud calling. Give my love to the girls! And the goats."

Kate watched Liza run off after Maud, thinking what a thoroughly decent person Liza was. If she'd been a little more patient, managed everything a little better, would Maud and Liza have stayed? It was only now that they'd gone that it was clear just how much they'd done for the Unit, and Kate felt guilty for mocking them for decorating their barrack. She'd misjudged them, horribly.

She'd misjudged a lot of people. But mostly Emmie. If Emmie left the Unit—she wasn't sure she could forgive herself for it.

Julia had tried to tell her, but Kate had ignored her, because Julia was Julia, and because, from the day they'd started Smith, she'd had an idea of what Emmie was, and she'd stuck to it, an idea compounded entirely of her own insecurities. She'd just assumed, she'd always assumed, that Emmie's name and position shielded her from everything, that being a Van Alden made her impervious, dancing obliviously through life, showering charity on lesser mortals. She'd wanted, if she were being honest with herself, to bring Emmie down a notch, to make her feel what it was to be small. Because Emmie's father belonged to private clubs and Kate's had driven a wagon full of beer.

But Kate's father had loved her. Her stepfather loved her. Even her ridiculous brothers loved her, when they weren't busy tormenting the life out of her. Her mother, who didn't approve of what she was doing, had come to see her off and sent her boots.

And what did Emmie have? A mother who cared for everyone but her. A father who ignored her. A friend who wasn't much of a friend at all.

There was no point in going over it again and again, Kate told herself. She'd finish her errands, get back to Grécourt as soon as Mrs. Barrett and the rail system would allow, and do her best to make up for the damage she'd done. In the meantime, she had fruit trees and chickens to acquire.

Florence had told her to see the national nurseries

about fruit trees, the next step in the grand replanting project.

A very nice lieutenant received Kate cordially, offered her coffee, showed her their survey of the area, and told her it couldn't be done.

"Why not? Is it the cost?" He'd shown her their maps of the region, estimating that to replace the fruit trees destroyed by the Germans in their villages would cost somewhere between six and seven thousand dollars. It was a sum that made Kate's stomach clench, but if there was one thing that she had learned in helping to run the Unit, it was that sums that had seemed unthinkable to her were well within the reach of Smith's alumnae.

"You are too near the front." The lieutenant shrugged, an entirely French sort of shrug that Kate had learned translated to something in between *c'est la guerre* and *why are you bothering me, you mad American?* "It is too expensive to do the work twice. If we planted now, the trees might be destroyed by shells. It is not worth the risk."

Nothing Kate could say would budge him.

If she couldn't get Florence trees, she could at least find her chickens. The Marquise de Noailles, who had found them their goats, had provided Florence with the address of an official she swore could help them acquire poultry.

"As many as you can get," Florence had told Kate. "I could sell three or four hundred if I could get them. They all need them so."

Which brought Kate to a very grand marble anteroom in a very grand marble ministry waiting to see a very grand officer who only gave audiences on Saturday afternoons and Wednesday mornings.

The assistant came out of the inner office and bowed to Kate. "Monsieur le General will see you now."

Kate straightened her hat (which had, in fact, been lightly chewed by Minerva; she'd been hoping people wouldn't notice) and tried to look like someone who was regularly granted special audiences by important military officials.

This office was the grandest of the many offices through which Kate had processed today. The desk was roughly the size of the SS *Rochambeau* and the man who sat behind it was wearing a dazzling array of medals. He'd been so decorated that his medals had medals.

Kate put her best rubber boot forward. "Thank you so much for being willing to see me. I'm only in Paris for another week."

The general rose in greeting. "We have heard of your good work in Grécourt, Mademoiselle"—he was very good; it took him only a second to consult her card—"Mademoiselle Moran. How may I be of assistance?"

"I've come about the chickens," said Kate succinctly.

"Chickens?" he asked.

Perhaps that had been a bit too succinct. "Madame la Marquise thought you might be able to tell us where we could buy chickens for our villagers."

"I would be delighted to be able to oblige you, but . . ."

Kate hadn't spent the past six months dealing with reluctant bureaucrats in Amiens and Noyon without learning that they always said that. There was always the *but*. The trick was getting in there before they could start making excuses.

"I know they're very scarce right now," said Kate, quickly running through all possible answers to all possible objections, "but we promise, they will be put to the best possible use. There's no need to worry about the cost; we have the money to pay for them. And there won't be any bother with shipping. I will convey any chickens we might acquire personally to Grécourt."

The general's mustache twitched in amusement. "You are, I see, a woman of great resources. And it breaks my heart to be unable to be of assistance, but, you see, I know nothing about chickens."

"But the marquise said . . ."

"Madame la Marquise, I fear, has mistaken one fowl for another. My province," said the general, unlocking a cabinet and proudly producing a brass bird, "is the carrier pigeon."

"The carrier pigeon," said Kate.

"A most noble bird, the pigeon," said the general, patting his bronze pet.

Kate was fairly sure that most of the statues in Central Park might feel otherwise but refrained from saying so. "So you really know nothing about where I might find chickens?"

"*Dommage*," said the general. "Now about the pigeon . . ."

The general waxed eloquent on the properties of pigeons and their use in warfare from the ancient Romans to the present. Kate managed to control herself throughout the recitation, thank the general kindly, apologize again for her mistake, and make it all the way out of the office, through the anteroom, and into the hall before covering her mouth with her handkerchief and giving way to a burst of hysterical laughter.

She had spent a whole day wrangling passes and arguing with petty officials to hear a history of the pigeon.

It was so dreadful it was funny, and she only wished Emmie were there. Even if poultry was rather a tender subject with Emmie at present. But it was just the sort of thing Emmie would find irresistibly hilarious.

Kate tried to share the joke with Julia, but Julia was not in a mood to be amused.

Julia was braiding her long, golden hair for bed. She paused to look over her shoulder at Kate, saying abruptly, "I was working with Dr. Clare at the Red Cross hospital this morning, and I think you should know, Kate—she's not planning to come to Grécourt."

Kate sat on the edge of her bed, feeling the mattress sag beneath her. "You mean she's waiting for her pass."

Julia gave her head a brusque shake. "I mean she's stopped trying to get a pass. She means to stay here."

Suddenly, the brass pigeon didn't seem quite so funny. Fruit trees they could lose; chickens might be had elsewhere. But they needed a senior doctor. "There must be some mistake."

Julia twisted a bit of ribbon around the end of her braid with brisk efficiency. "If you say so."

There wasn't any mistake.

Dr. Clare wasn't staying at the hotel on the Quai Voltaire. She had made her own arrangements at the Hotel Sylvia. Kate caught her there the next morning at breakfast. Their new doctor had an apple-round face, a pair of spectacles on a gold chain, and the hardest brown eyes Kate had ever seen.

She was delighted to make the acquaintance of the assistant director of the Unit—even one so young—

looked forward to seeing dear Mrs. Barrett again, and had absolutely no intention of going anywhere near the Somme.

"We're really most eager to have you at Grécourt with us. It's heartbreaking the number of patients we've had to turn away," Kate tried, cupping her hands loosely around the lukewarm black coffee that had been offered her.

"It's a pity, but it is what it is," said Dr. Clare, not sounding as though she thought it was a pity at all. "I have yet to be convinced that reconstruction work is either safe or worthwhile at present."

Kate stared at her in surprise. Reconstruction was what they did. It was the entire mission of the Unit. "But—you joined the Unit. Your trunks are at Grécourt."

"Do feel free to make what use you can of them," said Dr. Clare, with the air of someone making a great concession.

"We don't need eight trunks of someone else's belongings. We need a doctor." Just in case Dr. Clare was missing the point, Kate added, more insistently, "You signed on to be our doctor. Our work is at Grécourt."

"For the present," said Dr. Clare.

"There's every indication that the British will renew our passes," said Kate sharply, even though there was absolutely no indication. "We intend to carry on with our work as planned, including our medical department. But for that, we need you. In Grécourt."

"As to that . . ." Dr. Clare seemed perfectly content to sit comfortably in her chair, her coffee in hand, as if she weren't ripping apart all of Kate's plans—all the Unit's plans, that was. "When I enlisted, I had every intention of joining you at Grécourt, and would have done so had my pass been issued. But Providence, it seems, is wiser than we. I truly believe that my work is here, with our fine boys. The only way to give France any lasting relief is to keep our troops fit and well. Worming French peasants will have to wait."

They weren't peasants. They were people. They were their people. Kate made an effort to control her disgust. "You'd have worms too if you were living on a dirt floor, eating any manner of thing you could scrounge."

"Really, what can one expect of these people?" Dr. Clare seemed amused. Kate wanted to slap her. "I'm sure you girls can carry on bandaging cuts and bruises. The military situation seems to me far more important. After the war is time enough to do your relief work."

Your relief work. As if it weren't anything to do with her at all. "You signed a contract," Kate pointed out, trying to keep her voice level. "We were relying on you to join us."

"I can't very well join you without a pass," said Dr. Clare complacently. "It's more likely you'll soon be joining me. I'm sure the Unit can do excellent work here in Paris."

That wasn't the point of the Unit. It had never been the point of the Unit. But there was clearly no arguing with her. Kate found herself desperately missing Dr. Stringfellow, who might pretend to be a misanthrope but was always there when it mattered and never balked at anything, not even hiking five miles through drifts with her medical bag on her back.

Kate returned to the hotel in a state of deep agitation. She found Julia in the parlor, reading a medical journal.

"Can you carry on without Dr. Clare?" she asked without preamble.

Julia didn't look up from her journal. "My pass expired. Remember?"

Kate stopped, struck by a sudden, nameless suspicion. "You've gone to get your pass renewed, haven't you?"

"I put in my request." But Julia's hands didn't seem entirely steady as she turned the page of *The Lancet.*

Kate stared down at Julia, thinking of that giant duffel bag. "You don't mean to go back, do you?"

"I can't if I don't have a pass, can I?"

Kate was shaking; her whole body felt like she had

a fever, like Thanksgiving, when she'd been so sick. But this wasn't a fever; it was rage and fear. Fear that everything was falling apart, that she'd ruined everything. She couldn't even keep the medical department running, much less anything else.

"You're going to abandon us. You're going to let that cretin drive you away." Julia wouldn't look at her. Kate's chest felt tight. "I'm right, aren't I? That's why you don't want to come back."

Deliberately, Julia closed her journal and stood, taking full advantage of every extra inch between them to look down at Kate.

"What does it matter? The Brits are going to kick us out anyway. We're done, Kate. Admit it. There's no point in dragging it out."

Tossing her journal on the table, Julia stalked out, never once looking back.

Chapter Twenty-Two

The British question is what absorbs all our minds these days. With the exception of three American women in the Philadelphia Unit and three in the Red Cross hospital at Nesle, we know of no other British or American women in the part of the war zone controlled by the British—they're really quite strict on the topic.

You ought to see the British officers marching by with their troops. It's quite remarkable. Long, clean-cut, absolutely trim in appearance, well-tailored, they stalk along at the head of their companies through miles of mud in the most casual way as though they were out on a Sunday-afternoon walk; it would never seem to occur to you that they had any idea of fighting. I believe they are said to go to battle in the same casual way.

There are several "affairs" in the Unit at present, but it's an awful place to have an affair with so little privacy and such an audience. (Don't ask how I know!) There's a British officer who has been making eyes at Emmie Van Alden and for the sake of delicacy we all have to pretend we know nothing about it—while all secretly hoping it might weigh the scales in our favor. Not that one is supposed to admit such things, but . . . all's fair in l'amour et la guerre?

—Miss Eleanor ("Nell") Baldwin, '14, to her family

February 1918
Grécourt, France

"Colonel—Mrs. Barrett—"

Emmie glanced at Captain DeWitt and found it wasn't quite in her power to form his name. Her lips just didn't seem to want to move in that direction.

Emmie began backing toward the door. "I'm so sorry. I didn't realize we had visitors."

"Very welcome visitors," said Mrs. Barrett meaningfully. She looked at the colonel, who nodded. "Colonel Hayes has just been telling us that we're to be allowed to stay."

Emmie clasped her hands together, which at least gave her something to do with them. Otherwise, she suddenly seemed to have more arms than an octopus, and at least half a dozen legs. "Oh, that's marvelous! Thank you!"

She was trying very hard not to look at Captain DeWitt, which meant, of course, that she was alarmingly aware of his every infinitesimal movement. What did one say to someone who had kissed you two months ago—well, it was a war, these things did happen—and then sent long, thoughtful letters entirely failing to mention said kiss or said war? Emmie wasn't sure what the protocol was for that. Neither the more traditional governesses approved by her father nor the relentlessly progressive ones chosen by her mother had covered those niceties in their tutelage. She could greet ambassadors in three languages but she couldn't meet Captain DeWitt's eyes.

"I don't know if you should be thanking me or cursing me," said Colonel Hayes briefly. "I ought to have you out—but the French won't have it. I've been bombarded with visits from every petty official from here to Paris insisting that you be allowed to stay."

"Monsieur le Commandant Monin brought a book of newspaper clippings," said Captain DeWitt, straight-faced, but Emmie could tell he was amused all the same. "He said if we evicted you, we would be worse than the Hun."

"Typical Frenchman," muttered Colonel Hayes.

"He's been *lovely*," said Emmie with feeling, possibly a little too much feeling. "Everyone's been lovely. We're so very grateful."

"We are, of course, appreciative of your confidence in us," said Mrs. Barrett diplomatically. "We should like, if possible, to remain another six to eight months to see our work truly brought to fruition."

"Fritz might have a thing or two to say about that," said Colonel Hayes. "If you do stay—"

"We intend to do so," said Mrs. Barrett pleasantly. "As you can see, we have a great deal of work in hand. Have we told you about our spring planting?"

Colonel Hayes cleared his throat. Under the mustache, he was really fairly young, Emmie realized. And trying very hard to retain control of the situation. "As I was saying, if you do stay, there will be conditions."

"Naturally," said Mrs. Barrett, which meant, Emmie knew, that she meant to persuade him out of all of them. "Would you like more coffee, Colonel? Miss Van Alden, if you would be so kind as to ask Madame Gouge?"

"Oh, yes, of course." Emmie fumbled for the coffeepot, a rather pretty one, which Mrs. Barrett had brought with her from Paris.

"Let me carry that for you," said Captain DeWitt, and neatly scooped up the coffeepot before she could drop it. He held open the door for her with his other hand. "After you, Miss Van Alden."

"There was really no need," said Emmie as the door shut behind them. "I've spent the morning hauling bookshelves for Anne. I can manage a coffeepot."

"I know you can." Captain DeWitt paused on the path between the new house and the kitchen tent, which they were still using, despite Mrs. Barrett's determination to move the one working stove to the new house. "Don't you recognize a stratagem when you see one?"

"A stratagem? To abscond with the coffee?"

"It is very good coffee. But no." Captain DeWitt looked at her over the coffeepot, the sunlight winking off the badge on his cap. "I mean to abscond with you—at least as far as the kitchen."

Emmie didn't seem to be breathing properly. "That isn't much of an—is *abscomption* a word?"

"I don't believe so," said Captain DeWitt gravely.

They stared at each other over the coffeepot, like strangers but not. It had been two months since they had seen each other in person, two months since that bench by the moat. It was one thing to sit with someone at a party, flown on music and good food, and quite another to see them by day, in one's official capacity. And wonder if he still saw whatever it was he had seen then, if he thought whatever it was of her he had thought then. Or if it had just been Christmas and loneliness and the front and a sympathetic ear. Well, lips, really.

The silence stretched between them, if it could truly be called silence with artillery pounding in the distance and one of Emmie's roosters screeching.

It was so strange to be shy of each other when they'd been living inside each other's heads since Christmas. But there was a world of difference between being invited into the private world of someone's mind—all the odd thoughts and memories—and then presented, once again, with the living, breathing person in whom those thoughts resided, someone at once familiar and alien. And very, very much made of flesh. Emmie was strangely aware of the physicality of him, the way his uniform belted in at the waist, the breadth of his shoulders beneath the drab khaki, the ungloved hands holding the coffeepot.

"Or I can go away again," Captain DeWitt said, watching her very closely, "and write you a letter."

Emmie flushed. "That's an idea, isn't it? We could set up a postbox somewhere between here and the house and leave each other letters in it. You know, things like, 'hello,' and 'fine day, isn't it?'"

"It is a fine day," agreed Captain DeWitt.

Emmie wished her uniform were cleaner. And that she'd washed her hair more recently. "Thank you for letting us stay."

"It wasn't my decision." The captain shifted the coffeepot from one hand to the other. "The colonel really was driven half-mad by Frenchmen petitioning him on your behalf."

Emmie couldn't help but feel flattered. "On the Unit's behalf, you mean."

Captain DeWitt shook his head. "Not just the Unit. You. Your work in Courcelles is a shining model of what determination, hard work, and a warm heart can accomplish—I translate from the French, of course," he added drily.

There was something in his tone that made a little of the light fade from the sky. "You sound as though you don't agree."

"I wish I didn't. If you were a dilettante or a hobbyist, it would be much easier to urge you to get out. The trouble is that what you're doing is making a difference." He looked at her, his eyes shadowed by the brim of his cap. "You know the children have a game they play. They call it *Les Dames Américaines*. The heroine of the game is called Mademoiselle Aimée. That is what they call you, isn't it? Aimée?"

She who is beloved. Emmie gave an awkward sort of shrug. "It's only because they can't pronounce Emmie. Please don't tell me the game is something awful."

"It's not if you're six. Someone lies down and pretends to be sick and the others dance around and sing a song and the Mademoiselle Aimée character helps the first child up. It's a bit more than that, but that's the gist of it. I asked the little beasts what it was about. They said you were saving them."

Emmie blinked rapidly, trying not to show how close she was to tears. "All I did was get them milk and a village pump."

"And blankets and beds and shoes and clothes. They appreciate it, you know. We just march through, but you stopped for them. Half those children would have died this winter without you. Don't tell me I'm exaggerating. I'm not. You've done the hardest part— you've kept them going through winter. But winter is over. And the sooner you get out, the better."

"But there's still so much left to do—it's not just winter." Emmie looked at him appealingly, trying to make him understand. "There's still the rest of the planting. We've done a first round of distributions for basic needs, but that's only the beginning. We need to canvass everyone again and find out what else they need, and that takes time. It all takes time."

"Time is what you don't have." Captain DeWitt lowered his voice, looking over his shoulder. "There's going to be fighting—you must have heard talk. Haven't you?"

"There's always talk." He was standing so close that she could see the insignia on his buttons. "We've thought we were going to be shelled out at least a dozen times since we arrived. And we're still here."

"It's not like that this time. There have been rumblings across the line. There are trucks coming in from the east, trucks and men. We've caught the Germans studying our lines. They're planning something, and whatever it is, it's going to happen soon. We have plans in place to try to stave them off, but . . . I shouldn't be telling you any of this."

"No, you shouldn't." Emmie looked quizzically at him. "Your colonel did say the Unit could stay."

Captain DeWitt made a noise of frustration. "It's not the Unit I'm concerned about. It's you. I was half hoping you'd all be out—that I could know you were safely in Paris, on your way back to the States, anywhere but here."

"Because I can't be trusted to take care of myself?"

"Because the Germans can't be trusted not to shoot

everyone on sight," Captain DeWitt said roughly. "Do you think they'll care that you're only here to help? Or that you're American rather than French? You're at war now too. I can't tell you to go—I haven't the right to tell you to go—but there are nights when I wake up in a cold sweat, dreaming the Germans have come and you're here in their path. There's no protection for you here, nothing."

"Only you," said Emmie, looking up at Captain DeWitt, at his weathered, worried face. "You stand between us and them."

"I wish we were equal to that trust—oh, don't think we won't do our damnedest. We will. But numbers tell in the end. It doesn't matter how pure your heart is, no matter what the poets say."

"Are you trying to scare me?" Emmie asked seriously. It was hard to reconcile this talk of death with the sun shining down, with the smell of springtime in the air, with Zélie chasing Minerva across the lawn, trying to get back someone's winter underclothes.

"Would it work if I did?" Captain DeWitt asked hopefully.

"I'm not going," Emmie said. She hadn't even realized she'd made her decision until she said it. "I made a promise to the people here—and to the Unit. I can't just run away to save my own skin."

"I know," Captain DeWitt said soberly. "You have your duties and I have mine, and it's entirely beside the point that I want you to live. I want us both to live. Preferably together. If you could bring yourself to have me if this war ever ends."

"Emmie! Have you seen Minerva?" It was Florence, coming down the path, shielding her eyes from the sun.

"She went that way," said Emmie, pointing, and turned back to Captain DeWitt, who was looking quite uncomfortable and more than a little embarrassed. "Was that—are you—did you just propose to me?"

"No!" He winced. "Possibly. Could we say I'm proposing to propose? I can't propose to you like this. I'm holding a coffeepot."

"It's a very nice coffeepot," said Emmie.

Captain DeWitt grimaced at the item in question. "Never mind the coffeepot. That's the least of it. If something happens—when something happens—I don't want you tied to a man with no legs. Or no face. It would be one thing to be killed outright, but . . . you were there at the hospital at Neuilly. You know what the odds are."

"You know that wouldn't matter to me." Everything felt very unreal. Any moment now, she'd find she wasn't here at all, on the path with Captain DeWitt, but on her cot in the barrack, with Florence shaking her awake.

Emmie squinted up at Captain DeWitt, trying to read his expression. Tentatively, she said, "But . . . you can't really want to propose. Or propose to propose."

Captain DeWitt looked down at her, his expression very serious. "Are you going to tell me we hardly know each other? I've known people for years I haven't known nearly so well as I've known you in six months."

"It's closer to seven, actually. Not that I've been counting," Emmie added hastily.

"I don't want to deceive you—I'm really rather dull when I'm not in a uniform." His lips quirked in a crooked smile. "I used to collect stamps when I was a boy, not because they were valuable, but because I liked thinking about where they'd come from and where they might go. But the truth is, I probably won't go much of anywhere. I'd thought of it once, of roaming the world and going to the edges of the map, where the sea serpents stand sentinel. But I like my home too much, and my family."

He'd written to her about them all. About his sister at Somerville College, his little brother at Harrow, about the model village they were building for their biscuit factory workers, or had been, before the war.

"It's a good thing to like one's family," said Emmie seriously. She loved her brothers, but she wasn't sure that anyone in her family liked each other terribly much. "I used to do the same—not with stamps, but with maps. I used to steal the atlases from my father's library and imagine myself away, anywhere but where I was."

"Would a small village in Durham be far away enough for you? If it helps," he said diffidently, "we have turrets and gargoyles. My grandfather built a faux medieval monstrosity, complete with leaded windows and a priest's hole. We even have a secret passage— though I'm not sure it precisely counts as secret when everyone knows exactly where it goes."

There was nothing Emmie would like better. Wandering through a not-so-secret passageway with—and there was the problem.

"Do you realize, I still don't know your first name?"

"What's in a name?" Captain DeWitt caught himself. "Never mind, Romeo isn't an example we want to be following."

"That was Juliet." Emmie looked up at him, remembering a long-ago conversation in a Salvation Army canteen, what felt like roughly a decade ago. "You did promise not to descend to Shakespeare."

"I did, didn't I?" He looked at her in a way that made the world around them fade into nothing. No chickens, no trucks, no colonel waiting for coffee. There was nothing in the world but the two of them, here, on this scrap of duckwalk in the midst of the spring mud. "It's Fitzwilliam. My friends call me Will."

"That's not nearly so bad as Algernon," said Emmie softly, unable to look away.

"I'm glad it passes muster. You wouldn't mind seeing it on your stationery, then? At some point," Captain DeWitt added, "my father will shuffle off this mortal coil and you'd be lumbered with a *lady* in front of your name—but hopefully not for quite some time. He's a good old stick and I rather like him. I think you would too."

Emmie hated to say it. She hated to even think it. But someone had to. "Haven't you stopped to think . . . we're in the midst of a war zone. There aren't any other women within miles. You might change your mind when you get home. You might decide you'd rather not be saddled with—with an overgrown do-gooder with buck teeth. And an American," she added as an afterthought.

"You'd be surprised how many Americans there are in London. Lady Randolph Churchill for one. You'll fit right in. More to the point . . . what idiot told you you're overgrown?" he demanded, sounding every inch the outraged English lordling. "You're just the right height."

"For getting things off high shelves?" Emmie couldn't help herself; she always spouted nonsense when she was nervous.

"No," he said firmly, looking at her in a way that proved just how well-matched they were in height. In her thick-heeled rubber boots, they were practically nose to nose. And lip to lip. He brushed a strand of stray hair out of her face, his hand cupping her cheek. "For this."

"Don't mind me!" They jolted apart as Nell brushed past them. "Dave's ditched the Red Cross truck at the gate again. Marie is threatening bodily harm."

Captain DeWitt pressed the heel of his hand against his eye. "Good Lord, it's like Euston Station. Is there any privacy?"

"Not much." Emmie fought a disconcerting tendency to giggle. They'd gone from romance to farce, but, bizarrely, that made her feel better. It made it more real, somehow. More something that might actually happen to her, instead of a woman out of a book. "Come on, we'd best go get the coffee."

She took his arm, and it felt entirely natural to do so, to walk down the duckwalk together with the sun shining on their heads.

Captain DeWitt—Will, she reminded herself— looked sideways at her. "They'll all be talking about us now, won't they?"

"They already were," Emmie admitted, smiling despite herself. "We live in very close quarters here—it gives us something to talk about other than the war.

Nell has been sneaking behind the barracks with one of the engineers and Florence has been walking out with a Canadian forester who doesn't seem to mind that she hasn't washed her hair since Christmas. She says it helps to keep warm. Oh, and Gwen Mills thinks we don't know that she's been exchanging letters with one of the doctors at the Red Cross hospital."

"Emmie—" Will stopped her before she could lift the flap of the kitchen tent. "You do know, don't you, that this isn't just a wartime infatuation? This isn't your friend and the forester or stealing kisses behind the barracks."

Behind the barracks, Emmie thought, would be a much safer place than the duckwalk. She was rather sorry they hadn't thought of it. Because if this was a wartime infatuation—well, maybe it made her a hussy, or a fallen woman, but she'd rather have all the memories she could have to take home with her once it was over.

Will tried to take her hands and remembered he was holding the coffeepot. "Before the war, when life was an endless garden party and the worst that might happen was tea gone tepid, I made the usual rounds of Saturday to Monday and did my duty at the requisite number of debutante dances. I've met any number of women I'm happy to esteem as friends, but never anyone I wanted to share a breakfast table with for the rest of my life."

Before Emmie could say anything, he added firmly, "That's not the trenches speaking or the loneliness or delusion brought on by tainted food. That's you. Because you're like no one else in the world, and if the world had to come to this for me to find you—maybe the kaiser isn't all that bad after all."

"I really don't think you should be saying that," said Emmie in a voice that didn't sound like her own. "Doesn't that count as treason?"

"All right. We won't invite the kaiser to the wedding," said Will, his breath warm against her lips.

"That idiot of a Red Cross truck driver!" Emmie jumped roughly a foot in the air as Mme Gouge stomped up to them. "Pardon me—that man just makes me so angry. Did you want something?"

"Yes, some privacy," muttered Will in English.

Emmie took the coffeepot from her would-be lover's hand. She had very fond feelings about that coffeepot at present. She had very fond feelings about everything. But particularly the very annoyed Englishman standing next to her.

Demurely, Emmie handed the coffeepot to Mme Gouge. "Mrs. Barrett wanted a fresh pot of coffee for Colonel Hayes. And possibly a few biscuits?"

Chapter Twenty-Three

I want another month, perhaps two, to make sure the Unit is so firmly fixed in public opinion that no one could possibly contemplate sending them home again—or breaking them up into smaller groups and farming them out for canteen work, as the Red Cross is now threatening to do.

We are, as you may have heard, now officially under the control of the Red Cross.

Ruth Barrett is an expert politician and, I believe, equal to the task of making the Red Cross think they're in charge while going on doing exactly what she wants to do. I just wish I knew for sure that what she wants to do is what I would like her to do. . . . It is particularly annoying

having to run an organization through other
people. They persist in having opinions of their
own and those are not always what one would
want those opinions to be. I have hopes of Kate
Moran, but she's young yet, and wants steadying.

Give the girls my love and tell them I'll be
home as soon as I may. I miss you all terribly.

           — Mrs. Ambrose Rutherford
           (née Betsy Hayes), '96, former
           director, to her husband,
           Ambrose Rutherford, Esq.

March 1918
Paris, France

"You look like you need a biscuit," said Mrs. Rutherford.

Kate sat down gingerly on a silk-covered chair. Mrs. Rutherford was staying in a very grand house in the Faubourg Saint-Germain, the sort with ceilings higher than the heavens, windows that went on forever, and wall panels edged in gilt. Mrs. Rutherford's battered suit with its sagging skirt and pouching pockets was decidedly incongruous next to all the ormolu and marquetry. "I think you're confusing me with Liza."

"Nonsense," said Mrs. Rutherford, rummaging in a

large box and pulling out a battered packet of DeWitt's rich tea biscuits. "I couldn't possibly confuse you with anyone."

There was something reassuringly mundane about that crumpled pack of cookies. The same couldn't be said of the Greek gods holding court on the painted ceiling. "This is quite the place."

"It's on loan from an acquaintance. Cheaper than staying at a hotel," Mrs. Rutherford added, handing Kate a biscuit. "This way, I can contribute my hotel fees to the Unit."

She'd been here in Paris, all this time, donating money, chivvying reporters. But she'd left them on their own on one day's notice.

"Why did you let them make you go?" It wasn't what Kate had come to ask, but now that the question was out, she couldn't stop. "If you're still here, doing all this—why didn't you stay?"

Mrs. Rutherford hesitated over two identical biscuits. She finally picked one. "You know that I was asked to resign."

"Yes, but did you really have to listen?" There they had been, blundering their way along, freezing in barracks, desperately needing someone to give them guidance, while Mrs. Rutherford had been here, in this palace that looked like something out of the court of Louis XIV. "Or did you just not want to be there anymore?"

"Oh, my dear," said Mrs. Rutherford, which was somehow nearly as infuriating as the room itself. "Do you really think I would leave you all just when we'd finally arrived?"

"But you did." Kate felt like a child. All those hard months, all the desperation and having to be resourceful, all the trying and trying and feeling like she was always failing, every small victory followed by a new setback, rushed in on her, making her feel light-headed and close to tears.

"I didn't want to go. I wasn't left much choice." Mrs. Rutherford toyed with the handle of the coffeepot. Like the rest of the items in the room, it was a museum piece, whisper-thin Limoges, a world away from the thick red-and-white pottery of Grécourt. "I've had some . . . hiccups in my past."

"Hiccups?" Kate frowned at their former director. *Hiccups* seemed unnecessarily frivolous.

"*Peccadillos* might be the better word." Mrs. Rutherford looked up at Kate over the coffeepot. "Not everyone approves of women making their own way—and that includes some Smith women. My archaeological career has been a cause, in the past, for some raised brows."

Kate's cookie tasted like ash. "You were who you were when you founded the Unit. That didn't stop anyone then."

"You can't put anything past a Smith woman," said Mrs. Rutherford ruefully. "We train you all far too rigorously. More sloppy habits of mind might be a boon in certain circumstances. . . . You may have heard that I was caught in Greece during the Greco-Turkish War."

Kate eyed Mrs. Rutherford warily. "I heard you were decorated by the queen of Greece for your bravery."

"She's a wonderful woman, Queen Olga. I was." Mrs. Rutherford sat up a little straighter, folding her hands in her lap. She looked directly at Kate. "And then I spent six months in a sanatorium in Switzerland, recovering."

There was something about the way she said it. "For your health?"

"I was . . . not myself. The things I had seen—well, I don't need to tell you. It was deemed prudent that I undertake a rest cure." Mrs. Rutherford's back was very straight, but the corners of her mouth trembled slightly before she got herself back under perfect control.

Kate squirmed uncomfortably on her chair. "Surely, no one could hold that against you."

"Not that alone, perhaps." Mrs. Rutherford took a deep breath. "But there were other . . . incidents.

After my daughter was born—I was not in the easiest state of mind. I forgot things. I forgot my daughter. I left her in a stationery shop in Northampton. I got her back again," she added. "She was entirely unscathed. She had a lovely hour being cooed at by the staff in the shop. But it's the sort of thing that gets around."

"That hardly seems—" Kate began.

"Oh, there was more." Mrs. Rutherford crunched down hard on a biscuit. "I thought I could get through it by just carrying on, by working my way through the fog. I was teaching a class at Smith. There were days I couldn't get out of bed to come to class at all, and when I did—I cried all the time. I could never tell when it would come on; my students started bringing extra handkerchiefs to class. It became a great joke with the students—but they weren't terribly amused when I went to administer the final examination and found I had left all the examination papers at home."

"You were *that* professor?" Even Kate had heard the stories. It was a legend on campus, the batty classics professor, or possibly a botany professor, or maybe even a French professor.

"Yes," said Mrs. Rutherford resignedly. "I was that professor. People talked, of course. There were requests that I resign."

"But you didn't."

"Not that time. But that was different. That wasn't the fate of two thousand innocent people." Mrs. Rutherford drew in a deep breath. "That's what you're really asking me, isn't it? Why I didn't fight to stay. I didn't fight to stay because I knew if I did, it would tear the Unit apart. Or at least discredit our mission beyond repair. I had never imagined anyone would dredge up all that. It had been so long. But once they did . . . who wants a mission run by a woman society has condemned as unstable? That's what they were saying, you know. That I was mad, that I had always been mad, that I couldn't be trusted to make decisions."

It was hard to look at her, to hear the naked pain in her voice.

"Everything we had done, all of our plans—they were all in danger of being dismissed as the ravings of a lunatic mind. And who knows?" she added whimsically. "Perhaps they're right. In ancient Greece, there was a fine line between inspiration and madness—the sacred prophets speak truth and then run mad. . . . Biscuit?"

"No, thank you," said Kate. She was still holding the first one. It was gummy and slightly crumbly in her hand. "You aren't trying to alarm me, are you?"

"Perhaps just a little. But you see the problem?"

Kate could only nod. There had been a time or two,

she remembered guiltily, when she had wondered if
Mrs. Rutherford, with her enthusiasms, her sweeping
ideas, was entirely sane. Those whom the gods touched
indeed.

"So, you see," said Mrs. Rutherford. "I had no
choice. The only thing I could do was ensure that I left
the Unit in good hands."

"Dr. Stringfellow?"

"No. I mean you. I fought for you, you know. I made
it a condition of my going that you take on the baton.
Under Ava, of course."

"But why? We'd barely just arrived—I hadn't even
been sure about coming in the first place."

"Because I'm a very good judge of character," said
Mrs. Rutherford complacently. "And because you
made Madame find us all space at the hotel."

"Anyone would have—"

"No, they wouldn't. They'd have scattered to a
dozen other hostelries and broken up the Unit before it
even started."

Kate opened her mouth to argue and then closed it
again. It was true. But even if Mrs. Rutherford was
right about that, she was wrong about the rest of it.

"I managed the hotel," Kate said, feeling her voice
catch. "But that may have been the only thing I did
right. We barely made it through the winter—so many

members of the Unit have resigned—and Mrs. Barrett seems to think we need improvements."

"You made it through the winter. Barely or not, you did. You kept the Unit there and working. Did you think it was a foregone conclusion? It wasn't."

"But the resignations . . ."

Mrs. Rutherford waved that aside. "Maud Randolph and Ethel Ledbetter were going to resign after six months anyway. There was never any question of that. Where Maud goes, Liza goes; it's an inalterable law of nature and nothing to do with you. And Margaret Cooper was on my head." Mrs. Rutherford's face sobered. "I should have seen from the beginning that she wasn't up to the work. Ruth Barrett has suggested evaluating more stringently for both physical and mental fitness—and she's right."

"She's come in and changed everything," said Kate in a low voice. "Pianos and maids and new schedules. . . . I really did try to do my best for the Unit."

"Did?" Mrs. Rutherford sat up very straight, peering at Kate as though Kate were a particularly knotty Greek inscription. "The Unit still needs you. It needs you and Ruth. Hear me out. Ruth Barrett may seem frivolous, but she's a brilliant diplomat. She'll do what's needed to butter up the Brits and keep the Red Cross happy—without letting them eat us whole. But she doesn't have the sheer, dogged determination to wrangle the Unit forward. That's you. You're the one who holds it all together."

Kate thought of Emmie, who hadn't quite yet tendered her resignation, but might. She thought of Julia, hiding from Dr. Stapleton. "I wouldn't say that," she said hoarsely. "I've upset more people . . ."

"You can't let *that* bother you," said Mrs. Rutherford. "Not if you want to get anything done. If you want to be loved, don't take on responsibility. But you can't do that, can you? I've seen you. Your natural tendency is to lead. And to lead is to upset people. That's just what it is."

"What if you hurt people you care about?"

"To love is to forgive. I should know—I've been forgiven more times than I can count. Ava, for one. But that's not a story you need to hear." Mrs. Rutherford looked at her with a sisterly sort of compassion. "It's one of the great lessons I've learned over years of blundering gloriously. True friendship isn't abstaining from hurting one another, but forgiving each other when you do."

"You make it sound so simple," said Kate helplessly.

"Do I? It's really quite the opposite. We're all such masses of contradictions—we can barely understand ourselves, much less anyone else. And the more we care about someone, the more we have the capacity to wound them." Recalling herself to the present, Mrs. Rutherford smiled determinedly at Kate. "You can blame me, if you like. I put a great deal on you when I chose you. But it was because I knew you capable of it. And you're still capable of it."

Kate shook her head, wishing she could see herself as Mrs. Rutherford saw her. "I can't even get Florence her chickens."

"That," said Mrs. Rutherford, "is something I can solve. Bruised spirits are beyond my control, but poultry I can provide. Where did I put that pencil . . ."

The audience was over. Mrs. Rutherford provided Kate with a slip of paper with yet another address on it, told her not to mope, and chivvied her firmly toward the door.

"Thank you for the biscuit," said Kate. "And the address."

Mrs. Rutherford looked at Kate thoughtfully. "Do you remember the story of the oxcart of the kings of Phrygia?"

It took Kate a moment to remember what she was talking about. "You mean . . . the Gordian knot?" Closing her eyes, she recited what she could remember. "It was impossibly knotted and no one could figure out how to untie it—so Alexander the Great came along and sliced it open."

"In some versions of the story, he pulls out the linchpin of the oxcart to free the rope. But slicing has far more élan." Mrs. Rutherford rested her hands on Kate's shoulders, looking deeply into her eyes. "You, Miss Moran, have a remarkable capacity for slicing knots. Don't be afraid to draw your sword. Now go away and get on with the work that needs to be done."

Kate was left staring at the beautiful wooden panels of the door, thoroughly bemused. She'd forgotten Mrs. Rutherford's force of character. Mesmerism had nothing on it. The oxcart of the kings of Phrygia indeed.

But . . . it certainly had worked so far, this cutting of knots. Everything they'd accomplished had come of ignoring the official channels through which they were meant to do things and just going ahead and doing them, aggravating Red Cross officials and inflicting French bureaucrats with permanent dyspepsia. *Go away and get on with the work that needs to be done.* It wasn't a very elegant motto, but it was a functional one.

Feeling a little giddy, Kate wondered if it sounded any better in Latin. Or possibly ancient Greek.

In the spirit of knot cutting, she marched to the address Mrs. Rutherford had given her, and after a mere two days of being sent from office to office to office, she emerged triumphant with three crates of fancy fowl.

"Does that mean chickens?" Kate asked suspiciously. "I am only interested in chickens, not roosters or any other kind of poultry that is not a chicken."

"Would mademoiselle like to see them lay eggs?" the harassed seller asked.

"Your word is sufficient," Kate said, staring at him in a way that completely unnerved him and lowered the price by a good ten francs.

Buoyed by her success, she breezed past Madame at the hotel—or, at least, as much as one could breeze while juggling three crates of squawking fowl, inexpertly roped together with twine—and thumped the chickens down next to Julia's bed. Julia was propped against the pillows, reading a newspaper.

"Pack your things," said Kate briefly. "We're going back to Grécourt."

"Are you talking to me or the chickens?" asked Julia.

"You. The chickens have no choice in the matter."

"Do you mean to put me in a crate?" Julia raised herself up on her elbows. "You're not serious, are you? I have no pass, remember?"

Kate stuffed three clean shirtwaists into her duffel. "When did we ever let that stop us? Remember when you talked Liza through the checkpoint with that article from whichever paper it was?"

For a moment, Julia seemed to be listening. But

then she lowered herself back against the pillows. "We won't be able to bluff our way through with *Le Monde Illustré* this time. They've tightened the restrictions."

"We'll find a way." Setting down her duffel, Kate marched up to the side of the bed, folding her arms across her chest. "I will *not* let that Stapleton man drive you out. I don't care what I need to do. I'll truss him and fling him into no-man's-land myself if that's what it takes."

"He's a foot taller than you are."

"So was that *poilu* I punched," said Kate dismissively. "Height isn't everything."

Julia lifted her head. "You punched a *poilu*?"

"I'll tell you about it on the train." Kate tossed Julia's uniform jacket in the other woman's general direction. "You've been lying around all week and it's a terrible waste. I won't have it."

"*You* won't have it."

"I'm still assistant director," said Kate firmly. "If you don't pack, I'll pack for you."

"Someone is feeling autocratic today," commented Julia bitingly. "You do realize that assistant director is not the same as Lord High Tyrant?"

"That's assistant Lord High Tyrant." Kate paused in her packing and looked at Julia, who seemed more awake than she had for days. Julia was another one of those people who didn't do well when she wasn't busy. "I don't blame you for not wanting to be in the same room with Dr. Stapleton—"

"That's none of your concern." Julia's face was very white, her cheekbones very pronounced.

"But it *is*." Sheer, dogged determination, Mrs. Rutherford had said. That was what Kate brought to the Unit. And something else, as well. "Not just because we desperately need a doctor and you're a very good one. Although we do and you are. But because we're a Unit. We stand together. If that man tries to hurt you, any one of us will tear out his guts."

There was a long pause before Julia said, "You realize that's not as easy as it sounds. You can't just go around casually disemboweling people."

"I'm not feeling the least bit casual about it." Once, she might have thought Julia was just being standoffish. But now she knew better. She wouldn't let Julia down the way she'd let down Emmie. "You're not alone anymore. Your mother may have disowned you—but you've got all of us."

Kate saw Julia blink rapidly before turning away and saying, in a deliberately bored voice, "Just what I needed: a swarm of ill-assorted sisters."

"We could say *cousins* if you'd rather be more distantly related." Kate seized on the excuse to change the topic. "Speaking of cousins, that's another reason to go back. I'm concerned about yours. She's been getting letters from that British captain."

"Are you afraid she'll suffer a paper cut?"

Kate swept her hairbrush, hair receiver, and book of hairpins into her bag. "I'm afraid she'll suffer something. You know how impressionable Emmie can be. He's so—well, British. And he has a highly dubious mustache."

"A dubious mustache?" Julia's blond brows rose.

Put that way, it did sound rather ridiculous. But Julia was looking more human than she had in weeks.

"Look, are you coming or not?" Kate demanded.

Julia swung her legs off the side of the bed, moving reluctantly, but moving all the same. "We're going to be sent back, you know."

"You never know until you try," said Kate, shoving Julia's jacket at her. "Do you remember the story of the kings of Phrygia's oxcart?"

Chapter Twenty-Four

For livestock, there's not much change around
here. We have eight cows, nine goats, and never
enough chickens. We've been trying to make sure
that in each village the small fields, the fields too
small to be plowed by government tractors but too
large to be turned over with spades by the old men
and women who have to work them, are plowed
and made ready to plant. . . . The Unit bought
several plows and harrows and others have been
loaned by the French Service Agricole.

I thought at first we might be able to go out,
two or three of us, and do quite a bit ourselves, but
as I realized how much there was, and that
multiplied by fifteen villages, I started a hunt for
help. For a week, I went from one military

authority to another, and at last found a wonderful quartermaster general who, instead of looking at me as though I were mad, immediately said, "How many horses and men do you want and where shall I send them?"

In a number of villages the work is well under way and within a week should be begun everywhere. I hope we can see it through. . . . The war has been "hotting up" as they say—but I'm not meant to be writing about any of that. (Will the censor strike that through, I wonder?) No matter. You'll read about it in the New York Times well before you get this letter.

I have been so thoroughly enjoying my work, my play, my friends, and the weather, that I feel as though I should throw a ring into the sea to placate local deities—or is that only Venice?

— Miss Florence Lewes, '01, to
her brother, Mr. Thomas Lewes

March 1918
Grécourt, France

"It was three days before we could get a train and how those hens *cackled*."

It was an utter cacophony in the living room of the

new house. They'd just finished supper when Kate and Julia appeared out of nowhere, tugging three crates of hens between them. Anne had rushed to find some food to feed the prodigals, Florence was on her knees in front of the crates, inspecting the chickens, while Mrs. Barrett was looking on with an expression somewhere between apprehension and amusement, begging the chickens to spare the rug, which was only on loan.

It was amazing, thought Emmie, how very full the room felt with just two more people in it. She should be delighted, she knew. But instead, she felt vaguely apprehensive. Ever since the proposal to propose, she'd been living in a springtime sort of dream, all new grass and fluffy clouds. But Kate and Julia were—well, they weren't the dreaming sort. It didn't matter to Emmie that she wasn't entirely sure whether she was engaged or engaged to be engaged. All that mattered was that there was Will DeWitt in the world, holding the line, writing her letters that ended with *Yours to be yours.*

But Kate would think it mattered, she knew. Kate would question his intentions and ask questions about the future—and they had discussed the future, they had; it was couched in poetry and daydream.

Had we but world enough and time . . . We would sit down, and think which way / To walk and pass our long love's day.

Will was particularly fond of the metaphysical poets.

When they had world enough and time. That was one of their abiding preoccupations. Once the war was over, once they had world enough and time, what would they do with it? It was like a children's game, playing house in absentia. Walks, he suggested. Amateur theatricals. He'd played Titania in a wig and someone's sister's frock at Harrow, and Emmie had teased him about it by return post. *Oh Will, how thou art translated!*

It was Shakespeare, and therefore against the rules, but he'd brought it on himself.

It was all very silly and the censors probably thought they were off their heads—or engaging in the most Byzantine sort of cipher known to man—but Emmie had never been happier, had never imagined being so happy, even if she knew that it was a fool's paradise, that at any moment a German sniper or bomber could end it all with one well-placed missile. But they weren't to think of that; they'd promised each other. Like an old-fashioned sundial, they would count only the happy hours.

She didn't mistrust Will or his intentions. Only the war itself. And maybe, just a bit, herself. But she didn't think Kate or Julia would see it that way. And this new Kate and Julia, a Kate and Julia who worked together, who had shared jokes and seemed to understand each other's minds—that was more unsettling still.

Trying to make up for her ungenerous thoughts, Emmie took one of the odd, two-handled bowls from Anne and brought it to Kate. "Did you keep the chickens in the hotel all that time?"

Julia looked surprisingly human with her forehead smudged with soot from the train, her cheeks flushed from their long walk from the station, and her skirt stained with goodness only knew what from the chickens. "Madame would have dearly liked to evict us, but Kate fed her a dreadful line about war service and doing one's bit."

"It wasn't a line! It was all true." Kate's lips quivered with suppressed amusement. "But she couldn't very well throw us and our chickens out after that."

"I'm surprised she didn't just stick them in the soup pot," said Nell.

"And take away a chicken from the service of France?" drawled Julia, raising her brows dramatically.

Kate balled up her cloth napkin and lobbed it at her.

"Children, children," protested Mrs. Barrett, but she was laughing too.

And then the first bomb fell, making the walls of the house shake and George Washington fall face forward on the table.

"Oh no, we forgot the curtains!" Emmie stumbled

to the windows. She yanked the fabric so hard she nearly brought the whole curtain down.

Another crash followed the first, closer this time. The hens cackled in distress in their coops, and outside they could hear a dog yelping.

"The pantry!" exclaimed Alice, and made a dash to extinguish the lamps there. A moment later, the house was plunged into darkness. "Owwwwww."

"Are you all right?" Emmie called, bracing one hand against the piano to orient herself.

"The doorframe hit me," said Alice, groping her way back into the room.

"Better than a bomb," said Nell. For the benefit of their returning members, she added, "That's the great drawback of the new house. The lighted windows are a positive invitation to the Hun to use as target practice."

"It was careless of us to forget to draw the curtains," said Emmie remorsefully. "They keep telling us it will be the big push any day now."

"And by they, you mean your British friends?" asked Kate, and Emmie could practically hear all the things she wasn't saying.

"Well, they are the ones who would know," said Emmie.

They waited in silence in the dark for a few moments, listening. When no further bombs fell, Mrs. Barrett said, in bracing tones, "I think we can risk one lamp."

A moment later, a match was struck. Mrs. Barrett fiddled with the wick. A faint flame flickered and caught, sending a rosy glow throughout the room.

"Welcome home," said Nell, from her spot on the rug with her legs curled under her. "Aren't you glad you're back?"

"Yes. Surprisingly," said Kate, draining the rest of her soup. "Bombs and all."

Sitting on the piano bench, looking around the room in the dim light, at all the familiar faces brought into high relief by the interplay of light and shadow, Emmie thought how very odd it was what one was able to become accustomed to. Being bombarded had become merely a minor irritation, like midges at a picnic. They'd become too used to it to take it seriously.

Would she have ever thought that possible, back in New York?

She'd changed, she realized. They'd all changed.

Kate set aside her soup cup. "We weren't at all sure we'd be able to get back. My pass was all right, but Julia's had expired, and I wasn't sure I could manage all three crates on my own—and after what we'd paid for them, I certainly wasn't going to leave them!"

"I'm glad to know you only brought me along for the chickens," said Julia bitingly.

"So what did you do?" asked Anne, perched on the edge of a bench made by her own students. Anne was terribly proud of that bench, the product of her woodworking classes. She sat on it at every opportunity.

"Shenanigans," said Julia. "Skullduggery. Sleight of hand. Our Kate here turns out to be an accomplished charlatan."

"That's all nonsense," scoffed Kate, but Emmie could tell she was pleased. "When the man came for our passes, I might just have happened to drop one of the crates."

"Just happened? The thing practically exploded," retorted Julia. "There were feathers everywhere, people squawking, hens squawking—"

"Poor things!" Florence patted a chicken crate. "Were they all right?"

"Were *they* all right?" Emmie had never heard Julia so voluble. "They were having a grand time. They got into someone's lunch and scattered war bread everywhere. The guard tried to make a run for it and tripped over a piece of broken crate. After that, no one was going to bother with a little thing like passes."

"We did get them all back in the crate," Kate reassured Florence. "And strung the broken bits back together with twine. I never meant for the box to break."

"It was a good thing it did," said Julia cynically. "Or they'd have had me off the train, chickens or no chickens."

"Well, I know some people who'll be very grateful for these," said Florence. "One woman in Offoy told me that she desperately needs another chicken, because she has only one, and it's pining for company."

"Do chickens pine?" asked Kate skeptically.

"Why shouldn't they? It's miserable being left all alone," said Alice, with a little too much feeling.

"You could send the poor hen one of Emmie's roosters," said Nell mischievously. "A barnyard romance might take its mind off things. . . ."

"It works for some," said Gwen loftily, pointedly looking at Emmie and Nell, both of whom she considered sunk beneath reproach. Florence was too busy with the chickens to realize she was being included in the ranks of the fallen.

"Has the rooster a mustache?" inquired Julia blandly. "A dubious mustache, perhaps?"

"I'm sure the roosters will be delighted by the company—as are we." Mrs. Barrett stepped in, smoothly turning the conversation. "I had meant you to have a longer rest, but I'm beyond glad to have you both back. Pass or no pass. The number of people we've had to turn away from the dispensary is nothing short of heartbreaking. Dr. Stapleton has been doing his best, but with his own work at the Red Cross hospital . . ."

Kate looked at Julia, and some sort of unspoken message passed between them.

"About that," said Kate innocently. "Now that Dr. Pruyn is back, wouldn't it be best to release Dr. Stapleton to his regular duties? We wouldn't want to keep him from his war work."

"But we've still only one doctor—with no insult to your abilities, Dr. Pruyn," said Mrs. Barrett, smiling at Julia. "I don't want you collapsing from overwork."

"I won't," said Julia. She waved a hand imperiously in Gwen's general direction. "Miss Mills can assist me. She's more than capable."

Everyone, including Gwen Mills, stared at Julia. Julia had, in the past, been cutting about people who took one nursing course and considered themselves medical professionals and had done everything in her power to damp what she considered Gwen's medical pretensions.

"Why, yes, naturally." Gwen floundered. "I'd be more than delighted. . . ."

"You see?" said Julia coolly. "There's no need to strain the resources of the Red Cross."

"And there's Miss Van Alden," said Kate, turning to Emmie. "I've seen her administer first aid. She saved a child from extensive burns our first week here."

"That was just ambrine," said Emmie, confused and pleased. At least, she would have been pleased if she didn't have the feeling that she was being used as a pawn in an obscure game set up by Julia and executed by Kate. "Anyone would know how—".

"I didn't," said Kate. "After all her years of social work, Miss Van Alden is an accomplished practical nurse. And she's a wonder with children."

"Except for Zélie," said Emmie.

"Zélie is a law unto herself," said Kate fondly. "Zélie and that goat of hers."

"Minerva butted Dr. Stapleton last week," contributed Nell, grinning. "He was bending over a patient and—"

"We can make a trial of it," broke in Mrs. Barrett. "It's only until the rest of the Unit gets their passes. . . . Oh bother. There go the planes again. Do you think those are our boys this time?"

"Is the big push really coming?" Kate asked Emmie as they prepared for bed, having made a mad dash across the lawn to their barrack. Canvas was tacked over the windows, and the only light was the dim glow of the stove.

"That's what we've been told, but they've been saying it constantly since you left, so we've just been going on pretty much as normal."

Kate was shaking out her blankets, airing them after her long absence. "What does Captain Biscuit say?"

"His name is DeWitt." Maybe it was because she knew Will was sensitive on the topic, maybe it was because she'd spent her whole life bearing the brunt of being her mother's daughter, but it came out sharper than Emmie had intended. "And he doesn't say anything. He can't. You know that."

"All right." Kate smoothed down the topmost blanket. In the tone of one holding out an olive branch, she asked, "What else has happened since I left?"

"Well, you know it's mostly been the planting." Anything to keep Kate from digging into Will. Emmie found she deeply, deeply didn't want to discuss Will with Kate. Because Kate would pick and pick and pick and Emmie didn't think she could bear it. Emmie plunked down on her own bed, starting the complicated process of letting down her hair, which always wound up tangled around her pins. "We had the hardest time getting Canizy plowed—the French authorities were supposed to be doing it, but hadn't, so I had to find the man in charge of the region, who turned out to be all the way across the river in Buney. He said he'd tractors, but no idea where to send them. I finally had to set up a sort of parlay at the old railroad crossing at Canizy—you know the spot—with the *chef de tracteurs,* the mayor, and all the women who own land, and we had to walk the fields, actually pace them out, with the owners pointing out marking stones or drawing lines in the dirt with their spades. You wouldn't believe all the wrangling, but we finally got them all sorted out and the tractors in, and now they're plowing away like anything. Florence has come to some sort of arrangement with the British to get it all harrowed next—did you even know there was such a thing as harrowing before we came here?"

"No," said Kate. "Not at all. I thought vegetables came from the greengrocer."

Emmie babbled on. "Nell and Anne are going great guns on their social centers—you'd never know Verlaines and Canizy. They've got climbing ropes and ladders for physical education—and even a cinema machine! You wouldn't believe how popular it's been. We've had Tommies wandering in pretending they were just passing by."

Oh dear. She'd brought them back to the dangerous topic of Englishmen.

Emmie cast about for another neutral topic. "You'll never imagine—Alice taught me to drive!"

"You're driving?" Kate looked unflatteringly alarmed. "But you always said . . ."

"I know. But we can always use another driver. I'm

only taking the wheel when there isn't someone else." Emmie caught herself before she could keep apologizing. There was nothing to apologize for. Why shouldn't she drive? Will didn't seem to see anything odd in her taking the wheel. He'd encouraged her in it. Emmie squared her shoulders. "It's really not as hard as I thought it would be. Alice thinks I should go to Paris and get my license."

"Hmm," said Kate, and that single syllable hurt Emmie more than any number of words.

"We've been ridiculously busy since you left," Emmie said stridently, wanting to show Kate what they'd done without her, what they could do. "Mrs. Barrett put us all on a new schedule, so we could take over the villages for the girls who aren't here yet. I've had Douilly. It used to be Ethel's, remember?"

Kate paused in drawing off her boots. "Yes, she wrote an article about it, didn't she? All about the noble French peasant and the even nobler Smith woman."

Emmie couldn't help but bristle at Kate's casual tone. "Well, she should have been working at it instead of writing about it. The conditions there are unthinkable. We've been delivering beds and mattresses for months, but there were children sleeping on floors." It had broken Emmie's heart to see them, covered with chilblains and sores.

"She certainly didn't say that in her article," said Kate slowly. "Or in her reports."

"Are you sure?" It was the visitor's job to report this sort of thing, to make sure appropriate medical care and supplies were delivered. The reports went to Kate, who then allocated whatever was needed. "She must have said something—put in for supplies—"

"The store went there, of course," said Kate, putting her boots by her cot, lining them up ever so precisely. "I know milk was delivered. Other than that—Ethel didn't put in for many extra supplies. I'd assumed it must be in better condition."

"In better condition!" Courcelles, which had come to her in a shambles, with fifty children, none of them well, looked like a prosperous mecca in contrast to Douilly. Emmie could feel tears sting the back of her eyes just thinking of it, how it had looked when she had visited for the first time last week. "There was one old man with nothing to eat with but an old tin can. He hadn't even a spoon. Just that ancient tin can."

"Was his home out of the way? Could Ethel have missed him?" asked Kate.

"If so," said Emmie, "she missed nearly everyone."

Emmie didn't understand how Ethel could have visited, week after week, and seen only medieval ruins and quaint stories and never noticed that there were children shivering in rags. In Courcelles, which had been so terribly devastated, they had provided beds for all the children, small stoves to cook on, pots and pans and plates and blankets. Emmie had finished delivering the basic necessities before Christmas and had long since moved on to the second part of their plans: wrangling government barracks to house people living in shacks and shanties, a properly equipped schoolhouse, books, athletic equipment, and, of course, livestock and planting.

If Emmie had ever doubted that what they were doing made a difference, she had seen it then, when she had visited Douilly.

"I gave him the fork and spoon and bowl out of my haversack, and you would have thought I'd given him something marvelous and rare, he was so delighted. It made me sick, Kate." Emmie looked at her roommate, trying to impress upon her the seriousness of it all. "I'm not exaggerating, really, I'm not. There are people there living like our people were back in September. All of the children have lice, and not a washtub among them. I don't care what I have to do to get them, I'm going back with scissors and washtubs and fine-toothed combs. And a pump! They hadn't even a village pump yet, Kate!"

Kate straightened. Emmie could practically see her brain ticking away, listing tasks. "We'll need to put in a request with the Red Cross—"

"I put in a request while you were away in Paris." It was part of her job, making requests for materials, part of the job Ethel hadn't been doing. There was no reason for Kate to think Emmie was as slapdash as Ethel.

"Of course you did," said Kate quickly. "I'm sure you have it all in hand. It's a good thing the people of Douilly have you to look after them now."

Emmie frowned at Kate. "I am perfectly capable, you know."

Kate paused in putting clothes away in the trunk that doubled as nightstand and armoire. "Isn't that what I just said?"

"Yes, but you shouldn't have to *say* it," said Emmie. "When you say it, it sounds like you don't mean it."

Kate looked at her with genuine confusion. "Do you mean you don't want me to tell you when you're doing something well?"

She should just leave it, Emmie knew. She hardly knew what she meant herself. But she couldn't seem to stop herself. "When you keep telling me what a good job I'm doing, it makes me feel like someone's golden retriever. As if you're patting me on the head for fetching a stick." As if Kate were looking down at her from on high and judging. "You don't keep telling Alice what a marvelous job she's doing with the machines or Anne how special she is for teaching woodworking."

"They don't need to be told," said Kate worriedly. "You were so low this winter. . . ."

There was a reason she'd been so low. Because Kate had made her feel useless. "I'm not a child, Kate! You don't need to hand out treats to me for good behavior. I've spent years doing social work. You and my mother may not think much of it, but I did learn something from it. Not much, but *something*."

"I never said I thought nothing of it!" protested Kate.

"No, but you thought it." The way Kate went still told Emmie all she needed to know. "It's not just that. You never made a fuss about any of the others going off on their own. Ethel tramped all around the countryside without a by-your-leave. Anne walks by herself to Offoy all the time—"

"That's because I can trust them to find their way back by supper," said Kate, bright spots of color showing on her cheeks. "And not send me out looking for them after dark in a snowstorm!"

"You didn't have to come get me." Emmie had been thinking it for weeks now, without daring to say it. "If you hadn't come after me, I would have stayed the night in Courcelles. It was only because you came running after me that we wound up lost in a snowstorm with those dreadful men."

"Was I supposed to leave you unaccounted for overnight?"

"Yes!" Emmie was close to tears. "Yes! You should have trusted that I had the sense to stay in place! I'd told you where I was going—you knew where I was going. If you'd asked Red Cross Dave, he could have told you he'd left me there safely. There was no reason for coming after me as though I were a child who'd wandered off into the woods!"

"Bread crumbs and witches?" said Kate sarcastically. Kate always got sarcastic when she was upset. Emmie had always known that about her; she had always accepted it meekly before. "Pardon me for looking after the welfare of the Unit. Some of us have more to do than gadding about with plausible Englishmen."

Emmie wasn't sure which infuriated her more, the *plausible* or the *gadding*. "Englishman, Kate. One Englishman. And I'm hardly gadding! I've been working like a mule while you've been lounging in Paris."

Kate flinched as if she'd been struck. Nothing hurt Kate more than being accused of idleness. "You know I didn't want to go."

"But you did. And it was probably a good thing too—it showed us we could all get on without you." Emmie knew it was cruel, knew it even before she saw Kate's fine-boned face go white. That was the worst of it; they knew too well how to hurt each other. "As for that Englishman you so despise, at least he treats me like a person—not a golden retriever!"

"I never treated you like a golden retriever!" Kate veered back to the attack. "What do you know about him, really? Only what he tells you."

Emmie ached all over. But she couldn't seem to stop; neither of them could. The only way to end the fight was to give in, and she was sick of being the one giving in. "Because my judgment isn't to be trusted? That's what you mean, isn't it?"

"You've known him for such a little time and in such strange circumstances. He might have half a dozen wives in an attic in England, Emmie. Or a fiancée waiting for him. Or gambling debts or some other noxious behavior we know nothing about." Kate's hands were clenched into fists at her sides. "You know I only want what's best for you. . . ."

"Do you? Did you, all those years when you didn't write back?" Emmie could taste bile in the back of her throat. The old hurts pushed up from the very bottom of her gut, pushed up from where she'd hidden them all these years. "One minute you were my best friend in the world and the next you were just . . . gone."

"I took a teaching position," said Kate hoarsely. "You knew that."

"Did your students tie up your hands? Steal your ink? I wrote to you and wrote to you and wrote to you. Don't tell me you wrote back," said Emmie passionately as Kate opened her mouth. "Two lines every six months hardly counts. I told myself it was because you were working and busy and didn't have the time . . . but maybe it was that you just didn't want to be bothered with me anymore."

Kate's mouth opened and then closed again. She shook her head, entirely at a loss for words.

"I made you come out here. I know you didn't want to. And I know you feel obligated to take care of me." The words felt like knives; every single one tore at Emmie's throat. "But you don't have to anymore. I'd rather fail of my own accord than have you holding me up when you don't want to."

Kate's knuckles were white against the edge of her cot. "You say that now—"

"I mean it!" Stung, Emmie retorted, "I know I've made mistakes, but you have too, Kate! What about Douilly? You should have seen something was wrong with Ethel's reports!"

Kate's throat worked, as if she was finding it hard to swallow. "When was I meant to do that?" Her voice crackled with frustration. "When I was reading fifteen other reports? When I was driving the truck to take the doctors to every village between here and creation? I can't do everything!"

"No, you can't." Emmie sat back on her bed, feeling exhausted and sad. She wasn't angry anymore. She wasn't sure what she was. She felt about a hundred years old. "We're meant to be a unit, Kate. We're meant to work together. Not you running around trying to do everything and making yourself and everyone else miserable. That's what Mrs. Barrett has been trying to tell you. That's why she sent you away."

"So I wouldn't make you all miserable?" Kate looked absolutely ghastly, like someone in the last stages of consumption. "You try making all the decisions. . . ."

"But you shouldn't *have* to make all the decisions. That's just the point." Emmie clasped her hands together in her lap, trying to make Kate understand, trying to salvage something. "If you'd trusted any of the rest of us just a little—"

With a swift movement, Kate extinguished the small lamp sitting on her steamer trunk. She rolled herself in her bedroll, turning her neatly braided head away from Emmie.

"It's a good thing you have Mrs. Barrett, then, isn't it?"

Chapter Twenty-Five

I've been meaning to thank you for my Christmas boots. I got some strange looks for them in Paris, but I've got the warmest, driest feet in the Unit and wouldn't take them off for anything.

We may not have terribly much more time here. There's not much I can tell you without running afoul of the censor, but I'm well and working hard, and you're not to worry. We've had some measles in the Unit—I'm so glad I got it out of the way all those years ago, although I imagine it wasn't much fun for you. I don't remember much of it, but I do remember your reading me the same book over and over and over.

Things are a bit tense here, but the Unit has brave friends holding the line. There are even

*some of our very own boys from Brooklyn in the
engineers. We had a mass at the village church our
first month here, and the engineers sent over six of
the men who were Catholic. I'm pretty sure I
recognized at least one boy from St. Mary's—
although I'm very glad Matt and Timmy and Pat
and Johnnie are safe home and not here with us.*

*New York seems a long way off just now. . . .
I feel like a soldier writing his farewell letter
home before going into action—which is very
silly of me. I'll write again soon and you'll
undoubtedly hear from the papers whatever
happens long before this gets to you.*

*I'm sorry if this is muddled—the guns have
been going nonstop for two days, so it's hard to
think, let alone write. I know I don't write
enough. But I do love you all.*

> —Miss Katherine Moran, '11,
> Assistant Director, to her mother,
> Mrs. Francis Shaughnessy

March 1918
Grécourt, France

Mrs. Barrett left on a Monday.

"You didn't have to see me off," Mrs. Barrett

said, drawing on her gloves and checking once again to see that she had her *feuille bleue* and *carnet rouge*, the papers that gave her access in and out of the war zone. "I'm only gone for a week—it's hardly call for a committee."

Kate shielded her eyes against the sun rising over the ruined walls of the château. "No, but I just wondered if you had any last instructions. . . ."

"My dear." Mrs. Barrett put her gloved hand over Kate's. "You girls have the work well in hand. Just go on doing what you're doing. And take some time for play. Alice and Nell tell me the Englishmen quartered at Hombleux have a cinema going in an old barn. You ought to go with them once or twice."

Kate blinked against the sun. Since her fight with Emmie, she'd felt strangely raw, as though her shell had been pried off her like a lobster, and every passing breeze touched a nerve. "Is that an order?"

"Consider it a suggestion," said Mrs. Barrett. "A strong suggestion."

Which, thought Kate, was just what Emmie had been telling her. That leading didn't mean ordering people about. It meant trusting them to make their own decisions. But what if that didn't work? What if the decisions they made were the wrong ones?

It was fine for Emmie to complain about Kate treating her like a child. Kate had never wanted to be here in the first place; it was Emmie who had dragged her here, Emmie who had insisted she needed her. If she was treating Emmie like a child, it was because Emmie asked to be treated like a child.

But it hit Kate in the gut, all the same.

She'd thought they'd been happy at Smith. It had seemed to work then. Emmie provided all the affection and Kate provided the practical skills, and between them, they balanced out rather nicely. She'd been happy to help Emmie with her Latin, and if they joked about things like Emmie being hopeless at remembering directions—well, it was a fond joke. She'd never thought Emmie minded. It was Emmie who was always reminding everyone that she would never have got through Smith without Kate, which Kate had always taken as just another sign of noblesse oblige, Emmie trying to make her feel important, make up for the difference in their situations.

It had never occurred to her that Emmie might have actually believed it. Or that Emmie might have thought she hadn't written, after Smith, because she didn't want to be bothered with her.

She should tell Emmie the truth, Kate knew. But the idea of turning herself inside out, laying all her insecurities bare . . . She just couldn't.

She didn't have time for this, thought Kate savagely. Mrs. Barrett was leaving and there were a million tasks to be accomplished and a German army massing somewhere just to the east.

"When are you seeing Mr. Hunt and Mr. Folks?" Kate asked, trying to keep herself brisk and businesslike.

"Wednesday morning." Mrs. Barrett made a face. "The Red Cross might have picked a better time for a meeting. But at least it means I can work on our passes in person instead of wasting whole days writing letters which I am assured that no one ever bothers to open."

"We'll make sure to get the last of the harrowing done while you're gone," Kate said immediately. "And—"

"You don't need to tell me. I know you will."

Joseph, one of the soldiers loaned to them for heavy work, was waiting with a horse and cart to drive Mrs. Barrett to the train station. It might be only the eighteenth of March, but spring had come on with a vengeance. The ground was thick with early blooming anemones, and the air was fresh with the smell of plowed earth and growing things, which made most of them joyous and made Alice sneeze.

Mrs. Barrett paused for a moment, looking back at the park, dotted with anemones; the water tower, wrapped in red vines; the barracks, with their crooked signs reading "*Seelye*," "*Comstock*," and "*Burton*." They had named their barracks after the past presidents of Smith College. "I do hate to go just now. Grécourt has never been so hard to leave as it has been this week."

Don't go, Kate wanted to say. *Don't leave me to do this on my own.* Which was absurd. She'd never wanted Mrs. Barrett here in the first place. "You didn't see the best of it, coming in winter."

"No, but I saw the best of all of you," said Mrs. Barrett, smiling at her with warm, tired brown eyes. "Goodness, I can't think why I'm being such a watering pot. It's only a week. I'll be back with you all by Saturday."

"Don't stay away too long," said Kate, only half joking. "You don't want to miss the big drive."

"If we had a penny for every time we were told it was to be the big drive, we could afford to feed and clothe every child in France." Mrs. Barrett lifted her bag and started for the cart, keeping carefully to the duckwalk. She was wearing her Paris shoes, as if she were already gone, had already shaken off the mud of Grécourt. "I'll be very put out with the kaiser if he tries to visit before I get back."

"We'll be sure to tell him that," said Kate.

"Don't laugh," said Mrs. Barrett. "The force of the British Army is one thing; the fury of a Smith woman is quite another."

She climbed into the cart and was gone.

Kate stood there for a moment, watching as the cart trundled over the moat and down the long alley that had once been lined by poplars. She didn't delude herself that Mrs. Barrett had passed control of the Unit to her out of any confidence in her abilities; it was simply that she was assistant director and in the absence of the director, it was expected that the assistant would take charge.

It hurt her to admit it, but they'd all been happier since Mrs. Barrett had come. It wasn't just the creature comforts, like the new house and the housekeeper and a somewhat better quality of war bread. It was, Kate realized, standing there in the morning chill, the combination of having an ultimate authority—someone who wasn't one of them—and knowing that she trusted them to know what to do.

Mrs. Barrett had taken Julia's and Kate's word absolutely on sending Dr. Stapleton away. She hadn't asked any questions. She hadn't argued the point. She'd just done it, adding as her only provision that Julia not struggle in silence but tell her immediately if the work was too much.

The change in Julia had been wonderful. She'd set about ordering her medical department with ferocious satisfaction. Kate had never seen Julia this close to happy.

Kate stared at the sign next to the moat, the battered sign reading "*Bonne à Boire.*" It wasn't "*Bonne à Boire,*" this. It was a bitter draft, realizing that maybe Emmie had been right, maybe there was something to be learned from Mrs. Barrett, that maybe leading wasn't so much telling as trusting.

Kate wasn't very good at trusting. Her motto had always been, if you want something done, do it yourself.

But it seemed that wasn't what it took for the Unit to run.

It was only a week, Kate told herself, as she went in to join the others for breakfast. There was only so much that could go wrong in a week.

As Kate came in, Emmie focused hard on pouring cream into her coffee. Usually, when they disagreed about anything—or even when they hadn't—Emmie fell over herself to apologize. But not this time.

Nell raised a cup to Kate. "Hail our interim director! Do you have any directions for us?"

Kate sank into her seat—the seat at the head of the table that had been Mrs. Rutherford's, and Dr. Stringfellow's, and then Mrs. Barrett's, and was now, briefly, Kate's—and forced a smile. "Only carry on, as our British friends would say."

"Are you sure you're feeling quite well?" asked Nell.

"Gwen isn't," broke in Alice. "She's got a rash across her face and she's shivering like anything. She says the sun hurts her eyes."

That caught Emmie's attention. She looked up in alarm. "That sounds like measles. I saw a lot of it in New York—once it gets started in the tenements, it spreads something terrible. Whole families sick at once."

Kate had caught it as a child, in a building Emmie would undoubtedly have considered a tenement. Kate remembered her mother sponging her head with a damp cloth, wringing it out, and starting again. She remembered how her eyes had stung and the soft sound of her mother's voice, singing to her.

"Do we know how many of our people have had it?" Kate asked.

"Gwen's been working in the infirmary," said Alice, fidgeting in her chair. "She must have seen hundreds of people last week. She might have given it to any of them."

"Not the children, though," said Kate. Gwen was an excellent nurse—with adults. Children she saw as

small, inferior adults who behaved in unpardonably ir-
rational ways, and had no patience with them. "Emmie's been seeing to the children."

Kate looked at Emmie, feeling absurdly like she was
trying to curry her favor, to make up for everything
she wasn't ready to admit to doing wrong.

"Hands up," said Julia. "Who here has had it?"

Everyone raised their hands except Nell, who bit
her lip and fiddled with her coffee cup. "I haven't. My
brother got it, but my mother sent me away in time."

Kate put down her napkin. "The first thing to do is
get Gwen into quarantine. I can run Gwen over to the
Red Cross hospital in Nesle. If everyone agrees," she
added belatedly.

Julia pushed back her chair. "I'll come with you
to see Gwen settled, and then Emmie and I can start
making the rounds of the villages to check everyone
with whom Gwen came into contact over the last two
weeks. If our interim director permits this alteration of
the schedule?"

"Your interim director applauds this alteration of the
schedule," said Kate. "Nell, if you wouldn't mind . . ."

"I'll take over Emmie's classes for the next two
days," said Nell promptly. "Don't worry."

"There's always something to worry about," said
Florence, placidly eating bread and jam. "If it's not

measles, it's the big drive."

"On the plus side," Alice said brightly, "it's hard to worry about the big drive when we have a measles epidemic to worry about. My mother always used to say that if your head hurt, you should stamp hard on your foot."

Julia stared at her. "That's dreadful advice."

"It does stop you thinking about your head," said Alice.

"Yes, until you break a toe." Julia looked hard at Alice. "Don't break a toe."

Gwen would contract measles the day Mrs. Barrett left, thought Kate, bitterly and unfairly, as she drove to the Red Cross hospital in Nesle, Julia in the back with Gwen, who was covered in raised red spots and running a worryingly high temperature.

Alice was wrong, Kate decided. It was quite possible to worry about both a measles epidemic and the big drive. If this hit their villages—if this hit the troops . . . The planes thrummed overhead, the noise making Kate's back and shoulders tense, smoke like candy floss spinning through the air as men high in the clouds did their best to murder each other in the name of king and country.

It was a relief to arrive at the hospital, to hand Gwen off to a nurse in a white apron, who said cheerfully that she'd seen worse cases. The hospital had been a tuberculosis pavilion before the war. There was something about the airy rooms, the large windows, and the garden around it that made one feel inherently peaceful.

It was certainly better, decided Kate, than putting Gwen into quarantine in one of the barracks, where the thin walls and small windows let in a great deal of cold but very little light or air. She'd be more comfortable and better cared for here.

"Now let's just hope she didn't spread it," said Julia as they headed back out to the truck. "It's the nearer villages that are the concern—"

She broke off as a man stopped in front of them, on his way to the ward. "Hello!" said Dr. Stapleton. "I thought that was the Unit truck out front. Missing me already?"

It sounded so charming the way he said it, with a big, self-deprecating grin. If Kate hadn't known better, she would have smiled back.

Instead, she stepped in front of Julia, shielding her as best she could. "We just dropped off a measles case. Gwen Mills."

"She's worn herself out, I see," Dr. Stapleton said gravely, but he couldn't quite hide a hint of smugness. "I would have been happy to continue visiting. . . ."

"But we weren't happy to have you visiting," said Kate bluntly. It would have been easier to simply walk away, to pretend this wasn't her quarrel. But it was. She'd promised Julia. "You aren't wanted, Dr. Stapleton. You aren't wanted and you aren't needed."

He looked over Kate's head at Julia, then back down at Kate. "You're not listening to sour grapes, are you? If Julia's been talking nonsense . . ."

"I've known *Dr. Pruyn* for over a decade," said Kate sharply. "I've never known her to speak nonsense. And I'll tell you something, Dr. Stapleton. We know. We know what you are. If you ever prey on another woman again, we'll be sure every hospital in America knows it. You won't find a single practice to employ you. You'll be lucky to get a job as a navy surgeon in the South Seas, where there's not a woman within a hundred miles and nothing to stare at but the bottom of a bottle."

Dr. Stapleton's face was as white as his collar and cuffs. He gave an entirely unconvincing laugh. "I have no idea what you're talking about. But you certainly have a picturesque way of expressing it." As two nurses in Red Cross uniforms passed by, he added loudly, "You don't need to worry. I'll look in on your measles case for you."

"I wouldn't if I were you," Julia said from behind

Kate, sounding remote but entirely in possession of herself. "Measles can make you sterile—or worse."

Dr. Stapleton looked entirely discomfited. "Well, naturally. That is . . ."

"Goodbye, John," Julia said, and stalked out with Kate following behind.

Neither of them said anything until they were safely in the truck.

Then Julia glanced sideways at Kate, her mouth twisting with delicate irony. "A navy surgeon in the South Seas?"

Kate grimaced. "It was the first thing that popped into my head. I just wanted something suitably remote."

There was silence for a moment, as Kate maneuvered around a very large, extremely top-heavy farm cart.

Once they were past it, Julia said quietly, "Thank you."

"We stand together, remember? Besides, you didn't need me. You should have seen him sweat when you mentioned he might lose his manhood!"

Julia permitted herself a little smile. "I knew that would hit him where it hurts. He mentioned once that he hadn't had measles. . . ."

"At least we know Gwen's safe from him," said Kate. "But this means you're back to doing all the medical work on your own."

Julia looked at Kate levelly. "Not entirely on my own," she said. "Oh, don't go all sentimental on me! You're getting as bad as Emmie."

Over the next three days, with Emmie on hand as nurse, Julia examined every adult and child in Hombleux, Esmery-Hallon, and Breuil, the three villages with which Gwen had had contact.

Julia delivered her report over a late dinner on Wednesday night. They'd kept dinner back for Alice, Nell, and Florence, who had been to the "movies" in Hombleux that night. With only seven left at Grécourt and the constant hiss of aerial battle overhead, the Unit was clinging together as much as possible, reduced to its core.

"What's the diagnosis?" asked Kate, trying to sound jaunty, even though she was really, truly, desperately afraid. A measles epidemic could decimate their villages.

"Eight cases of pneumonia, two of tetanus, and more syphilis than is socially acceptable," said Julia, spearing a braised turnip from the serving platter. "But no measles."

"Thank goodness," said Kate, with feeling.

"Don't break out the fatted calf yet," said Julia. "There's still time. We'll know in about two weeks if Gwen spread it to anyone. Fortunately, there was a brutal epidemic last spring—anyone who was going to get it got it. It's only the children under the age of one we have to worry about. And the troops, but they have their own doctors. They're not our concern."

"Speaking of the troops . . ." Alice poked at her stew, trying to sound casual and failing utterly. "The Esmery-Hallon boys couldn't join us tonight—we got word they'd received marching orders."

The room suddenly seemed a little darker, the shadows cast by the lamps more ominous. The tension in the room was palpable, like the heavy air before an electric storm.

Defiantly, Nell shoveled more stew onto her plate, as though to show she wasn't the least bit concerned. "Colonel Hayes came over midway through the movie and told us that the big drive is starting tonight. It didn't stop him watching the rest of the film, so I can't imagine there's anything much to worry about."

"Well, if he has time to go to the pictures . . ." began Kate, but the rest of her words were lost as an enormous blast shook the walls of the new house. Nell dropped the serving spoon, splattering stew across the tablecloth.

Anne stared wildly around the room. "What *was* that?"

"It didn't—it didn't sound like a bomb," said Emmie, wide-eyed.

"Whatever it was, it's ruined Mrs. Barrett's linen tablecloth." Nell scrubbed awkwardly at the tablecloth with her napkin. "Oh, bother. Does anyone have some salt before it stains?"

"Try some water first," suggested Florence.

Alice had gone an unfortunate greenish color. "My m-mother swears by a mix of b-baking powder, talcum, and cornstarch."

Kate looked down from the head of the table at the other six remaining members of the Unit. Nell was scrubbing maniacally at the tablecloth. Emmie was clinging to her water goblet for dear life. Even Florence, imperturbable Florence, had cocked her head, listening, and her usually placid face had a strained look about it. They were all scared out of their wits, but determined to pretend, to their last breath, that they were quite all right and it was just a bit of bother, with nothing more to worry about than a stained tablecloth. And Kate was just as bad as the rest of them.

What's wrong with us? Kate wondered. Maybe, she thought madly, it would be easier if they just admitted they were all scared out of their wits, instead of all desperately pretending to be fascinated by the best method for getting grease out of linen.

Another boom, as loud as the last, made them all dive for the ground.

"At least it's not bombs," said Anne when the vibrations subsided. Her teeth were chattering nearly as loudly as the plates on the table. "I do hate when they try to drop bombs on us."

"That sounds like an English gun," said Julia, picking herself deliberately up off the floor.

"It's most likely a trench raid," offered Emmie. "Don't you think?"

"Goodness, listen to us," said Alice with a high-pitched laugh. "We've become such military experts."

"We could teach a class at Smith," said Kate, her own voice as unnatural as the rest. "English and German gun noises, the differentiation thereof."

They all sat still, listening. Kate could feel her nails cutting into her palms. But the guns, German and English, had gone silent.

"You see? It was a raid and they're done," Emmie said quickly, but Kate noticed she was shredding the edge of her napkin.

Florence dropped her own napkin next to her plate. "I'm going to go see to the cows. It's another full day tomorrow."

"Bed for me too." Nell smothered a yawn, and stood, stretching her back. "If that was the big drive, it wasn't much of one."

"Don't tempt them," said Kate, doing her best to

keep up the casual tone. "Shall we take bets on when the next big drive will be? My money's on a week from Tuesday."

But it wasn't nearly that long. Kate had barely fallen into an exhausted sleep when she woke to a tremendous pounding, the walls of the barrack shivering around her.

"What time is it?" Kate asked hoarsely.

Emmie was sitting up in the next bed, her knees pressed to her chest. "It's just past four."

The noise was like nothing Kate had experienced before. It was terrible, crash after crash after crash, unceasing, unrelenting, driving out all thought, leaving nothing but raw fear and a dreadful instinct to huddle and hide.

Emmie lifted her face from her knees and shouted over the din. "Will—someone told me they meant to pound the Germans to keep them from advancing. If it ever came to it."

"I hope they can," said Kate through numb lips, but her words were lost in the sound of the guns.

The barrage continued all that day and into the evening as they went about their rounds, visiting villages, directing the teams harrowing the fields, hauling furniture donated by the Red Cross to the poor of Douilly, trying to pretend this was just another day.

Julia doled out headache powders without comment, possibly because no one would have been able to hear it if she had commented.

When the guns finally stopped, a little after breakfast on Friday morning, the very silence made Kate's head hurt.

It felt very strange to hear the normal everyday noises, like the sound her boots made against the thin floor of the barrack, or the way her breath seemed to rasp in the suddenly still air. Next to her, Emmie was filling her rucksack with handkerchiefs, soap, and combs for her weekly hygiene class at the new civic center in Verlaines.

Kate took a deep breath. "I guess your Englishmen beat them off."

Emmie paused, looking at her over the rucksack. "I only have one of them," she said. "One Englishman, that is. I can't take credit for all of them."

"You can take credit for whatever you like." Kate bit her lip, trying to find the right words. "Emmie. I never thought you were a child—I never meant to treat you that way. If I did, I'm sorry."

Emmie's rucksack hung off one shoulder, the empty strap dangling. "I know you didn't *mean* to."

She hesitated, but before she could finish her thought, Florence barged through the door as though she still lived there.

"Kate? Kate? Those blasted guns spooked the horses. Emmie, Alice is waiting for you with the jitney. She says you're going to be late."

"Thank you," said Emmie. She looked at Kate and gave her head a sad little shake. It felt like farewell.

"If you look east and I look west, we should be able to find the horses," said Florence, cheerfully oblivious.

At least tramping through the mist hunting for horses gave Kate an excuse to stomp heavily.

By the time she'd been hunting for an hour, Kate was sweaty and cross. Her hair was falling in scraggles from her chignon and her shirtwaist clung damply to her back in a most unpleasant way. Kate just hoped Florence was having more luck than she was. They had parted ways somewhere just past the water tower, Florence going left while Kate went right.

The blasted horses could find their own way back as far as Kate was concerned. She was meant to have been out with the store an hour ago.

Except that they really did need those horses for plowing.

Sighing, Kate flapped her jacket a few times for some cool air, shook a stone out of her boot, and trudged forward, through what once had been woods and was now mostly scrub. The mist was so thick she could scarcely see a yard ahead of her, making her flounder and trip over things. She had just stubbed her toe on yet another felled tree—another thing she could hold against the Germans—when she heard the incredibly welcome sound of hoofbeats.

"Well, thank goodness for that," she muttered.

It was certainly coming on very fast for a plow horse. Out of the mist not a yard in front of her emerged a magnificent beast, all heaving flanks and glossy withers.

Kate had a healthy dislike for horses—one tended to when one's father was kicked in the head and died—but even she could tell that this was a beauty of its kind.

The horse's rider reined in sharply at the sight of her.

"What are you doing out here?" demanded Emmie's captain without preamble. "Didn't you get our message? The colonel sent a groom an hour ago."

Kate put her hands on her hips, sweaty, disgruntled, and generally not in the mood to deal with high-handed Englishmen. "I've been chasing horses," she said sharply. "So I have no idea what your colonel wants. If it's tea, he'll have to call another day."

The horse sidled. Captain DeWitt got it back to where he wanted it to be. "Where is—the rest of your Unit?"

"If you mean Emmie," said Kate, "she's gone to Verlaines to teach a class."

The captain said something he really ought not to be saying in front of a lady, even if that lady was covered in mud and sweat.

"What is it?" Kate noticed, for the first time, that the captain looked decidedly disheveled, as if he hadn't slept and certainly hadn't bathed. There was dirt on his face and mud on his uniform. "What's wrong?"

"They've broken through," he said. "We can't hold them. They're coming on, thousands of them."

Kate could feel all the blood draining from her face. "Broken through. The Germans?"

Captain DeWitt gave a curt nod. "Get your Unit and get them out."

Chapter Twenty-Six

Right after breakfast on the twenty-first,
Emmie Van Alden and I started out in the jitney
for Verlaines, where she was holding classes and
I was visiting. As we got close, we began to
meet refugees fleeing from Ham. You can't
imagine the state of those roads. The army
retreating, the infantry so tired it hurt to look at
them, great guns, wagons full of supplies and
equipment, ambulances evacuating hospitals,
and, along with them all, hundreds and
hundreds of refugees, pushing wheelbarrows or
leading a mule with a wagon if they were lucky
enough to have one.

In spite of all the racket, it never entered our

heads that the Boche could possibly break through. . . .

> —*Miss Alice Patton, '10, to her sister, Mrs. Gilbert Thomas*

March 1918
Grécourt, France

E mmie knew something was wrong even before they got to Verlaines.

The road from Ham to Verlaines was crowded with people, dozens of them, hundreds of them, heads down, shoulders bent, old women pushing wheelbarrows piled high with linens, agitated mothers pulling children by the hand, trying to keep out of the way of the military trucks bumping toward the front, the dispatch riders on their motorbikes whizzing to and fro.

"What's happened?" Emmie called out, leaning out the side of the truck.

No one really seemed to know. All they knew was that the Boche were coming and they were getting out, as far as the road would take them.

"Have you been evacuated?" asked Emmie, exchanging an alarmed look with Alice, who had pulled the jitney to a stop by the side of the road.

They hadn't been evacuated. They were just leaving. The army was too busy to bother with them, and why should they bother waiting for the British Army? It was safer just to go.

Alice's lips were very white. "Do you think it's serious?" she whispered.

"I don't hear the guns." Emmie looked at the people with their bundles, all their worldly possessions piled on their backs. "It might just be an excess of caution—but maybe we ought to go to Ham and find out. So we can tell our people what to do."

If Ham was in danger . . . but it probably wasn't, Emmie told herself hastily. Will was there holding the line. Will and all those brave boys whom they'd had to tea and impromptu dances with a temperamental Victrola and rubber boots for dancing slippers.

"If you go on to Verlaines," Emmie told the woman she'd been talking to, "you can get something to eat and drink—and we'll take you on after if you need to go on."

A camion honked sharply at them.

"All right, all right," muttered Alice, her hands trembling on the wheel.

She'd had a harder time than any of them with the bombardment; Emmie had found her resorting more than once to her little silver flask of sherry, writing endless letters home that she always crumpled up again.

Alice managed to get them back on the road, weaving her way between the refugees going one way and trucks going the other. They were all of a quarter of a mile from Ham, but at this rate it would take them an hour. It was worse than Fifth Avenue on an opera night.

"What's taking so long?"

"Ambulances," said Alice, her lips barely moving. "Can't you see them? Up there."

The jitney inched forward and Emmie saw it, the steady line of ambulances bumping into Ham, battle-scarred, shell-marked, mud-smeared ambulances, tires shot out, riding on their rims, pulling forward one by one to a makeshift casualty clearing station. Alice swung the jitney to the side so they could go around, past the row of ambulances, into the town. As they passed, Emmie could see stretchers being unloaded, endless, endless rows of men on stretchers, men in pain, moaning and calling out, men with limbs twisted at strange angles, faces covered with mud and gore, as the stretcher bearers worked stolidly on, carrying more and more and more.

Emmie heard someone make a noise and realized it was her. In all their time in the war zone, she had never seen anything like this. The copper stench of blood clung to the back of her throat. Thick black flies buzzed around them, their sound horrible in her ears.

On and on and on they came, the *blessés*, each ambulance turning and going back to the front for more, as Tommies, blank-faced with exhaustion, wrestled with sticks and canvas to make more tents to house the onslaught of wounded.

Was Will somewhere, in one of those tents? Emmie had never asked him, she realized with sudden panic. She'd never asked him what exactly they *did* at the front, where he was to be stationed, how he was to serve. They'd never talked about that, only about nonsense. He was in the Durham Light Infantry, he'd told her that much, with its insignia of a bugle surmounted by a crown. But she had no idea what any of that actually meant, where he was, what his part had been in whatever battle had taken place.

Why hadn't she asked?

Because he couldn't tell her, because he wasn't allowed to tell her, and because neither of them had wanted to think about it, about the reality of all this, only the newly harrowed fields and the latest exploits of Zélie's pet goat and the woman Emmie had found in Douilly who hadn't any bed but somehow, for some inexplicable reason, had ten chairs, all piled one on top of the other.

"I think I'm going to be ill," said Alice faintly. She was holding the steering wheel very hard, her hands as white as wax.

Emmie took one of Alice's hands between her own. "You're not going to be ill. Let's go to headquarters and find out what's going on."

At headquarters, everyone was packing up, hastily sweeping documents into dispatch boxes, yanking out telephones and telegraph wires, running this way and that and bumping into each other. Emmie managed to catch the arm of a lieutenant who had been to tea at Grécourt. She couldn't remember his name, but he had a friendly, freckled face.

"What's happened?" she asked.

"Oh, Miss—" He couldn't remember her name either. "You didn't hear? The Boche have pushed down from Saint-Quentin. We're trying to pack up and move HQ to Nesle before the Boche get here."

"How long?" Emmie thought of all those people on the road, all the people in Verlaines and Eppeville and Villette who had no idea what was coming toward them.

"I don't know—you'd have to ask—"

"What is this? A tea party?" His commanding officer strode in, staring at Emmie and Alice with unconcealed fury. It was the horrible major who had interviewed them all back in January, to make sure they weren't spies. "What in the devil are you doing here? This is no place for women! We sent a messenger. You were meant to clear out—not walk right into the path of the ruddy Germans!"

"Wait." Emmie grabbed him by the arm. "What about the neighboring villages? Have they been warned to evacuate?"

"How the devil would I know? They're like rats, they can tell when to leave the sinking ship—but you clearly can't, so I'm telling you now. Get. Out."

They got.

"We need to get back to Grécourt and warn them," said Alice, turning the crank of the jitney with all her might.

"No." Emmie wasn't sure where the certainty came from; she just knew. She knew what she had to do, even if she was scared out of her wits. "Didn't he say someone had sent a messenger? They'll be all right at Grécourt. But the people of Verlaines won't. Once the Germans take Ham, the next place they'll go is Verlaines. We can't just leave them there."

Alice paused, her hand on the crank. "But the major told us to get out."

"He told us to get out of Ham. He didn't say anything about Verlaines." They'd been with their people this long; they couldn't abandon them now. "What he doesn't know won't hurt him. The British Army clearly has a great deal on its hands right now. I say we leave them to their work and we do ours. We can move people in the jitney faster and farther than any of them can go on foot."

Alice straightened, her eyes meeting Emmie's. "We'll need gasoline," she said, and Emmie felt her heart lift, a crazy sort of energy pulsing through her. "I think I know where we can get some."

The boys at the supply dump were packing up, but when Alice explained the need, they stumped up fifty gallons of *essence*, strictly under the table, no ration books required.

"Saves us carrying it," they said, and Emmie had to resist the urge to hug them.

All along the road to Verlaines, they stopped to pick people up—women with toddlers clinging to their hips, an old woman clutching a sack of linens, an elderly man hobbling with a stick who told them he had lost his leg in the last war against the Prussians and he'd be damned if he'd let them take another one—until the springs of the jitney were groaning with the weight and Alice warned Emmie that the old truck couldn't possibly manage another. They decanted their burden in the town square of Verlaines, urging them to wait, that they would take them on farther when they could.

They'd never seen Verlaines like this before. The square was pulsing with troops and refugees, with frightened people running out of their houses, begging for news. When the jitney pulled in, they were inundated with a rush of children. Emmie hugged and hugged and hugged them, holding as many of them close as she could, telling them not to worry, it would all be all right, they would make it all right, and could they please, please tell their mothers to pack up anything they needed and come to the square?

A horrible booming filled the air, closer than any guns Emmie had ever heard before, followed by a dreadful whistling noise.

"A shell," whispered Alice, staring at the sky as though she might see it, even though the mist had burned off and the sky was fine and clear and there was nothing at all to be seen. "That has to be a shell."

They'd never been close enough to hear the actual shells before. Only the thrum of the guns firing them.

Verlaines was only three miles from Ham, and the Boche were nearly at Ham.

Emmie could feel her palms go cold with sweat. A girl started crying, and Emmie cuddled her close, a toddler boy bumping his head against her shin to get her to hold him too. She wasn't strong enough for this. She wanted to curl up with the children, curl up and shake.

But she couldn't. They were depending on her, these children. All of them. Emmie forced back her panic. What would Kate do? She had to think like Kate.

"Take them to Ercheu. It's only . . ." Emmie did the mental math. "It's eight miles. That should be far enough to be safer but not so far we can't get there and back. If you ferry the first load, I can pack people up. We'll be faster that way. All of you," she said to the children, "go, now, tell your mothers it's time to go. I have candies in my bag for everyone who does what I say."

The magic word had its usual effect. Propelled by the power of sweets, the children scattered to their homes, the homes they had worked so hard to rebuild, and that the Germans were threatening, again. They had worked so hard for this, all those long, backbreaking days of hauling furniture and tacking up canvas and tramping through miles of mud and fighting with the trucks when they broke down, and now it was all going to be knocked down again in moments, all their hard, hard work. Anger lent Emmie new energy. If the kaiser thought they'd roll over, he had no idea. They'd get everyone out, everyone, and then come back and build it up again, even better this time, and serve the kaiser right. He had no business being here in the first place.

Buoyed with righteous fury, Emmie stalked to the nearest home, a hut that had once been a *tabac*, and began the lengthy process of coaxing the inhabitants to pack enough, but only just enough, and no, they couldn't really take the stove with them, and yes, it was a lovely stove, but it would be here for them—hopefully—when they got back. She helped them pack their clothes and chase their hens; she held babies and soothed anxious children as the shells whistled overhead and the guns got louder and louder and Emmie wondered where on earth Alice was and why it was taking her so long.

Alice came back from her first run with the jitney loaded with bread, milk, and eggs. "For the refugees—we can at least give them a solid meal. I stopped back home," she added defensively. "That's where I picked up all this. You were right. They'd been warned. They're all fine there. Kate says to carry on and God-speed."

Emmie was beginning to understand how Kate felt. *But we didn't have time!* she wanted to scream, but it was too late for that, the time was spent, and they could use the food. She had only so much chocolate in her bag.

"It was clever of you to think of food," she said as calmly as she could, and knew she'd done the right thing when she saw Alice's shoulders relax. "I've got the next bunch waiting for you."

The town was thick with English troops, setting up headquarters in Anne's beloved social center, pulling down the white-and-yellow curtains of which Anne was so proud, tossing aside her rag rugs.

They were very understanding about Emmie coming in and collecting all the books and medical supplies. "God bless," they told her. And "good luck." Many of the men were familiar. These were the men with whom they'd watched the makeshift cinema in Hombleux, officers who had drunk tea in the barrack with them, and Tommies who had helped lay their duckwalk. Soot-stained men now. Scarred, bloody, battle-weary men, getting ready to fight again.

"Do you know if the Durham Light Infantry was in the battle?" Emmie couldn't help asking as she piled books into her rucksack.

Their captain shook his head. He was friends with Florence, Emmie knew. He'd loaned Florence his mare for riding, since he couldn't use it at the front. "It was all such confusion. They came on us out of the mist. We never saw them coming." He looked at Emmie, his face twisted in anguish. "They got our guns."

"You'll get them back," said Emmie, as she might have to one of the children. "If there's anything we Americans know about old England, it's that you never let go of what you think is yours."

The captain mustered a weary grin. "And if there's anything we know about you Yanks, it's that you never let well enough alone—and thank goodness for it." They both snapped upright as a dispatch rider hurried in. "Yes? What news?"

"What is it?" Emmie asked anxiously as the captain scanned the short message, his face going very, very still. Whatever it was, it couldn't be good. She mentally began to calculate how many loads they had left. Alice had gone three rounds so far.

"We're to retreat," he said, looking around at his weary men. "They're five miles away—or were, half an hour ago. All right, men. Onward."

From house to house Emmie went, urging people out, trying to stay calm and reassuring even as the sound of the guns became louder, knowing that every minute brought the Boche closer to Verlaines.

"Would you like a book for the journey?" she asked, knowing that Nell would understand, that she wouldn't mind her books being given away. It broke Emmie's heart to see a fourteen-year-old boy hug a battered book of fairy tales close to his chest, holding tight to the book as he was forced to leave his home, again, never knowing if he would ever come back or what there would be to come back to.

Emmie hurried people to the town square, distributing milk and boiled eggs as they waited for Alice to return with the jitney, hunting up one woman's missing hens and another's misplaced sack of clothes, trying to guess how many more loads it would take, how many people they could fit on the jitney before the springs gave way. One elderly couple refused to leave. Emmie begged and pleaded but they were obdurate.

"My wife is ill," said Monsieur Philippot. "She is dying. I cannot move her."

"I'll take her on the mattress," Emmie promised recklessly, hoping they could fit the mattress into the jitney. She'd deal with that when they came to it.

Monsieur Philippot shook his head. He had been a prosperous man before the war and his dignity hung around him like an old suit that was too large for his wasted frame. "This is our marriage bed, the bed in which our children were born. She cannot leave and I will not leave her."

Emmie left them some milk and bread and begged them to come to the town square if they reconsidered. The jitney was loaded and loaded again, packed as full as the springs would bear, but it wasn't enough, they couldn't fit everyone on, especially not when Mme Lebrun refused to be separated from her prize hens. Emmie might have fought with her over it, but there was no point to it; they'd have to do another round anyway.

It was a terrifying feeling watching Alice drive away, trying to be bright and cheerful for the group that remained, who all looked as terrified as Emmie felt.

Emmie looked for her watch, which she always kept pinned to her breast, but it must have come off somewhere, abandoned with all the other debris of lives interrupted. Not knowing the time made it worse somehow; she was aware of time working against her, every minute stretching into hours as the shadows grew longer and the guns grew louder. A Boche plane flew so low over their heads that Emmie could see the black cross on the tail.

How long did it take a German army to march? How much time did they have left?

Even with books and toys scrounged from the social center, the adults were getting anxious, the children restless. Some were threatening to just return to their houses, others to take to the road by themselves. The British troops were marching out, all of them. Emmie had never felt anything like the fear that came with the sound of those retreating feet, knowing that at any moment they might be left to their own devices with the German army pushing down upon them.

Where was Alice?

The jitney rattled into the square, looking even more dilapidated than usual.

Alice was covered head to toe with dust, her lace collar askew, thoroughly frazzled. "I didn't mean to take so long—the roads are nearly impassable. Everyone in the world seems to be going in both directions at once." She looked down at Emmie, suppressed fear in her eyes. "One of the men told me they're sending every man they can to the front."

Emmie took a deep breath. "Can we fit everyone on, do you think?"

The sun was setting already, the village abandoned except for the Philippots, back there in their marriage bed, waiting for the Germans to come. Emmie just managed to cram everyone on, the jitney riding low on its sorely pressed springs. Somehow, it moved. Slowly, but it moved. The road from Verlaines to Ercheu had never been so lovely. It seemed unfair that it should be so beautiful, just now, when they had to leave it, when a German army was coming to wreck it all. The sky was rose and gold and purple over the fields they'd worked so hard to plow, those fields with all their promise.

It was twilight, that most melancholy hour of the

day. Her crazy rush of energy was gone; Emmie felt her spirits plummeting with the sun, as the warmth of the day waned, leaving her cold and spent, here in this broken-down truck filled with people who had lost their homes yet again, who they had tried so hard to help, only for it to come to this.

"Mademoiselle Aimée?" It was one of her students, nine years old but suddenly very young again. Emmie could see she was trying not to cry, hugging a makeshift sack to her chest like a doll. "Mademoiselle Aimée, will we come home again?"

"As soon as the English get rid of the Boche for us," Emmie said, trying to sound as encouraging as she could.

But it was hard. It was so hard. She'd never seen anything so weary as the British troops they passed as they made the achingly slow journey from Verlaines to Ercheu.

They were lovely, those troops. They moved aside to let the jitney go through, lifting their hats when they could, waving, and raising ragged cheers.

"Good old America!" called out one officer, lifting his cap to them as he and his men rumbled past in an open truck, and Emmie waved back, trying not to cry.

"It's nice to be appreciated," she said, to cheer herself as much as Alice.

"Ye-es," said Alice, looking worriedly over her shoulder. There were shells whizzing overhead, English shells, aimed at the Germans. "But I'll be very glad to get back. They won't make it as far as Grécourt, will they?"

"They can't," said Emmie, but they'd only just dropped that last group at Ercheu, painfully late, nearly nine, when they heard the rumble of a big gun coming from quite the wrong direction.

It was dark now, full dark, the night broken only by the flashing lights of airplanes overhead, battling to the death. Emmie squinted into the darkness, feeling cold to the bone. "Was that—did that come from Grécourt?"

"It can't be," said Alice, but she coaxed the jitney as fast as it could go. She made a little noise that was somewhere between a laugh and a sob. "I'd go faster if I could, but I'm not sure the poor old jitney could take it."

"They're all right—I'm sure they're all right." It was impossible to think of the Germans at Grécourt, their Grécourt. This was their little bit of Smith in France, and to think of it being invaded was like trying to imagine the Germans marching their way into Northampton. Emmie harbored a momentary fantasy of a phalanx of professors fighting off the Germans, beating them off with umbrellas and Latin textbooks.

There was an army camion stuck in the ditch by the gate—a British one. Emmie felt light-headed with relief. She'd half expected to find the Germans there, ready to march them off into a German prison. This was a Grécourt transformed, dotted with lights, like something out of a fairy tale, people moving about, carrying flashlights, striking tents. The area around the moat was so thick with vehicles Alice could barely get the truck through. It was like every tea and every dance they'd ever had multiplied by ten, the courtyard swarming with uniformed men, except that their guests didn't usually bring a giant antiaircraft gun with them.

Kate came hurrying out. "As you can see, we have visitors, about two hundred of them." She paused by the side of the jitney, working very hard at refraining from expressing alarm or concern or relief. "Alice said you were taking villagers from Verlaines. You got them all out?"

"All except Monsieur and Madame Philippot. They wouldn't go." Emmie lowered herself out of the jitney, feeling about a hundred years old, every muscle aching. "Poor Anne—we had to abandon her curtains. And I gave away Nell's books."

"They'll understand," said Kate. She started to reach for Emmie and then let her hand fall. "I can't tell you how glad I am to have you back. Both of you."

Emmie swallowed hard and gave Kate a big hug, as if they were at Smith again, when life was simpler. In a muffled voice, she said, "We heard the gun and thought Grécourt was under siege."

Kate swiped at her eyes and gave a crooked smile. "You could call it that. We have two hundred hungry Tommies billeted on us. Julia is dealing with scratches and fevers, Nell is making up beds, and Anne is running the canteen. I've sent our *basse-cour* people on to Roye, with Marie to boss them." Some of Kate's brave facade crumpled. "Zélie may never forgive me for parting her from Minerva. She had to be carried protesting into the wagon. I felt like Lady Macbeth."

"It had to be done—they couldn't possibly have taken the goat with them. You can't imagine what the roads are like. You did it for her own good." With all the khaki uniforms bustling about around them, their insignia indistinguishable in the darkness, Emmie couldn't help but ask, "Will—Captain DeWitt—he's not here, is he?"

"No, he's not," said Kate with genuine regret. "He did come by this morning—he wanted to make sure we knew the Germans were coming. He came riding out of the mist like something out of one of your books. Young Lochinvar and the Scarlet Pimpernel all rolled into one. Poor man. It was utterly wasted on me—he pretended he was here for all of us, but it was you he wanted."

It was so hard when Kate was being kind. "Did he leave any message for me? Did he say where he would be?"

"He had to go back to the line. He told me to tell you something about compasses," Kate added as an afterthought. "The points of the compass always come together in the end."

"It's John Donne," said Emmie, her throat scratchy. "'A Valediction: Forbidding Mourning.' The two points of the compass always come together in the end, so true lovers can never really be parted, even when they run around in circles."

Except in the poem, the author was speaking about death. Emmie didn't want to think about death. It was all very well to talk about not loving as sublunary lovers love and expansion of souls and all that, but she'd really rather not have to commune with a soul. She wanted the whole person back.

He'd been alive this morning, which meant he'd survived the dawn assault, but if he'd gone back to the line . . .

"There's been no word since?"

Kate shook her head. "No one really seems to know anything. Only that there was heavy fighting. You were closer to it than we were."

Emmie thought about the ambulances, those endless ambulances, bearing their gruesome burden.

"I'm sorry," said Kate.

She couldn't let herself cry now. Not when there was so much to be done. Will was away somewhere, but these men were still alive and needed her. Emmie blinked hard. "What can I do?"

"You've done so much today already. . . ." Kate saw the expression on Emmie's face and quickly changed whatever she had been about to say to "Anne could use the help—she's in the kitchen."

"We've been making gallons of tea," said Anne distractedly, pushing a strand of ginger hair back behind her ear as Emmie poked through the canvas flap. Every pot they owned appeared to be in use, the big old stove smoking like anything. "They've been without rations for twenty-four hours, these poor boys. We've been cooking and cooking for them since three o'clock. We've opened every can of beans in the place and boiled every scrap of macaroni we could find. But mostly it's tea they want, poor men. One nearly cried when I asked him if he wanted milk. He says he hasn't seen milk for months."

Emmie sliced bread and brewed tea and sliced more bread and brewed more tea, going back and forth to the dining room with tray after tray after tray as one group was fed and another came in.

Work helped. It was easier not to think of Will out there in the mist with the Germans coming upon them when her hands were busy making up beds or carrying trays. They were so grateful, those men. Emmie, Anne, and Nell went back and forth between the kitchen and the dining room, cooking, collecting dishes, washing dishes, and filling them up again, while Florence saw to the animals, and Kate and Alice turned the dining room and the Orangerie into makeshift dormitories, stripping the mattresses and blankets off their beds to make pallets for the soldiers.

"Was that really the last of them?" asked Anne, sitting down heavily on a stool, her feet sticking out in front of her. It was two in the morning and everyone had been fed and put to bed except the seven remaining members of the Smith Unit, who were collapsed in the kitchen, among a stack of dirty pots and dishes.

"Merciful heavens, I hope so," said Nell, yawning. "If I never see another tin of beans, it will be too soon."

Kate rubbed her eyes with the back of her hand. "They'll need breakfast."

Julia pushed herself off the wall against which she'd

been leaning, half-asleep on her feet. "We'd best get started, then, hadn't we?"

"Noooo . . ." said Nell, but Julia gave her a light shove.

"If I can make oatmeal," said Julia, "so can you."

Emmie had no idea what had happened between Julia and Kate in Paris, but whatever it was, she had never seen Julia pitch in like this before, like she was actually part of the Unit and not just there for medical experience. Julia tucked up her sleeves and boiled and scoured with the rest of them. Her sharp-tongued jibes galvanized them into moving when they needed it, and Emmie didn't even mind the sting.

Oatmeal. Cauldrons of oatmeal. Lakes of coffee. They left it all sitting in buffet form in the Orangerie and staggered down the duckwalk to their barracks, only remembering just in time that they'd given up one barrack to officers, shoving Alice's and Florence's cots into Kate and Emmie's room. There was barely room to move between the cots and their bulging duffel bags.

"You packed my duffel?" said Emmie, looking at Kate.

"Just in case." Kate paused for a moment and then added, reluctantly, "The major said we should be ready to go if needed."

Their eyes met. They both knew what that meant.

"They meant us to evacuate this morning," said Emmie. "Alice and I just ignored them and carried on."

"So did we—and then we weakened their resolve with tea and beans," said Kate. "They were hardly going to insist once we started feeding them. But I doubt that will work again if the Germans come closer. We should get what sleep we can. While we can. Alice, what on earth are you doing?"

Alice shoved another paper into the fire. "I'm burning my letters so the Germans won't get them."

"Mm-hmm," said Kate, nobly refraining from pointing out that the German infantry probably wasn't terribly concerned with Alice's private correspondence. Emmie had to tamp down an entirely ridiculous fit of the giggles at the thought of the Boche puzzling over Alice's letters from her sister, looking for codes in crochet patterns.

"I've got the chickens in their crates," said Florence heartily as she plumped down on her own bed. "And I've sent the cows and goats on to Moyencourt in care of Marie's son. We don't want the Boche to get them. Just a precaution, of course."

All just a precaution. They knew it wasn't, though. They'd moved past precaution somewhere around nine that morning.

Emmie lay down on the bare springs of her bed,

pulling her coat over herself in lieu of a blanket. The mattress was currently on the floor of the dining room, as was the blanket, both being used by exhausted British soldiers who needed them far more than she did. She was still wearing the shirtwaist and uniform she had put on to teach a hygiene class in Verlaines a lifetime ago, before the world had exploded in blood and ash.

In the silence, Emmie thought she could hear the sound of marching feet, the German army, thousands of them, bearing down on Grécourt, pitiless, unstoppable, laying waste to everything in its path like a beast from a child's nightmare.

"Good night," she whispered, and closed her eyes and tried to pretend it was yesterday, when Will was well, and all was well, and the Germans weren't marching inexorably toward them.

Chapter Twenty-Seven

I was never afraid before I met you. But now I am. I know we said we wouldn't speak of the war, but the war is here, the war is coming for us, and I'm afraid as I was never afraid before, when there was only my own miserable life at stake. I'm afraid for you. I'm afraid for myself. I'm afraid I'll never see you again, never hear your voice again, never have the chance to tell you, in my own weak, miserable words, how much I love you.

I've been trying to take solace in others' words. I have my John Donne here with me (not Shakespeare, I promise), reminding me that our souls are joined even if our bodies are parted, circling like the points of a compass. I never told you that you are all the points of the compass to

me: *my east, my north, my south, my west. My*
America. My newfound land. My Emmie.

I'm babbling now. I can't seem to think clearly
in the midst of all this, and time is short. So if you
can hear only one thing through the rubble and
the noise, I hope you hear the echo of this:

I love you.

I love you.

I love you.

—*From a letter, unsent, found*
among the things of Captain
Fitzwilliam DeWitt, 2nd
Battalion, Durham Light
Infantry

March 1918
Grécourt, France

They'd scarcely been asleep an hour when the guns started again.

Kate struggled up, trying to make sense of where she was and what was happening. It was Grécourt, but she was in her clothes, the room was jammed with extra cots, and the guns were rumbling nearer than she'd like.

Feeling hot and cold all at once, Kate sat up, reaching for the coat-covered lump that was Emmie. Alice and Florence were already stirring, rubbing their eyes and pinning up their hair, but Kate knew from college that Emmie could sleep through just about anything. Even, apparently, a machine-gun barrage.

"Emmie—Emmie."

Emmie grumbled, trying to stick her head under her pillow.

There was a rat-a-tat-tat on the door, and the major entered, manfully averting his eyes, even though it was pitch-dark and they were all fully clothed. "I'm awfully sorry," he said. "But the Boche seem to be on the move again."

"Then I guess we ought to be too." Kate's voice felt scratchy. It hurt to even think of leaving. But the guns—they were close. Closer than she had ever heard them. Three miles away. Five if they were lucky. She wondered what had fallen in the night, which of their friends were dead. "We're already packed. We can be out in fifteen minutes."

Alice stuffed her knuckles into her mouth, making a muffled sound of distress.

Kate fished in her pocket, digging out a set of heavy keys. "Here." She thrust them at the major. "These are the keys to the cellar. You'll find our supplies down there. Take anything you can use. Give any blankets and food to the soldiers, and medical supplies to the hospital corps. As for anything that's left . . . if you have to retreat, burn it. Burn it all."

"The seeds—" said Alice faintly, and stopped. They'd all spent weeks sifting seeds into tiny little packets, thousands and thousands of them. Weeks of effort, gone. All their hard-won supplies, all their Hague parcels, all the extras they'd wrangled from the Red Cross, gone.

"What Kate said," said Emmie, heroically coming to Kate's aid. Her hair was out of its pins and half-down around one shoulder. "We'd rather lose everything than have it fall into the hands of the Boche."

"I suppose so," said Alice, hugging her duffel to her chest. "It does seem a shame, though. Think of all those nubias the Bangor Committee collected for us."

"Oh heavens, not the nubias," said Florence. "Even the Boche couldn't possibly want the nubias."

"What's a nubia?" asked the major, sounding so politely bewildered that Kate had to bite her lip to keep from laughing. Or possibly crying.

"I'm just going to take my duffel to the truck," Kate said in a muffled voice, and staggered out before she could disgrace herself.

Behind her, she could hear Alice explaining, "A nubia is a sort of woolen hood—they're not worn very much anymore."

"Ah, I see," said the major gravely, as if she were explaining a military tactic of utmost importance.

Kate paused just outside the barrack, her shoulders shaking, her chest tight. She was about to cry over the blasted nubias, and she couldn't, not now, not when they needed her to be strong, even though she had no idea what she was doing, what she was meant to be doing.

She wanted Mrs. Barrett; she wanted Dr. Stringfellow; she wanted anyone who could tell them what to do and where to go. Grécourt looked different already, the anemones churned up by the tread of two hundred soldiers, tents dotted around the lawn. Maybe, if she closed her eyes and wished hard enough, she could make it a week ago: the ground bright with flowers; slipping into story time and holding Zélie on her lap while Nell read to the *basse-cour* children in French about Little Red Riding Hood and the Big Bad Wolf; joking with the Unit around the supper table about their amazing ability to differentiate between types of guns.

But it wasn't a week ago. The Big Bad Wolf was here, he was on the march, with his big, big teeth and big, big guns, and maybe she wasn't the best the Unit could have, but she was what they had right now.

"Is it too heavy?" asked Emmie, coming out, lugging her own duffel.

Kate fumbled for the bag, grateful for the predawn dark that hid her face. "N-no. Just awkward. I can't seem to get a good grip."

Outside the Orangerie, a surprise was waiting for her, all three trucks as spick-and-span as could be, the mud and dust of the previous day scrubbed off, everything oiled and greased and shining.

"Did the Tommies do this for us?" asked Kate wonderingly.

"I did," said Alice, heaving her duffel into the White truck, with the hard tires they had acquired at such cost. "Last night, while you were all cooking oatmeal. They're all greased and oiled and filled with *essence*. And there's extra *essence* in cans in each machine."

Kate goggled at her. "How on earth did you get the gasoline?"

Alice gave a little half shrug. "They were packing up the supply dump in Ham yesterday, so Emmie and I went along and asked them. They were really quite nice about it."

Nice didn't even begin to describe it. Kate hadn't even thought about fuel. There was so much she hadn't thought about. "Alice, you're a wonder."

Florence staggered up, holding a large crate in each hand. "I've got the hens."

"I thought we might need food for the people on

the road," said Emmie breathlessly, bent nearly double lugging two five-gallon drums of milk. "I've packed our entire supply of milk and all the bread, biscuits, and chocolate I could find. The major has some Tommies carrying the rest of it over for us. I told him to put it in the jitney."

"I've got first-aid supplies and gas masks," said Julia briskly, swinging her doctor's bag into the back of the jitney.

"I brought blankets," said Nell, balancing a large pile of the aforementioned item on her head. "Someone is bound to need blankets."

"And I've brought a portable stove," said Anne. "And my tools. Just in case we need them."

Kate felt her throat close up. "You're all wonders," she said.

She looked at the six other remaining members of the Unit, huddled together around the trucks, each and every one of them a wonder, each and every one of them her sister. They had been strangers to each other when they arrived seven months ago, but now she knew each of them down to the bones, just as they knew her, better than she had ever known anyone.

The Tommies were loading the trucks, piling in the food and duffel bags and crates of hens. It felt horribly, dreadfully final.

Kate drew herself up to her full five foot one, looking at all that remained of their Unit. "They won't drive us away," she said fiercely. "We're not leaving, not really. We're just stepping away for a bit. The Boche have no idea what they're up against in us."

One of Florence's roosters stuck his head out through the slats of his crate and let out a loud, defiant crow. It pierced the dawn, resounding over the guns and the thrum of the motors.

Nell let out a shout of laughter. "Chanticleer agrees. Take that, Boche!"

"Even the Unit's hens don't admit defeat," said Alice nobly. "Nell, you're with me in the White truck?"

"That one's a rooster, actually," said Florence, swinging up behind the wheel of the Ford truck. She grinned at Kate. "Mr. Buff Orpington himself."

"You'll never let me forget that, will you?" asked Kate, settling herself behind the wheel of the jitney, Emmie next to her and Julia behind.

The major touched his hand to his cap. "Good luck. Godspeed."

"And you," said Kate. She had no idea what awaited him or them; all she knew was that all of them needed all the luck they could get. Luck and—what had Mrs. Rutherford called it?—grim determination. She nodded curtly at the major. "Kick those Boche back to Berlin for us."

The small procession of trucks bumped over the moat, through the great gates, down the long alley of fallen trees. Kate was glad she was driving; it kept her from craning her head back to look, to try to memorize it all: the ruin of the castle in the mist; the Orangerie, where they had kept their trucks and held classes and their clinic and their parties; Marie's tumbledown house, where she had cooked for them on her trusty stove before they had set up the kitchen; the church where they had sung their canticles and celebrated mass.

Just a few days, Kate told herself. The British never let go of anything. And there were the foresters and the engineers and the aviators—all the men who had danced and come to supper and drunk soup out of their tooth mugs—all those brave men holding the line.

But then they hit the road to Ercheu and saw the soldiers, companies upon companies of them, dragging their way wearily down the road, away from the front. There was a Scots band, their drums silent against their chests, their bagpipes furled, and somehow that struck Kate as the most haunting thing of all, their silence, when they had last seen them marching bravely toward the front with kilts swirling and bagpipes screeching.

And alongside the retreat came the refugees, villagers from their own villages, villagers from farther on, family groupings and people on their own, big sisters minding little siblings, an old woman clutching her cat, stumbling down the road in the pitiless light of the rising sun.

"Stop! We have to do something for them! Can't we take them up?" Emmie pulled on Kate's sleeve. The sun was rising, burning off the mist, revealing all the horrors that had been softened by the dawn.

"We'll have to drop our things and come back." Kate didn't want to tell Emmie that she didn't like the noises the jitney had been making. "But we can give them something to eat at least."

They paused by the side of the road, handing out milk and bread and eggs to hungry children and soldiers, promising again and again that they would be back to take people up.

Behind them, Florence honked. "We're blocking the road!" she shouted. "We need to get moving."

"She's right," Kate said as Emmie twisted to stare back at the new waves of villagers, more and more, trailing out of the war zone. "We can set up in Roye at the Red Cross hospital and ferry people back. We can do more that way."

It felt good to have a plan. They weren't running away, Kate decided; they were doing their job, and would go on doing it. It made her feel less like a refugee herself.

But when they got to Roye, a little after six in the morning, Dr. Baldwin was packing up the hospital. "We're evacuating," he said, in between giving orders to harried orderlies. "We've been told to go on to Montdidier. It's not safe here anymore."

"But—surely—they can't just be retreating," said Alice. "They must mean to take a stand somewhere?"

Dr. Baldwin paused, turning to face them. "The best I've heard is that the English have been forced out of their last trench. It's hand-to-hand combat now, in the open. The Germans are mowing down everything in their path."

"Everything?" said Emmie, her face chalk white. "But surely some of the men in the front lines—not everyone can have been—"

"If they do take a stand," said the doctor, misunderstanding her concerns, "it will be at the line of the old Battle of the Somme—which means we're on the wrong side of it. Let's hope there are enough left to hold the Germans there. In the meantime, we need to move our sick. We've mainly children here."

Kate turned to the rest of the Unit. "We have two choices. We can take our things and move on. Or we can stay and help."

Emmie was still pale, but resolute. "There's no question. We stay."

"I always wanted a good story to tell my children," said Nell bravely.

Alice looked like she strongly wanted to disagree, but controlled herself.

"Is it unanimous, then?" asked Kate. Even Alice nodded. "All right. We have three trucks and seven of us. If we empty the trucks and leave all our bags here, we can use one truck to take the children from the hospital to Montdidier, and the other two to go back and pick up as many people as we can."

"I'll take the children," volunteered Alice quickly, taking the job that involved driving away from the active fighting.

"If they're evacuating Roye, we won't be able to use this as a base. We'll need some sort of refugee center in Montdidier." Kate was struck by sudden inspiration. "Emmie, could you go with Alice and take charge of setting up a refugee center?"

"Y-yes. Of course." Emmie lifted her head, some color returning to her face. "If we can find a hotel to take us, we could use Nell's blankets for pallets and Anne's stove to heat milk for babies."

"Brilliant. If you can organize that, Florence and I

can take the other two trucks and ferry people from the villages between here and Ercheu. Nell can come with me and Anne with Florence."

Alice was twisting her lace-edged handkerchief back and forth between her fingers, fear warring with conscience. Conscience won out. "It's a long way from Ercheu to Montdidier. If you bring people here, I can run back and forth between Montdidier and Roye."

"That will double the number of people we're able to move," said Kate gratefully. "Shall we?"

The Unit dispersed to their tasks, dumping their belongings in the courtyard of the hospital, distributing their remaining foodstuffs between the three trucks to share out among the refugees. Florence looked mournfully at her chickens but agreed there was no way to take them; they would have to be donated.

"Trust me, I mind as much as you," said Kate. "After the trouble we had getting those horrible hens from Paris! I thought I was going to be pecked to death!"

"They can tell you don't like them," said Florence seriously.

"I like them in soup," said Kate.

But that was the last moment of levity they had for a long time. The day stretched on, endless, getting brighter and hotter. It felt like July on the road, and the dust rose in a choking cloud, coating their clothes and hair, sticking in the backs of their throats, mixing with sweat to make tracks of mud down their faces.

Kate had never imagined anything like what they saw on the road that day, as they stopped and stopped and stopped again, loading as many people as they could into the truck, giving milk until the milk ran out, distributing every last scrap of bread they could find in their haversacks. There was an old man wheeling his paralyzed wife in a wheelbarrow. They made a pallet for her out of someone's mattress and got her into the truck, her husband next to her. Dispatch riders on motorbikes zoomed past them in both directions, raising more dust. Army camions lumbered past, and above it all, the guns thundered on, closer and closer.

A colonel they knew honked from his truck, going the other way. "Don't stay too long!" he shouted. "We're going to blow the bridges up!"

"How long?" Nell shouted back, clinging to the side of the truck, but they couldn't hear the answer.

"As long as we can," Kate said grimly, and they went on, back toward the guns, back against the wave of people flowing in the opposite direction.

Back and forth they went, back and forth along the road, picking up the people they had told to wait for them before, going into the villages past Roye and collecting anyone who looked like they might need help, which amounted to roughly everyone. It made Kate furious to think that these were the survivors. These were the few who had managed to remain after the first German invasion, to cling to their homes, to stay together, and here they were, on the road in the dust and confusion with the Germans bearing down again, losing one another, losing everything.

One woman was hysterical over a sack of clothing she had misplaced, all her smocks for her children, everything she had for them in the world.

"We'll look for them," Kate promised, because she knew the woman had to hear it, had to have something that was hers, even if the world was exploding into ash mile by mile, and they had bigger problems than baby clothes.

"It's one thing seeing the aftermath months later," said Kate soberly as they dropped another group off at the hospital at Roye to be ferried on to Montdidier by Alice, "and quite another to watch it in progress, all these people being wrenched from their homes."

"It's such a *waste*," said Nell, and climbed into the back to see how much food they had left to distribute.

Half the people on the road were people they knew, people from their villages. All they'd done to make them comfortable again, lost. They'd tried so hard to give them some security, some hope—and now the best they could do was try to help them find a place where they could sleep on a floor for the night before being sent off to goodness knew where.

Kate wondered how Emmie was getting on with the refugee center in Montdidier. She wished with all her soul that Emmie were here—Emmie was so much better than she was with people. She'd know what to say to a mother who had nine children on nine separate gun carriages, frantic with trying to collect them. She'd know what to say to the woman who refused to leave without her cat, which had run off.

Nell was unflaggingly cheerful, a brittle sort of cheerfulness that might shatter any second, but the children responded to it and followed her, and Kate was insanely grateful to have her along, jollying the children and comforting the adults as Kate drove the truck.

They picked up an eleven-year-old girl, a loaf of bread sticking out from under each arm, her hands holding tight to two little sisters, one on each side. She refused to be parted from either bread or sisters until they promised they only meant to help them up into the truck, together. They'd lost their mother, who was blind, and two little brothers, who were with their mother, in the confusion of the evacuation.

"We'll see what we can do about finding her for

you," said Nell cheerfully, and then crawled over the baggage piled high in the back of the jitney to Kate in the front. "Kate, we have to find some way of getting families back together. We have no idea who Florence and Anne have picked up—these girls' mother might be in her load."

"What about the crossroads? We're dropping them there to wait for Alice anyway. We can set up a reunification center." Kate scrubbed her forehead with a dusty hand. Most of them knew only the people in their assigned villages, but Anne, with her special carpentry and sewing classes, knew pretty much every child in all of them. "If Florence can spare Anne, she can do it—she knows more of these children than anyone."

The next time the two trucks met outside Roye, Kate shouted her plans across. Anne began sorting families by the crossroads and Florence went off alone, down the road to Margny.

"Be careful!" Kate shouted after her, and Florence waved her hat at her in response as the dust rose in her wake.

Kate was putting the jitney into gear when a sentry hailed them.

"Is something wrong?" asked Kate, and then realized what an idiot question it was. Of course something was wrong. Everything was wrong.

"It's Albert, isn't it?" Nell called down. "You directed the traffic for us in Ham!"

"Yes, miss," said the sentry, showing crooked teeth as he grinned at Nell. "Well, you see, it's like this. They want me to guard the Nesle–Roye road, but someone's needed to direct traffic here."

"I've always wanted to direct traffic," said Nell, putting on her old ebullience like a cloak. She stood up in the jitney, shaking out her dusty skirt. "It's a lifelong ambition of mine. You'll be all right without me, Kate?"

"Right as rain," lied Kate in the same cheerful tone, and left Nell standing at the crossroads, moving her arms left and right, shouting at camions and scolding cart drivers.

Kate's shoulders were stiff and aching from fighting with the jitney. There was something wrong with it; she'd have to get Alice to look at it later. But there wasn't time now. Every minute counted, every minute meant another person saved. It was harder without Nell, so much harder, and she was painfully aware of time passing, of the sun moving and the shadows gathering and the Germans coming on and on, unstoppable.

Mme Chevrier, from Bacquencourt, wanted her to tell Emmie that she had saved the curtains she was making for the social center in Canizy. Kate congratulated her and tried not to think that there probably wasn't a social center left for curtains; she couldn't let herself think like that.

A British soldier blocked her on the road to Ercheu. "It's not safe anymore, miss—you can't go that way. The Boche."

Had they got everyone out? Kate hoped so. Her cheeks stung with sunburn and her eyes with dust as she drove the last load back to the crossroads.

She found Alice there, helping Anne get families into the White truck. "They say it's not safe to keep going back," said Alice anxiously. "Florence has gone on to Montdidier with the truck."

"Does anyone know what's going on?" asked Kate in frustration.

Alice shook her head. "Only that they're closer."

How much closer? What did that even mean? Kate was sick of rumors and half news, of not knowing what was going on. She felt as if she were in a snow globe, being shaken about, while someone was peering in from outside, watching her dance.

"All right," said Kate hoarsely. She was stiff and grimy and, she hadn't realized it before, sick with hunger. Her watch said it was past seven. She had been driving for thirteen hours straight. "We'll regroup in Montdidier."

618 · LAUREN WILLIG

They left Anne and Nell—Nell still directing traffic, Anne staying to keep her company. "It's all right," Anne promised them, as Kate took up her last load of refugees. "Dr. Baldwin says he'll take us to Montdidier with him when he finishes closing down the hospital."

In Montdidier, Kate found that Emmie had taken over a hotel. "The owner has been splendid," said Emmie. "She's let us have the whole building and found us straw for pallets. Julia's taken over a room for a children's infirmary. Mrs. Goodale—she's one of Dr. Baldwin's nurses—got onto someone she knew and came back with a regular bonanza of condensed milk for us, so we've been able to feed the babies now that we don't have our cows anymore."

"Emmie—" Kate looked around, dazed and amazed. There was a full canteen running in the courtyard, and rooms lined with pallets like dormitories. "How on earth did you do all this in one day?"

Emmie flushed, looking pleased and flustered. "It wasn't just me. Some of our Quakers from Ham came by and have been helping. We managed to find enough stoves to make sure everyone's had some warm food— there's a schoolmistress who let us have the stove from her school and someone else donated tables and chairs for a canteen in the courtyard. . . ."

"Is that Marie?" One of the groups clustered around a table in the courtyard looked awfully familiar.

"Yes! Florence brought our *basse-cour* people in just an hour ago. . . . Oh dear, yes? What is it?"

One of the Quakers needed Emmie. She gave an apologetic wave and bustled away, leaving Kate to Marie, who embraced and scolded her all at once, wanting to know what Kate had been doing to get her uniform into such a state, and after Marie had washed it so nicely for her too.

"But weren't you—you left on Friday," said Kate dazedly. It belatedly dawned on her that Friday had been yesterday. It couldn't possibly have been only yesterday. Yesterday morning, they had still been going about their business. That couldn't be right. But it was. "You ought to have been here ages ago. What happened?"

They hadn't really thought the Germans would come, so they'd gone only as far as Moyencourt. But then with the morning, they'd been told they had to go, so they had joined the other refugees on the road, and might have made it faster, but there had been that trouble with Zélie—

"What trouble?" Kate wasn't tired anymore. She was suddenly, desperately scared. She could see all the other *basse-cour* residents eating in the courtyard, but not Zélie. "Where's Zélie?"

"It was that goat," said Marie defensively. "My son brought the animals to Moyencourt, but we couldn't bring them farther, so we went on without them, but that Zélie, she ran off when no one was looking."

"Ran off. After the goat?"

Marie stepped back, folding her arms across her chest. "I always told you that goat would be trouble, treating it like a pet. Now you see what happened."

"Where did she go? Back to Moyencourt?" Kate could see the map of their villages in her head with horrible clarity. Moyencourt was farther from the front than Grécourt, but not by much. Not nearly enough.

"She's probably sleeping in a barn somewhere with that goat," said Marie, but she didn't sound sure.

"Alone, in Moyencourt." Kate didn't stop to think. She grabbed a piece of bread from the table. She had water in a thermos in the truck. "If anyone asks, I've just gone on one last run."

Chapter Twenty-Eight

In the dark, with our roosters to crow us on our way, we rolled out of the gate and headed to Roye with the other refugees.

All along the road we kept meeting men we knew, men who had come to dinner or tea with us. They were retreating steadily, and it did all look a bit black. They told us what was ahead of us on the road, where the Germans were, what risks we took, and then left it to our judgment. We were one of them now. I can't tell you—I could never in a lifetime show you—how fine people are when all the external, superficial barriers are stripped away by a great emergency.

We went back and forth all morning, carrying refugees. It was heartbreaking to see the babies one and two days old, the sick and the old, and always the soldiers and the guns and the planes. For the rest of the day, Nell directed traffic for the Great Retreat, and I did my best to "match up" families. Nell and I stayed on at the crossroads until Dr. Baldwin came to bring us into Montdidier to join the rest and we discovered Kate was missing. . . .

—Miss Anne Dawlish, '07,
to Miss Ruth Minster

March 1918
Montdidier, France

E mmie had left Will's letters at Grécourt.

It was such a stupid thing to be thinking about. There were so many things to be done. There were blankets to be stuffed with straw to make makeshift beds, milk to be warmed for the babies, and tin after tin of sardines to be opened.

But as Emmie hurried around the hotel in Montdidier, making sure all of their refugees were fed and had places to sleep for the night, she found herself slowing and thinking of that packet of letters in her trunk in Grécourt with a sharp pang of grief that hit her right in the center of her chest.

Emmie paused with her arms full of blankets, hugging them to herself as hard as she could, reminding herself that she needed to be strong for the Unit, for all their people who needed them. They'd been finding their own people all day; there were families she knew from Canizy and Courcelles, and it had been a solace to have the children run to her and hug her and know that seeing her there eased their fear a little, that if their Mlle Aimée was there, then everything couldn't be all bad.

The grown-ups were harder. Some of their questions were relatively simple ones: finding missing baggage or, worse, missing family members. Emmie could say, "Well, the cars are still coming in, we'll see who Alice brings," or "Where exactly was it that you left your sack of *linge*?" It was the other questions that were harder, the big questions, the ones who wanted to know when they could go back again, what the Unit would do to replace what had been lost, when they could rebuild again, would they be back in time to finish the spring planting.

I don't know, she wanted to say. *I don't know, I don't know, I don't know.*

But part of her job was to give people hope, to make them feel like there was some certainty, some safety, in this horrible, mixed-up madhouse of a world into which they had plummeted, so she smiled and said things like, "As soon as we know more, we'll be sure to tell everyone," which meant the same thing, really, but sounded so much better, because it made it sound like the Unit had some control over the situation when they hadn't really, not at all. All they had was this hotel, for which they were paying a rather alarming amount, and one duffel each—and Alice didn't even have that, because her duffel had got lost in the transfer from Roye to Montdidier, goodness only knew where or how, so she would have to borrow clothes from Emmie and Anne, because she was too tall for Kate's or Florence's or Nell's, and Julia hadn't bothered to bring much in the way of personal possessions, instead cramming her bag with all the medical supplies they could manage. Alice, of course, was pretending this was all very well, but Emmie knew she minded horribly, that her frills were her armor and she was as cut up about it as Emmie was about leaving Will's letters.

Will. Somewhere on the front lines. It didn't mean he was lost. People survived, they did, she'd seen it. She'd seen them survive in all sorts of ways, some almost worse than not surviving at all. Emmie pushed back that horrible thought, hating herself for it. Nothing could be worse than Will not surviving.

She tried not to think of the men in the American hospital at Neuilly, having their faces rebuilt, like a child's exercise in clay.

No one knew anything. No one could tell them anything. She'd stopped asking, because it was all the same, from everyone she'd asked. There'd been fog and the Germans had come out of nowhere, overwhelming them, and no one knew where his own messmates were, let alone another regiment.

Only that the Germans were pushing on and on and on.

They'd heard conflicting accounts throughout the day. The Germans were bombing Paris. The Germans had been stopped at Cambrai. The English were all fleeing. The English were making a stand. Only one thing was solid and true—there were people here, living, breathing, lonely, scared people who needed help, who had been pushed from their homes and separated from their families. Emmie rolled up her sleeves and scrounged stoves and badgered the Red Cross for supplies and tried not to think too much of what was happening a dozen miles away, what Kate and Florence and Anne and Nell were driving back into again and again and again.

Or Will. Out there at the front. Riding up out of the mist to warn them and then riding away again, gone.

Useless to remind herself there were other women's sweethearts out there too. It was hard not to be selfish when you'd found the one person in the world whose mind marched with yours, who made you feel in all ways better than you could ever possibly be.

"—the blankets?" someone was saying.

It was one of their Quaker friends from Ham, who had worked so hard at rebuilding the roofs that the Germans were at the present engaged in tearing back down. They'd shown up at the hotel earlier in the day, offering their services in getting the refugee center up and running, and had been working like troopers ever since.

Whenever she looked at them, Emmie saw in their eyes something she was desperately afraid of seeing in her own: a bewildered sort of grief, confused and desolate all at once.

Emmie blinked rapidly and handed over the bundle. "Sorry—I have them here. Is everyone tucked up?"

"Almost. Madame Lenois's two-year-old is rampaging all over the place pretending to be an elephant. We may have to tie him to his cot." The young man hesitated and then said, "Would you like to go take a rest? We can hold the fort for you for a bit."

Alice had staked out two rooms for the Unit, insisting that they needed to sleep if they were to help anyone. The idea of going upstairs, of pulling the covers over her head, was tempting beyond belief. Every muscle in her body felt sore with tension. This morning, she'd had enough energy for fifteen people, but it was beginning to wear off, leaving exhaustion and achiness and a horrible, howling sort of emptiness.

She had to keep moving, she had to keep working, or the emptiness would grab her and pull her in. If she let herself close her eyes in the darkness, she would have to acknowledge everything that had happened, that they had lost Grécourt, had lost everything they'd worked and worked and worked for, that their people were homeless again.

That Will was missing, likely dead.

"No, that's all right," said Emmie brightly. "You go on. Kate and Anne and Nell are still out there and I don't want to go to bed until they get back."

Kate had come back for five minutes and then gone off again. One minute she had been there, and the next the jitney was gone, presumably back to Nell and Anne. Florence, coming back dusty but cheerful as ever, had said that Nell was directing traffic and Anne was at the crossroads, reuniting families. Neither of them drove, so Kate must have gone back for them.

Emmie reached for the watch at her breast before remembering it was lost, lost since yesterday, which felt more like ten years ago.

Mme Lenois came to ask her for warm milk to settle her son, who was driving everyone mad with his elephant impression (Nell had taught him that, and was entirely unrepentant about it). Emmie went to dilute and warm the milk, glancing at the clock in the kitchen. Nearly ten. Surely they should be back by now? Alice and Florence had already gone to bed, leaving the White and the Ford parked outside.

A truck rumbled to a stop outside. There were voices. American voices. Thank goodness.

Emmie popped the door open, but it wasn't the jitney outside. It was a Red Cross truck, with Dr. Baldwin at the wheel and Anne and Nell saying their goodbyes. Emmie looked behind them for Kate, but there was no sign of her.

"Hello," she said to Dr. Baldwin. "Did the jitney break down? Where's Kate?"

"Isn't she with you?" asked Anne, rubbing her gritty eyes with the back of her hand. Her hair was straggling out from under her hat. She looked thoroughly done in. "She came back here hours ago."

"No," said Emmie slowly. "She came here and then she left again. I thought she went back to you."

"Maybe she went straight to bed." Nell staggered as she stepped down from the truck. "My legs feel like they're about to give out. I never knew it was such hard work directing traffic."

"Alice saved two rooms for us upstairs if you want to go up." Maybe Nell was right; maybe Kate had gone upstairs. There had been confusion with a woman whose husband had been hit by a cart during the retreat, who insisted on bringing in the body to be resuscitated even though he was clearly well past saving, and that had occupied Emmie's attention for some time, trying to gently get the woman away from the body and find a friend to sit with her.

Dr. Baldwin was asking about his patients. "Oh, yes, this way. Julia's set up a room as a children's hospital. We've added quite a few to your original patients, I'm afraid. Julia and Mrs. Goodale have been working tirelessly." Pausing, Emmie looked back at Nell, feeling silly but worried all the same. "Would you mind seeing if Kate's upstairs? I'm sure she is, but . . ."

It wasn't like Kate to just go to bed when there was work to be done. But even Kate was human, and ferrying refugees was a bone-wearying test of endurance, emotionally and physically trying. It would, however, thought Emmie, cheering up a bit, be very like Kate to just sit down for a moment and be so tired her body gave out on her. She was probably asleep in her clothes right now, still thinking it was four hours ago and she'd just nodded off for a moment.

"We have twenty-two children here at present," Emmie said, taking Dr. Baldwin into the infirmary. "There were three cases from Sancourt that looked like measles, so we've put those children into a separate room and Marie—our mayor from Grécourt—is sitting with them."

Marie and Mme Gouge, the cook/housekeeper Mrs. Barrett had hired, had been in competition to show who could do more for the Unit. In the end, they'd had to separate them, leaving Mme Gouge in command of the kitchen and Marie in charge of the infectious diseases, which had the added benefit, as Julia had acidly pointed out, of getting them both out of her infirmary so she could actually care for her patients without having spoons of broth being thrust under her nose every three seconds.

Julia was kneeling next to a pallet, listening to a boy's chest. At Dr. Baldwin's entrance, she pushed herself stiffly to her feet and began briefing him.

Nell popped her head in, saying in a stage whisper, "Kate's not upstairs."

Julia turned sharply, pausing mid-sentence. "What's that about Kate?"

"She went back to Roye and doesn't seem to have come back." Emmie tried to sound casual about it, but she couldn't. "Could she still be there? She might be looking for Anne and Nell. It's like something out of a French farce, isn't it? Everyone looking for everyone else and going in circles."

"It's nearly eleven already," said Julia. "She would come back here if she couldn't find them."

Emmie tried not to sound as panicked as she felt. "Maybe we should go back for her."

"No one's going back. Army's orders. If she's still there, she's probably bunked down at the hospital for the night," said Dr. Baldwin dismissively as he moved toward the basin to wash his hands. "I wouldn't worry."

"No, of course," lied Emmie. "If you'll excuse me?"

Julia followed her out. "Where are you going?" she asked bluntly.

Emmie hesitated, knowing Julia would mock her. But she needed to confide in someone and there was no one else. "Kate would never just leave Anne and Nell. What if she went to the crossroads to look for them and the jitney broke down? It was making strange noises this morning—Kate said she'd have Alice look at it, but I don't know if she did. We were all so busy. . . ."

Julia didn't mock her. She said, "Who can we get to drive?"

"I can drive," said Emmie, heading out the door. "Alice taught me. Wait, what are you doing?"

Julia had climbed up into the White. She sat there, ramrod straight, her medical bag in her lap. "Coming with you."

"But they need you here."

"Dr. Baldwin is back." Julia shrugged, and then said, with deliberate provocation, "You need me more than he does. You've never been able to read a map. You got lost once in the garden of your own house."

"It was a maze," Emmie protested, knowing she should make Julia stay but selfishly relieved not to be going alone. The street was so dark, with no street-lights and all the windows blacked out. She would have to somehow navigate, in the dark, without headlights. "It was designed for people to get lost in."

A gun boomed somewhere miles away, and Emmie felt the car swerve as she flinched. They'd been under fire so much, but it felt different being out at night, in the dark, at the wheel. The walls of the house weren't much protection, but they were something.

Emmie took a deep breath. "You shouldn't talk. You were the one who led me into the maze and left me."

Julia balanced her medical bag on her knees. "I told you all you had to do was keep going left."

"Yes, but you know I can't tell my right from my left."

There was an army camion coming straight her way, also without headlights. Emmie clung to the wheel, wrenching the White out of the way just in time, narrowly evading a collision with an ambulance. The road was busy with traffic, complicated by everyone having their lights off. All she could see were shapes in the dark.

"You never told on me," said Julia unexpectedly as Emmie wrestled the truck back onto the road. "About leaving you in the maze. Why?"

"It was easier to let Nanny scold me for being silly than to have her punish you." Nanny wouldn't have punished the Van Alden children, but an unpleasant child who was dropped into her care without a by-your-leave was another matter entirely. Julia had been sentenced to cold baths; locked in dark rooms; and, when none of that had any effect, treated to the horrifying slap of birch against flesh. "It wasn't hard. Nanny expected me to be silly."

Not far away, a plane plummeted from the sky, flames billowing from its tail. The light momentarily lit the scene, the road, the trucks, the scrap of metal falling like Icarus. A cart horse neighed in panic, nearly oversetting the cart it was pulling.

"If I get through this," Emmie said, her teeth chattering so hard she could barely get the words out, "Fifth Avenue won't have any terrors for me."

Julia looked at her hard but didn't make fun. "There's the crossroads. There's a sentry on guard. I'll ask him if he's seen the jitney. Stay here."

Emmie stayed, using the time to try to get her

breathing under control. She could see Julia, a dim figure in her gray uniform, having a long conversation with the sentry, interrupted, from time to time, as the sentry paused to direct traffic or stop a truck. Emmie's fingers were tingling with pins and needles. It seemed so silly to worry about pins and needles when the guns were rumbling and she could see the lights flashing in the sky that meant air battles, and where, oh, where, was Kate?

"She's not here," said Julia, hauling herself back into the White. "She went through here four hours ago, headed east."

"East?" East was the front. East was the guns and the shells and explosions of gas that turned the air to poison.

"East," repeated Julia grimly. "She said something about going to Moyencourt after a lost child and a goat."

A lost child. And a goat.

"Zélie? It has to be Zélie. But they all arrived. . . ." Emmie tried desperately to remember who she'd seen at the refugee center. She could picture Marie's son Yves, the nine-year-old girl who helped milk the cows, and Mme Lenois's toddler, of course—but not Zélie. She stared at Julia, feeling a growing sense of horror. "Oh no."

Moyencourt. Three miles from Grécourt. It was

where Florence had sent their animals. Including the goats. What had Kate told her yesterday? Zélie had been devastated. She was only five. A five-year-old with no family. With nothing but that goat.

"Oh no," Emmie said again, feeling the guilt all the way down in her bones. "I never realized—I just assumed she was with the others. But Kate—"

"It's been four hours," said Julia remorselessly. "Even on these roads, it shouldn't have taken more than an hour each way."

"If something happened to her, we need to find her." Emmie started the White, praying the engine would catch.

"We don't know how far the Germans have come."

The night was terrible with the sound of battles being fought to the east, the crack of rifle fire, the rumbles of explosions, the sound of booted feet marching, the whine of airplanes overhead, as the Germans tried to bomb the railways and the roads, and their boys, American and British and French and Canadian, took to the skies to stop them. The Germans could be anywhere, crossing the canals at Canizy, fighting hand to hand in the woods near Offoy, creeping through the fog toward Moyencourt.

It was madness to go forward, into goodness only knew what.

"We can't leave her," Emmie said stubbornly. "If you want to wait for me here, you can. But I'm going."

Julia leaned back with something of her old air of insouciance. "Lead on, MacDuff."

"It's *lay on*," said Emmie, her breath catching on a sob.

"I don't think it matters," said Julia, picking up a gas mask and setting it down next to Emmie. "Do you?"

The sentry wasn't pleased with them. "What are you doing?" he demanded as Emmie accelerated past, as fast as the White would go, dust rising in her wake. "Miss! Miss! You don't want to go that way!"

Emmie ignored him, bumping the car down the rutted road, trying to remember the way to Moyencourt.

"Left," said Julia. "Your other left. We need to go north."

Emmie wrenched the truck left, trying to keep her eyes on the road and search the verge at the same time. "When she left, I never thought—I was so busy—there were so many people to feed—"

"Spilled milk," said Julia succinctly. "Think. Which way would she have gone?"

Emmie took a deep breath. "The road to Ercheu."

There were side roads, cart tracks, really, but Kate was more likely to have stuck with the road she knew. She'd been back and forth on the road to Ercheu for a good part of the day.

They had come down this same road only this morning, on the way from Grécourt. In the last eighteen hours, the landscape had grown infinitely more desolate, with wheelbarrows and luggage abandoned by the side of the road and a downed German plane smoldering in a field. Emmie could smell burning metal and acrid smoke.

There were signs of accidents everywhere, twisted bicycles and burned-out trucks. Emmie thought of the woman whose husband had been run over by a cart, and wondered if Kate was lying somewhere, broken and lifeless.

She hunched over the wheel, drawing as far to the side as she dared to avoid an army camion. "It's my fault Kate's here. I made her come."

"Ha," said Julia roughly. "Have you ever seen anyone make Kate do anything?"

The driver of the camion braked, leaning out the window. "It's the Smith Unit, isn't it? There's no one here to collect. Go back. It's not safe anymore."

"We're looking for one of our own." Emmie wished her voice sounded less wobbly. "Have you seen a Ford jitney?"

There was a brief consultation. The head reemerged. "There was a truck abandoned by the road at the crossroads just east of Ercheu—it might have been a Ford."

Emmie appreciated that he didn't try to stop them, just gave them a quick précis of everything he knew of current troop movements, which wasn't much.

"It might not be the jitney," Julia warned her as they rattled on, past Ercheu, which didn't look at all like the village it had been only two days ago, empty now, echoing in its emptiness.

But there, at the crossroads just outside Ercheu, on the road that branched one way to Esmery-Hallon and the other to Moyencourt, Emmie saw the familiar outlines of a Ford jitney, with the dent in the side where Liza had hit the gate back in October.

Emmie braked hard, hard enough to make them both jolt forward, and was out of the White and running before she even knew what she was doing, shining her flashlight at the jitney, calling, "Kate! Kate!"

No one answered.

Chapter Twenty-Nine

Wednesday in Mr. Hunt's office, I met with half a dozen delegates from the devastated regions, all of whom wanted the Smith Unit in their own districts, as the Red Cross considers our work at Grécourt nearly done. Each man thought he had just the place for us in his territory.

Thursday, Williams, White, McCoy, and McMorris finally secured their passes to Grécourt. Liza Shaw, who had previously been with the Unit, asked if she might rejoin, and as her pass was still good, we cheerfully welcomed her back.

Friday morning's paper told us of heavy bombardments, but upon inquiry, Mr. Hunt told us he didn't think it ought to impede our getting back. Just as our train pulled out of the Gare du Nord at 8

a.m. on *Saturday, we heard two heavy explosions,
and while, at this time, there is still some uncertainty
as to their origin, they are thought to have come from
a massive gun seventy-five miles away. . . .*

*At the station in Noyon, we were met by Mr.
Barbey (the man who got our new house for us)
and the first thing he said was "Grécourt has been
evacuated." Just then a shell burst near us. I don't
know which alarmed me more.*

*We have been trying to get word of the rest of
the Unit. . . . A young doctor of the AEF told us
he had heard they had been doing wonderful
work, evacuating civilians through Roye. He kept
telling us he was sure they would be all right, until
I was quite ready to tell him that I thought we
knew more of them than he did!*

I do hope they are all right. . . .

> —Mrs. James R. Barrett (née
> Ruth Irwin), '02, Director, to
> the Paris Committee

*March 1918
Montdidier, France*

Zélie whimpered in Kate's lap.

Kate felt like whimpering too, but that wouldn't

be the responsible thing to do. Not that anyone was watching her, here on the outskirts of what had once been a village, protected only by the dubious shelter of an overturned farm cart. It was better than nothing, she supposed, trying to tuck the blanket from the truck closer around Zélie without moving the girl's leg, which, even to Kate's inexperienced eyes, looked very bad indeed.

She'd found Zélie fallen in a shell hole, looking like so much crumpled laundry, not far from Moyencourt. It had been hellish getting her out, and even worse getting her back to the truck, with Zélie clinging to her neck, in such pain with every movement. Kate had wrapped the leg as best she could—she was afraid to even touch the bit of bone sticking out—and tried to drive as gently as she could on the rutted road, but they'd made it only as far as Ercheu when the jitney gave out entirely.

Which would never have happened if she'd done what she ought to have done and taken it to Alice to look at.

Kate sat with Zélie on her lap, doing her best not to move—or cry. She'd been unpardonably thoughtless. Blame it on lack of sleep, blame it on the confusion of the retreat, blame it on whatever one liked, she ought to have known better.

Kate looked down at the child in her lap. She looked so small, so fragile. They all joked about how bossy Zélie was, but, sleeping, her face was rounder and softer. Kate was forcibly reminded of just how young she still was, just one step away from babyhood. But what a babyhood. Zélie's entire life, her entire life as she remembered it, had been lived under the shadow of war, one long litany of loss. No wonder she had gone back into a war zone after a goat. The goat was all she had.

She ought to have known better. She ought to have known that Zélie would do something like this.

They'd made a joke of Zélie following her around. Kate had been touched and flattered by the little girl's affection. But when it came down to it, she had failed Zélie. She could tell herself that it had been the right thing to do, sending Zélie off with the rest of the *basse-cour*—and it had!—but she might have taken the extra time to explain to Zélie what was happening, to ask Marie or Mme Lenois to take special care of her. Or to find a way for them to take the blasted goat. Instead, she'd just waved them all off and told herself her duty to them was done.

And now here they were. With a broken truck. In the dark. Troops moving all around, German planes overhead, explosions coming from the east. She could try to carry Zélie, but she didn't think they would get far that way. Even if she weren't so worried about jarring Zélie's leg, Kate wasn't sure she could carry her—how far was it back to Montdidier? Fifteen miles? Twenty? Too far. Even a mile would be too far.

Kate smoothed the little girl's hair back from her brow and tried to think. In the morning, when it was light, it should be easy enough to get help—they could flag down a dispatch carrier, send word to the Unit. But who knew what the morning would bring? The Germans might be moving already, now, under cover of darkness. She'd heard explosions before, and thought, hoped, that it might be their British friends blowing up the bridges across the Somme, but there was no guarantee that would hold the Germans for long.

Who would get to them first? Their friends? Or the Germans?

"Kate?" Kate shivered with cold and misery. She must have been drifting off to sleep, dreaming. She'd thought she heard Emmie calling her name.

"Kate!" There it was again, and it really did sound like Emmie, unless it was the auditory equivalent of a mirage, panic creating false sounds, or just ears gone tinny with the constant booming of the guns.

Gently, as gently as she could, Kate wiggled out from under Zélie, who winced and muttered, her sleeping face creased with pain. Kate's right leg had gone completely numb; she had to drag it along, trying to flex her toes to drive the blood back into it.

Light arced through the night, half blinding Kate. She heard the sound of a scuffle and then Julia's voice saying, in a harsh whisper, "Turn that thing off! What do you want to do, send an engraved invitation to the Boche?"

A wave of sheer joy flooded Kate. She might hallucinate many things, but not Julia telling Emmie off.

"Emmie? Julia?" Kate staggered around the cart, so giddy with relief she hardly felt the pins and needles in her right leg.

"Kate!" Emmie grabbed her, hugging her so enthusiastically she couldn't breathe. "You can't imagine how worried we've been! What happened? The sentry said something about a girl and a goat—"

"I came to find Zélie," Kate said at the same time, both of them speaking over each other, "and I've got her, but the jitney broke down, and Zélie's leg is broken, and, thank heavens, I've never been so glad to see anyone in my life!"

Julia cleared her throat. "This reunion is very touching, but may I suggest we remove ourselves to an area a little farther away from the battlefield?"

Kate wiped her eyes with the back of her hand, giving a laugh that wanted to be a sob. "I'm glad to see you too, Julia. I've left Zélie behind that cart. She's sleeping. She's got a broken leg. I had thought I could carry her to a road where we could get a lift with an army truck, but it was hurting her too much. So I thought we'd find someplace to wait until morning."

Julia borrowed Emmie's flashlight to twitch back the blanket and look at Zélie's leg. "You're an excellent administrator, but you make a lousy nurse. I'm going to need to reset that."

"How bad is it?"

"Bad." Trust Julia not to sugarcoat it, thought Kate. "Let's get her into the truck. The sooner we get you both out of here the better."

They all froze as everything around them shook, lights dotting the sky from miles away. It was like all the Fourth of July fireworks all together, sparks setting off sparks setting off sparks, a crazy funnel of electricity lighting the sky.

Kate stared, half-blinded. "What *was* that?"

"They've been blowing up bridges. . . ." offered Emmie.

"That wasn't a bridge," said Julia.

There was a choked, whimpering sound from their feet. The noise had startled Zélie awake, jarring her injured leg. Any other five-year-old would have howled. Instead, she had crammed her hand into her mouth, trying so very hard not to be heard. It cut Kate clear through to the heart, listening to her try to choke back her pain so the Boche wouldn't get them.

"We're getting you out of here," Kate said contritely, kneeling by the little girl. "Do you remember Dr. Pruyn? She's going to fix your leg for you. And then we're going to scold you like you've never been scolded before for scaring us like that."

"I needed—Minerva—" Zélie rasped, her eyes wide with fear and pain.

"You'll just have to make do with us," said Kate, trying to smile. "I know we're not as good as a goat, but we'll try. Oh dear. Please don't cry."

"Of course she's crying. She has a compound fracture," said Julia impatiently.

Next to her, Julia had been having a whispered consultation with Emmie. They arranged themselves on either side of Zélie, the flashlight lying on its side on the ground so that it shone directly on the girl's leg. Next to Julia were two broken boards from the cart.

"Hold her hand," Julia said tersely to Kate.

Kate had never felt so helpless, clinging to Zélie's hand, burying the little girl's head in the folds of her skirt as Julia did something truly horrible to her leg. Zélie gave a muffled cry and then went limp, her forehead cold and clammy.

"Julia?" whispered Kate.

"Hush," said Julia, fitting the two boards around the girl's leg and wrapping the blanket around and around. "Not what she needs, but it will have to do. They didn't teach us field dressing at Johns Hopkins. What? She's fainted, that's all. You can lift her now. Emmie, brace her legs. One . . . two . . ."

They got Zélie into the White truck, Julia putting Zélie's head on her lap and improvising a makeshift cradle for her legs, as Emmie squeezed Kate's hand and said, "Don't worry, it's all all right now," before, improbably, going over to turn the crank and start the car as if starting a car were something she did all the time.

Kate climbed up onto the bench seat, shivering with cold and reaction. "Thank you," she said belatedly. "Thank you for coming to get me."

"Thank Emmie," said Julia from the back. "Dr. Baldwin was all for leaving you."

"Don't be silly. We couldn't leave you." Emmie,

with a look of great concentration, was backing up, making her way as carefully as she could around the broken jitney.

Kate's hands felt like they belonged to someone else. She flexed them, just to see if she could. "I've been impossibly stupid. You can tell me what a fool I was, if you like."

"It wasn't just you. I should have realized she was missing," said Emmie apologetically. "If I hadn't been distracted . . ."

Somehow, Emmie apologizing just made it even worse. It was just like Emmie, taking the blame when it was Kate's fault, when it was all Kate's fault. And Kate had let her. For months and months, she had made herself feel important at Emmie's expense. But not anymore.

"It wasn't your fault. It was mine." Kate dug her nails into her palms, welcoming the pain. "I was the one who said we shouldn't go off alone. I'm the one who said we should never get attached. I'm the one who should have known better."

Emmie looked at her in surprise. "But of course you had to go. You couldn't have left her there—any more than we could have left you."

Kate couldn't help herself; a little whimpering noise came out and then another. She clamped her hands over her face, trying to hold the sobs in, but they forced themselves through anyway, all the tears she hadn't let herself cry before, ugly, gasping, panting tears, ripping through her, tearing her insides out.

Of course, Emmie said. Of course. As if it were obvious. It would never occur to Emmie that Zélie was just a French orphan or that Kate might have gotten them all killed or that, as their acting director, Kate had responsibilities to the Unit that ought to have kept her from haring off on a whim. And Kate didn't know if that was wonderful or awful, but she did know that her heart was a shriveled, stunted thing compared to her friend's because she would have thought those things, she had thought those things.

"It's all right now," Emmie was saying, as though Kate were Zélie, as though she were five and could be comforted with a pat on the arm.

"Why are you being so kind?" Kate shook her head blindly, her face contorting. "I've been dreadful to you. I've been a rotten friend."

The truck slowed as Emmie waited for a row of gun carriages to pass, trundling along to the front. "What are you talking about? You know I would never have gotten through—"

Kate gave a hiccupping laugh. "Smith without me?"

"Well, yes, that too. But what I meant was all this."

Emmie waved at the guns. "I know I was selfish to ask you to come but—you've been a rock for all of us."

Kate didn't feel like a rock. She felt more like sand, shifting and shiftless. "It's the other way around. It's always been the other way around. I would never have gotten through any of this without you. I would never have gotten through Smith without you. I probably would have been back in Brooklyn within six months." She'd never admitted it to herself before, but it was true. She'd been so scared and lonely. "Do you have any idea how afraid I was of you all? You all spoke right and dressed right, and there I was, embarrassing myself with every vowel and terrified of anyone finding out I didn't belong."

"But of course you belonged! You passed the entrance exams. That's more than I can say. They had to make an exception for me."

Kate pressed her lips tightly together to try to stop them from wobbling. "If it hadn't been for you, I wouldn't have done a thing at Smith other than study. I would never have joined a literary society or the dramatic society. I would never have thought I could. All those picnics and ice cream socials—I would never have been invited on my own. But because you took me up, other people did too. That was all your doing.

All the best things were your doing. And you never once took any credit."

The camions had gone. Emmie slowly eased the truck back on the road. "Because there wasn't any credit to take. You were secretary of the literary society, Kate! You were voted in fair and square."

"Because you told me to run for it. Do you think I would have, myself? Everything I had, everything I was, came from you." All the walls Kate had built so carefully were toppling, one after the other, leaving her as much a ruin as Grécourt, jagged on the outside and empty within. "I didn't stop writing because I thought you were a burden. I stopped writing because I was afraid people would think I was hanging on your coattails. I was afraid you would think I was hanging on your coattails."

Emmie was squinting at the road, scanning it for potholes. "I always thought I was hanging on *your* coattails. And that you just couldn't stand it anymore."

"I never minded helping you—I liked being useful. And you always made everything so *fun*." It sounded so trivial put like that. But it wasn't. There had been such joy in the world in their Smith days, and so much of that joy had come from Emmie, from her ability to laugh at herself, to make anything a joke. Afterward, in Boston, Kate had felt like half the light had gone out of the sky. Everything was grim and gray and serious. Even amusement had felt like work. "I missed you so much. It was so lonely without you."

Emmie gave an audible sniff. "I missed you too. But I didn't want to be a bother, so I thought when you didn't write back—"

"You had your debutante year and all those parties and your work—"

"You had *your* work and I was sure you were making all sorts of friends who were so much better than I am—"

Kate twisted on the seat, feeling the tears making tracks down her dusty cheeks but not bothering to wipe them away. "There couldn't *be* a better friend."

"D-don't b-be f-f-foolish." Emmie was crying too, swiping at her eyes with the back of her hand, the truck wobbling unevenly across the road, causing a dispatch rider to shout something very uncomplimentary at them.

"If I might interrupt your effusions for a moment?" Julia's voice rose from the back of the truck. "This is all very lovely, but please try not to crash the truck. I can set other people's bones, but I don't want to try it on my own."

"I don't want you to try it on me either," said Kate,

drawing in a long, shuddering breath and trying to wipe her face with a corner of her sleeve. She looked sheepishly at Emmie. "I guess thinking you're about to die makes you realize what's important."

"Not crashing the truck," said Julia firmly, holding on to Zélie to keep the movement of the truck from jarring her leg. "Not crashing the truck is important. You can indulge in all the sentimental rubbish you like once we're safely to the hotel."

"It's not rubbish," said Emmie indignantly. "Look, there's the crossroads. We're through the worst of it now."

"Yes," agreed Kate, looking at Emmie—Emmie!—confidently driving the truck and Julia cradling a five-year-old French girl. Everything was going mad around them and they had no idea where the Germans were or what the morning would bring, but they were all together, and that was enough. "I think we are."

Kate was awakened the next morning by someone nudging her arm, hard.

Rubbing sleep out of her eyes, Kate blinked up to see Marie-Rose, one of their most faithful milk customers, standing over her, poking Kate's prone form with her foot, her baby held in one arm while her toddler peeped out at Kate from behind Marie-Rose's skirt.

"I have come for my milk," Marie-Rose said.

"Your milk," said Kate groggily, pulling herself up to a sitting position.

She didn't remember falling asleep, but she must have. She remembered getting to the hotel just after midnight and finding it locked and Julia banging on the door until Nurse Goodale came and opened it. She remembered Dr. Baldwin and Julia rushing off with Zélie and holding Zélie's hand while they did something deeply awful to her leg and wrapped it with proper splints and bandages and gave her something to make her sleep, while Kate knelt next to her on the floor, holding her hand. She must have fallen asleep that way, because here she was, still in her dust-coated uniform, on the floor of the parlor of the hotel. Zélie, her leg propped on cushions, was asleep next to her.

"Yes, my milk," said Marie-Rose as if it were the most natural thing in the world that the Smith Unit would go on with the business of supplying her baby. It didn't seem to matter to Marie-Rose that they weren't at Grécourt anymore. They were the Smith Unit and they were here, and that was what they did.

There was something strangely reassuring about that.

Kate hauled herself to her feet, wincing at bruises she hadn't remembered she had. "I'll just go find that for you," she said.

Emmie was already up, opening tins of condensed milk, diluting them, and warming them to feed all the children in their care.

"Marie-Rose is here for her milk," said Kate, and the next thing she knew, they were both giggling helplessly, like undergraduates again.

"I'd best bring it to her or she'll wake the whole house," said Emmie, expertly decanting warm milk into a bottle. "Dr. Devine of the Red Cross Refugee Bureau came by and wanted to know if someone could go help at the station. He says it's an absolute scrum over there, worse than the New Haven Line on Yale-Harvard weekend, and they need someone to sort people out and get them on trains. Oh, and someone from the French Mission sent a note, asking if we could spare someone to evacuate Margny."

Emmie stayed on at the hotel, running the refugee center with help from Mme Gouge, who declared herself in charge of the kitchen, washing dishes and sterilizing bottles and scolding them about having something to eat. Marie, deeply chastened, promised to watch Zélie—not that Zélie could possibly go anywhere now, with one leg entirely immobilized, but Kate appreciated the sentiment. Under the guidance of the French Mission, Florence and Alice went off with the trucks, to evacuate any villagers who couldn't walk on their own, while Kate, Anne, and Nell went down to the station, which was just as much of a scrum as Dr. Devine had claimed, with people milling everywhere, looking for lost relations and lost luggage, yanking hungry, hollow-eyed children, elderly people sitting on their bags on street corners, looking lost and hopeless, frantic mothers searching for children who had become separated in the retreat.

Kate begged a stove and supplies from the Red Cross and got Anne started running a canteen at the station, with soup for the adults and milk for the children. Nell worked the platform, helping people onto trains, finding lost baggage and lost children, and generally cheering everyone up, while Kate found herself acting as a sort of general information bureau, taking notes on people who had been left behind and families that had been separated, directing the confused people wandering into the town toward the train station, and telling them to stop by the canteen for something to eat.

It was relentless, heartbreaking work. Some of them had been days walking on foot, from villages all the way past Ham. When Kate would ask where they were going, the answer was always the same: *Je ne sais pas*. I don't know. They looked so lost, clinging to their little bits of baggage, torn from their homes for a second or even third time, with no idea where they were going or when they would be back.

But a strange thing happened. Some of their villagers started working alongside them. The blacksmith and his wife from Hombleux took over the task of feeding the refugees being herded onto trains, running up and down the platform, handing food through the windows. Mme Chevrier, the seamstress from Bacquencourt, became a one-woman lost-luggage bureau, hunting up misplaced baggage. The farrier from Canizy told stories to the children to keep them entertained. And when Kate directed old Mme Didier from Verlaines to the station, the woman pressed five francs into Kate's hand.

"To buy milk for the babies," she said imperiously when Kate tried to give it back.

Alice and Florence would swoop in, drop off a load of people, check with Kate for directions, and drive off again, bringing with them news of the outside world, of troops on the move, of villages filled with soldiers preparing for one last stand. Alice came back all excited because a group of French gunners had taken her to their emplacements to see their guns in action, which had been deafening but thrilling; Florence was indignant about the animals she found abandoned en route.

Sunday bled into Monday, Monday spilled into Tuesday, feeding and sorting and getting people onto trains, opening tin after tin of milk, slicing loaf after loaf of war bread. The camions rumbled past, endless rows of them, and the cannonading grew louder and closer, but their work had taken on a kind of rhythm, everyone doing their best, so it came as a dreadful shock when the Unit stumbled in to breakfast Tuesday morning to find a delegation composed of a British major and two Red Cross officials with orders that they were to evacuate at once.

"At once?" echoed Emmie. She looked to Kate for support. "But we couldn't possibly, not right away. We have a house full of people who can't be moved, most of them children."

They'd gotten most of their able-bodied refugees onto trains, but the hotel was crammed with the sick and the wounded, ranging in age from a two-day-old baby to a ninety-seven-year-old grandmother. And Zélie, thought Kate, with a sick feeling in her stomach. Zélie with her badly fractured leg.

"And there's my livestock!" protested Florence. "All of our cows and goats. I'll need to see them moved."

"And the station canteen . . ." began Anne.

Mr. Jackson, the Unit's Red Cross delegate, looked

hunted. "You can have until the afternoon, and then you really must go."

"Right. We can set up again," said Kate, rallying her troops. "We'll simply move on and keep going, just like we did when we left Grécourt."

"About that . . ." said Mr. Jackson.

"Where are you sending us?"

"We don't know. But you can't just keep on. It's not safe."

"But—" Nell looked from one man to the other, furious. "We're doing absolutely useful work! We could keep on doing the same. Just move us a few miles west and we can go on getting people out. We can keep doing what we're doing."

"No. I'm afraid you can't," said the major calmly but firmly. "Fritz is moving much faster than anyone expected."

That was the British Army speaking. It was no use, Kate knew.

"Then we'd better do as much as we can with the time left to us," said Kate.

"I'll get breakfast for everyone and tell them they're going to be moved," said Emmie bravely.

The morning was a disaster. Florence stormed in fuming because someone had filled her gasoline can with water and she'd poured it into the truck without noticing and now the truck wouldn't start and the whole engine had to be overhauled. Anne scalded herself heating milk and had to be tended to by Julia, whose bedside manner was even more acerbic than usual, a sure sign that she was worried. Kate, meanwhile, had the job of getting all their patients into Red Cross trucks, seeing them settled on mattresses on the beds of the trucks, trying to think what to tell them when they asked, again and again, where they were going.

Zélie clung to Kate's neck, refusing to go. Kate was half-frantic with knowing there were a million things to be done and not wanting Zélie to hurt her leg. Marie had promised faithfully to stay with Zélie, wherever they were sent, and Kate had to be content with that, because there was no other way.

"Please," she begged the little girl. "It will just be for a little while. We all have to go. I'll find you once this is all done, I promise."

"Why can't you go with me? You promised you'd stay with me." Her face crumpled, a five-year-old driven beyond endurance. "I want Minerva."

That, at least, Kate knew something about. Florence had gone to see the cows and goats rerouted to Clermont, on the grounds that they would need them when they went back to Grécourt. When. Not if. Kate wasn't sure she believed it, but she had to try. For everyone's sake.

"Minerva is being sent to someplace safe." Kate tried to pry Zélie's arms from around her neck, as the Red Cross driver waved frantically at her, anxious to be off. "You can see her again once the Boche have gone. Once the Boche have gone, we'll all be together again. We'll all go back to Grécourt and be together again."

But Zélie wasn't consoled and neither was she.

"I don't even know where we're going," said Kate with despair as the last wagon rattled away. The hotel felt eerily empty with the canteen packed up and all their patients gone. Their duffels sat in a pathetic pile in the courtyard, ready to be loaded into the White truck. "How can I tell her?"

"Amiens," said Emmie, wiping her hands on her apron. "Dr. Devine just sent word that we're to go to Amiens."

"That's not so very bad." Kate looked at Emmie with new hope. "If they let us stay that close, then maybe things aren't as bad as they made it sound."

It wasn't as bad. It was worse. They'd just made it to a hotel in Amiens and begun eating supper when there was a tremendous crash and all the lights went out.

"I think—I think we're being bombed," said Alice in a small voice.

Another terrific crash shook the building. Kate found herself part of the general rush to the cellar, which was very small and very crowded. She sat in the dark with Emmie on one side and Julia on the other as the bombs fell continuously all night.

"It feels like the whole world is falling down around us," said Emmie worriedly.

Kate shivered, leaning closer to Emmie for warmth. They'd thought they'd known what it was like being under fire in Grécourt, but it had been nothing like this. She was terrified of the house collapsing on them, terrified of being buried alive. "I feel like a mouse in a hole."

They sat there, holding hands in the darkness, listening to the never-ending drone of engines, the rumble of bombs blasting houses to shreds, wondering if they would be alive come the morning.

"Do you remember how scared we were when we first got here?" said Kate.

"And on the ship," said Emmie. "Do you remember how we thought we were going to be torpedoed?"

"And that first air raid." Kate remembered standing out there on the balcony of the hotel, watching the planes, feeling awkward and out of place. She'd never been so scared as she was now, but she didn't feel out of place anymore. These were her people. Even Julia.

"Maybe," said Emmie bravely, "maybe six months from now we'll be sitting somewhere, saying, remember that time we were bombed in Amiens."

Another tremendous crash shook the walls of the cellar.

"You mean while we're being bombed somewhere else?" said Kate shakily. "Or maybe we could have some machine-gun fire, just for variety."

"This war has to end sometime," said Emmie, although she didn't sound quite sure.

"This night has to end sometime," said Kate, although she wasn't particularly sure of that either.

But it did. At dawn, the last of the planes flew away. They emerged on shaky legs into a ravaged world of crumbled buildings and people being borne away on stretchers, firemen racing to put out blazes, people mourning their dead.

"I don't think we should stay in Amiens," said Nell very seriously. "It really isn't healthy."

And that was how Dr. Devine found them, outside the hotel, holding on to each other and snorting with laughter.

"Oh, good. Your hotel is still standing," he said. "I've come to tell you that you're being sent on."

"To another safe place?" said Julia sarcastically.

Dr. Devine looked rather embarrassed. "We could

hardly know. . . . We'll let you know shortly where you're to go."

But first there were people to help in Amiens. There were refugees at the station who needed to be fed, and wounded who needed to be evacuated. Dizzy with fatigue, scarcely knowing what she was doing, Kate handed out blankets and condensed milk. Florence had the bright idea of paying the refugees for their rabbits and hens, since the money would be more use to them than the livestock, and turning the meat into stew on the spot. The next thing they knew, the station was thick with feathers as Florence wrung necks, Emmie plucked, and Anne stewed, while Kate organized people into orderly lines and handed out bowls.

She was so tired that everything was starting to blur a bit on the edges. It felt as though she'd always been in this train station, like some sort of purgatory, always heating milk and ladling soup, always helping endless rows of bewildered people onto trains, headed they knew not where.

It was the old question and answer: *"Où allez-vous?"* *"Je ne sais pas."*

Except this time it was the Smith Unit who didn't know where they were to go, half-dead on their feet, ladling soup in their sleep. Kate couldn't remember the last time she had brushed her hair. Or changed her clothes.

"I feel like one of the hags from *Macbeth*," she told Emmie as she took over from Anne at one of the big soup pots.

Emmie gave one of her unexpected laughs, bubbling out of her. "Can't you just see us cooking up eye of newt and toe of frog when we run out of chickens?"

"They're French," said Kate, feeling immeasurably cheered, even if she was beginning to see double. "They eat frogs anyway."

By the time Dr. Devine came to collect them to take them on to wherever they were going, Kate wasn't quite sure what day it was anymore. She was half-asleep in the back of the truck, her head on Emmie's shoulder, with Nell asleep in Anne's lap next to her, and Alice asleep on Nell. Julia sat hunched over her medical bag, trying desperately not to yawn, while Florence snored next to her, sleeping like a horse sitting up.

She hadn't slept, not really, at least she didn't think she had, but when Kate opened her eyes, the truck had stopped in front of an entirely unknown building on an unknown street. They were in a town, that much was clear; there were tall streetlights and proper sidewalks. But she had no idea what town it was or how far they had traveled.

"You can put their bags in here," a familiar voice was saying. "We've beds made up for everyone."

Kate blinked at the woman silhouetted in the light from the open door. "Mrs. Barrett?"

"Welcome to Beauvais," said Mrs. Barrett. Kate stumbled down, out of the truck, and Mrs. Barrett enfolded her in an embrace that smelled like lavender and laundry soap. "We've been worried sick about you all. You remember Williams and White and McCoy and McMorris, don't you? And, of course, I know you know Miss Shaw."

Liza waved at Kate from behind Mrs. Barrett. Kate had no idea what Liza was doing there. And Dr. Clare, who was, inconceivably, there as well, wearing a violently patterned silk wrapper with her hair braided for bed. Kate began to wonder if she was still asleep and if there were going to be dancing aardvarks next.

"But—where—"

"We've taken over a girls' school," said Mrs. Barrett. "This is our headquarters now and I'll tell you all about it in the morning, once you've had some sleep. My poor girls, what you've been through!"

There was something rather wonderful about being fussed over by someone who reminded Kate strangely of her mother, even though Mrs. Barrett looked and sounded nothing like her mother. Maybe it was the way she took charge, bustling them all inside, counting heads, ordering their duffels upstairs to the dormitory, talking all the way.

"If you can imagine, they actually let us on a train to Grécourt on Saturday—the wires had been cut by bombs Friday night so we had no word that the drive had happened. We got as far as Noyon, and then they sent us back to Paris. You can imagine we were frantic to know what had become of you. Everyone has been asking about the Unit, and they're all very keen to help. We've been offered everything from motorcars to Victrolas. Mr. White of the White Motor Company called personally to offer a car to us."

"That's good," said Kate, her voice rather creaky. "Because I'm afraid I lost the jitney."

"Not to mention all your things." Mrs. Barrett looked sympathetically around the remains of the Unit, all of whom were blinking like moles in the light, looking distinctly disheveled and travel worn next to the new girls. Someone came up to Mrs. Barrett, one of the new girls, White or Williams, Kate didn't remember which. "Yes?"

"We've just had a message from the stationmaster," said the new girl breathlessly. Her uniform was so clean it made Kate's eyes ache. Or maybe it was just that Kate's eyes were aching already. "There are loads of refugees coming into the station—no one knows what to do with them—and they wanted to know if we could find them something to eat."

Kate looked at Mrs. Barrett, and at Emmie and Alice and Nell and Anne and Florence and Julia, all battered and war-worn, all half-asleep on their feet.

"I could manage to open a few more tins of milk," Emmie said, rubbing her gritty eyes with the back of her hand.

"Me too," said Nell, smothering a yawn, and Kate felt so full of love and pride for her friends that she thought she might burst with it.

Turning to Mrs. Barrett, Kate said, as briskly as she could, "We're ready. What do they need us to do?"

Chapter Thirty

Dear Ma,

It's Mother's Day here at the "club." We helped
160 servicemen write letters home today, and now
we're writing our own.

So much has happened over the last two
months. The night we got here, we were called to
the station to help feed the refugees coming
through—just a big freight shed, two smoking
stoves, cases of unopened and unlabeled supplies,
thousands upon thousands of wretched old men
and women and children and invalids crowding
in, and a cluster of exhausted Smith women
rushing about diluting milk and desperately
trying to find cups and bowls enough to serve
everyone. After a night of that, we came up with

a system of eight-hour shifts, and got in some more stoves and supplies, so we had that all pretty well up and running within three days. With every train of evacuees that leaves the station, we try to make sure each person has a packet containing a can of meat or sardines, bread, chocolate, and a can of condensed milk.

We'd just got that in order when one night a doctor came to our door asking if we could give his blessés something to eat. So off we went and the next thing we knew we were in the business of providing hot milk and soup and cigarettes to the trains of wounded that go by. They try to put the English-speaking men together, so we gather up all the daily papers in English we can for them. Our own boys were so happy to see American faces again that one thing led to another, and now, on top of it all, we've been doing hospital visits, taking writing materials and treats to "our boys," and have made a sort of club for the men where they can come as they convalesce, with a parlor and a reading room and sing-alongs for the boys two nights a week (it's become a general theory around here that if they can survive Dr. Clare singing Gilbert & Sullivan at them, they can survive anything that battle has to offer).

As you can see, we're quite safe here in Beauvais and keeping busy. One of the Red Cross men told us yesterday, "We don't need any more women who want to hold the dying soldiers' hands; we need ones like you, who can wash dishes." If you'll believe it, he meant it as a compliment. He told me that it gave him hope to see women of refinement (that's me, apparently) have the spirit to take on the ugly jobs, cleaning up messes, scrubbing floors, and washing dishes.

I know you wanted something more for me, Ma. I know you scrubbed because you had to and not because you wanted to. Everywhere we've been, there's been squalor and confusion and we've been able to plunge in and turn it all around—and that's something I learned from you. Even when we were poorest, you took what little we had and you made it work, somehow. You always found a way. I'll never be able to thank you enough for showing me that it isn't what you have, it's what you make of it—whether it's turning a can of sardines and some condensed milk into a *supper or turning a group of strangers into a band of sisters.*

I don't know when I'll be back—the work keeps coming and coming and sometimes it seems like this war will never be over, and I haven't quite given up the hope that we'll be able to go back to Grécourt and set that to rights again too—but I'm sending love to Dad and the boys and particularly to you. Happy Mother's Day, Ma.

> *With love, your Katie*
> *—Miss Katherine Moran, '11,*
> *Assistant Director, to her*
> *mother, Mrs. Francis*
> *Shaughnessy*

May 1918
Beauvais, France

"Have you written your letter yet?" Kate asked Emmie.

Emmie looked down at the crossed-out piece of paper in front of her. In the hall of the club, a large sign had been posted: "To-day is Mother's Day. Have you written your letter?" Emmie had spent the morning visiting hospitals, helping the boys there write their letters home. Some had been lovely. Others had been heartbreaking: the boys who couldn't hold a pen, the boys who could hardly speak because their lungs were so groggy from being gassed, the boys who were never going home again, no matter how they pretended.

But no matter how she tried, she couldn't seem to write her own.

Dear Mother, she had written. And then she stuck. Because what could she possibly tell her mother of their life here? Of the calls from the station, the trains that went through, unloading the lost and the wounded. They knew all the trains now: the improvised trains for the *petits blessés*, the lightly wounded, who needed to be fed with rich soups and brought cigarettes and a hard bread they sarcastically called *gâteaux*, who would thank them for the English papers and joke and laugh with them. Then there were the permanent trains for the *grands blessés*, those who were grievously hurt, who could only be tempted by oranges and chocolate, and who needed letters written with alarming urgency, to send their last messages back home.

The *grands blessés* were the saddest, but even the *petits blessés* were a heartbreaking sight, crawling out of the straw, their uniforms so matted with dirt and blood it was nearly impossible to discern the original color.

The Unit was doing good work—Emmie knew they

were doing good work. They were busy and useful and together and working in a terribly organized way, sleeping in proper beds, and eating proper meals, and she couldn't remember the last time she had been so unhappy.

It wasn't just unhappiness. It had taken Emmie some time to identify the feeling, because it was so unexpected. She was angry, with a horrible, snarling, brooding sort of anger that colored everything. It made her resentful and hateful.

She hated that they'd had to leave Grécourt. She hated the work. She hated the new people, with their cheerful assumption that this was what they were here for, this was what they were meant to do. She hated seeing the broken men with their broken bodies and broken spirits, the huddled refugees passing through, headed goodness only knew where. She hated all the articles praising the Unit for being angels of mercy and towers of strength when she didn't feel either merciful or angelic. She just felt furious.

She hated that she'd found the one person in the world she'd wanted to spend her life with, the one person in the world who looked at her and saw something wonderful, and now she hadn't the faintest idea where he was or if he was alive or dead.

It wasn't heroic or patriotic. It was wasteful and horrible.

And now, this letter to her mother, it was the very last straw. Emmie couldn't, wouldn't write what she knew her mother wanted to hear—how marvelous it all was, what a fine showing they were making. She couldn't speak of the people they served as statistics, so many fed, so many outfitted, so many sent on.

Alice had been collecting funerals. They'd seen so many men die, so many without family—Scotsmen from remote islands, boys from Kentucky farms, New Yorkers, Liverpudlians, and Nova Scotians—that Alice had taken it on herself to attend every funeral she could, to make sure someone was there to bear witness. She wrote to all the next of kin after, a personal letter in addition to the official one. Emmie had promised she would help her—with the letters, not the funerals—but she found it so very hard. She found it all so very hard.

Emmie wanted to be back at Grécourt, with her chickens who were really roosters, and with the hope of summer to come. She wanted to deliver milk to adorable, pink Boche babies, not cigarettes to men wounded beyond bearing.

Maybe that made her unpatriotic. Maybe that made

her ungenerous. She wasn't sure. Mostly, it made her moody.

Kate had taken to checking in on her. Not explicitly. Just stopping by throughout the day, saying a word or two, giving Emmie a chance to fume if she needed it. That, at least, was one good thing that had come of all this—she had Kate back again, not in the old blithe way of the Smith days, but in a new, more concerted way. They'd stopped taking each other for granted. They listened to each other now, really listened. And sometimes, like now, it was enough just to be, to know the other was there.

"Is that your letter?" asked Kate, perching on the arm of Emmie's chair.

Emmie grimaced at the marked-up page. "I haven't gotten very far. Do you think it counts if I write to my brothers instead?"

"Or you could just give an interview to the papers," said Kate blandly, and Emmie made a horrible face at her, because, of course, that was just what Emmie's mother had done, after the evacuation, when the Smith Unit was in all the papers. She'd told the *New York Times* that it was no more than she would have expected of her daughter and it was time the world recognized the potential of the modern college woman.

Emmie wasn't sure which bothered her more, the idea that this was somehow a measure of her being her mother's daughter, or the idea that she was meant to be an archetype of the modern college woman, a bloodless model of an ideal, rather than a person who had tramped through mud and gone two weeks at a time without a shampoo and cried over spilled chickens and found immeasurable joy teaching children to sing rounds in French.

There was a time, not so very long ago, when she would have been delighted to have made her mother proud, whatever that meant. But now—

She was just so *angry*.

"She hasn't the faintest notion," said Emmie. "Of course, why should she? No one would who hasn't been here. But . . ."

But the thoughtlessness of it all, the complete lack of any attempt to understand, the idea that they were just grist for her mother's mill . . . Emmie was certainly happy that people were seeing the potential of the American college woman, and it didn't at all offend her when Mr. Hamlen of the Red Cross said the exact same thing, or when Major Perkins wired that they needed more college girls like the Smith Unit in France—but when her mother said it, said it to a paper, it made her want to snarl.

"I keep thinking about that night in Amiens." Emmie looked up at Kate, struggling to put her emotions into words. "You remember. That horrible cellar, with the bombs falling and falling."

"Oh, I remember," said Kate with feeling.

"That was the first time I really thought we might die—actually die, not just talk about it. Those bombs didn't care who we were. It didn't matter to them that we were Smith girls or *les dames Américaines*—they were just falling anywhere they landed, obliterating everything in their paths. We might have been anyone. Maybe that's what's bothering me. I don't think my mother has ever, in her whole life, been somewhere where she's been just anyone. All those railings she chained herself to—no one was ever going to arrest her, not really."

The police were never going to haul Mrs. Livingston Van Alden off to the Tombs or beat her with a nightstick, not when she was the niece of a senator and second cousin to a former president.

"I know that doesn't make it a sham, precisely," said Emmie slowly. "None of it changes what she's done—we probably wouldn't have the vote in New York now if it weren't for her, and if we ever get to vote nationally, it will owe something to her, so I suppose she has done more good for more people than I ever could, but . . ."

"But it doesn't seem quite so heroic anymore?" offered Kate.

Emmie nodded. All her life, her mother was the model she'd striven to follow. She was Lady Liberty and the entire pantheon of Greek goddesses all rolled into one. Emmie had tried so very hard to contort herself into what her mother wanted her to be, to follow her mother's example.

Emmie looked down at her unwritten letter, the ink blurring in front of her. "It makes me so angry that she's trying to take credit for our work when she hasn't been here, when she hasn't done any of it—and it's nothing to take credit for. It was just surviving. The things that we did that were good, the things that matter, those are the things she doesn't care about. Like getting pumps for the villages and making sure there were enough combs to go around. And teaching the children to play again. Those were the things that mattered. And that's what no one seems to care about now."

"You could always write her that," said Kate.

"She'd never read it." Emmie was fairly sure her mother had never read any of the letters she'd written home from Smith. "And I'd just feel silly and petty for writing it. We're meant to be keeping our end up."

"I don't think keeping our end up means pretending everything is wonderful when it isn't," said Kate. "It's a war. It's meant to be awful."

Emmie managed a wobbly smile. "I just—I hate the work we're doing here. You don't, do you?"

"I don't hate it, no. Not the way you do. If we'd done this from the beginning, I'm not sure I would have minded it so much. But I feel like Grécourt spoiled me for other things."

"I know this is what's needed. But—it's just so disheartening. I keep thinking of all our people and wondering where they are now and whether we'll ever be able to keep our promises to them." It had all seemed possible in Montdidier with the mud of Grécourt still fresh on their boots. But that had been in March, and now it was May, and the Germans still pressed on. The idea of going back, rebuilding, seemed impossibly remote. "Sometimes I wonder if there was any point in it. We worked so hard and then it was all swept away again."

There was silence for a moment as the wheels of ambulances rumbled by on the street outside, bringing more wounded, always more wounded.

"If we had never come," said Kate, "hundreds of

people would have died this winter. They may have lost their homes again, but they're alive. They can go back. We can go back for them."

"Can we? The new girls have no idea—they seem to think this is what the Unit is for. Nursing and canteen work."

"But we know what it's for," said Kate, and Emmie had never been more grateful for Kate's determination, that streak of mulishness so entirely at odds with her fine-boned delicacy. "Florence would go back in a moment. She's held on to the cows and goats for just that purpose. She takes it as a personal affront that she wasn't able to finish the planting. And Liza too."

"Liza?" Emmie looked up at Kate in surprise. "But she always wanted to do canteen work."

"She says she misses the store. And being outdoors. And fresh air." Kate glanced over her shoulder, checking to make sure no one was listening. "It was always really Maud who wanted to do canteen work—and now Maud's left, Liza doesn't have to listen to her anymore."

Emmie sat a little straighter, feeling a faint, dangerous spark of hope. "What about Nell and Anne and Alice?"

"I haven't spoken to them yet. I know Anne misses her school in Boston. I doubt she'll want to stay on that long. Nell might, but I'm not sure." Kate looked at her seriously. "It wouldn't be for a while, you know. We're not going to make it back to Grécourt until the war is over."

If the war ever ended. Emmie stared down at her hands, large-fingered, calloused, bare of rings. "Will and I used to talk about what we'd do after the war. It was like a game—only it wasn't."

She felt Kate's hand on her shoulder. "Has there been any word?"

It was amazing how hard it could be to choke out one syllable. "No."

She'd searched and searched the casualty lists for Will's name. Of thirty officers from his battalion, twenty-two had been officially reported dead. Emmie wasn't quite sure what that meant for the other eight. Will wasn't marked as missing—there was that. Did that mean he was sick somewhere? Wounded? Or simply serving wherever it was he had been called to serve? The censorship of the French papers was so complete; it was almost impossible to get any information. They had no idea who was doing what where; only rumors.

It was at times like these that being engaged to be engaged seemed a rather flimsy thing. If they'd been engaged, properly engaged, she might have done what her mother would have done, and badgered every relative who had contacts anywhere in the State Department or at the Court of St. James's. She would have had the phone lines buzzing, diplomats calling hospitals— but it was very hard to explain to the authorities that a pile of letters signed *yours to be yours* counted as at all the same thing as an engagement announcement in the *Times.*

Not to mention that the letters themselves were now somewhere behind enemy lines, in a locked trunk in an army barrack behind an abandoned château, most likely torched by the Germans.

"I ask on every train," said Kate. "And Julia knows to keep a lookout when she does her rounds."

"I know. I suppose it's better that he hasn't turned up? It means he's off fighting somewhere." Or dead. Emmie made a show of checking the clock on the mantel. "Oh dear. If we don't get moving, we'll be late for our shift at the station."

She left the letter to her mother unfinished. If her mother wanted to know what they were doing, she could read it in the papers. It was a small defiance, but it made Emmie feel better in a petty sort of way.

She did write to her brothers, though. For them, she wrote a cheerful letter talking about the unexpected visitors who would stop by, the group of aviators knocking on their door saying, "Hallo, Smith Unit! Just wanted to say hello. We're the Lafayette Escadrille."

She wrote about the sing-alongs they had twice a week at the club, with Dr. Clare pounding out a combination of hymns and light opera. *We go from "Onward Christian Soldiers" to "I Am the Very Model of a Modern Major-General"—the only thing they have in common is that they're both martial and we can't sing either of them on key.*

One group of men who had come through the club sent them 346 francs to buy a Victrola.

"So other poor boys won't have to listen to Dr. Clare singing," suggested Kate, sotto voce, making Emmie choke on her coffee.

The Smith Club of Japan sent two boxes of supplies, including the most beautiful writing paper Emmie had ever seen, silky and whisper thin. It made her think of gossamer and butterfly wings and the stuff of dreams, the sort of paper that should be used for writing poetry and love letters, like something out of that Keats poem—or was it Coleridge?—with casements opening upon fairy lands forlorn.

Nothing like the sturdy stuff on which she and Will had exchanged letters, a motley collection of stationery cadged from Paris hotels and paper torn from notebooks and on one occasion, when nothing better could be found, brown paper packaging cut into squares.

Emmie gave the paper to Alice for her condolence

notes, which were multiplying at an alarming rate as May raged into June and the Germans kept on and on. Sirens screeched overhead; there was something far more fearsome about an air raid in a city than in the countryside. At Grécourt, they'd managed to make a joke of it, but here, in Beauvais, the planes screaming overhead were fearsome things. The cannon boomed, the antiaircraft guns fired, and the church bells rang in frenzied cacophony as the Boche planes screamed past on their way to Paris, dropping bombs in their wake.

The wounded poured into Beauvais. The train station was a terrible thing, trains belching out the dead and the dying in a fog of smoke and blood. Emmie had only just fallen into bed, still wearing her soiled uniform, when Mrs. Barrett shook her awake.

"We're all needed at the hospital."

They made their way through a nightmare landscape of smoldering houses and shattered glass, dodging craters in the pavement, whole streets blocked off by rubble. There were American nurses in the hospital, just shipped in from Paris, some just in from the U.S. One was being sick in a corner. Emmie couldn't blame her. The floor was thick with stretchers, with hungry, filthy, thirsty, feverish men, all dropped wherever the stretcher bearers had been able to find room. It was almost impossible to see; lights were allowed only in the operating room. For the rest, there were only shuttered lanterns, creating more shadows than sight.

Across the way, in the operating room, under the glare of the lights, all three tables were full, Dr. Clare bending over one, Julia over another, and a French surgeon manning the third. Someone was carrying men out of the operating room, someone else lining up stretchers waiting to go in, the men so bloodied they looked less like human beings than like meat hanging out in front of a butcher's shop.

"Anne," Mrs. Barrett was saying. "There are forty-five *grands blessés* just out of surgery in there. If you could tend to them. Emmie, this lot has just come in. . . ."

Emmie didn't even bother to take off her hat or her gloves. She found a container of drinking water and began making the rounds, one by one, checking each for fever and wounds, offering water, wiping their faces as best she could. The whistles were still blowing and the bombs falling, the walls shaking with each explosion, but the noise seemed to recede as she worked, the horror outside less than the horror within. She had never imagined anything like this, not in Grécourt, not in the evacuation, not even in Amiens.

She was balling up a blanket to try to use as a bolster for a wounded man when Kate tapped her on the shoulder. "Emmie. Emmie! Come with me."

"But I'm not done here. . . ."

"It's your captain." Kate had blood on her face and her dress; her usually neat hair was straggling out of its pins. "I think it's your captain. I've been helping in the operating room—"

Emmie was on her feet in an instant, feeling sick with hope and fear. "But these men—"

"Nell says she'll stay with them." Emmie hadn't even noticed Nell, but there she was, behind Kate, taking over without a word, Nell, who usually had a pithy comment for every occasion, her eyes burning hollows in her white face.

"Go," Nell said, and gave Emmie a little push.

They had to step over more stretchers to get there, to the operating room, where a man lay on Julia's table as she dug a needle in and out of his flesh.

Emmie had only a glimpse of his face—a face pitted with burns and scrapes from exploding shrapnel—before there was a tremendous crash and all the lights went out.

She could hear Julia cursing, and then a flashlight was shoved into Emmie's hand.

"Hold that," she said crisply, and Emmie held the flashlight as still as she could, that momentary glimpse of his face burned into her memory, trying to resist the urge to turn the beam of the light and look again.

"How bad?"

Julia shoved wadding into the wound. "It missed anything important. He'll live. As long as it doesn't go putrid on him. What?" she demanded, as someone came up behind her.

"The alert has sounded," said Mrs. Barrett grimly. "The officer in charge has suggested you stop and seek a place of safety."

"*Jamais!*" protested the French surgeon working at the next table. "I operate all night."

"While there are wounded here, I stay here." Julia snapped her fingers at the stretcher bearers. "Take him away and bring the next one."

On her other side, Dr. Clare, who had been operating for twelve hours straight, her usually immaculate hair matted with sweat, her apron covered in unspeakable fluids, was wordlessly humming "Onward Christian Soldiers" as she bent her head over the man on the table.

Handing off her flashlight to Kate, Emmie took one side of the stretcher, helping the stretcher bearer lower it to the floor in one of the wards. The room was humid with sweat and fear, the air acrid with the smell of burning things. The darkness was horrible, making all the smells and sounds more acute, playing tricks of perspective. The room might have been the size of a closet or a baseball field; she couldn't tell. All lights were needed for the operating room. The men in recovery would just have to lump it.

Emmie touched what she thought was his shoulder. "Will?" she whispered.

"Emmie?" His voice was hoarse, but it was his. "Emmie? I can't—I can't see."

She felt like laughing, which was an entirely inappropriate reaction, but she couldn't help it; she was such a mix of joy and fear. "It's the lights," she said. "The Germans have shot the power out."

She heard him draw a shaky breath. "Thank God. I thought I'd gone blind. I thought I was never—going to see—your face again."

"Where have you *been*?" As soon as she said it, Emmie realized it was really a rather ridiculous thing to ask. He'd been fighting. She groped for his hand, clutching his cold fingers. She didn't like that they were so cold. "I couldn't get any word—I only heard that most of your battalion—"

"Slaughtered." His voice was very weak. "I had pneumonia. Out of my head with it. I'd been knocked into a trench hole and apparently lay there for three days before some Frenchies found me. That's what they told me. I don't remember any of it. When I came to—they declared me fit for service and sent me out again. It's all been a bit of a blur."

Emmie clung to his hand. It was so strange, to be able to hold him but not see him, to feel the shape of his palm, the calluses on his fingers, as if she were learning the geography of him one small isthmus at a time.

"I left your letters in Grécourt. They were all I had of you and I left them."

"They were only paper and ink. The words—the thoughts—whatever was in them of any value—you have already. It all amounted to just one thing, anyway."

"Yes?" The bombs were still falling outside; there were roughly forty other wounded men packed around them, nurses navigating as best they could in the dark; but right now there was nothing in the world but Will, here, with her, the rasp of his breath, the feel of his fingers around hers.

"I love you," he said in his beautiful voice, scratchy now, faint, but still his. "Whatever happens, wherever we go. In this world or the next."

"You're not going to any other world but this," said Emmie fiercely, swiping away tears with her free hand and giving an entirely inelegant sniff. "Julia said it was a perfectly incompetent shell and missed anything that mattered. So you're not allowed to go all elegiac on me."

"'A Valediction: Forbidding Mourning'?" he managed.

"Yes, Kate gave me your message about the compass." Emmie's throat was so thick with emotion she could hardly get the words out. "It's all very romantic, but you've got it all wrong. I'm not forbidding mourning. I'm forbidding dying. I simply won't have it. You're not allowed."

He gave a shaky laugh that turned into a gasp of pain. "I'll do my best."

The sirens were wailing for all they were worth. Some of the men were crying, others praying. Another bomb crashed down, closer now. Emmie could hear glass shattering and someone screaming, screaming and screaming, alarmingly close.

Will pressed something into her hand, something hard and round and cool. "This is my signet. If I promise to try not to die, will you promise to wear it? I'd go down on one knee, but since I'm already prone . . ."

Emmie leaned over and kissed him. She didn't quite get the right part of his mouth, but they got that sorted out rather quickly. She couldn't embrace him because she didn't want to tear his stitches, and they both reeked rather strongly of sweat and blood, but she found that didn't matter in the slightest.

"Emmie." Kate squeezed her shoulder. "Emmie, I'm so sorry, but we have to go."

"We're engaged," Emmie said, the words feeling very small in the darkness. Will's ring was loose on her finger. "For real this time."

"Congratulations." Emmie couldn't see Kate, but she could feel the hem of her uniform skirt swishing back and forth, a clear sign of anxiety. "I mean it, I do. I'm very happy for you both. But we're all being evacuated. Now."

"I don't understand." Emmie sat back on her knees, clenching her hand around Will's ring to keep it from falling off. It was too loose. She would have to wrap string under it to keep it on, or maybe hang it on a chain around her neck. "What happened?"

"Part of the hospital is gone." Kate was trying to sound calm and businesslike, but Emmie could hear the panic under it. "They want us to get our things from the hotel. It's not safe in Beauvais anymore. You're being evacuated too, Captain DeWitt, but I'm not sure where."

"Will . . ." Emmie stared down at the dim shape on the stretcher. It seemed such a cruel trick to not even be able to see him, to see his face before they were parted again.

"I'm sorry," said Kate. "I'm so sorry."

Behind them, Emmie could hear people bustling about, stretchers being lifted, men moaning, Dr. Clare protesting about something.

Will squeezed her hand, and then, very deliberately, let it go.

"Go," he said. "Be safe. I'll find you, wherever you are. Remember? The compass."

"The points always come together again." Emmie leaned over and kissed him, one last time, not caring who saw, knowing Kate would understand. "When the war ends, come find me at Grécourt."

Epilogue

May 1919
Grécourt, France

Dear Everyone at Home,
We've been busy as clams since we got back to
Grécourt in January. Or do I mean happy as
clams? We've been working pretty much dawn to
dusk getting everything up and running again.
You should have seen the havoc those Boche
wreaked on our poor old barracks—it's as if they
didn't think they did the job properly the first
time! But this time, at least, we have plenty of
supplies and men to help us. All those French
soldiers home from the war, and the men and
women who were away avec les Boches have been

filtering back home, and they've been building
and plowing just as hard as they can—we've even
got a bunch of German prisoners of war working
for us, which is a little unnerving, although they're
sweet as lambs, most of them. I kept thinking
they'd have spikes growing out of their heads and
teeth like the wolf in Red Riding Hood, but
they're pretty much normal boys and bewildered
as can be.

Kate claims she still can't get used to being
called director, which is nonsense, since she was
pretty much director anyway, even when she
wasn't. Mrs. Barrett sends love and packages from
home. Her husband was sent back home to the
States after the armistice in November, so she felt
she had to resign and go back with him, but she
says she'll always be with us in spirit and as long as
the mails keep delivering. There are only four of
us Old Contemptibles left—Florence Lewes is
having a ball with chickens and cows, Emmie Van
Alden is in charge of social work, Julia Pruyn is
our medical department, and you'd laugh to see
me in charge of the store, peddling away like
anything. I've been setting up shops in all the
villages and helping the locals to stock them.

The new girls are a good lot, even if they do

keep asking us to tell stories about the early days at Grécourt and what it was like to be here under fire, which makes me feel like the Ancient Someone-or-Other from that poem.

We've had a rash of romances. Alice Patton—from the old crew—wrote that she's married one of the engineers! The Unit sent her a silver dish as a wedding present. There's an aviator from the Lafayette Escadrille who's been calling on Kate—he shows off flying around in circles—although Kate claims he's just a "friend of the Unit" (ha!). Oh, and you'll never imagine who came riding in on a farm cart last week, with eight boxes of chocolates, five rosebushes, and a luxury assortment of DeWitt's biscuits? None other than DeWitt's Biscuits himself. (Although Emmie has asked us to please stop calling him Captain Biscuit; for some reason, she doesn't find that the least bit funny.) He was demobbed in April, and they're to be married next month from St. George's Anglican Church in Paris, with Kate as maid of honor, and Florence Lewes, Julia Pruyn, the groom's sister, and yours truly as bridesmaids. The dresses were a problem, with rationing, but in the end we decided we'd just wear our uniforms and brighten them up a bit with some flowers, of which there's no

shortage right now. We've got enough growing
wild on the lawn to stock a shop. That little
French girl Zélie is going to be flower girl and toss
rose petals.

We were worried about losing Emmie, but she's
promised to stay on with her captain until we get
the work done enough to hand off to the French,
so we think of it not so much as losing a Unit
member as gaining a source of biscuits.

Oh dear—Minerva's got into the wash again
and Marie is throwing a fit and threatening to
have her turned into stew. At least, I think that's
what she's saying. It's in French and there are
still some phrases I haven't picked up yet. . . .
More later.

With love,

Liza

— Miss Liza Shaw, '09, to Mr.
and Mrs. Robert F. Shaw Jr.

June 1919
Paris, France

I can't imagine why I bothered to go all the way to
Paris for Emmaline's wedding. It was a most
irregular affair—such a peculiar collection of

women as bridesmaids, all dressed in those hideous gray uniforms instead of proper dresses. I know one can't expect much of these college women, but you'd think they might have made an effort for the occasion. When I asked, they told me they'd done it on purpose! Emmaline had requested it! I can only imagine Emmaline thought it would make her look better by contrast, choosing a bunch of dowds as bridesmaids and putting them in gray wool.

I could have wept to see Julia there in that dingy gray. She ought to have been maid of honor—anyone would agree it was her right—but that honor went to that horrible little charity girl Emmaline dragged home with her from Smith instead of her very own cousin. When I pointed out to Julia what an insult it was, she only looked at me and said I knew nothing about it. I don't know why anyone even bothers to have children when they behave like this.

In any event, you would think Cora would be delighted that she finally found someone to take Emmaline off her hands. There's a title there, even if it is a new one, but with those feet, it's a miracle that Emmaline found anyone. I suppose nearly dying does lower a man's standards. Instead, Cora seemed positively disappointed that Emmaline had chosen to marry instead of demanding the leadership of that poky old Unit of theirs. I don't understand it. There's Emmaline, as plain as shoe leather, married to DeWitt's Biscuits, while my Julia is off poking the tonsils of French peasants. There's no justice in the world.

The only consolation is that the groom's family seems quite as mad as Emmaline. There must be insanity in the family; it's the only explanation. The father—Lord DeWitt—only wanted to talk about model villages, whatever that means. The sister, who was one of the bridesmaids, was the most militant sort of New Woman—all she could talk about was her college at Oxford and the vote for women and other perfectly boring things. She and Cora took to one another immediately. It gave me a crushing headache. Or maybe that was the champagne. I had to drink a great deal of it to alleviate the boredom.

There was no call at all for Cora to tell them to stop filling my glass.

There were a number of men at the wedding, including one of the Nelson boys (mother a Stuyvesant, father in railroads), who would do very nicely for Julia. Not as much money as the DeWitt boy but a far better pedigree. Union Club,

Knickerbocker, etc. Yale '08. Did something with airplanes during the war, but of course that's all over now. I might have pointed Julia in his direction once or twice, but—just to spite me, I'm sure—she practically shoved him at that horrible little mouse of a Moran girl.

What's the use of even trying? Julia's complexion is quite ruined from tramping about the French countryside. When I gently suggested to her that some face cream might be in order, she only laughed at me and told me that her patients didn't care what she looked like.

It has been a most trying day.

There's no point in staying in Paris. There isn't a person I know here anymore—at least, no one anyone would want to know. Besides, I can't afford it. Cora refuses to pay my bill at the Ritz. She had the gall to suggest I stay somewhere within my means.

At least Emmaline has some family feeling. She's booked me a first-class cabin back to New York and I mean to take it. Julia will just have to manage without me. . . .

> —From the diary of Mme la
> Comtesse de Talleygord (née
> May Van Alden)

June 1919
Paris, France

That was a three-handkerchief wedding—the right sort of crying, not the wrong sort. Miss Van Alden floated down the aisle (yes, Lawrence, I know that's not physically possible, but allow me some license). Her groom stared at her like he couldn't believe his luck. Some might call it shell shock, but I'm pretty sure it's love. Yes, I know, I'm just an old romantic. I married you, didn't I? Betsy, being Betsy, claims full credit for the match, on the grounds that if she hadn't formed the Unit they would never have met, and spent the whole time beaming maternally at them when she wasn't using up my handkerchiefs because she'd forgotten to bring her own.

I'll admit, it made me a little weepy to see the old crew again, from our new director all the way down to little Zélie, who served as flower girl and took her petal-tossing very seriously. They made her a junior version of the uniform to wear and you've never seen anyone look more pleased. With a bit of cutting of red tape in the right places, she is now officially the ward of our director, Miss Moran, although she's really been adopted by the whole Unit. She has a bit of a limp from her experience during the retreat, but Dr. Pruyn did an excellent job of patching her up. (I may have taken a look during the reception.) I've told Julia that there's a job waiting for her in Philadelphia at College Hospital whenever she's done at Grécourt. She pretended not to be interested, but I think she'll take it. Eventually.

It was a beautiful thing to watch the bride rush back to hug everyone again and again. Even yours truly came in for a hug or two. She was the sort of happy that wants everyone to be happy with her, and it was wonderful to see how delighted the Grécourt crew were for her and how they welcomed her husband (well, roasted him, really, but that's how they show their affection, these girls). When I think what these girls were when they arrived—it warms even my flinty heart to see how they've come together, particularly Dr. Pruyn, Miss Moran, and Miss Van Alden, whom I must try to remember to call Mrs. DeWitt now. The way they look after each other is something beautiful to behold. It seems a shame that they'll be separated once the work is done, but I don't imagine they'll let anything keep them apart for long. . . .

*Oh, bother. Now I'm getting weepy again and
Betsy's walked off with all my handkerchiefs.*
　　　　　　—Dr. Ava Stringfellow, '96,
　　　　　　　*to her husband, Dr. Lawrence
　　　　　　　Stringfellow*

*July 1919
Grécourt, France*

Darling Emmie,

*Yes, we have everything in hand, and no, you
don't need to come back early! Please do stop
writing us and just enjoy your honeymoon. That's
a request as your friend, not an order as your
director, but don't think I won't pull rank if I
have to.*

*Zélie loves the beads you sent her from Venice.
She won't take them off, which means we can
always hear her jingling everywhere she goes. Julia
loves the ticket you sent her mother. She'll never
tell you herself, but she's terribly grateful to you
for sending her packing.*

*There really isn't anything to say about
Lieutenant Nelson, but I promise to tell you
whatever there is when you come home.*

I won't say you aren't missed, because you are,

but we want you to have a little time for yourselves before we put you both back to work. You're always so busy taking care of everyone else that you never stop to think of yourself, so we're going to think of you for you and absolutely forbid you to return for at least a month. We'll set Minerva on you if you do.

> *All my love,*
> *Kate*

P.S. Tell Will we've proclaimed him an honorary Unit member and Mme Gouge is sewing him a uniform as we speak.

> *—From Miss Katherine Moran,*
> *'11, to the Honorable Mrs.*
> *Fitzwilliam DeWitt (née*
> *Emmaline Van Alden), '11*

August 1919
Grécourt, France

Venice was lovely and so was Rome, but I've never seen anything so lovely as sunrise through the gates of Grécourt. . . .
It's a wonderful thing to come home.
I wish I could shrink it all and put it in a snow

globe, to put in my pocket and take with me when we're done here. Kate says we have it anyway, in our memories. Julia tells me not to spew sentimental tripe.

And Will—Will made me a snow globe with the gates of Grécourt in it.

Has there ever been anyone as lucky as I?

— From the diary of the Honorable Mrs. Fitzwilliam DeWitt (née Emmaline Van Alden), '11

Historical Note

Back in 2018, I was trying to find information about Christmas customs in Picardy during World War I—as one does—and stumbled on *Ladies of Grécourt*, a memoir by Ruth Gaines of the Smith College Relief Unit. It turned out that her book was absolutely useless in terms of Picard Christmas traditions, but I was fascinated by the fact that there was, somehow, a group of American college women in the Somme, right next to the lines, arranging Christmas parties for French villagers. It wasn't what I was supposed to be working on at all. But I couldn't help myself. I plowed through that memoir, captivated by Gaines's account of how the Unit came to be, what they did, how it all turned out, and I was tantalized by a few enigmatic comments and inconsistencies.

Why did their director, the force behind the whole expedition, resign less than two weeks after they arrived at Grécourt? What exactly was Gaines getting at when she wrote: "The only limitations to that high experience were the limits of comprehension, of endeavor, of fellowship, set by our own personalities"? I'd attended an all-girls school. That carefully phrased line about the limits of fellowship set by personalities sent out a bat signal to me. I smelled drama. So I did what any procrastinating author would do: I started digging, first into the publicly available sources, which raised still more questions, and then into the vast piles of letters and journals by Unit members housed in the Sophia Smith Collection at Smith College.

The story I found in those letters is the story that you read in this book.

Basically, leaving aside the emotional dramas of my own pretend people, if something happened in the book, it happened to the Smith Unit. The Unit was founded in April of 1917 by Harriet Boyd Hawes, a highly eccentric and volatile pioneering archaeologist and humanitarian who delivered a stirring speech at the Smith College Club in April, pulled together volunteers, backers, and supplies with record speed, and embarked on the *Rochambeau* with a brand-new Smith

College Relief Unit in uniforms of gray (with touches of French blue) in late July.

Wherever I could, I stuck with their own experiences and timeline. There wasn't enough room in the inn when they arrived at Paris; they did wrangle an attic to sleep in. The chauffeurs did have to go to Saint-Nazaire to put their trucks together. Their agriculturalist, Frances Valentine, was delayed in DC, leaving another member to fill in—and that other member did accidentally buy roosters instead of chickens. The Unit did visit the American Ambulance Hospital in Neuilly, where a member fainted, and later dropped out entirely. The incident with a small child, who was hit by a ball and began screaming, thinking it was a bomb, was taken from a letter by a distraught Unit member. Kate and Emmie's terrifying experience with the *poilus* at a deserted inn, including rescue by Canadian Foresters, came directly from the letters of Marjorie "Pidge" Carr and Catherine Hooper. Two Unit members were indeed sent to ask a very important official about acquiring poultry and wound up being lectured about pigeons.

Most dramatically, I discovered that, yes, there was a coup within the Unit and the sudden disappearance of the director, Harriet Boyd Hawes, was not, as it was put out in the public materials, for health reasons, but because of a deliberate campaign to remove her, a coup driven partly by personality, and partly by a disagreement about the nature of the Unit. As in the book, the faction succeeded in removing Hawes, who was replaced as director first by the Unit's doctor, Alice Weld Tallant, and then by Hannah Andrews (the Mrs. Barrett of the book), but not in altering her vision for the Unit. And, yes, the Smith College Relief Unit did ignore British orders to evacuate during a German onslaught and, instead, drove right into the fray and evacuated their villages. Everything you read about the March 1918 invasion in the book, the Smithies did, including directing traffic for the Great Retreat. Even more remarkable, they all came through unscathed in real life as well as in my fiction.

I did bend the truth in places. You may have noticed that although there are references throughout the book to there being eighteen original Unit members, if you count the named characters, there are actually only fifteen. That was because I found it impossible to keep eighteen personalities straight—and if I couldn't keep track of them, how would my readers? It also replicated my experience reading the letters, where some members certainly stood out more strongly than others, with a core of perhaps ten who seemed to play the largest role in the Unit's dramas and made for the best copy. My apologies to anyone who actually did the math and realized I was three characters short.

If there's an incident in the book, it almost certainly happened, but I may have moved it or conflated events for simplicity's sake. In the book, all of the women drive down to Grécourt together. In real life, one chunk of the group went to Grécourt on September 11, as described (issues with a pass, breakdown, loaned *poilus*, and all), while another chunk stayed in Paris and came down a few days later. In the book, Emmie is delighted at having wrangled benches for their schoolhouses (keeping a French bureaucrat from his lunch!) in October. In real life, that exact incident happened in January. In the book, Margaret has a breakdown after seeing a boy who had been deliberately maimed by the German occupiers. In real life, that didn't happen to the girl who dropped out. It did happen, but to a different Unit member, and later in the year (that Unit member wrote home that she'd seen something so shocking it had changed her whole life and made her decide to stop shilly-shallying and accept the proposal of the man she loved). And so on.

I also used real events as inspiration for fictional twists. Kate going missing at the end of the book was my own invention, but it was inspired by two Unit members being left at the crossroads in Roye and other Unit members defying Dr. Baldwin's instructions and going back for them. There was, in fact, an English major (not a captain!) who gifted the Unit with duck-walk, but Captain DeWitt was entirely my own invention, even if Unit romances were not—there was at least one marriage that came out of the Unit's adventures. As one member reported in her letters home, there were a number of "affairs" in progress between Unit members and their various admirers but very little privacy in which to conduct them.

I could go on and on, comparing each incident in the book with its antecedent in real life, but then this historical note would be as long as the book. I have never had the privilege of dealing with as rich a source of anecdote as the chatty, snarky, fascinating letters written home by the members of the Smith College Relief Unit. My only regret was that I couldn't include even more of their adventures and mishaps in the book. There were times when I was highly tempted to abandon the whole project and put together an annotated version of their letters instead, because the truth was even more incredible than fiction. The letter excerpts at the start of each chapter, some very closely paraphrased from actual letters, are my nod to the amazing corpus of material left by the real members of the Smith College Relief Unit.

However, since I did go on with the novel, this is where the book departs from the historical record: the events are real, but all the women in this novel are fictional. Some are more fictional than others. Some, like Kate and Emmie, were entirely the product of my imagination; others were more or less closely inspired by the characters of the actual members of the Unit as they conveyed themselves to me from their personal letters.

Mrs. Rutherford is based—with some fictional flourishes—on Harriet Boyd Hawes, the real founder of the Smith Unit, a pioneering archaeologist and war nurse who once forgot her baby in a stationery shop in Northampton. Dr. Stringfellow was a stand-in for the amazing Alice Weld Tallant, who did have really quite dramatic eyebrows, but was not, in fact, Mrs. Hawes's college roommate or even her same class year. Nell Baldwin, the Unit's librarian, was inspired by the letters of Alice Leavens, who wrote movingly of begging for books for the children. Florence Lewes was my answer to Frances Valentine, the Unit's agriculturalist, who, like my imaginary replacement, wasn't able to arrive until November (and wrote home about how it was much warmer not to attempt to wash). Liza Shaw was inspired in part by Catherine Hooper, who wrote home so feelingly about food—and who did such a marvelous job with the traveling store.

My two heroines, Emmie Van Alden and Kate Moran, and Emmie's cousin, Julia Pruyn, are really quite genuinely fictional, although the inspiration for Kate did come from two real members of the Unit. When I first read Ruth Gaines's memoirs, I was struck by the subtle difference in attitude toward Maud Kelly, the Unit's junior doctor, the only Catholic member of the Unit. The underlying vein of anti-Catholic sentiment came out even more strongly in some of the private letters of a handful of the Unit members. Looking into the history of Smith College, I was struck by the fact that the number of Catholic students in any given class at the turn of the century was in the single digits. What would life have been like for a Catholic student at Smith? Or after?

The other inspiration for Kate was Marie Wolfs, '08, a Smith grad whose home is listed as Newark, New Jersey, but who was of Belgian parentage and was in Lieges when the war broke out. Marie's letters are just as colloquial and "Smithie" as the rest of the women's, but she is frequently referred to in both articles and the private letters as a Belgian refugee or that Belgian girl, something that sets her apart from the others, even though she got along with everyone and seems to have neatly avoided factions and feuds. Like my fictional Kate, Marie Wolfs was appointed assistant director of the Unit and wound up in charge of the evacuation as their director, Mrs. Andrews, had been summoned to Paris for the week for meetings with the Red Cross. Like Kate, Marie Wolfs returned to France as director of the Unit after the war to oversee the rebuilding of their villages.

Emmie was inspired by the many references in the women's letters to both the suffrage movement—the winning of the vote for women in New York was something that was followed by the members of the Unit with great interest, and the New Yorkers in the group crowed mercilessly over their less fortunate companions—and their background in settlement house work, which deeply informed the whole structure and nature of the Unit. Briefly put, the settlement house movement was a charitable initiative in which upper-middle-class women would move into an underserved urban neighborhood and provide services and educational opportunities—much as the Unit did in their villages in France. It also provided an outlet for the talents of educated women at a time when work outside the home was not yet the norm for women of means. Many of the real members of the Unit had a settlement house background. There is a score of books on the settlement house movement, including Domenica Barbuto's *American Settlement*

Houses and Progressive Social Reform and Harry Kraus's *The Settlement House Movement in New York City: 1886–1914.*

Because there were so few secondary sources, I relied very heavily on the Smith Unit's own letters, trying, when necessary, to make allowances for unreliable narration, and to cross-reference with other contemporary accounts whenever possible. The members of the Smith Unit, I noticed, had a tendency to downplay the danger to themselves when writing home, something that was highlighted when I compared accounts of being bombed out of the hospital in Beauvais by, on the one hand, the Smith Unit, and, on the other, an American nurse (not a Smithie).

For anyone wanting to hear the voices of the members of the Smith College Relief Unit, I highly recommend checking out the 1917 and 1918 issues of the *Smith Alumnae Quarterly*, which are sprinkled with letters written home by Unit members. I was deeply amused, reading their private letters, to find them scolding family members for sending in their letters to the alumnae rag, and, for heaven's sake, these were for private consumption only. Apparently, some letter recipients didn't listen, because you can find excerpts of their letters included in the alumnae magazine straight through 1918. These issues are freely available online through the *Smith Alumnae Quarterly* archives. You can also find a compilation of letters—including some gems not included in the *Alumnae Quarterly*—in a 1968 pamphlet by Louise Elliott Dalby called "An Irrepressible Crew: The Smith College Relief Unit."

You can find glancing references to the Smith Unit in books such as Dorothy and Carl Schneider's *Into the Breach: American Women Overseas in World War I* and Ed Klekowski and Libby Klekowski's lively (and sometimes laugh-out-loud funny) *Eyewitnesses to the Great War: American Writers, Reporters, Volunteers, and Soldiers in France, 1914–1918*, as well as a few other places, but there has not yet been a monograph written entirely about the Smith College Relief Unit—an omission that Professor Jennifer Hall-Witt of Smith College is in the process of remedying.

In the meantime, for those wishing to know more about the real Smith College Relief Unit—as I hope you do!—you can find a Readers' Guide on my website, www.laurenwillig.com, which contains pictures, maps, and other items of interest.

I hope you find the Smithies who went to war as fascinating and inspiring as I do!

Acknowledgments

Every book has its list of people who helped it on its way. In this case, this book wouldn't have existed—wouldn't even have had a hope of existing—without the incredible generosity and kindness of the librarians at Smith College Special Collections. It is a truth universally acknowledged that librarians are heroes. These librarians aren't just heroes, they're superheroes. I stumbled on the Smith College Relief Unit back in 2018 via Ruth Gaines's *Ladies of Grécourt,* an account of her time in the Somme. The incongruity of it struck me. A group of American college women in the Somme, right in the middle of World War I. What were they doing there? Who were they? I gobbled up all the publicly available material, with their tantalizing scraps of period letters, and then made the happy discovery that there was a treasure trove of primary sources in Northampton. There was just one wrinkle. I had, at the time, a one-year-old and a five-year-old. There was no way I was spending three months in the archives in Northampton. A day trip was a stretch; a week was an impossible dream.

I emailed Smith College Special Collections. Without blinking an eye, the amazing super-librarians of Smith College digitized thousands of pages of material for me: letters, journals, reports, lists, photos. There were faded music scores of the canticles the Smith Unit learned to sing for mass with the villagers. There were doggerel poems handed around on Christmas Day, memorializing each Unit member. There were photographs with handwritten inscriptions. I could see the stationery they'd used, cadged from Paris hotels; the colors of ink; where they'd crossed things out. There are no words for how grateful I am to Roxanne Daniel of Smith College Special Collections for bringing the archives to me when I couldn't come to them. This book wouldn't be here but for you.

I am also very grateful to Professor Jennifer Hall-Witt of Smith College who is currently writing a monograph about the Smith College Relief Unit and was kind enough to answer emails from a random person claiming to be a historical novelist. Anyone wanting to know more about the real Unit and the context in which it was formed should run and buy her book as soon as it is available. (I, for one, cannot wait to read it.)

As always, huge thanks to my agent, Alexandra Machinist, who encouraged me to go chasing Smithies in the Somme. So many thanks to the team at William Morrow: to Rachel Kahan, editor extraordinaire, who took the Smithies to her heart (and coined the working title *Smithies at War*, which I'm still trying to remember is not the actual title of the book); to Elsie Lyons, cover design genius, who managed to work real Smithies, the real Grécourt gates, and real French villagers into the cover, and make it everything I ever wanted this cover to be; to Danielle Bartlett in publicity and Tavia Kowalchuk in marketing, there is no way to ever calculate how much I owe both of you for all you do and for your incredible patience with the five zillion "so I just had this thought . . ." emails you've fielded over the years.

I owe a special debt to my good friend Vicki Parsons, who, when I got stuck and wanted to scrap the whole thing, read the first few chapters and persuaded me to put down the coffee and step away from the delete button. (Okay, maybe not put down the coffee.) Perpetual thanks go to my sister, Brooke Willig, and my college roommate, Claudia Brittenham, who have now made it through twenty-one books' worth of "are you around so I can talk book at you?" and haven't yet blocked my number on their phones. I love you both. And your book instincts are impeccable. Speaking of talking book at people, hugs to Carlynn Houghton and her World War I literature class at Chapin who let me babble about Smithies at them for a whole class period (and didn't make a break for the door).

Mille mercis to Professor Jessica Sturm, Chair of the French Department at Purdue, who served as French language consultant for this book, preventing me from any number of *bêtises*. All remaining Franglais is entirely the fault of the author and of the members of the Smith College Relief Unit, who persisted in peppering their letters home with French phrases of varying degrees of accuracy, some of which I suspect they made up to confuse future novelists.

Book people are the best people. I am endlessly grateful for the support, friendship, epic text chains, and unabashed enabling of my writing sisters, Beatriz Williams and Karen White; any excuse for lunch or a coffee with M.J. Rose, Lynda Loigman, and Alyson Richman; the fellowship and joy of the New York writers' cabal, including, but not limited to, Amy Poeppel, Sally Koslow, Susie Orman Schnall, Fiona Davis, Jamie Brenner, and Nicola Harrison; wise advice and industry gossip with Andrea Katz, Suzanne Leopold, Bobbi Dumas, and Sharlene Martin Moore; and all the book bloggers, booksellers, and librarians to whom I owe so much (you know who you are!). Huge hugs to all of the readers I've gotten to know over Facebook, Instagram, and my website. I can't tell you how much it means to know you're there.

And, of course, there's my family. With only a month until deadline on this book, New York plunged into lockdown and I suddenly found myself confined in my apartment with a two-year-old, a six-year-old, and my husband—and a Nespresso machine. (It's very important to note the Nespresso machine, my first and best pandemic purchase, without which this book would not be here.) But, primarily, without my husband this book would not be here. He kept the kids at bay for three hours a day so I could work. Thanks are also due to my children, who only flooded the apartment once while I was trying to cadge extra writing time. And it was really only a small flood. So much love and thanks to my parents, who heroically took us in when my husband had to quarantine for two weeks and I still had Zoom book talks to do and deadlines to meet and no one to watch the kids while I did it. And to my siblings, who spend endless hours on FaceTime with my kindergartner while I sneakily try to get work done. I won the lottery when it comes to family members.

This book also owes a great deal to the Chapin School and its legendary headmistress, Mildred Berendsen. Full disclosure: I am not a Smithie. But I did have the incredible privilege of spending thirteen years at an all-girls school run by a Smithie. Our headmistress had been a scholarship girl at Smith. Every year, she would call us together and tell us how Smith had changed her life and how much we owed the world in exchange for the great gifts and opportunities that had been given us. When I stumbled on Ruth Gaines's memoirs, when I read Harriet Boyd Hawes's stirring call to action, when I dug into the Smith Unit's alternately earnest and breezy accounts of their incredible work in the Somme, I could hear Mrs. Berendsen's voice in my head, exhorting us to do more, to do better—but to do it with grace and dignity and a sense of humor. Smith shaped Mrs. Berendsen; Mrs. Berendsen shaped Chapin; and Chapin shaped me. Reading about the Smith Unit, I felt moved and grateful beyond words to be part of that lineage. It also struck me forcibly, while researching this book, how very much the Smith Unit belonged to the same world, shaped by the same ideals, motivated by the same principles, as their contemporaries: the founders and first generation of students at Chapin.

I owe both Chapin and Mrs. Berendsen more than I can say—including my deep feeling of kinship with the women of the Smith Unit. *To thee dear Alma Mater*, indeed.

Last but not least, I would be remiss if I didn't express my gratitude for the true heroes of this book: the real women of the Smith College Relief Unit, who plunged into a war zone, risking their lives to bring help and hope to women and children crushed between two armies. I only hope I did them justice.

Thank you all!

About the Author

LAUREN WILLIG is the *New York Times* and *USA Today* bestselling author of more than twenty novels, including *The Summer Country*, the RITA Award–winning Pink Carnation series, and three novels cowritten with Beatriz Williams and Karen White. An alumna of Yale University, she has a graduate degree in history from Harvard and a JD from Harvard Law School. She lives in New York City with her husband, two young children, and vast quantities of coffee.

HARPER
LARGE PRINT